The Irish Rebel

The Journal of My Great-Great-Grandfather

Peter L. Crawley

The Irish Rebel
The Journal of My Great-Great-Grandfather

iUniverse books may be ordered through booksellers or by contacting:

iUniverse LLC
1663 Liberty Drive
Bloomington, IN 47403
www.iuniverse.com
1-800-Authors (1-800-288-4677)

ISBN: 978-1-4502-2831-2 (sc)
ISBN: 978-1-4502-2830-5 (hc)

Printed in the United States of America

iUniverse rev. date: 07/24/2014

This work is lovingly dedicated to my four wonderful daughters; Erika, Holly, Mareva and Eileen who frequently have caused me to reflect on the following: while the finished work of the painter, writer, chef, musician and sculptor is obviously to be admired, I am oftentimes left to marvel more at the artist's fundamental decision to pick up his brush, pen, ladle, instrument and chisel than at the finished work itself, for based on their initial decision to create they have reaffirmed for me our human condition—one of inspiration.

PART ONE

Chapter One

The western state of Minnesota-May, 1893

Catching it up like a song forgotten,
Filled the air with the Rebel Yell.
The last war cry of the land of the cotton.

Till all the resonant fibers of pines
Every power of sound enlarging
Rang with the thrill of a shout

That never sprang from alright
But the terrible lines
Of the dauntless grayness fiercely charging

Echoes it back from the mountain's brow
From tallest pines and stunted sages
A shout that shall echo through future ages:
'To lower the flag is treason now—
From Appomattox on and forever

                        H. W. Taylor

"I say, damn them—damn them all to hell!" Coming as it did on the heels of a most rigorous Roman Catholic and apostolic Latin mass, was all the impetus I needed to look around, wondering if indeed the Apocalypse was now upon us. Or, at least a severe heavenly reprimand was due at any moment. Perhaps, in the form of an impending run on the bubbly, gas-induced liquid everyone around these parts called a "cherry soda" that was my one weekly indulgence, since spring had returned to the Midwest.

The younger man next to me muttered the above blasphemous sentence to no one in particular, as we cleared the big brass framed doors of St. Patrick's Catholic Church in downtown Lanesboro, Minnesota. I moved aside to let him pass into the springtime weather first. An extended gesture I hoped, of an older man being polite to another man quite a few years younger, and not out of fear of being verbally lambasted as I had just witnessed. Still, his exhortation that someone be given a free and everlasting ride to Hades, kept drifting back to me over the pregnant morning air. He might have been one of those *holier than thou* ex-"Yankees", the way he kept twisting his elongated, crushed, slightly-dimpled-on–the–crown, black, felt hat back in forth, in evident frustration. This he did, while at the same time declaring that a particular person or group had done him an irreparable harm, and therefore should be punished. It struck me that all this time, his pestiferous attitude conjured up the image of one who was destined to submit to inquisitional measures. On the other hand, what was evidently more likely given his stocky and menacing manner, to possibly mete them out. Finally, and indeed what was probably akin to the beatific truth more than anything else on this magnificent, Midwestern, springtime morning was the fact this young man owned a ticket to a boxing match. Which he just found out he could no longer attend. Or, if he did attend the boxing match, it was with the threat of religious excommunication hanging over his head. It was that simple and unequivocal.

I assumed his theological dilemma was due to the fact that our parish priest, right before giving out his benediction at the ten o'clock mass that morning had made a very important announcement to all of his parishioners. His announcement consisted of declaring the upcoming, bare-knuckled, match-fight between our very own hometown hero, "Fightin'" Jim Sweeney and some monster of a backwoods Georgia man, as off-limits to any practicing Catholics such as ourselves. Our parish priest I suppose, didn't want to see us encouraging the conduct of someone, who earned his daily bread traveling the countryside living off wagers. And those wagers consisted of betting he could knock the daylights out of any man who could don a pair of pants without pissin' in them first. You see, Father Helmut Guber doesn't exactly see things the same way you and I might see things. First off, just like our parish's patron saint, Father Guber is from someplace other than Minnesota, and in particular the ex-Holy Roman Empire. Where, and from what I have been told, unless you are wearing a hair vest, chewing locusts, and on your swollen knees a good six to eight hours a day in prayer.... Well then, you might just as well forget the idea that one is "saved". The "one" in mind of course, is yours truly, along with the rest of our dubious and apparently unrepentant congregation. Indeed, from what has been preached to me by Father Guber, as well as from what I have been able to surmise on my own, the conclusion is quite upsetting. For it seems to me, during the last dozen or so years that I have been a parishioner at St. Patrick's, I've been taught there is still a fifty-fifty chance that I won't make it to any celestial paradise. This morbid conjecture is based solely on my self-indulgent, almost heretical practice of using snuff more or less on a daily basis.

You can be a member of good standing in the *Father Matthew's Total Abstinence Society.* Make a point of giving a plate of food out the back door to the hungry traveler stopping through our lonely town. Even take time out to visit the saintly man who is in prison for setting fire to Killiwick's Apothecary shop. While in prison, he admittedly set fire because he'd refused to allow his youngest daughter to go a-courting with the son of that "Orangeman" Killiwick. Still in all, it doesn't amount to a hill of beans to our saintly priest. He'll call the shots concerning our collective spiritual welfare, and nowhere on his list of anointed things to do is there the least mention of assisting at boxing shows. Even though, most of us are pretty sure "Fightin'" Jim Sweeney can just about lower the boom, on any Southern straggler, who comes to Lanesboro, Minnesota claiming otherwise.

The only time I saw our priest close to being enthralled by my attitude was the curious moment when I'd stayed up all night assisting in a difficult birth. Being a dentist by trade, and with Dr. Fount gone over to St. Paul's for a bladder and spleen convention, I had no choice in the matter. Thus, he mistook the bags under my eyes to be the result of some sort of mystical hallucination, or even revelation for that matter. As such, Father Guber kept coming up to me at five minute intervals during the poor child's emergency baptism (she miraculously came through after having the umbilical cord twisted this way and that around her neck) asking if I'd seen an angel, and if I had...was the Kaiser by any chance with him?

I have no doubt that our parish priest is a fine and holy man. It's just that as a close-to-being-retired parishioner I'm worried. I am more than a little concerned that my final debt as a salvation-bound Catholic is to be a last, all-out crusade to free the Holy Land one more time. And this all to be led by none other than our own Father Guber, perhaps with the concordance and fidelity of ravaging Templar Knights hiding out somewhere in the simmering back country of Minnesota.

Now, I am by no means a rabid boxing enthusiast. Except for the few times my older brother, Paul Francis Daniel was inclined to illustrate a black and blue tattoo around one or both of my eyes. This he did for some insalubrious remark I made concerning his carrot-colored hair. Nonetheless, it isn't to be that even the weighted remarks of such a holy man as our own Father Guber can keep me from going this afternoon. To witness the fate of such two talented pugilists as our own, "Fightin'" Jim Sweeney and whoever this Southern pretender to Sweeney's throne might be.

With that plan in mind I set off for my own home, not more than two blocks away from St. Patrick's, displaying a measured swiftness to my gait that

I hadn't enjoyed for quite some time. It was as if the salty, sweet taste of the pickled herring that was to be my lunch was already in my throat, and only needed to be swallowed for my sense of well-being to be complete.

If the truth be known, I haven't felt such a sense of inspiration, nor for that matter something to look forward to for these last many pendulous months. Not since my own dear wife, Katherine Louisa Maddox was called to her heavenly home quite suddenly last December. In effect, her departure left me alone once again, for the first time since I'd been abandoned by my father. Thus, I ended up on a boat as a *gossoon*[1] with my mother departing Castlewarren, County Kilkenny, Ireland for the United States. This all happened when I was of the wizened Abraham-like age of seventeen. That doesn't seem so long ago when measured by the time spent next to my beloved Katherine. Now alone again, it's as if that Dakota Indian saying: "that the departure of a loved one is like the Northern goose that hovers and hovers...trying to find his bearings over some recently spaded field. Confused, batting its wings convulsively while instinctively knowing it will not make its Southern heading before winter comes much too early, and all is lost."

Yes, that's how I feel now, without Katherine, all is lost. Indeed, that's me—without my beloved Katherine; I'm hovering in flight once again while being inexplicably disoriented and invariably lost.

Also, and in spite of Father Guber's mid-sermon exhortation to the contrary, "Everyone remain close to your family's hearth tonight, for Satan is most likely to be up and about. He'll be dressed up in boxing attire while offering watered-down whisky to anyone who is foolish enough to partake."

This of course, brings to mind the question that only a true corned beef and cabbage fed Irishman like myself can answer. Which is to say; if the whisky isn't watered down then can one of *Erin's* own partake? The response came back suddenly, as if the sainted Patrick, who had chased the snakes from our sacred island, had answered me himself; 'Most willingly!' That response was all I needed to hear. Therefore, indeed, now that I had decided to attend the boxing show, I left the church's steps not so much echoing my fellow parishioner's sentiment that everyone be damned, but rather happily so. Contented in fact, realizing I wouldn't have to attend the evening staring at the parlor wall while dreaming I was off shooting Northern "Yankees" with Katherine at my side fixing lunch. With that in mind, I descended the final, graying, interlaced, granite stone steps of St. Patrick's towards my more modest dwelling over on Second Street.

On Coffee Street, I headed directly past the Phoenix Hotel that borders the red-bricked Rayon Wheel Company. This place of business presented no immediate concern to me other than the fact that the proprietor, Mr.

---

1   Young boy

4

P. W. Blatterman and I are veterans of the blue-grey conflict between the states. He in fact, being one of the more stubborn and most cussedness sort of man on the face of God's illustrious, green earth obviously fought for the North. While, myself, as only befitting someone who had been reared to hate the all-encompassing tentacles of the British Empire, had defended the courageous and fiercely independent South. There, to have indelibly stamped on my heart a love and respect for a certain Mr. Jefferson Davis which has not diminished in the least little bit. Not since I last took off the uniform of the Third Kentucky Cavalry, or as we were known throughout the Southern counties back then; "Morgan's Raiders". If I was able to lay claim to an old man's last desire, or could wish it were so, besides tasting one of my dear Katherine's corn-fed and rum-marinated tripe and kidney pies.... It would be to clear Mr. Davis' name from the cruel and unsuitable view that he turned his Free-Mason's back on us. Or, somehow, left us to face our unflinching Yankee fate without so much as a pair of proper trousers to our name. This, President Davis was accused of doing while supposedly off in some quaint Richmond hotel. Thereby, biding his time before joining up with those rich Northern industrialists who had only one purpose in mind; that of squeezing the last ounce of profit from our exhausted and destitute *état*.

I spent many a cold and wheezing night thinking these same exact thoughts through and through in my disoriented mind. This occurred amidst my embattled internship in that barren, heartless prison known as the Rock Island Barracks. A lonely prison, cast aside somewhere in the cheerless state of Illinois, as if we were the North's invective after-thought.

You must understand how it was back then; we were something the North would attend to...when and if the North found the time to do so. But with the war at an end now, and so much to be decided, rebuilt...reorganized along more consequential and therefore favorable geopolitical lines. This being the case, the Federal government decided we'll get to you prisoners when we can. Other than that, we as prisoners just had to wait until we were noticed once again amidst the North's preoccupying state of disemboweling the South. Like so much inheritance to be divided up...and the quicker the better.

So much for their nauseating spiel they proclaimed *sans fin:* "Now that Appomattox has put the conflict behind us, let's come together, we're all brothers once again...." Still in all, a lot of our Southern soldiers died from consumption at the Rock Island prison. Due in no small way, I believe, because our Northern "brothers" had forgotten to hand out enough blankets when all was said and done. Indeed, there was more than enough to be said for their Northern brotherly reconciliation, and the way our blue-clad, former adversary extended an olive branch—right before they buried a lot of us.

Yes, we as Southern prisoners-of-war were declassified somewhere in Rock

Island, Illinois, left to rot so to speak. If for no other reason than to chase away anyone desiring to visit, or sharing a little sympathy with those of us deemed responsible, for embodying slavery in such a disgraceful way.

Why it wasn't that way at all, I swear to it. Most of us common soldiers didn't give a sprig of heather for slavery one way or the other. What got caught under my keel was the fact that the Northern United States, having over-developed and outgrown their industrial factories and cities to such a devastating extent that in doing so, they could no longer feed themselves. The Northern states then turned a wanton eye towards the South and their agricultural venues. That without which, the North could no longer exist, having overextended themselves in their lust for riches.

Of course, I didn't know anything about these matters back then. But only from what I've learned since the end of hostilities almost forty years ago that has convinced me of the following; it wasn't so much the slave question that vexed the Northern boys. But rather, how are we going to feed ourselves, if we let the South go independently on its merry way to pursue its own goals? Slavery, I've concluded was the last thing on the Northern boys' mind. If, it was there at all in the first place. No, it became simply the question; *Why hadn't we thought of it first?*

They say it's the writers of history that determine the truth. Well, from what I've read, and been lectured on these last forty years or so, the following becomes rather apparent. You can damn well bet your life on one regrettable fact. That most of what's been written about this supposedly decisive and glorious war that abolished the Southern practice of human enslavement once and for all; as a matter of course, was written by men, who'd been dipping into the *poteen*[2] in voluminous increments. Thereby, considering themselves all *shanachies*[3]. Thus, these narrators of history could write and say just about whatever they felt like as long as it followed their one hallowed rule of thumb: that whatever they said or wrote had absolutely no bearing whatsoever on the truth.

I swear to you this day, by all that I hold sacred in this life, over thirty-five years to the day that hostilities have ceased. I never owned or knew of any of my fellow soldiers who possessed slaves. It just wasn't to be. And that includes Longfellow Mortlock who served with me in "Morgan's Raiders". Even though it's true, he kept a Negro boy around our soldiering camp at his beck and call. Longfellow claimed he paid the young Negro an honest thirty-five cents a week to make sure he was shaved properly every morning. This Longfellow insisted upon. Regardless of the previous evening's circumstances, for he'd promised his mother back home in Donegal he wouldn't die during

---

2   Irish home brew
3   Story teller

battle unshaven, like a Protestant. Still, being around Longfellow Mortlock as much as I was, I never heard him employ the use of the words; 'banshee-whooper', 'shagger', 'thin lips' or 'frizzy head' in all our time together.

You can see now, what kind of man P. W. Blatterman is. For, if by simply walking past his place of business, can set a man to roaring so, and getting under way like some maniacal carnival preacher, you can imagine what it must be like to actually meet the lunatic ex-"Yankee". Even to try and have a conversation with him; something akin to inviting the devil over for tea, as far as this Irishman's concerned.

Next to Blatterman's wheel factory, and abridging the corner which leads onto Second Street where I live, is the office of the village clerk. This lime-colored building has recently been renovated, and includes solemn, red, brick-enclosed, flower beds both upstairs and downstairs. These flower beds are gilded, forged, black iron and mortar affairs from which nothing has ever grown. It's because the mortar initially had been poorly cured, gradually breaking up into a lot of holes. That being the case, now every time it rains, the water takes the topsoil away, and deposits it onto the street below in various clumps. From these clumps of dirt, lovely pink and crimson geraniums have sprouted with astounding success. So much so, that for awhile our mayor considered closing off half of the sidewalk, and declaring the other side, the geranium side, a public park.

In Lanesboro, for awhile anyway, there was some debate as to which group should be responsible for watering this so-called *geranium park*. Should we call on the emergency fire pumpers or several of our politicians? For as one of the local businessman pointed out, "They have nothing to do but yap all day long anyway. They might as well do their yapping, holding onto to a sprinkling hose." At which point, the idea was shelved.

It is also my office, for I had been sworn in as Lanesboro's village justice of the peace, for a period of two years since October 19th, 1882. That was eleven years ago. Since then, every time an election has been for my successor, it was cancelled due to some very serious municipal affair. By a serious municipal affair, I mean, the German Brook trout running in excessive numbers up at the reservoir, or on occasion, even something more dramatic. It could very well be the widow Klamecki had over-extended herself once again, in effect, producing more than she could hope to sell. Therefore, unless one hurried at breakneck speed to her pastry shop over on Fifth Street.... Well, in that case, there might not be any more brown sugar n' cinnamon coffee cake to go around. Thus, the elections were called off, and I continued in my bi-annual role of village justice.

Turning the corner onto Second Street where I live, and neighboring my own place of business and home is Mr. Britton, with his shoe manufacturing establishment. I refrain from calling Mr. Britton a common shoe maker, although, I personally see nothing wrong in that. However, upon the severe admonishment of one Mrs. Britton, I will refrain from calling her husband a common shoe maker. And instead, will continue to refer to Mr. Britton's place of business as a shoe establishment. Regardless of its name, or the ambiguity referred to herein, Mr. Britton is a very cordial neighbor. He is also an excellent shoe maker and despite the daily, intermittent wailings of his socially aspiring better half, he never lacks for clients. He even told me, he has a mail order business with wholesalers as far away as Duluth and Little Falls.

My own home and dental office is squeezed in between the Britton's shoe establishment and the Lanesboro Fire House while at the same time, it sits just above Daulton's stables. This of course, brings the never ending string of questions, involving the latest dental device of using chlorophyll gas to extract teeth with. The smell of this gas is often confused with the fertilized odor emanating from the ground floor horse stables. This of course, causes some patients to remind me that they haven't come for an extraction. But rather, for some other noble dental affliction, and wouldn't I be so kind as to turn off the chlorophyll gas machine. I then feel obliged, and take it upon myself, to inform the distraught client that riding lessons will be over in another hour or so. And in the meantime, offer them a white hospital mask to put over their faces. It seems to work well enough I suppose, except in the case of Mrs. Schumaker, who always claims she never can trust a dentist whose mouth she can't see. At which point, I find myself reminding her the mask is for her own visage, and not for mine.

My bedroom, kitchen and parlor make up one half of the upstairs while down the hallway at the other end remain my small suite of one dental office or consulting room, operating clinic and kennel. Yes, a kennel. I have heard that in other states, and even when I practiced dentistry in Maysville, Kentucky, pets are frowned upon in most dental offices. However, if I want to practice dentistry, and be successful about it in Lanesboro, Minnesota, I, by all rights must have a kennel. This is for the simple reason that with Lanesboro winters being a six to seventh month loathsome affair, a common dental appointment could very well turn into an overnight, or even several nights' engagement. This could be due to the sudden arrival of one of Lanesboro's customary, yet ill-timed snow blizzards. As a matter of course, this is why some of our townspeople think ahead, and bring with them to my office their canary, hamster or Labrador dog, along with their own clean sheets and pillows. Once I even welcomed an extremely tame, yet exuberant wolverine. Which, when she had her first pup (not in my office thankfully, but several months later), the owner, a certain Mrs. Darnall, was kind enough to name the wolverine pup, "Dr. Ruth", after yours truly. To which I felt myself in no small way honored, and accepted by my fellow citizens of Lanesboro.

I walked into our parlor with its two massive, tan-brown, Danish-leather chairs. The worn, darkened leather is protected by a long, hem-less piece of hand-woven, white, Irish linen. These chairs are pulled up in uncertain, forty-five degree angles from our hearth. There is a round table that jettisons the left hand chair, my chair, upon which is heaped my reading material. To be truthful about it, our house is a series of piles. There is the one on my reading table, the one I just mentioned. There is also the one in the cookery. There is also the pile of clean clothes, just at the beginning of the dark-green carpeted hallway, waiting to be folded and put neatly away. I don't bother with all of that. Why should I? I'd rather push and poke into the pile, until I find what I am looking for, then set the pile right side up again. These are not piles of trash, but, rather just piles where the hand of a woman has once been, and is no longer. Her absence magnified by the distance between the piles as if a small attempt at order has been made, and then just as abruptly forgotten. To put it bluntly, it is no longer worth the effort on my part.

I took off my thin, yellow and brown checked, spring coat. And for some reason, rather than throwing it across the sofa as is my disloyal want, I went and adjusted it on the coat rack. This Katherine would have required had she still been with me, and not as she had unknowingly left me; an orphan for the second time in my life. I did this while my eyes rested on a poem framed and hanging on the wall. I read it carefully, although I didn't really have to for the words had long ago been memorized by my heart:

My Wife

> *She who sleeps upon my heart*
> *Was the first to win it;*
> *She who leans upon my breast,*
> *Ever reigns within it;*
> *She who kisses oft my lips,*
> *Wakes their warmest blessing;*
> *She who rests within these arms,*
> *Feels their closest pressing.*
>
> *Other days than these may come;*
> *Days that may be dreary,*
> *Other hours shall greet us yet;*
> *Hours that may be weary.*

Still this heart shall be thy throne,
Still this breast thy pillow;
Still these lips meet thine as oft,
As billow meeteth billow.

Sleep, then, on my happy heart,
Since thy love hath won it;
Dream then, on my loyal breast,
None but thee hath done it;
And when age brings grief and change,
With its wintry weather,
May we in the self-same grave,
Sleep and dream together.

I still haven't been able to kick this feeling of emptiness that's been hounding me, for quite some time, these last, aching months.

I put the tea kettle on, and went about fixing myself something to eat. I kept asking the question if "Fightin'" Jim Sweeney has it within himself to put that big bloke of a Southerner somewhere down on the paddock floor. I guess no one would really know until we'd all seen the Southerner, and could tell for ourselves just exactly what he's made of. I know for sure, Sweeney is one of Lanesboro's toughest lads around. He keeps order over at our local tavern, and can bale hay most days without once looking over his shoulder for the water wagon. Besides his fists and all-around ruggedness, he is assuredly most sought after for his mastery of our Sunday hymnal. It might seem incongruous to the reader and all, but the sweet truth of it is, Jim can put a feverish baby to sleep with that tenor voice of his. Everyone agrees the way he intones, "Closer My Walk to Thee" is as if an angel himself had come down to lend a hand. It is that clear and beautiful. Hopefully, "Fightin'" Jim has decided not to play the part of an angel today.

I walked down the hall to my office, and retrieved my weekly appointment book, before sitting down at the kitchen table. I leafed through my list of appointments for the next day. The kettle on the stove began to whistle, and I made my tea.

There, heading up the list for Monday morning is Mr. Perry Rudy, due in tomorrow for a readjustment of his new plate of dentures. I had written a note to myself several weeks back reminding me that Mr. Rudy still owes me five dollars from his last appointment. This is because he made the appointment for himself, yet I devoted more than half the allotted time to setting his wife up nicely with three gold fillings. At that time, Mr. Rudy argued he wouldn't pay my voucher for the three gold fillings, because the appointment had originally been made for him. He further contested, I had spent most of my time on his wife's perfunctory palate at her request, so why should he pay for his appointment? Continuing to berate me, he asked, 'what kind of a dentist was I anyhow, if I couldn't help out a close friend in need, now and then?' I made a note once again to bring up the question of the three dollars required at least to cover the cost of the gold, I had used on Mrs. Rudy.

After I finished with Mr. Perry Rudy, I had an appointment to see Mr. Coblish. This gentleman had been after me for several weeks now to clean his teeth, and repair one or two of the more unsightly ones. It seems as if Mrs. Coblish won't kiss him anymore, for his breath has turned increasingly sour, because of his disintegrating teeth. Mrs. Coblish even made the poignant remark that she felt as if she was engaged to be living in the married state amongst four brick walls and a snorting mule. That's how bad the situation has become. Mr. Coblish told me in a matter of the strictest confidence if he didn't clean up his mouth and its accompanying odors that Mrs. Coblish was threatening to leave him. Her menace included going back to Butte, Montana, where fresh mountain air would remind her of happier times. It is an urgent matter for all of us, as they are newlyweds as well.

The rest of my morning and perhaps late into the afternoon will be taken up by my appointment with a certain Mrs. Fitzgerald. Besides being an imposing woman with a robust figure which could rival that of a plains-nesting bison, she is as persistent, as well as the most demanding patient a dentist could ever wish to avoid. Mrs. Fitzgerald had originally retained my services for a complete set of upper teeth to replace the ones that the "shyster" down in St. Paul's had recently fabricated for her. She told me at the time of her initial appointment, when she arrived with her uninspiring husband in tow that she was tired of "wobbling" her way through the holiday season. By that, Mrs. Fitzgerald explained to me, she meant she wasn't sure of what meat or skin she could bite into, and what she couldn't, for fear of losing her ill-fitting dentures. However, the way her spindly husband eyed her, unabashedly frightened, showing more than a little apprehension while she made that statement, left me wondering just exactly whose *hide* she had a mind to bite into. At that time, she related the story about the dental offices down in St. Paul's. The "shyster's office", as she put it, "the ones who had tried to swindle me"—who had originally outfitted her with false teeth. Who, insofar as he could, had reminded her that no one could make a set of false teeth as good as God had made the original ones. This she should try and understand while keeping more of a tight lid on her mouth. "Not to open it too frequently", was the way the dentist from St. Paul's had put it. In some way, inferring that we'd all be a lot better off if she did what he had suggested; "to keep a tight lid on her mouth", that is. This in no small way displeased Mrs. Fitzgerald. Who by then, had not only come to my office for a new set of teeth, but also to relate to me, how rudely she'd been treated by "that shyster dental pioneer" down in St. Paul's. It was only after I had contacted Doctor Briggs, the "shyster" down in St. Paul's, to have him send me the lady's dental history and prints was the following story offered to justify his side of things. That apparently, it was at the end, after the exasperated palate and false teeth man had tried to readjust her upper plate for the umpteenth time, and to no avail that he offered the following explanation. When his client, Mrs. Fitzgerald complained for the final time, "They are still too loose—like mackerel in a fish basket," she said. Upon hearing this, Doctor Briggs swore, if ever he found Mrs. Fitzgerald in his dental office again complaining that her false teeth didn't feel quite right, he'd be furious. In fact, should this ever come about, "He'd pound her false teeth into her mouth with one inch-thick railroad spikes where they wouldn't budge anymore!"

I closed my appointment book, and put it back in its place. But not before making a little note to myself that if time was available, Lanesboro's Protestant representative, a certain, tortured Reverend Mason, needed an extraction done. And if at all possible, the sooner the better, for the good man had reported searing pain. I would tentatively put him down for tomorrow's very late afternoon. I pitied the poor man, for by experience I remembered he would take nothing to alleviate the pain of the extraction. This included even a myopic drop of camphor oil. For as he had expressed himself to me before under similar circumstances, "The Almighty wants us to suffer, He needs us to suffer—we should be willing to suffer—so pull my good man, P-U-L-L!" That being the case, and since I wasn't the one to pass out of consciousness from one of these ordeals, I couldn't in good conscience pass judgment on the man. Still in all, and upon the insistence of the patient, I always performed the extraction without any assuagement whatsoever. Except for the comforting thought; the Reverend Mason would soon be running out of his natural teeth, and therefore the means with which to suffer.

My tea finished, I went into my room, and fished about in the upended clothes pile, for something appropriate to wear to the boxing show.

Chapter Two

Not yet was it treason when we flew,
to arms for a question vexed and nettled,
from times of the Colonies on and through,
to Appomattox—but there it was settled.

Author unknown

The boxing show or competition if you prefer, was scheduled to get under way at three o'clock sharp in the afternoon at Harcourt's Paddock. Harcourt's Paddock is just off the end of Twelfth Street, where the apple orchards and walnut groves started, and the civic boundaries of Lanesboro ended. This boundary plan was due no doubt to the fact that Lanesboro had strict laws against traveling merchants and their vendor-laden shows. In part, to protect an immigrant population which bought up every new article that any hawker could come up with. This included draughts for taking back pains away, or for that matter, draughts for bringing on back pains. If you were of a mind or had any inclination to acquire incriminating back pains, for whatever reason.

I can certainly recall an interesting case in point, with an out-of-town visitor, a Mrs. Ebstein, I believe was her name. This lady displayed chronic back pains from her bed in the recesses of their travelling sales wagon. In order to promote her husband's new pharmaceutical concoction of dried ocean water plankton and grated filings of desert cactus roots. This according to the ingredient's label was all mixed together, with a generous measure of one hundred and twenty proof grain alcohol. Unbelievable as it may seem, this concoction supposedly took away any lumbar discomfort a person might have with an uncanny one hundred per cent cure rate. Unfortunately, for reasons never fully explained, Mr. Ebstein never marketed his "sure-fire" remedy. Nor from what I heard later did he ever forgive himself, for having overindulged his suffering wife with his remedial medicine. In effect, taking away any back pains she might have had while reducing his wife's memory to that of a weaning infant.

In that regard, the city's boundary became a sort of last minute defense for a population that otherwise couldn't defend themselves. Due to the fact, upon having stumped the local inhabitants, there is the imposing Root River flowing alongside our town, marking out one of its boundaries like a pulled-up draw bridge. This river, would by necessity, require some last minute, hectic navigation should the need arise. Along with half of Lanesboro's population in pursuit, forming a retroactive lynching party, if one couldn't coherently navigate in a timely manner, our last bastion of defense—the Root River.

There was one story which I infallibly remember, whereby, a traveling merchant by the name of Hocklestein had suckered half the population into buying religious relics of a distinct and humid flavor. I believe the story goes somewhat as follows; these relics belonged to an Italian grocery store owner from somewhere in New Jersey, who had brought them over from the old country. At the time he sold them to Hocklestein, he insisted that by tapping them anywhere on the ground a source of water would issue forth immediately, and in gushing volumes. Mr. Hocklestein, while collecting our money cautioned us however, clearly admonishing those of us interested in his relics not to tap too indiscriminately and with too much force. He cited a township over in Michigan that had initiated a flood, wiping out half their farms by doing just that. In the end, Hocklestein gave back all the money he'd sequestered from us, in return, for a more appropriate breathing spell than once every thirty seconds while being ducked over his head in our local Root River.

I arrived at Harcourt's Paddock just as I guess everyone else was arriving as well. The afternoon, springtime weather was deliciously golden with the sun distinctly shining somewhere above us. The sky painted blue, hung by itself with a few bellicose clouds scudding about, creating a lovely diversion in the invigorating, spring time heat. There, just outside the paddock, booths had been set up and already the youngsters were having a go of it with candied red apples, and plates of iced, vanilla-flavored cream. Here and there, couples strolled around the stable grounds aimlessly, or so it appeared. Their hands entwined, with nary a thought for the circulating world around them, lost to themselves and their private joys. This didn't surprise me, but on the contrary left me enraptured, for I have always been deeply impressed with your everyday peoples' love and unabashed concern for one another.

The closer one got to the paddock however, the closer one sensed that things were meant to be taken seriously today. Just outside the white-washed fencing and the makeshift bleachers was Mr. Ogden S. Cassidy, who was taking wagers, and from the looks of things doing a good business as well.

Ogden Cassidy was a pot-bellied man, whose suspenders strove mightily to hold up what looked to be two cast-iron pipes from a stove, or in this case, Cassidy's thick torso and stumpy legs. His bowler hat was crooked to one side over his half-smiling, swarthy face. His darkened moustache seemed to be gleaning with sweat as he extolled the pugilistic virtues of "Fightin'" Jim Sweeney. He explained to one and all that Jim had never been out-punched by anyone, as far as Cassidy could recall, and that included his mother. Who, everyone round–a-bouts knew, could wallop just about anyone. This included, as well, her four sons, one of whom (not Jim) worked the smithy, and owned forearms the size of cannons.

To be on the safe side, once in awhile Cassidy would shift his derby to the other side of his head, and proclaim in a hawker's penetrating voice the boxing prowess of the man from Georgia. Who, Cassidy claimed, had once stood in a bog, "Somewheres down in the South for two and a half straight days, fighting it out with an alligator, until the busted gator gave up and swam away."

After that, I saw a lot more money going down on the Georgian.

Maybe fifteen to thirty yards away, and laid out just in front of the makeshift turnstiles, someone had thoughtfully organized an outdoor fruit and vegetable stand. Pulled taught amongst two giant ash trees was a red and yellow awning. Underneath the awning, and stretching out in several directions were wooden crates of every fruit and vegetable our countryside had to offer. There was one woman wearing a daring, open at the shoulders, off-white, summer shift using a tan-colored, springtime bonnet to protect her head from the sun. She happened to be riding a bicycle with a bushel of giant oregano leaves strapped down over the back fender. Although, for the moment, the lady had stopped her bicycle. Thus, she was leaning over, using one straightened leg to keep her bicycle from falling down. She appeared to be waiting for another woman, who was fingering tomatoes in a pulsating manner. As if they were willing, or even able to bite back. She had a peculiar way of grasping a tomato firmly in her hand, and staring at it as if daring the tomato to give her its best shot. In the meantime, the other woman was now standing next to her bicycle, and kept calling out for her sister, or friend to hurry up with her purchases. She kept on insisting the fight would soon be starting. Next to the two of them a man wearing a blue shirt and brown dungarees stood planted there like a ladder. He kept eyeing everyone who passed by suspiciously, his hands stuck in his back pockets, as if at any moment the woman would make a desperate run for it, armed with an apron full of stolen tomatoes.

Further on, and lying at arm's length to anyone passing by, although there was no proprietor within hailing distance that I could see, were haphazardly stacked boxes. These boxes contained green onions and cabbages, bright yellow squash as well as long-stemmed, pale-green, Romanian lettuce. Most of the people were finished looking over the vegetables, or purchasing them. It seemed as if everyone now, was making their way towards the paddock, for it was just about three o'clock in the afternoon.

Just behind one of the ash trees, out of line from the makeshift stream of spectators, and curiously equivalent to something from the French countryside, were two couples sitting around. They graced a wrinkled, white coverlet which had been carelessly thrown over the rumpled, grass-covered ground. One man was lying down on his side, one foot slightly underneath the other one, his pale, sky-blue shirt sleeves rolled up to his elbows. Separating him from the makeshift coverlet and his companions was a wickered hamper. In that regard, he appeared farther away from the ground strewn coverlet and food hamper than his friends. While everyone else was sitting together, he lay on his side, and with one arm to support himself was lifting up a glass of a deep-red burgundy wine. He continued on, raising a toast to their small group. The woman opposite him in a somber, red blouse and egg-shell white, summer bonnet was having difficulty slicing her loaf of bread into two halves. Either her knife wasn't sharp enough, or as I suspected more to the point; our Midwestern sourdough could either be eaten, or used in resoling our crude farming shoes. Our bread had that kind of multi-purpose reputation, for being that tough and resilient. The other woman who was hatless, therefore, everyone could tell she was wearing her red hair in a behind-the-head bun, kept peering through her wire-framed glasses following her neighbor's actions. She studied them so intently, it seemed as if she was the product of a two year university program, involving the cutting and slicing of French bread. And that somehow, according to this woman's calculations, her neighbor needed to be precisely guided through her cutting actions. Lying on the spread ground cloth was another, as yet, uncut loaf of bread sitting next to a wine bottle with perhaps a glass of shaded, ruby-red wine still left within. The man wearing a grey derby was saying something in French to his friend raising the toast, although I didn't have a clue as to what either one of them were discussing. I recognized both couples as being French, as well as being patients of mine, and walked by announcing a hearty *bonjour* as I did so. I was greeted in kind by, "*Bonjour Monsieur le dentiste, comment allez-vous?*"

Having purchased my ticket, I found a seat next to a fellow I knew from town; the inimitable, mustachioed and slightly balding, energetic R. J. Laughorn. He moved over and I sat down, acknowledging his presence with a firmly pressed handshake. I looked out over the paddock, and took into account the bright red, blue and white bunting which had been placed around the white borders, giving Harcourt's Paddock something of a fourth of July look and feel. All of a sudden, I felt a gentle nudge in my ribs, and leaning suspiciously close to me was R. J. Laughorn. He pushed next to me while at the same time, proposing a bottle hidden in a canvas sack, with only the burnished, abruptly-short, green neck of the bottle showing.

"Hey Doc,—want s'um?" He asked me.

Then he confessed to me in a low-slung drawl while continually shoving the bottle at me. Seemingly, as if we were both to become involved in a desperate conspiracy, "Why with this stuff, Doc, you can just about take anyone's teeth out with a hammer, and they won't even know what hit 'em for a good solid two weeks!—Long enough anyways to collect your money and get outta town!"

Having said that, R. J. Laughorn took to wheezing and slapping his thigh, choking and laughing all the while, as if he'd never heard anything funnier. He sounded like one of those new steam engines I'd seen working over at the Anchor Oatmeal factory. The way Laughorn cackled and clamored, he was only missing several puffs of white smoke before his whole being backfired, then sputtered resolutely into life.

I politely refused the bottle. Although, for just the briefest of moments, I wanted with all my heart to have one last go of things. That's right, to sit with the menfolk and swap tales, listen to their bluffing, good-natured stories, tell mine, and laugh when I felt like it. Even if it didn't seem appropriate to laugh. I knew with the men they wouldn't care, they would be happy to see me laugh and enjoying myself...just to laugh...even if it was over absolutely nothing at all. That would be fine with me, to drink a good stiff one; then... nothing at all. How delightful it would be. Whatever it was which made us forget our momentary trials while giving us a rejuvenated impetus to get back into the thick of things. Like an old pack mule that once pushed and coerced into starting out, would set back into a constant pace that could go on forever and ever. I'm telling you that sure would be nice. The feeling for good–tasting, run-like-the-devil, sour mash *poteen* always made me feel this way. But I couldn't, to be honest, I'd had my trials with the accursed *bottle* some years before, and will never forget that amber colored liquid which I couldn't stray from. It wouldn't let me go very far...no matter how hard I tried to make my getaway. The wanting haunted me, and for awhile stayed closer to me than my own shadow. I seemed to always come back for more with a disgusting promptitude, I might add. You could say it cost me my Katherine... for awhile anyway. My body involuntarily shuddered at the thought. Getting a hold of myself, I forcefully pushed the canvas sack back towards its owner, and mumbled something with asperity about maybe some other time.

Laughorn circumventing my uneasiness happily replied, "Suit yourself, Doc," before taking a great big swig from the bottle. He exposed just the stumpy neck of the green bottle to let the refractive sunlight play on the glass, for just a moment. Then turning the bottle over slowly, he gazed at the sun's reflection hypnotically, seemingly to discover, up until now, some withheld secret of the universe.

Just then, there came a shout from down below. I straightened up while straining forward to see what should have been the boxers, making their way into the paddock. Just in front of me, and a little to my left was the man from church, the one who was willing to damn us all to hell, if he couldn't watch the fight.

For someone with the threat of excommunication hanging over his head, he seemed to me somewhat overbearing in his exuberance. Or, even prevaricating for that matter, for he kept hollering out, "Come on Sv-ee-ney you lousy Irishman; show us vat you're made of."

I couldn't tell whether Jim was listening or not. For there were more than a few catcalls like that one, making there way down, from where we as spectators were sitting.

You have to understand one thing though. For those of us living in Lanesboro, Minnesota, which was really just a township of immigrants, as I mentioned earlier, we barely had anything to get excited about. Well of course, if there was a fire or tornado that burned down, or blew everything away; yes, then everyone got excited. If an accident like that happened, hold on; you heard more collective dialects than what supposedly went on at the tower of Babel. But if you wanted some sort of distraction. Well then, besides the once a year *Red Bluff-Indian Folk Dance and Revival Festival,* in which for three days there was a not so subtle message, celebrating what Sitting Bull did to General Custer at the Little Bighorn. Or, later on in the year, Buffalo Bill Cody's *Wild West Show* depicting in graphic detail what we should have done to the Indians, at the Little Big Horn. We, as citizens of Lanesboro really didn't have much to get worked up over. This in a sense suited most of the townspeople just fine. We were a quiet, sententious, God-fearing folk who respected one another, and our various backgrounds and cultures. Still in all, when the time came like today for a change, a chance to get lathered up over something as inconsequential as a donnybrook....Well brother, let them have at it, and may the best man win. For on the morrow, we'd all be back at our planting or forge or mercantile trading or whatever it was which kept each and everyone of us in our daily bread.

The big moose of a Southern man sauntered into the paddock area first, leaving a trail of dust that floated up and away from his army-issued, scarred and tattered, cowhide boots. He wasn't very tall, just a skid over my cousin Pauli's dwarfish ears. But what got us all was the width and thickness of his bare shoulders. He looked like one of those Conestoga wagons, the way he ambled around the paddock paying no never-mind to the crowd. Heck, he could have been a snotty, wet-nosed ox in pants, for all we knew.

Myra Hutchinson, the thin-boned, strawberry-blonde, sales clerk from the emporium screamed out, "Why he looks like the devil himself!"

In the meantime, she pointed to the Southerner's adherence of a tattooed eagle which draped over his right shoulder and halfway down his back. So much so, that every time he moved, or extended his right arm, the eagle appeared to beat its wings in an attempt to fly away. The Southerner was naked to his waist, with shoulder-length, sun-bleached, blonde hair and a gristly, blonde beard that hadn't seen the smooth side of a bar of soap, since Moses set to preaching. The Southerner didn't open his mouth, but seemed to glare ferociously at each and every one of us. And all at the same time as well. As if he could; he'd put the lot of us in his repulsive, oversized mouth, to chew us all up. And then, take his own bloody time about spitting out our collective bones. He was accompanied by a small, hairless individual (his "corner" if you will), who followed the Southern boxer around the paddock. During this time, he kept dabbing at his champion's face with a towel. That for some unknown reason was blackened with charcoal on one side. The upshot of this was, every time he toweled his man off he kept darkening his face. So that before the fistfight actually started, the Southern boxer was peering out between two dark, elliptical saucers around his eyes. Almost like a raccoon caught dead to rights in a great, blinding light.

A tremendous hurrah arose from all of us, when our own Jim Sweeney appeared some twenty yards on the other side of the paddock wall. He had leaped the fenced enclosure himself, with spontaneous alacrity. And now, stood there in place, aloof and alone, no longer approaching his opponent. Instead, he kept shadowboxing while on occasion letting out an immense, vacant uppercut. This phantom punch started somewhere around Sweeney's knees. Thus, by the time his uppercut was finished, the force of the empty punch lifted Sweeney right off his feet. While simultaneously, he let loose a tumultuous roar which indicated to those of us sitting in the grandstands, he'd bag his opponent on the first go-around. Those of us admiring our local hero took up the cry as Jim finished his.

What a sight it was! No sir, Jim Sweeney was no slouch as I've mentioned earlier. He was wearing baggy, blue-denim breeches with an undershirt that sported maybe three sizes too big, for a man of Jim's bantam-like size. Now, knowing Jim Sweeney the way I do, this could only be considered part of his sporting psychology to outwit his opponent. Which is to say, armed with a duffel bag of an undershirt, Jim looked like he was undernourished. And except for the sinewy, corded muscles around his shoulders and biceps, Jim seemed too thin to be boxing his way past much of anything. This included a gator-swallowing Southerner who looked like he lived on raw rattlesnake meat, and not much of anything else.

Anyway, Jim starts to working his way across the paddock, spewing and fuming like an undernourished baby bull. As he moves, Jim's always crisscrossing the air with first his right then his left uppercut. As a result, by the time he gets to where his blonde-haired opponent is waiting, Jim all of a sudden stops, lets his arms hang down loose along his sides like he's all boxed out. Again, knowing Sweeney the way I do, I chuckle to myself, figuring my fellow Irishman has more or less duped the Southerner into thinking; he doesn't have much left in reserve. And with his long, droopy, innocent-enough, freckled, choirboy face, Jim looks more like he's fit to rearrange the drapes at a revival meeting, than knock the wind out of someone. Still in all, Jim stands there for a moment, breathing rather heavily, his brown hair dangling in a thick cowlick over his freckled forehead.

At this point, the referee, a man by the name of P. McCardle steps into the middle of the paddock, between the crowd and the boxers. He announces to everyone almost politely, as if we had all been invited to Sunday scones with jam and tea amongst other things, "Well, noo-ow...." He pronounces in a matter of fact tone, "Welcome, I say welcome one and all. I say welcome one and all to a most goo-lew-rii-ous Sunday afternoon."

P. McCardle, in which the "P" stands for Patrick, something he wasn't willing to be let known, at least until the fight was no longer in doubt. He was garbed in a white shirt with stripes of green and black. It was probably the only formal shirt available to our local undertaker at that late hour on a Sunday. He sported two black elastic bows on each upper arm, to hold his billowing shirtsleeves into place. Everything else was pulled into brown pants with his pant's legs being tucked into his socks. Thus, he couldn't trip over himself, out in front of everyone, running around after the fighters. His buttoned shoes were ankle-length, and besides new suspenders, McCardle had on his best Sunday bowler. It was easy to see it was his best Sunday hat, for he wasn't so inclined to take it off, and administer a whack with it to emphasize what he was saying. This most definitely would have been the case, had McCardle been wearing his ordinary, work-a-day bowler. The man's face was long and clean shaven, almost wax-like in its smoothness. Yet, his muscled jaw stood out in relief, as if he continually clenched it as a means of keeping his feelings to himself. His eyes were small and penetrating, separated by a nose which had been broken more than once. McCardle, as well, owned a set of eyebrows that appeared to be made up of three or four hairs and little else.

In any case, the referee McCardle gets to yelling and screaming, "Come on, come on over here now, gen-teel-men, and let's get to commencin' this here fight."

This happens until both fighters are almost within arm's length of each other, when McCardle suddenly demands, "Should either one of you fellows have any last words—something to be remembered by—for the crowd?"

Boy, talk about being an undertaker to the end. You'd a thought it was a public hanging, the way McCardle kept staring first at Sweeney's knife-like hands, then back to the Southerner while shaking his head sadly. All this time asking, if anyone had any last words, before once again looking directly into the eyes of the out-of-town opponent.

The man from Georgia never caught on. He just stood there kind of pawing the ground, like he was anxious to get started hitting someone. I should have seen it coming. It was as neat a fix as anyone could have drawn up. Now, I'm not saying Sweeney was part of it. No, that's not what I'm saying at all. What I am saying is this; McCardle like or not, was favoring his Irish countryman as much as he could, without actually cold-cocking the big Southern lout himself. It was as fair as fair could be, Irish-style. Especially for one, who, so I was told after the whole show and debacle was over, didn't exactly take time out to explain how things were run in Lanesboro. Not in any honest sense of the word, as far as I could see, to the alligator-killer. Well then, and with your forgiveness, it appears as if I'm getting ahead of myself, once again.

At length, Patrick McCardle, the referee, after making sure the big Southerner didn't have anything to say (in any case, McCardle wouldn't give the man the time of day had he asked for it), turns to Sweeney and asks him in a voice that might have brought down a sweet, gentle dew from heaven upon us all, "And you, "Fightin'" Jim Sweeney, what have you to say for yourself?"

Well, wouldn't you just know it, but Sweeney tells McCardle that rather than saying anything at all, he'd just as soon sing a song. However, this impromptu bit of theatrics doesn't please the Southern man at all. In fact, he then declares to McCardle he's changed his mind, and now all of a sudden, he would like to recite a poem entitled, "The Fall of Atlanta." At which point, McCardle gets to waving his arms up and down, claiming the lugubrious visitor had his chance. That he could have had the paddock floor to himself so to speak, but now with a little respect, we should all like to standby, quiet-like while "Fightin'" Jim partakes of a tune.

Still in all, the referee McCardle, to show his newly-acquired fairness, seemingly threatens Sweeney when he inquires seriously enough, "The song you're 'bout to sing wouldn't be from the *Land of Erin* now would it, Jim, me boy?"

To this Jim immediately chirps up, "Why, yes, Mr. McCardle, it certainly is."

All of sudden, McCardle, who can no longer restrain himself, starts hopping around on one foot, then the other, proclaiming, "Well noo-ow, and did 'ja hear that folks? He says it's a fine ol' song, from the ol' country!"

At length, as if he would drop off and fall asleep, McCardle discards his hat to somewhere above his breast, and stands there expectantly, his half-closed eyes turned heavenward. Now, this doesn't please the boxing man from Georgia in the least, for he gets to tearing around the paddock, gesticulating both arms in opposite and equally flailing movements. While all this time, the big black and yellow eagle on his back gets to moving its wings something fierce. As if the eagle tattoo had just discovered a field mouse scampering around out in the open right there in the paddock, and was eager to detach itself from the Southerner's back to chase after it.

Mr. P. McCardle quietly readjusted his hat on to his head once again. At which point, as if he was lecturing someone on the poignancy of a long and drawn out funeral wake, tells the Southerner, who by now, is just about ready to box McCardle, Sweeney, as well as those of us sitting in the grandstands that this is all part of our Midwestern heritage. Indeed, it was right, fitting and proper, for Sweeney to sing his song. And it certainly couldn't be blamed on any one of us, as a case in point, if the man from Georgia probably sounded like a wounded alley cat, if called upon to sing.

The Georgia boxer started to bellow almost unintelligibly, given his sudden frustration over what had become something of a circus act. When in a deep Southern drawl he declared, "Why I never said I couldn't sing, you—you folks never gave me half the ch—"

But he was abruptly cut off by McCardle, who sententiously expounded, "Never let it be said that I, P. McCardle, never gave a man his fair due. In any case, who under the blazin' heavens wants to hear about Atlanta falling down—one way or t'other—? Come on, be honest 'bout it no-oow. Who cares, or has even heard 'bout Atlanta?" Afterwards, with a much more intelligible expression on his face primly commanded, "That being that, for the love of mike, be quiet my good man, for you've had your chance!"

For some untold reason, this abruptly silenced the sulking, now somewhat confused Southerner, for he took to alternatively looking at the sky, and scratching himself somewhere around his sweating armpits.

McCardle, at last, turned his full attention on Sweeney, "Enough's enough. Now that's been taken care of—go ahead Jim, what'll it be?"

The man everyone hereabouts had nicknamed "Fightin'" Jim Sweeney, called out to us as if we were all front and center at the Duluth Opera house. He announced with his clear, tenor voice, half-singing and half-talking that he'd like to favor us all with "Mrs. McGrath". So he did, he started right in, his oversized undershirt billowing backwards and forwards like a luffing sail caught up on some distant, vagrant, lee shore;

> *"Oh, Mrs. McGrath, the sergeant said,*
> *Would you like a soldier to be your son, Ted?*
> *Scarlet coat with a big cocked hat,*
> *Oh, Mrs. McGrath, wouldn't you like that?*
> *Ah-too-raa-roo-raa-roo-ah-ehh*
> *Ah too-raa-roo-raa fiddley-ehh—*
>
> *Now, Mrs. McGrath looked on the shore,*
> *And after seven years or more—*
> *She spied a ship come in one day,*
> *Bearing her son from far away.*
> *Oh, Captain dear, where have you been?*
> *You been sailing the Med-it-err-a-ne-an.*
> *Have you news of my son, Ted?*
> *Is he living or is he dead?*
> *Ah-Too-raa-roo-raa—roo-ah-ehh*
> *Ah-too-raa-roo-raa-fiddley-ehh—"*

"Ah, the man can sing—t'is nee-ew doubt," chortled the referee McCardle to no one in particular, and commenced to singing the chorus as it came around again. This he did while dancing an Irish jig on one leg. Pretty soon, the Celtic members of the crowd started joining in as well. Still, not knowing the song as well as Sweeney does, we had to wait for the chorus before we could let our vocal chords warble unrestrained;

> *"Then Ted comes in without any legs,*
> *And in their place are two wooden pegs*
> *She kissed him a dozen times or two*
> *Then said, "Oh my God, Ted, but is it you?"*
> *Were you drunk or were you blind,*
> *When you left your two fine legs behind?*
> *Or was it walking upon the sea,*
> *That wore your two fine legs away?*
> *Ah-too-raa-roo-raa-roo-ah-ehh*
> *Ah-too-raa-roo-raa-fiddley-ehh*
>
> *Now, I wasn't drunk and I wasn't blind,*

When I left my two fine legs behind.
A cannon ball on the fifth of May
Tore my two fine legs away.
My Teddy boy, the widow cried,
Your two fine legs were your mother's pride.
Stumps of a tree won't do at all,
Why didn't you run from the cannonball?"

Well, by this time and in between verses, things were starting to heat up, for one man hollered out in a heavy German accent, "Is this a boxing show, or a Sunday afternoon at the park with the missus?"

"He's right!" Cried out someone else, "I didn't pay two quarters to get a melody of the old sod,—you old sod—."

"Vell, if you love it so much—vy don't you go back to the "old sod"?"

This came I knew from the gentleman at church. The one who didn't mind being excommunicated as long as it came onto blows from the boxing combatants first.

"Hey, and take some Indians with you when you go!" Someone else added.

From out of nowhere, a drunken voice spewed forth the following, "The Indians? Hell, take all the Irish potato–lovers, French-speaking aristocrats, German beer-guzzlers and Italian mongrels, and throw the whole lot of 'em, including the Indians over the side,—once and for all!"

Above it all, Jim did his best to finish,

"All foreign wars I do declare,
Live on blood and a mother's pain,
I'd rather my son as he used to be,
Then the King of America and his whole navy....
Ah-too-raa-roo-raa-roo-ah-ehh
Ah-too-raa-roo-raa-fiddley-ehh—"

As Sweeney finished his song, Laughorn my neighbor turned to me, and told me confidentially with breath that smelled like the inside of a boarded-up tavern, "With a voice like that, I'd marry 'im meself if I could—just to 'ear the bloke sing each and every mornin'."

I took a long, hard look at his bottle, and noticed it was empty, at least what was showing from deep down in the caverns of his canvas sack.

With Jim sweetly intoning the final note, Myra Hutchinson yelled out,

"If you can't box 'em Jim Sweeney, then croon 'im to death. That's what I say. Come on—let's get the fight started before next you ask 'em to dance!"

All of a sudden, the referee, as if awakened from a dream, donned his hat before confirming to one and all that fair play is the order of the day. He then beckoned with both arms to the fighters to get on with it. Which they do, circling one another while pawing the ground, and snorting their foreheads up and down, like a pair of truncating mountain rams.

My first reaction was; *Jim's got the big Southerner alright.* For Jim was slicing back and forth, cutting swathes of fine dirt into the air, all the while displaying a lethal quickness much like a stealthy bantam cock. Simultaneously, weaving and bobbing, offering an insidious opening to his opponent by his tantalizing movements, yet never getting too close. As the big Southerner kept taking the bait from Jim, he continued throwing out a bare-knuckled, left jab that found nothing but air. Jim took to biding his time, occasionally feeding off of one of the Southerner's empty jabs, to pepper him with four or five well directed counter-punches. That by the sound we could all hear, appeared to make solid contact just above the man's abdomen. However, it only caused his opponent to cough lightly once or twice before resuming his spurious offensive. This went on for about a half-minute or more with no one gaining the advantage. Twenty or thirty seconds into the second minute of the fight have gone by, that's all, before Jim decided to strike. He danced in tantalizingly close once before backing away. Then abruptly a second time, offering his unguarded silhouette a tempting target, before retreating just as quickly, away from the thick, brutish forearms of his frustrated, yet angry opponent. Jim approached the Southerner a third time, and just as quickly made as if to dance away like before. However, this time, he only took one step back, prior to hesitating for a full second in a seemingly half-winded feint. In a heartbeat, like a coiled cobra, Jim struck forward in a pugilistic explosion. He blasted the Georgia boy with a fearsome clout into the fatty tissue just below, and to one side of the man's ribcage. You could tell Jim had let go with all of his reserves, so much so, that he took to rocking in place for a full measure or more. It seemed clear to all of us that Jim needed the time to gather himself together once again. To be quite honest about what happened next; to our collective surprise, the Southerner didn't appear in the least bit piqued. Rather, his face registered a fleeting discomfort like one might find from a mosquito bite, or an unintended brush with one's forearm and the corner of a chipped, wooden cupboard...perhaps even less irritating.

At last, the Southerner, having decided that boxing is quite impossible, coming as it does against the likes of a lithe and disappearing opponent, such as Jim Sweeney, decided he'd had enough of Jim's taunting manner. He bull-rushed Sweeney, figuring there was no way "Fightin'" Jim could wriggle himself out of his iron grasp once he got those gator-wrestling arms around Jim. Well, not only does Jim anticipate the man's rushing charge, but fixed him with a decisive right hook which would have moved the Southerner's nose several inches closer to the state of Wisconsin. Except he saw it coming, and turned his head to one side in the nick of time. Then the two of them went down in a mound of paddock dust, with the Georgian on top of Jim. That being the case, we no longer had a clear view of our local champion, hidden as he was by a monster of a man with a tattooed eagle on his back. This eagle seemed to be beating his wings with every movement, as if to lend a hand (or wings as it were) to Jim's downfall. However, it was too much play at close quarters for the Southerner to do any real damage, for he couldn't get any recoiled range into his punches. This also might have been due in some small part, to the fact that Jim had relinquished any hope of gaining ground at such close quarters. And therefore, had decided his best chance lay in viciously biting the elbow of the arm used in pinning him to the paddock's earthen floor.

Seeing all this, the referee McCardle didn't like much of what was happening to Jim Sweeney. For he started to dance around the paddock kicking up the mulched, brown dirt, all the while proclaiming, "There's no call for any of that noo-ow, I'm tellin' ya. No call a—t'all. Let the man up, let 'im up I say!"

McCardle must have been furious with the direction the fight had taken, for he suddenly took to throwing his own fists about, and declaring the first boxing round over. He started waving his best Sunday bowler impudently at the fighters, all the while, trying to instigate a reprieve from the grappling down on the paddock ground.

McCardle kept crying out, "It's over—the first round is over! Let the man up—good heavens, Sir! I say let Sweeney up—he may never sing again!"

Still, the gator-swallowing fighter from Georgia didn't pay any never-mind to what the referee had to say. For the Southerner, by now, had decided in the absence of a solid fist to Jim's face that he would use his propitious weight advantage. Therefore, he started gyrating his horizontally flattened body back and forth like a rocking chair, slowly squeezing the life out of our "Fightin'" Jim Sweeney. So much so, that Jim stops biting the man's elbow to concentrate all his energy on hanging onto the man, enabling both bodies to take the invective blow, and not just Sweeney's.

Well, McCardle saw what was going on and kept insisting, "T'isn't fair—t'isn't fair, I tell you!"

At length, he invoked some obsolete boxing rule while with the use of his Sunday-best bowler proceeded to buffet the Southerner about his ears and neck, until the man released Jim. The Southerner, then, turned and growled at

McCardle to stop pestering him, unless he, the referee, would like a helping hand as well of some unconventional Southern hospitality.

Using the momentary relaxation of his opponent, Jim struggled backwards and away from the man's wrestling hold like a bear cub from a snake, giving up ground so he could at least regain his breath amongst other things.

"We can all take a water break if ye's a mind, Jimmy," McCardle yelled out. This he did while simultaneously dodging the thick forearm of the Southerner. Who by now had decided, he'd just as soon get in as many licks as he can. Knowing the fight was no longer, indeed, if ever had been, a fair one.

At this point in the fracas, I'm remembering to myself the prophetic words used in times past by our parish priest. The infamous Father Guber, who once claimed, he wasn't against the use of fisticuffs so much, just as long as they were used to teach any wayward-leaning Protestant a lesson or two. It appears to me, there is always something theological as well as a little theatrical in everything our priest says and does.

This didn't mean the paying customers all around me, were watching what was going on down in the paddock like so many petrified rocks.

First one, then another took to calling out insults like, "Come on McCardle, let Sweeney take his whipping like a man."

Another one foretold, "I've still got a sawbuck here that says Jim won't go down before supper!"

Someone else jettisoned, "Let Jim's mother fight for 'im. At least with her, we've gotta better chance of coming out on top."

"She can't you big dope. His mother's back at home—doing the cookin'!"

And so it went back and forth.

Even Myra Hutchinson couldn't keep her tongue quiet, for she kept crying out, "Give Sweeney a piece of solid timber—and make it a fair fight."

"Make it a fair fight? Then let Sweeney hit 'im with the wood when he ain't looking!" This came from Laughorn, my neighbor, who by now had the dried out look of a trout that's been out of the water much too long.

Now, I'm not so blind that I couldn't make out a certain hostility amongst the crowd members. As if finally, people were taking up sides.

There was Fred Bateman from the ironworks, who began by yelling at the boxers. Then for some unaccountable reason, he took to turning his irritation on the German man. Bateman made a point of singling the man out, "If its cheese you want—all you have to do is look between your own Bosch ears, you big luffer!"

Down in the paddock area, both combatants were leaning on the whitewashed fence. Their chests going up and down at a frantic beat, like two air bladders one could see over at the lumber mill. Indeed, resembling broken metronomes, both boxers stood in place, wheezing like old men. Their overextended lungs took turns making a strange sound; each time filling then releasing air, filling and releasing.

Jim Sweeney looked for all the world like a drowned cat. In so far as he still hadn't quite recovered his composure, after having been practically dismantled, by the overbearing weight of the Southerner. Jim, his hands straddling the wooden planks for support, with a glassy look about him, kept staring at one of the upright posts used for the fence. As if by fixing his gaze on it, things just might come back into focus. I noticed as well, his thirteen-year old sister, Francine had approached him by straddling the fence. She took to whispering something fiercely into her brother's ear. Right afterwards, Jim started flattening his oily and out-of-place hair down with one hand. He continued on, pushing his wayward cowlick back over his forehead, so that he started to resemble a choirboy once again. Still, one could tell even from where we were sitting that "Fightin'" Jim was hurting, and not all together himself, at least for the time being.

I shifted my gaze to where the man from Georgia was calmly picking at his teeth with a long stem of grass. McCardle, in the meantime, was trying to emphasize to Jim's opponent, the illegality of trying to squeeze the air out of one's adversary during a boxing display.

He didn't appear to be making much headway. For the Georgian barked back at him, "If we wait any longer to get to boxing once more, we just might have to cut the hay back. So's we can see one another again!"

At that moment, Jim Sweeney shifted his weight away from the fence, declared he never felt better in his life, and began striking up his familiar boxing position. Which is to say, he flexed down in a half-crouch, with his arms extended out, and his balled fists a little upwards, as if daring his opponent to approach.

Jim's sister, Francine, saw the change come over her brother. I believe she took it as a good omen, for she uttered the following encouragement, "I'll tell her to stay at home and finish supper. Even Ma couldn't whip you today, Jimmy-boy!"

She then cast off from her precarious position on the fence. Francine made a gruesome face at the Southerner, in which she revealed most of her adolescent tongue. This she did, before heading back into the grandstands where the rest of us were.

The Southerner cleared one nostril in a demonstrably vulgar manner, by holding his index finger over the other one and blowing. At length, he wiped his hand off on his breeches, eventually pointing the guilty member at Sweeney, before warning him, "I stood with a dad-gum alligator all day and all night in the swamps back home. I can certainly pass the time of day with an Irish choirboy."

To which Francine, Jim's sister, who as yet hadn't quite made it back to her place in the grandstands turned and furiously stammered back, "Our...our j—j-Jimmy might look and fight to you like a s-s-schoolboy. But today, he's t-t-the headmaster—giving you a lesson in manners, you b-b—big oaf."

Upon which, the two boxers took to half-circling one another. Until it looked like the ground would wear away from so much pivoting and torn-up earth sliding back and forth. From where I was sitting, I thought to myself, Jim's got to make a move. Otherwise, the big ox from Georgia will slowly corner Jim into the paddock's fence, prior to taking his punishing time about finishing our local champion off. Apparently, I wasn't alone with those thoughts. Indeed, every time the Southerner forced Sweeney to back-pedal towards the fence, there was the referee McCardle trying to aid poor Jim. He did this by pointing his hat at the Southerner violently while at the same time, warning him it was against the rules to do what he was doing.

Consequently, the Southerner muttered at one Patrick McCardle that he was, in effect, out of his mind for taking sides. In fact, he had never heard that backing an opponent in against the fence, was in violation of any kind of boxing conduct. This was followed by a short, blistering jab and crisp uppercut to Sweeney's mid-section. This lethal attack caused Jim to fall back closer and closer to the fence, where we all correctly assumed that he'd be mauled once and for all by the Southerner.

Showing whose side he was on, P. McCardle wasn't to be denied. "It is so—just as I say—right here in Minnesota," he answered back.

The Southerner stopped for a moment. He guffawed lightly while imitating McCardle in a most irreverent and mocking tone, "It is so—says so too...right here in Minn-e-sod-i."

The Southerner turned his head slightly to the side, in order to be heard by P. McCardle, giving Sweeney the opening he needed.

Jim stepped away from the fence, and put everything he had into his right hand dynamo. Even those of us in the stands heard the sharp crack of bone against bone. Still, the Southerner barely recoiled although there was now blood trickling out of the corner of his mouth.

Myra Hutchinson couldn't contain herself, "Will ya look at that?" She hollered out, "Ain't nothing gonna stop that bear of a man, but some buckshot 'tween the eyes."

Not satisfied with her previous remark, Myra took her bonnet off, the one lined with a purple-dotted, white sash. She then pointed her hat at the ring, her exhortation rising above the other catcalls, "Come on, Jimmy, knock 'em down and I'll kiss ya—ya big galoot!"

I'm not sure Myra's intended promise of a victory kiss was necessarily the impetus Sweeney needed to out-punch the Southerner. For Myra's front teeth were split far enough apart that one could slide in a one inch thick, wooden plank, between the two, without giving anything away. Or, for that matter, causing any discomfort whatsoever to Myra. In addition to this frontal gap, I had spent many a frustrating dental session, trying to correct an overbite which was probably best suited for irrigation projects, involving fully-grown, mature beavers.

Now, the Southerner, as if finally woken up to the fact that things had taken a stunning turn for the worst, started to land first one fist then another on Sweeney's taut, rib-showing chest. The Southerner would let go a punch, push his wet, stringy, blonde hair from his face, before staring at Sweeney waiting for him to go down. When Jim didn't, well, his opponent would launch another massive blow, and watch again, waiting for Sweeney to go under.

With each blow Sweeney took to coughing. At the same time, Francine, his sister, kept telling her brother to hang in there that as yet nothing had been lost.

She yelled out forcefully, "If the Southerner has to cheat to win, then so be it."

She added something else; about it probably being a good idea to send someone home to get their mother—even if she was cooking. During all of this, the referee Patrick McCardle could only stand by and watch, as Sweeney collected more and more punches, mostly around his upper chest.

In the meantime, things weren't exactly quieting down in the stands. For once again, the German man yelled out, "Vy don't, Sveeney, and zee rest of the Irish go back from vere they came from. Und take zere flimsy boxing technique vith them as vell?"

In defense of my neighbor, Laughorn, for he was pretty well drunk, thus, I don't believe he would have said the same thing sober, suddenly turned mean. Laughorn menaced the German man with, "They may's all go back to Ireland—just so's you can all go to hell! You bunch of aristocratic, butter-churning bastards!"

Now, it came uneasily to my mind that as a beckoning location, 'Hell' had been used much too frequently on this day for my liking. For, I had been taught as a young *gossoon;* you keep repeating something or somewhere long enough, and *the little people*[4]—daft as they may be—will find a way to take you there, like it or not. So you'd best be careful with what you say.

The man from church, possibly feeling threatened now that Laughorn

---

4   leprechauns

had stolen his line, called out to all of us, "If it's a punchin' you vant, then it's a punchin' you'll get."

He abruptly launched himself from his seat. Standing up, the man from church hitched up his suspendered pants, as if he was preparing to head down himself into the paddock area, and join the melee. Apparently, any sober thoughts which Father Guber had proposed earlier in the day, concerning basic Christian charity and mutual respect for one another, were forgotten. Now to be found neatly stacked along side the building plans for Noah's second ark.

I'm a bit lost at this point in the proceedings. For these are people I see almost every day. And for neighbors to be talking to one another like they are doing upsets me. I guess it's the ugly side in all of us. Like when there's one buttered scone left, and as a famished *gossoon* you look around carefully, before taking it. In a sense, making sure no one is there watching, to take note of your heathen selfishness.

Just at that moment, someone screamed out, "Jimmy's down."

I looked out towards the paddock floor.

Sure enough, our local boy was on the paddock ground, and lying there quiet-like, undisturbed, as if he was engaged without a care for the world, in a tranquil Sunday afternoon nap.

Myra Hutchinson was beside herself. To begin with, she let loose with her bonnet, throwing it in the general direction of the big Southerner, as if it would do him some harm. Seeing that her bonnet didn't even clear the spectator-filled grandstands, she began taking off first one shoe, before removing the other. At last, she threw them awkwardly, after her bonnet, with all the force her short-statured femininity would allow.

By this time, the referee McCardle was on his knees next to Sweeney, quietly whispering in his ear, "Jimmy, are you there? Are you okay, Son? Can you hear me, Jimmy-boy?" Finally, in desperation he pleaded, "Sing something for me Jimmy-boy—anything t'all? Please?"

Without a response, he turned to face the crowd, his until then, smooth and waxen face, all crumpled up and teary-eyed. Before he asked aloud, "What'll we do without Jimmy-boy to lead us in song on Sundays?"

Now, I'm as peaceable as a man can get, my Irish blood notwithstanding. My Katherine used to tell me, "Edward my dearest, had you been there when the Nordic men stole down upon our beloved shores to rape and plunder.... Sure-'nough, and wouldn't you have taken them all to *Lockhearts' Tavern,* for some stout and meat pie—trying to understand, just what ailed these poor misunderstood invaders."

Still, it took all the self-discipline I owned when I heard that fatal, "Let the dogs out on this cherubim-voiced bastard of a leprechaun!"

I looked over to my left wondering how a crowd could turn so unruly in such a short time (and never mind the empty bottles strewn about). When I noticed a woman dressed in high fashion starting to descend the grandstands where we all sat. She wore a velvet-composed half-jacket, exhibiting a crème-colored pattern and lavender half-circles thrown about on a matching ankle-length skirt. This ensemble was followed by a neck-buttoned, white blouse which must have been murderous to wear on such a sunny day. She didn't own a sun bonnet like the other women. Instead, the lady in question had chosen a hat piece that looked to be taken directly from a prodigious flock of peacocks. The reason why I say this is; because there were more feathers coming off her hat than one had the right or obligation to wear. Unless of course, you were from the Pawnee nation, and you were preparing yourself for an ambush of sorts.

As an afterthought, I got to thinking that whoever had decided to rustle up all the peacocks in the great state of Minnesota, to make such a woman's hat, could only be thankful for their premonition. In that it was still May and therefore, there was time as yet, for the feathers to grow back. Thus, giving the hunters something to aim at, by the time the fall hunting season returned.

Yet, there she was standing up, the very definition of elegance. As if to make her way out of there, and away from the spectators, who by now had turned quite ugly. Just about everyone around me, was hurling insults as well as throwing things, totally lacking in what we normally knew in Lanesboro, as 'redeeming social graces'. Now, I'm not claiming this lady was the spitting image of my Katherine. But she was darn close enough to where a man, who claims to have an ounce of gentlemanly pride, gets up and offers his assistance. Which is exactly what I did. I even pushed aside R. J. Laughhorn's feeble attempt to dissuade my early exit, with a sort of rugby-like, drunken tackle. This caused him to miss me completely while falling headlong into the remnants of Myra Hutchinson's potato salad bowl. His head came up in a flash covered with salad. He rubbed his face with one hand while looking at me quite ironically. Laughorn swiped at the streak of yellow mustard painted across his forehead and nose, with a mouth that was beginning to dissolve, into a silly, protracted grin.

This woman I believe, recognized immediately my thoughts and intent were of a Christian manner. Therefore, she didn't hesitate in giving me her arm, enabling me to guide her away from Harcourt's Paddock. And to what was rapidly becoming civil disobedience in the fullest sense of the word. I looked back over my shoulder, searching desperately to see what had become of the boxing match. To my dismay, all I could make out was Patrick McCardle, the referee, blocking Jim Sweeney's inanimate form from the big Southerner's victory celebration.

The referee kept insisting, "How can the fight be over, and you declared the winner, if the man's still breathing. Which he is—isn't he? I know Jim Sweeney, and he'll be right as rain, if you'll just stand back and give the man some room to breathe—. Come on, let 'im have the full ten count!" While he was saying this, McCardle kept alternating between gently tapping Jim's face to see if he'd come around, and frantically peering into his lifeless eyes.

To be quite honest about what happened next, I apologize to you, the reader, yet I can't recall exactly. One moment, I was admiring her perfectly shaped mouth and illustrious, high cheekbones while wondering how could such a gentle creature be found by herself, alone in Harcourt's Paddock. This I was thinking, just before some weight bearing projectile flew out of nowhere, and not only put me down succinctly on my backside, but set me to rights as well.

For an instant, my head stung like a pack of bees that had been let loose from within. Or, like the time Johnny Cauthers stole some of his uncle's *poteen,* and we drank the lot of it. Only to wish we had died the next day, so as to forget our miserable and fractured state. It was then I felt something wet and clammy just aft of my left ear. I looked up from where I lay a hundred questions vying for my immediate attention. Her eyes were wide open, and of an undaunted, grayish-blue, soft, yet quizzical demeanor, in what I hoped to be her sole concern for me. Before I closed my own eyes; I took in as much of her perfumed femininity as my lungs would allow. At length, right before passing out of consciousness, I believe I deliberately called the lady "Katherine"...while asking for her help.

PART TWO

Castlewarren,
Ireland-1851

Chapter Three

Aye, ye can go back, hoping one can he told me,
Go back to where it all started
Go on and see if it's the same, he warned
To where youthful palsy and trembling manhood parted.

Author unknown

Now, now, I beg of you, please bear with me.... I must incite a most humble pardon from my reader, for I am skipping ahead of myself, as I often have a want to do. Could it be due in some small way to my age? That this stumbling buffoon can no longer remember...what I heard the other day? It was just the other day as well, not so long ago—eh...? Oh yes, that this stumbling buffoon can no long distinguish his rear end from a hunting knife. Yes, that's it. A rather colloquial saying I might add. Although, if the truth be known; my posterior region isn't quite as sharp as a hunting knife, and has yet to skin a mountain cougar. Perhaps my confusion or imminent rambling is due in no small way from seeing my beloved Katherine once again, at the aforementioned boxing match. Still in all, I am altogether miffed as to why she didn't recognize me right away.

Nevertheless, to exonerate Mr. Jefferson Davis' or our own General John Hunt Morgan's name, cannot be too quickly aspired to. Nor lightly dismissed, in regards to what happened afterwards, by those who are required to write history. However, in all fairness to you, the reader, I had best start at the beginning which certainly appears the logical thing to do. And indeed, is confirmed by one of our professional tenets. In which, we as dentists, being a group of some of the more laconic and mundane group of individuals one is likely to come across, can only confirm our dour personalities by reciting the following tenet. Which at the same time may also be considered a summation of our collective banality: "if we don't start at the very beginning with a comprehensive examination, then we are most likely to cause our patients a great deal of untold pain and grief....For suturing can have no value whatsoever, if the tooth in question, hasn't been extracted. Or at the very least, set to rights with a minimum amount of ether gas or a vial of chloroform before commencing any operation."

That being the case, before I go any further, please let me explain who I am. As well, what in tarnation an Irishman like myself is doing out west. Amidst the fortune hunters and societal recluse who seem to haunt in abundance the western territories, of these very same United States.

If I am to establish any liens with the truth then I must, by obligation, take you back with me to my boyhood. Which according to the Reverend John Bowe, and his well-kept, Gowan parish records started sometime around my baptismal date, in the non-Celtic year of 1835. As well, this all took place in the small village of Castlewarren. Now, our village, Castlewarren is part and parcel of the larger County Kilkenny, which along with the neighboring counties such as Carlow, Wexford and Tipperary, help to make up central Ireland, or as the locals call it: "The Land of Erin".

A place, I've always heard talked about, and referred to as *God's own backyard*. It's also been described by others as; "a dirty, ragged town some of whom would think it a folly to throw away a penny on the place whilst others made it their home—not having that penny to throw away." Then again what do they know? For there are only two real truths in all of Ireland; the Catholic truth and the Protestant one, and your belief in one or the other decides if you'll eat that day or not.

I don't know if this following story will help shed some light on what went on in our *clachan* or crumbling village. Or what happened to most of us afterwards. Still, it's been retold to me so many times over the years by the *children of the Gael*[5] that I'm thinking it should be situated in the good book, somewhere between Mark and John. In any case, here's how the story goes:

"Now then, it seems a passer-by from Wexford was reminiscing to one of our own farmers when he made the remark, "His majesty Satan seems to own a great deal of property amongst these hills, judging by their names, Hanging Rock, Black lion?"

"Indeed he does Sir," confirmed this son of Erin, "But he is like most of our landlords, he makes his headquarters as well in London, Sir."

I'm not sure which way to lean, for I was quite happy growing up in Castlewarren. Therefore, as far as this Irishman's concerned, if it hadn't been for the *skibbereens*[6], over at the *Poor Law Commission*, who'd gone ahead and

5   The Irish themselves
6   Poor folk

made a pact with the devil to rape everyone of us. This they did, prior to taking away what precious little else we had. If it hadn't been for those cruel folks, I'd still be planting *lumpers*[7] on the hillside, and figuring out ways to bring the English down.

Castlewarren might have been an uneasy group of public houses and small shops, attracting broken lines of donkey carts loaded to the crib for market day. At the same time, it was also a lovely place where a young boy could run forever. Once the chores were done, for they came first...always. The chores were something you wore around your neck everyday like a halter. They chafed and chapped you undoubtedly, seemingly without remorse. They were a constant reminder that although we may be living in God's own backyard, and therefore, in accordance with the holy book; "The birds of the air need not sow or reap".... We on the other hand, not knowing how to fly, had better plant, weed, prune and harvest to avoid the swollen bellies of a lot of our diced countrymen. However, in all fairness to everyone concerned, once these tasks were completed I was free. Then I would run. It took only five minutes to cross the village at a heady sprint. For in truth, the village consisted of one street, with a hodgepodge of little lanes leading back into the hills. In truth, once through our crumbling village, I could then make for the fields which were cut deep into the surrounding hillsides.

The hills canvassing our village appeared to me to be like the needlepoint stitching that set off the intricate handiwork of fine Irish linen. This was due, no doubt, to the crisscrossing nature of the mortar-less stonework. There were no forests or trees to be seen anywhere thanks to the myopic English. Apparently, for some cantilevered reason, the English decided they needed the wood more than we did. Thus, they cut and hauled the lot of it away saving us the unwarranted need for leafy shade and its annoying comfort. This is also why everything that we built, including houses and fences, were constructed with stone. For there was nothing left to us, with which to build.

Everything was gentle and sloping except for the stone hedges. Granite bay stones were used as dams to lock up a field, and prevent it from spilling over onto a neighbor's plot. Or worse still, allowing the precious topsoil to disintegrate, and slide as it were, down into the contoured glens that lay like inoffensive, sleeping giants separating our hills. Beyond these hills stood more undeniable ones. Undeniable for the fact that craggy granite was the imposing order of the day, and wouldn't allow even the heartiest of farmers or the sharpest of plows to till imbedded rock. I didn't think about it, nor was aware of any of this when I ran. I was young back then, and it was just how things were. Little did this *gossoon* know that he was absorbing more so than

---

7   potatoes

he deserved, for someone so young. Only to be asked to spit it all up later, for the price of a sailor's jig and a piece of steaming pork pie.

What I loved about running were the liberated leg muscles which were no longer cramped from being indoors, or contracted under some injured sheep's, slimy flank. What I loved about running, as a village *laddie,* was the formidable smell of dampness from the stagnant fog mixed with the aroma of a peat fire. Truly, a most glorious inhalation that called to mind our St. Patrick's feast day with its special food, including *Sunday's kitchen* of a calf's head and pluck with *fadge* or potato bread. What I loved were the various hill paths leading forever upwards and away from an absentee Lord Tenant's fostered tale of chronic insufficiency and boggy, turf-fed woe. As if it was my personal duty to thank someone that our collective, blarney-filled rear ends were up to it in muck, with no forthcoming way out. My mother, somehow knew this and in her feminine Gaelic way let me run our hills and glens to let things out. Disintegrate my passions as it were, lest I turn into a *spalpeen*[8] for the hated British.

The village sheepdogs would put up their heads and bark only to give way to a wagging welcome as I passed by. They were of no particular breed that I can recall. Still, they were as smart as some of their dull-witted owners, and probably could have run the farms just as well, given half the chance. I have a vivid picture in my mind of a mongrel with brown on her flanks, black on her backside, with a white marking in the form of an arrowhead on her chest. She stands there in the middle of the lone, intersecting, village road early in the morning, waiting. I see her as I set out to collect our milk. She hasn't seen me, but seems intent on following an elderly man, who is working his way home. The man is slightly hunched over as if giving into the never ending fog, or the fatigue of a laborer's plight somewhere over on the Galway coast. I'd heard tales that they harvested the very ocean's growth over there, to eat, when families had to stretch things between harvests. I believe the common words they used were; "weeds from the sea" or "seaweed". And if, for no other reason than it doesn't sound right to my palate, I decided I'd stick to my mother's potatoes and buttermilk.

The whiteness of the rock-bordered fields, set as they were against the dung-enriched, green plots of land, when mixed with low-lying fog, sent my legs a flying. I would shoot out past the two storied, lime-colored house where the Burtons lived. Just opposite the Burton's place was an empty field, although on the eastern side of the field was a blackened wall. It was not blackened by fire, but rather from moss which had once covered the wall. The moss had slowly died, sucking up from within, whatever nutrition the wall could provide. No one knew why the wall was there. Just as no one knew why

---

8   Migrant agricultural laborer

we shouldn't go there to play, except that the elderly villagers said *the little people* (I believe the term they use stateside is "leprechaun") lived there. That we should leave them alone if we had a lick of sense about us, which was good enough for me. Down the lane, perhaps one hundred meters or so was another two storied house, the last one in Castlewarren, before the open fields. This house resembled the Burton place in appearance except it was white-washed and on only one side. As if some tragedy had struck the family, and they had left things as they lay. Far off in the distance past the planting fields was the last hedge stone wall. This low-lying, stone hedge followed the village for two kilometers or more. In that way, it separated where we lived and planted from the Northern hills, which as I mentioned earlier couldn't be tilled. Sectioned onto the beginning of this wall was a small, outdoor shrine. This, then, is where during Lent and before Candlemas, we would visit the shrine and pray to our God. To be truthful about it, He didn't answer all my prayers. I would have been happy with a solid sixty-percent rate of return that we reserved for the top kickers in our national sport of rugby. When I asked my mother; why didn't God answer all my prayers—was He away on holidays most of the time? Or, living on the other side of the Irish Sea, and couldn't be bothered with us like our Lord Tenant? I received a good crack on my backside for my purported theological insolence.

Finally, my mother (or "Ma" as we called her), in a moment of judicious confidence, told me God couldn't listen to everyone, what with the Protestants taking up most of His time, in Northern Londonderry.

At least twice a fortnight, I would take our donkey breached with several baskets, and lead him up into the neighboring foothills. We did this to collect turf from the outlying bogs for the hearth. I didn't like to do it, as our long-eared, obnoxious, untrimmed donkey named "Job" was a master at dragging his heels. Thus, he would see to it that our trip would take as long as he could possibly make it last. Of course, I tried to explain all this to Ma, yet her white ash cane explained in rebuttal, amongst great detail to my fanny, the reason I must go anyway.

To be fair and all, I've heard some people in passing by, spoke how we lived in "the bogs of nowhere", those of us from Castlewarren. Most of the time, saying it with their upper lip curled back and a marked look of disdain about their unkind faces. Seemingly, as if we were a people to be looked down upon, like that O'Byrne fellow over in County Carlow. A man, who was forever claiming his ancestors were of the purest Irish nobility, to anyone he could find who would listen. Nevertheless and in the meantime, this O'Byrne fellow spent most of his waking hours hiding out fearfully, in and amongst bushes of blackberry like a finch, begging his daily bread from the travelers who happened by.

41

Well now, and if so, that "nowheres" is a place to catch fish, to steal fruit from our absentee landlord, to play tether whip with John and Frankie Scullum, before hiding in and amongst the Druid caves which pocketed the hills. All this we did, while the wind that comes scuttling down from these same hills sang out the Druid's ancient rites. Then I must disagree. I loved Castlewarren and never wanted to leave. I'm thinking my mother, sisters and brother were of the same frame of mind as myself, all except for my pappy. That's what I'm thinking. I prayed long and hard on it too over at the shrine. Still, the good Lord must have been working overtime, due to those Protestant bastards up in Londonderry, because in the end, we moved just the same.

My lone recollection of my father is a man bent over as if in a continual struggle with our land. He is wearing a knee-length and dark, shepherd's rain coat taut over his shoulders and back. His coat then, falls free to hang straight out off his duff-end, like a sheave protecting him from the constant drizzle. He has a tool in his hand, and is planting just back of a crumbling, half-a-meter in height, belly-up, stone hedge. There's a low-lying haze, not very thick which surrounds him. This foggy air appears to me that if given half the chance, would engulf my father, and leave him stranded in that position. Perhaps hunched over and poking in the dirt for all of eternity.

The stone hedge isn't really tall, but just enough of a border to separate our thatch of brambles and *lumpers* from our neighbors. His yellow and red, tartan-patterned cap is slatted down like bent, corrugated roofing hiding his face. But in any case, you can't see his visage. For my father is studiously, it seems, peering intently down at the ground, specifically at what he is trying to stick into the earth. He is wearing a glove only on his spading hand while the other one holds the potato seedling to be laid in. His feet are spread apart as if they were a pair of *jimmies* or trestles, and he was being asked to bear the weight. *The weight of what? Perhaps, the impossibility of it all...of being a man without any help so to speak. Of knowing none was ever going to come, the patriarch of our destitute family, without any resources of any consequence, especially during those undeniably trying times.*

Aye, the poor man.... My heart goes out to him for the way the blight came on and the manner in which the English handled it. For they did a masterfully poor job of it which history has already recorded. Incredulous as it may seem, our colonial masters made a point of doling out misery to the Irish, three times a day, and on our own soil as well for God's sake.

Off in the distance, perhaps a good half of a mile or so away, is a well laid out field, plowed and furrowed with clean, symmetrical rows. It was almost insulting, lying there, just to the west of ours in its emphatic, well-maintained and thoughtful, geometric existence. Then there is the one in which my father is trying to keep the weeds, and who knows what else at bay while he waits for the crop to come in. The only parcel of land my father can work on is a twenty by fifty meter patch that he has hand-cleared, in which he is now planting alone. My father didn't have a chance to succeed. And probably not a clue as to how to succeed anyway, had it come right up and belted him over the top of his *croppie* head. It just wasn't in the cards.

I called out and all my father did was raise a single hand to acknowledge my shout. Other than that he didn't move a muscle, but just kept hacking away at the fuzzy, moss-colored earth. Heck, he didn't even call out for me to come and help lend a hand, like he couldn't have cared less. He probably had realized long before then the futility of it all. Still a man has to keep on going, maybe bearing his share of the pain as well. If not at that point in time, then sometime later on, maybe even years later. When you're before a fire with a solid glass of bourbon whisky, and you're feeling good with your world. Then all of a sudden it happens, it hits you, you get to thinking—*what about the others? The ones I left to grapple alone. Are they okay? Did things work out for them?* At length, with the help of the bourbon, in unrestrained quantities I might add, you can convince yourself that what you did was right. You can convince yourself they were better off without your help—that no one needs a lazy, in the tank, son-of-a-bitch father around anyway.

Now, I'm not condemning my old man for what he did, nor am I exonerating him either. But as a general rule, I'm damned put out against someone pulling on well-aged, sipping whiskey while the rest of us starved.

So that's the way it's to be then is it? You see? Now *the little people* have gone, and got me convinced I know what other people are thinking, including my old man.... How in God's good name could I possibly know what went through that poor man's mind? The two of them must have suffered greatly. Even though I didn't know my father all that well, I certainly saw the scars he left on my dear mother's face and heart. Aye, it was as if a milk wagon had burrowed its way back and forth over my mother's loving heart. In a sense, crushing the very life out of her, yet still maintaining enough pulse for it to keep on beating. This in addition to, leaving wheel tracks across her heart the size of the neighbor's nicely planted, furrowed rows. The thought of which (the planted rows and not ma's heart), I've been told, kept the old man awake and feverish most nights when he was still at home.

The reason I say he suffered, even though I didn't know the man, is because I've learned as a general rule no one could do what he did. And afterwards, be left alone to go about his own ways with an innocent enough conscience. A situation, which upon closer reflection, appears to me, to be very similar to an idle Scotsman, or a Connemara pony skittering shamelessly about the highlands. It just doesn't tabulate. There's a price to be paid later on in the year, for not planting in the early springtime right after the deep, infiltrating rains come. And there sure in hell is a price to be paid in abandoning your family, for the great whore of whores—becoming a politician. For that's exactly what he did when he came to his decision, without fully understanding it. He unknowingly condemned himself to middle years of shameful excuses and an unremitting conscience which finally broke him. Or, so I'm told from everyone who knew my father back then.

This of course, brings to mind our home and me mother and me sisters and my one older brother Paul Francis Daniel Ruth. The likes of whom would just as soon blacken one of your eyes than give you the time of day. My brother wasn't always like that, but turned sour and angry, all grey and threatening, like one of our vicious highland storms—it seemed to me the day our father left home.

Indeed, as far as this Irishman's concerned it was like that sheepdog I mentioned earlier, the one who waited patiently at the intersection of the lone street in Castlewarren. He'd be asleep right in the middle of the lane, when an echoing sound would announce something was coming down the lone stretch of road. His ears would prick up in anticipation, his forelegs would grapple the aggregate–bound pavement tense-like, and he'd wait. The dog and his whole being appeared patiently in place, everything straining to see who or what was up and about. As was mostly the case, the person coming through wasn't the sheepdog's owner, or at the very least someone he cared to see, like Owen Robins the Castlewarren butcher. So then he'd hunch back down, slipping his tail around his back legs and continue to wait, all expectant-like; still keeping one bent ear aloft for any sound which might bring his owner back. That was my older brother Paul Francis Daniel, except he wasn't wagging his tail in upturned anticipation. No, he turned ugly and cold, haunted by something akin to revenge when the old man left, like I mentioned before, and never came back.

My brother was tall and thin, somewhat frail with delicate features. His blue eyes were of an extraordinary brightness that stood out in stark contrast to his sallow, facial countenance. A countenance, I might add which went poorly with his full head of carrot-colored hair and thin-ridged, protruding cheekbones. A look I might add that later on prompted more than one American to ask if my brother didn't have forefathers, who were Norsemen, and rode the seas looking for lands to conquer. If my older brother had a discriminating feature, it was his un-abiding hatred for the British and anything they could dream up. This included some empirical idea that the sun never set on their aristocratic backsides. This thought, in and of itself used to turn my brother senseless with anger. Years later, I heard the American-born expression: 'that a man was carrying a chip on his shoulder'. That being the case, my brother had a whole bloody rock quarry on his. This he backed up with a set of fists which seemed to me to be a matching set of thongs. When you'd pretty much figured out that one was set to come your way then just the opposite would happen. Eventually, leaving some of the pain to dissipate once you asked yourself, *How come I never saw it coming?* He had a cynical or sarcastic tongue which he couldn't control. This seemed to go hand in hand with his inviolate ability to want to fight anything and everyone over the slightest provocation. I told him on more than one occasion he should have been a priest, like Father Daniel O'Shea over in Wexford County. Father Daniel O'Shea had the reputation of taking the penitent one outside the church; before, during, and even after a full confession to beat the living daylights out of the man seeking absolution. And God help you, should the penitent one make the mistake of coming to confess the same sin, he had already confessed the last time he had visited Father O'Shea seeking pardon. Back then, it wasn't so much God and his forgiveness who we needed, but a skilled "corner man" to stop our collective, spiritual bleeding between rounds.

Paul Francis Daniel was in the habit of spitting out irony whether one liked it or not. He was forever calling us, "The children of the Gael"[9], but one could tell the way in which he pronounced it, with his mocking tone and all, it appeared to be more of a curse on us than anything else. He was my brother, we grew up together, yet for all our trials and adventures together (if indeed they can be called that), Paul Francis Daniel had a short fuse which as I mentioned earlier came to life a short time after the old man left us. I'm not sure if it's a good thing or not, nevertheless, on the tolerable side of my calculation, his anger at least, showed no partiality to anyone, be they kin or otherwise.

Now, this doesn't mean we weren't a happy group. It seems to be part of our Irish personality to seek out the fuller side of life, regardless of our present circumstances. We could all be staring at the last bit of broth, but that there wouldn't be someone (including myself) to lay hold of a poem or song to help quiet our appetites. Indeed, my mother, who only spoke Gaelic, our Irish language (as befitting one of *the children of the Gael*, regardless of how my brother saw it), when the mood would take over she'd mete out the following, her an uneducated country girl and all. I'd be so astonished that I remember asking myself; *how could my dear mother know and remember such verse?* She'd recite:

> *Home!*
> *T'is the paradise of infancy.*
> *The tower of defense to youth*

9   Ireland's own people

The retreat for manhood
The city of refuge for old age
Recollections, associations cluster round it.
O how thickly—
Enjoyments are tasted there whose relish never dies from the
    memory.
Affections spring, and grow there through all the turns and
    overturns of life.
And which last on, stronger than death.
The thought of its early innocence has kindled anew the flame
    of virtue
Almost smothered beneath a heavy mass of follies and crimes.

For you see, to the Irish including myself, our love of poetry is the one thing the English couldn't tame, or take away from us. To us—*the children of the Gael*, it meant everything including our integrity as a people. Why to cheat the English out of something, they've figured they've got pretty much locked up in hand, is just about as important as waking up in the morning to find out you're still alive. That you've hood-winked the devil himself one more time, in a manner of speaking. This is also why, in the end, we will win our freedom. Which of course, is also the reason we must never let our love of poetry sleep and turn to ash. For our eventual freedom is intrinsically linked to our formidable love of letters. Indeed, the entire key to taming the Irish people lies in the fact that the English knew only how to grow the potato.... They never, ever learned to properly cook it.

Our home was a cottage, situated on little more than a quarter of an acre of land. Our cottage or cabin (to an American) measured a quaint four by six meters. I'm being unpretentious in that I don't mention the servants' quarters or the racing stables, or the bloody billiard parlor for that matter. This space included three compartments; a bedroom, also, sandwiched in between the bedroom and the roofing thatch was a loft, and intended as sleeping quarters for those of climbing age. This of course, meant it was used by my sisters (until they left), my brother and myself. I made a practice of sleeping next to my sisters, or as close as I possibly could get, before I would be pushed violently away, the two of them claiming I smelled too much like "Job" our donkey. This I must admit, I had attributed to my brother, which is why I made my way to their side in the first place. They had a clean and joyful smell, which combined with their flannel sleepers emanating warmth, helped me to sleep long before the evening fire quit. The rest of the cottage served as a workplace, sitting room, dining room and parlor, such as I was to see many years later, in some of the better homes in Boston. The one difference being that the parlors I eventually visited in Boston, were furnished with deep, thick carpeting and not the tamped-down, dried-out, mud flooring we were used to walking on. I've often asked myself in the ensuing years, if the good people of Boston could renew their expensive rugs as easily as we did our floors, simply by getting fresh dirt from the outside garden.

At the same time, near the bedroom door and the open hearth was the chimney corner. This part of the cottage was given its name because as children, we were constantly scrambling to find a perch on the closest *creepie* or small stool next to the hearth. There we would wait for mother and our meals trying not to fight too much amongst ourselves.

We took our meals on an old, carved-up, pine table which separated two waning oak dressers from each other, like matronly aunts who could no longer tolerate to be seen with the other one. In both of the dressers my mother had laid out her chipped and cracked crockery. This I suppose, was to show the Lord Tenant, should he arrive one day that we were fine examples of what responsible farming tenants could produce. Besides our illustrious tableware, this included according to my brother; churlish, undernourished vegetables and poor man's, vagrant, seamy breath. Paul Francis Daniel also mentioned that if ever the Lord Tenant should come, it wouldn't be because of our fascinating turnips or gleaming cookware, but more than likely to throw the lot of us out of our cottage and off his land. I didn't understand back then what my brother meant, but my mother sure in hell did. She threatened him with a short life at the end of a leather strap if he didn't hold his tongue, and quit his eternal fishing around to upset everyone.

There weren't any pictures on our walls, but that my brother didn't propose he could set to right some reddish pigment, and paint the great pyramids of Egypt. This he said he could do, on the empty wall space, between the oak dressers. With a certain flourish, my brother explained, his paintings would then show the other *croppies*[10] that we were a lot better off than those so-called 'cultured' Egyptian folks, who must build something in overwhelming detail before dying. Whilst the Irish could pull off death, simply by laying down their swing plow, and falling into the recently dug hole, without having to ask anyone's permission.

As I recall, there was the permanent smell of *shag* and potato skins from over in the sieve, in the corner of the room. I would be remiss in my duties if I didn't mention the line of laundry hanging right down through the middle of our parlor. The laundry had to, upon occasion, be pushed to one side of the room in order to prepare a place for the center of our winter's industry.

---

10   farming tenants

This of course, being the wheel or spindle, with which my mother and sisters used to make yarn.

Now, this was strictly woman's business. Insofar as that goes, we could only wonder, my brother and I; why with so much yarn to spin, how the women couldn't keep from becoming daft due to the monotony of the repeated cycles. It wasn't until years later I reached the conclusion that an inordinate amount of feminine gossip is required to keep the hands free to spin. Therefore, the man about the place, in order to promote the production of yarn, must keep quiet while he is supposedly being enamored with the story of the growth of a boil on Auntie Cecilia's foot, the size of which could be placed in a basket and sold by the dozen.

As I mentioned earlier, and without dawdling too long on the subject, ours was a poor man's lot. As such, we bought wool for one shilling a pound with the collective admonition that one day we'd have our own mutton to shear. The wool was then scoured and well-greased. Afterwards, it was laid out on wool-carders which are wooden squares, bearing handles with pliable wire bristles centered within, like the bristles of a hairbrush. The wool is brushed backwards and forwards at a canter's pace, between the carders, until the unevenness and tangles are gone. The remaining wool is finally brushed into light, fleecy curls about six inches in length. These lengths are spun into yarn by the simple process of holding the end of the curl on the spindle. A few turns of the wheel fasten and commence a thread, which is drawn with the left hand while the right hand is occupied in turning the wheel. Now, this all might sound fairly Dublin easy-like and squared-enough away, similar to a downhill run through the heather. Nonetheless, I can tell you, having given the whole operation a good settle myself that I'd much rather be given the task of explaining the book of Genesis to "Job" our donkey, than to have to fight the unmanageable wool into yarn. This is because the yarn, so cumbersome at times, it appeared to have a mind of its own. Indeed, the wool seemed to me, to be much like my sister Ann Horian, when she's made up her mind about something. In that way, much like our wool, exhibiting her blasphemous, Irish stubbornness, as if it was something to be aspired to, like the tapered forelegs of a swift racing horse.

It was only me mother, who had the nimbleness of thumb and brain to be able to spin each length of *skein*[11] in the correct manner. By this I mean, she could even out the yarn, yet at the same time harden it, by passing the length between her fingers while with the same stroke turning the wheel rapidly. My sisters couldn't do it. For the simple reason being; one of them would get to giggling over some silly thing or another which would make the other one cackle, thus causing the spindle to slow down and the *skein* to turn in against

11   A cut or length of thread

itself. The end result would be an unmanageable tumble of yarn, as well as, the uncompromising flash of me mother's backhand. When all was said and done, it was then time for the weaver to make an appearance. This he most always did, right before our supper was served out. Our mother would also keep a small draft for ourselves which she would knit into stockings to sell, using a variety of vegetable dies for color.

As I mentioned earlier, most spinning is done during the winter months. Oftentimes, it appeared to this young *gossoon* as the means to maintain a certain pace for gossiping amongst the women. This more often than not, seemed to occur, whether or not there was wool on the spindle to be spun. Even though I'd heard the same story before, it seems the womenfolk in our cottage either had extremely short memories, or a propensity for the McGrady brood, and what they were most oftentimes about. The smoke from the peat would be hanging around our heads, the loft nice and warm after an icy day outside, and the sound of the female Ruth's voices wafting up from below, keeping pace with the steady clack-clack of the wheel;

"Ma, did you know about Susie McGrady having finally left the village?" Susan, my sister, made it sound like a question, when in fact, it was more of a frontal assault.

"She went where, me-Darlin'?" My mother asked absentmindedly.

"Why down to the Scillin place so's n' to go with their son Philip!"

I can imagine the knowing looks my sisters gave one another, as if the entire world had cracked straight down the middle and right before their very own Catholic eyes as well.

"Without the sacraments, heavens-above? what are we comin' to? I know the good, Mrs. Scillin. She's a *dacent* woman—she is, with a good, honest head on her shoulders, which has suffered long enough, 'oldin' her poor family together, what with her husband still in the Dublin 'ouse."

All the while she's speaking, the clack-clack of the spindle is keeping time, albeit somewhat quicker then before, as if the spindle could feel the anxiety rising in our mother's voice.

"But Ma, it's not to be livin' together like man and wife, but only to be seein' if her n' Philip Scillin can be getting along first-off, without tearin' into each other, like a couple of Curragh bucks, let loose."

Now, the manner in which my sister Susan brought up these intimate remarks, made it sound as if it was nothing more than a breezy outing, an impromptu promenade to our local market-place.

There was a pronounced sigh from ma, first, before she explained, "Me own mother and pappy told me long ago, long before you were born that is; you don't need to be treatin' the married state like the purchase of a horse-drawn cart; clip-cloppin' your way down one street or t'other trying it out, gettin' the feel of things, wasting the good Lord's precious time. But that you should set it to knocking up the first *dacent* hill you both comes to. To see if the two of you, as man and wife, have the innards, the heart and courage, the good Lord's stamina to pull correctly together, right from the start."

My brother leaned over to me, quiet-like, lying there in the loft, as if he as well had to add his two bits to what was being said down below, "What if the first hill we comes to is a real damned bit of a *blower*? What'll we do then? Get some extra hay for the little lady to chew on? To give her some extra force? Or, head over to the pub and have some ale while she pulls alone?"

I couldn't see him lying there in the dark. But, I could distinctly imagine his lips pulled back, forming that sneer of his, the sneer that made a mockery of everything me poor mother said.

He then hissed in a calculated half-whisper, "Well then, and if we're to be married one day and all, it's good to know that if the little woman doesn't pull the cart like she ought to—then the man has the right to exercise his whip, if only to show her which direction to take."

You could tell by the way he said it, my brother had extrapolated some basic truth from what our mother had just told us, and was now using it to justify his insane sense of physical domination.

This then, was my brother, sisters and mother and those eclectic, winter nights spinning wool into yarn. Some of us, trying to keep the wool curls a necessary length while others were entertaining thoughts of a descending whip on our future wives. If somehow, she decided not to pull our cart up the first imposing hill we came to; Philip Scillin with an appropriate apology to the contrary, notwithstanding.

As far as my sainted mother was concerned, everyone or at least most everyone was a "decent" or give her pronunciation; a "*dacent*" person, this included half-wits and Presbyterians. Her maiden name was McCormick, and she hailed from a tenant's farm just north of Kildare. Ma was fond of saying when she was a young maiden, she was wooed by countless suitors. In so far as that goes, she could have had her pick of the lot, were it not for the fact so many of these so-called suitors lived in the "dark", as she called their infirmity. Or, as it is known today, this illness, by the common *croppie* term of "blindness".

Ma was short and circular, not unlike an oak barrel, with strong, rounded shoulders. Her face, although of a kind countenance, was full of wrinkles which hung in lopsided half-circles from her eyes down to her jaw, giving her a faded, washed-out regard. Like so many of our villagers, her days were spent in finding something for us to eat. She never wore shoes that I can recall. And when she spoke, it was through a mouth full of missing teeth which allowed her to engage in expressive, formal spitting while keeping her jaws tightly closed. She owned three dresses; two were for normal, everyday wear and the third was a blue and white, flowered-print affair. This one she kept for church, as well as for the day, our Lord Tenant, a certain Feargus O'Connor, would come to visit. In any case, he never did, only sending his manager, a disgusting man named Bailey Burke, to do his dirty work.

Ma claimed she didn't hold it against our father that he'd left us. That she'd have probably done the same thing herself—given a similar situation, in a turn-about way. Neither I, nor my siblings believed she was capable of doing such a thing. That in fact was how she was; always trying to justify, to try and understand, as well as forgive, the bad-enough behavior in others, including the father of her children. We knew she didn't hold it against him for she always precluded any story about our father by calling him "a *dacent* man". When pressed about it, she'd lob her tongue around inside her sagging face, before explaining that any man was "*dacent*" enough, who kept the *poteen* drinking separate from the beatings.

She told us the story over many evenings, when we'd queue up for our broth, of how the man who came to be her husband had gotten taken up with political fever, like so many horse beans left to simmer.

I told her impertinently perhaps, but I said it nonetheless, "He left us Ma, to fend for ourselves. The man couldn't have been much to look at."

With her swollen, raised hand beating her bosom, she admitted half-heartedly I had a point. Still, it wasn't in her personality to condemn our father, so she tried to justify to his children what he had done.

"Times were different back then." She told us before explaining, "Cries of *Home Rule* filled the air. It was the Catholics versus the Protestants, Home Rulers against the Unionists. You see, ever since the Englishman took away our rights to everything but the right to 'shit', every man who I knew wanted to give something back. Preferably at the end of a pike, to the people who had crushed us so severely in "ninety-eight" and that included your father. It's been our curse, the curse on all the true sons of Ireland—there's no doubting it, t'all."

She added, "The local lads have always had their way in that regard. They never stay around near their loved ones, but are always dreaming about going off somewheres, far enough away, to seek revenge without a never-mind for their own families. Even before Theobald Wolfe Tone led his ill fated uprising, why there's a saying even from way back when, in me own village, concerning such intimate matters." Then she scrunched up her worn-away face, as if she was reciting some national hymn, all solemn-like and afraid to forget one single word of what she was about to recite; "The men are there for the laying of the keel alright, yet seldom do they show up for the launching...." She finished with a hysterical, un-mitigating, crone-like screech, as if she was a demented, Druid priestess, finishing up some multifarious incantation. The thought of what she had just finished saying, must have released some pent-up anxiety or even fantasy, for it was so unlike our ma to act in such a way. At the very least, it shocked me to my bones.

Ma must have known that as a country-boy, I couldn't possibly have any idea what she was talking about. So she went on, explaining while spitting at the same time, "When *the little people* have told you what it's like to be with a woman, then you'll understand, Edward."

I could only hang my head in confusion and red-eared embarrassment, for I didn't like me own ma to be talking in such a manner, especially about *the little people* and what went on between a man and a woman in private.

"Aye, those were the days of *the troubles* here in Ireland. Once the English got through trouncing us, denying us our basic dignity, your father called us a nation of "able-bodied paupers"."

My brother called her to accounts, "If you ask me, our father weren't no better than that himself or for that matter, a Catholic turned Protestant. All laid in, neatly-alright and just-so, in order to curry favor with Mr. Feargus O'Connor, or that rat he employs Bailey Burke. T'is all the same, the Irish people nowadays, would turn their back on their own kind, for a bowl of mullet or *stirabout*[12]. And you can't tell me, t'ain't-so!"

To our unbelief, she continued to defend the man, who we all believed, had turned us into a bunch of nameless heathens. "When the English bastards took away our rights to own land, to vote, to practice the one true faith—we had to do something."

"We didn't know running away could change all that." My brother hurled back.

"Who's to say your father ain't coming back?" There was now an unmistakable edge to her voice. "Do you know what he did first thing off?" She put the question to all of us.

We all knew the answer to her question, but I guess the retelling of it would in some way bring back our father, at least for the time being.

My ma recounted it as if we'd never heard the tale before, "When your father found out Bailey Burke had left the church and became a Protestant, in order to take up gainful employment with Mr. O'Connor, our Protestant Lord Tenant; why he was so furious with Burke's treason he cornered and trapped a wild, trash-eating, Curragh buck and let him into Bailey Burke's house through a corner window while he was sleeping. When Bailey Burke finally got the buck out of his place near unto dawn, the buck had staged such a riot that it took Burke a fortnight or more, to make heads or tails of his home once again. Which is another reason your old man left—he had no

12   Irish porridge

choice—he'd pretty much publicly announced Bailey Burke was a turncoat to the Irish cause. That and the letting loose of the Curragh buck—was something Bailey Burke wasn't about to forget. Your father had no choice, but to leave Castlewarren afterwards."

For an instant, her face portrayed something of her youth again. A glimpse of unbridled pride, even if it was for the briefest of moments when she whispered from the side of her mouth, "There's not a person in the village who's forgotten it either; what your father did, and who he stood up to, and that includes Bailey Burke!"

Ann Horian spoke up, "Did you ever hear from father after he left?"

Her continued looking down at the soda bread she was kneading didn't betray, if she was really interested in what had occurred to our father, or if she was just making conversation for our mother's sake. Indeed, it was rare mother spoke of such things.

Ma sadly shook her head, "Aye, t'is the shame of it t'all. I finally got word he was road-making, way over and down, Donegal way. Sure 'nough, that was no place for him." She added softly, "He wanted to be one of the new, Irish leaders—the ones to take back our island from the English."

"They'll never give this place up, as long as they can have all our buttermilk for the taking." This my brother said, acerbically tongue-in-cheek as was his custom.

"That may be all true in what you say. Still, tomorrow is market-day, so you'se may as well get your fat and sassy rear-ends to bed." This ma told us chuckling ever so slightly.

We bade one another good-night, before trundling our "fat and sassy rear-ends" up into the loft, for our nocturnal rest.

Our ma then trundled over to the corner of our cottage, her waddling mass a bent-over vision to behold. With the virtue-like economy of the peasant that she was, she took to cooking tomorrow's food with the last of the evening's peat fire. From an iron basket she grabbed a hold of one of our only precious foodstuffs—the Irish potato. Then what followed; the unleashed and unrehearsed curse was in fearsome, garbled Gaelic, but her meaning was as clear as if she was addressing those words to almighty God Himself. She watched the potato split in two, top to bottom from her firm grasp. Finally, it turned into a spotty, bluish liquid which spewed forth a rank smell as it showered to the earthen floor. For a woman of a certain age and girth, her agility was surprisingly lithe as she hopped back from the soppy mess spreading about on her dry clay floor. For it appeared as if she had just come face to face with one of *the little people* dancing there and about, without a thought as to whom might be watching.

There were no four horsemen galloping up from the ends of the earth that night with colorful, wind-driven, medieval-embossed, military banners to announce it; the *malheur* which was about to descend upon us all. To proclaim the final Apocalypse would be decided in this gestating, little island a stone's throw from the coast of continental Europe. It should have been that way though. Who had decided to unleash hell and its gnashing of teeth on Erin[13] and her peoples? Had the sainted Patrick chased the demons from Ireland with such ignoble fury only to have them return in force, to "a place swept clean" as it were? Had God decided to punish us for our excessive ways? To make us realize we were a people frozen in time; too dumb to know we were stupid and too stupid to care. While the anti-Christ in London regurgitated *ad nauseam* that all men, including the Neanderthal ones from Ireland, were brothers.

In just such a way, the potato blight came upon us, killing over a million Irish, and exiling just as many from our shores, of which I was one.

13   Ireland

Chapter Four

1852-Castlewarren, Ireland
(My seventeenth year)

In nothing is God's goodness more evident than in the fact
That the greatest blessings of life are as open and free to the poor as to
the rich,
The loving sunlight falls impartially on all.
No locks or bars confine the fragrance of the flowers
Or the sweet breath of summer airs.
There is no pre-emption of the beauty
Which blushes in the sky and blooms on the earth,
And health greatest blessing of all,
Abides more constantly in the cabin of the poor
Than in the mansion of the rich.
                                        Author unknown

I was just starting to sit myself up in the loft. This I did prior to rubbing my eyes every which way to free them from whatever had glued my eyelids together during the night. It was during this morning exercise when I heard a contradictory sound that I knew from experience could only spell trouble.

"God save all here." Still, the way Bailey Burke intoned what he was saying, it came out as more of a foreboding curse than anything else. This he exclaimed while beating on the door with one hand as if to break it open. I didn't see him do it, but I distinctly heard the sound of him spitting when he finished speaking.

I looked out through the loft's opening. The darkened, chilly, thickening mist was still upon us descending from the silent, prehistoric moors which surrounded our quaint village. In this way I knew morning was still more than a lark's call away.

My mother, doing her best at a curtsy, gathered the pleats of her faded dress about her. This she did before vigorously nodding her bushel of filthy, blonde hair on an uncombed head, as she opened the door to the man who held the power of God over us. Her greeting was due in no small way, to the fact that Mr. Bailey Burke was the manager and sole representative of our landowner, one Mr. Feargus O'Connor.

"Please come in, Sir," she answered back, all the while holding her skirts together as if England's royalty was there before us all. Yes indeed, right before us in the flesh, there in our cramped cottage.

Bailey Burke was a tall and saffron-looking fellow, including an indentured look about him. He owned bushy, black eyebrows that met over his twice broken nose culminating in strange, shrewd, cat-shaped, black and yellow eyes. These very same eyes which seemed for the moment to peer out at once, from each of us to the surrounding cottage walls. As if he was measuring out something, calculating, and as yet unconvinced that his calculations jelled. Still whatever it was, couldn't have been to his liking, for his stretched, unshaven, harrowing cheeks flexed in and out, creating a sort of popping sound making him quite unintelligible when he spoke. We all knew that he was half-deaf, because if one spoke to him in a normal tone, Bailey Burke would fix the speaker with a questioning gaze. This he would do before rapidly turning his nervously-taut neck this way and that, in the manner of a duck. As if he'd concluded he was being mocked upon, or at the very least convinced things were being said about him behind his back. The way he first glanced at me mother and then our cottage upon having entered it, as if she was a sheep with a fifth leg, reminded me of the same attitude the health authorities portrayed when they'd arrived in Castlewarren some months back. They had arrived to quarantine half the village because rumors of "Irish Fever" or typhus had reached their ears in Dublin.

"'av you been 'aving trouble with this year's crop of potatoes or not?" He wheezed while a firm and profound silence descended all about the room, as we strained to make out what the man had to say.

"We be paying our rent, same as always, if that's what your coming here is all 'bout." Our mother stated defensively. She pulled at her skirts nervously, as if she felt threatened; she also appeared slow in her motions as if she was deliberately acting drunk.

Burke reacted as if she had pointedly insulted the man. And not only him, but raising hellish questions tracing back to three or perhaps four generations of Burkes.

In this way Bailey Burke practically shouted back his answer, like a summer blow was upon us, with lightning to boot. "I don't give me backside for your rent. You'll pay, or I'll have your starving Catholic asses thrown off this land. That's not what I'm here for. I asked if you're 'aving trouble with your potatoes. Now that's a simple question, even for a papist now, isn't it?"

Sitting next to me in the loft was my brother. He was unaware as to what had transpired the previous evening with our potatoes. In any case, Paul Francis Daniel made a snapping sound with one hand, and when I moved my head closer to listen he whispered, "Aye, we be having trouble with our potatoes alright. The trouble being; do we decide to eat our potatoes boiled for lunch first? Then have some more stewed up right away, and after that for dinner? Or, should we break things up a wee bit, with hearth-baked potatoes in between, for breakfast?"

Paul Francis Daniel then brandished a fist up in the loft which Mr. Burke couldn't see. I saw it though, and had to hide my mouth behind a hand to keep the smallest sound from escaping.

The man was wearing tweed jumpers with an over-sized, garden coat that he kept brushing back with one arm. As if at any moment he would pull a gun out, and have done with us. This I likened to a newspaper photograph I saw once, depicting what had transpired between the British army and the Irish folks, who had caused some sort of rebellious uprising in Dublin. It was explained to me at that time, this is what happened to those of us who spoke out-of-turn, to the governing and therefore, all-powerful English.

I didn't know then (back in Dublin) how to read. But I listened anyway as my brother asked the question of a stranger standing there, "When we will know when it's our turn to speak to the mighty English?"

The man standing there, whose horrific newspaper had inspired our conversation, folded up his newspaper quietly.

Then, and before turning to leave, faced my brother and I, forcing a sad smile as he told us, "Ah now, don't worry none 'bout that Laddies—neither of ya,—for it'll never be your turn."

My mother didn't possess the intellect to remind Bailey Burke that he had been one of those disgusting "papists" himself, once upon a time. And even if she had, it wasn't part of her make-up to be purposefully mean or vengeful to someone else. Nevertheless, she had the inbred notions of a *croppie* which forbade the admission of any information whatsoever to the Lord tenant's agent. To the point it would have meant a very serious, moral dilemma (for our mother) concerning the divulging of any specific information, as to whether or not she had gone to sleep the night before, if the question had been asked by the Lord tenant's agent.

"Trouble with our potatoes? I think not, Mr. Burke." She stood there in place, fidgeting with her skirt, as if waiting for the almighty Himself to pronounce judgment upon us all.

For awhile Bailey Burke stood there next to the hearth, slowly batting his riding crop against one hand, as if he was undecided about something. At length, he took to stirring the previous evening's ashes with his riding crop, as if to call up some sense of warmth into our parlor. This is a regrettable act for someone, who should have known that *croppies* didn't waste the peat on a fire, unless we had something to be cooked over it.

My mother defended our lack of heat, "Ya see, Mr. Burke, we'd be needing no fire this fine morning. For it's market-day, and we'd be leaving just as soon as the boys get "Job", that is—the donkey, loaded with our goods, for to be a-trading."

She then forced a smile which resembled more of a convulsion than anything else. To show him she wasn't hiding anything, or in the least way trying to contradict the man. Finally, she spat from between her closed teeth with surprising accuracy into the vacant hearth. In such a way that Bailey Burke jumped back with alacrity, as if he'd just seen one of *the little people* staring up at him, from somewhere down in the ashes.

"Ye won't mind then, if we go outside to the shed, and see your store of potatoes," he pronounced as a matter of fact. This he did while eyeing the inside of the cottage, as if he was the new owner, and would knock out one wall then another, just to get things to his own liking.

"Well, now and again, if ye's a liking to seeing our potatoes—in God's own time then, we'll show you what you've come to see—but not today, Mr. Burke. For today is market-day, and we've a mind to be going as soon as we can see daylight."

Her voice remained neutral...surprisingly so. At last, she clapped her hands together as if she was a hen, and we as her mindless chicks, should fall in line, so as to get things ready for our trip to the village and market-day.

The man ceased his aimless stirring of the ashes. Turning to face our mother, with what appeared to be cinder-born sparks flying from his eyes, he declared, "There'll be no market-day t'all, until I see your winter stock. And decide for myself, if you'se been having problems or not with your potatoes, one 'n all. Now, don't contradict me any longer!"

Bailey Burke started making his way to the door. He continued, smashing his riding crop about most fiercely indicating his impatience, although exhibiting a marked prudence not to touch anything. This he did while waiting for my mother to come to heel. And heel she must, for she was being treated no better than a dog by our Lord tenant's manager and his pestiferous attitude.

My brother, perhaps defensively, perhaps out of some instinctive urge to cause mayhem...I still don't know till this day why he said it, blurted out, "We ain't so sure about the potatoes—. But what do you say now to a little Curragh buck, along with its trash-filled trimmings to go with your tea this morning, Mr. Bailey Burke?"

Paul Francis Daniel, realizing a little too late what he had just said, upped and covered his face with his pillow. This he did before sinking back in the loft, probably feeling that if he lay as quietly as he possibly could then the inexcusable thing he'd just blithered out, would somehow be laid aside and hopefully forgotten.

Burke pulled up one sleeve of his garden coat then the other sleeve in the manner of a remonstrative headmaster, before he made his way over to the ladder which led to our loft.

"Come d-ooo-wn here this instant," he thundered up to us in the loft, his cheeks moving in and out like a tiny set of bellows while making stabbing motions at me with his index finger (as if I was the one who had said such a horrible thing).

In my fright, I could barely utter a muddled, "It wasn't me."

Still, this only made matters worse. In his not wanting to admit to his hearing defect, Burke had no choice, but to turn his scarlet face to my mother and pretend that he'd understood me to say, 'I'm not coming down.'

This led to Bailey Burke making a dangerous popping sound with his cheeks, as he sucked in a very uncompromising, "I'll show the distempered, little papist who runs thing around 'ere."

He started hesitatingly up the fragile ladder that led to our loft.

My brother, with eyes bulging from their sockets like two swollen eggs, stared incoherently about the loft, similar to a water-logged rat I'd once cornered in the shed. Indeed, slow and lackadaisical in his movements, with no logic to his actions, my older brother impulsively kicked at the ladder while at the same time my mother screamed out for him not to do so. Burke was halfway up the ladder when it tipped backwards, his hand thrust out, feeling indiscriminately for my brother's leg. However, without a firm grasp, he slid away from the kicking appendage, sending him hurtling back through space, a most disconcerting look on his normally moribund, sinister and authoritarian face.

What saved the man was me own sainted mother, and her disregard for her own well-being. This she did, by wedging herself between the falling ladder and the earthen floor. Yes, Mr. Burke did hit our floor after a fashion. But with nothing like the force which nature intended, had my mother not broken his fall when the ladder slapped across her back and cracked in two. This allowed Burke to slather to the floor like a drunk that had finally lost the evening's battle. He ended up sliding down to the floor in complete disarray, like a drunk, in the hope that good times, would, eventually—come 'round again.

The man lay there on the floor, his leg twisted up and behind him, in a position I'd always attributed to manageable, red hot iron fresh from a forge, a most unsound angle to be sure. Mr. Burke's arm was draped around me mother's neck as if they were both sweethearts, and were about to bid one another a fond and gentle goodnight.

This then, was the predicament my brother and I saw before us while my sisters both whimpered in unison, "Ma's dead, ma's dead."

My brother, rising faster than I thought possible, jumped to the floor, and fetched a kick into the side of Mr. Burke. This sudden, violent pressure set the man's eyes from being completely white, and turning in upon themselves, to finding their naturally evil, sinister, black and yellow color again. Bailey Burke took to spewing out such obscenities that I imagined the sainted Patrick would come down from heaven himself to administer a justifiable punishment, for a man on such amiable terms with the devil. In the meantime, Paul Francis Daniel ran out the cottage door while my mother struggled to right herself, resembling a suspended, half-circling teapot which somehow the cat had knocked over.

"Aye, there won't be a stone left here for you to call home, once I'm finished with the likes of you and your insubordinate household." This Mr. Burke stated emphatically while at the same time, by flailing his hands back and forth, he tried to disentangle himself from me mother's fleshy, fat arms.

He stood up alright, but with less dignity than he once imagined. For as he tried to address equal weight to both feet, his left ankle buckled, thus it kept sliding back under him, forcing the man to lean against my mother. This must have been physically painful for him, but was just as equally embarrassing to a man of his stature and position. Finally, he hobbled to the entry cove, where he spent more than a minute searching for the door latch that would allow him his freedom. Our mother resembled a shooting star or a night-flung comet, as she flew after the man insisting she hadn't known what had came over her son.

Mr. Burke, once in the saddle, turned his horse sharply towards ma leaving her little room to turn in our sad, dismal, little courtyard. "I'll be back tomorrow to see your potatoes. You can count on that. And this should give you more than enough time to pack your things, before I run you off this land. They're forming a spinster's club throughout Kilkenny where you can all waddle together, like so many Catholic sows, after the *skibbereen* men who left you all to starve by yourselves."

At last, the man gathered the reins, jerked his horse around and departed.

Knowing how important market-day was to us, me mother didn't miss a beat, but that she didn't commence to harnessing "Job" right after Mr. Burke and his resounding threats left us. This she did while my sisters and I searched everywhere for Paul Francis Daniel. I found him alright, letting into a stack of old *lumper* sacks with his naked feet followed by his fists. He appeared to me to be a spring which had been compressed way beyond its capacity, and was now unwinding nonstop, without a thought as to what or whom was in his way. It was quite beyond my own physical capability to try and stop my older brother. Regardless, as his feet went every which way, with a shock of red hair that belatedly followed the direction he had chosen, I called out for him to stop. I told my brother that Burke had left, and now ma was trying to get us ready for market-day.

The phrase or a word that I said must have triggered something in my brother. Aye, although he kept lashing out with a fist or foot, he stopped long enough to exclaim, "You wait and see. You just wait and see old man Burke, but that I won't give you me other foot in your ribs—hard enough next time that you won't be getting up so easily, as you did today."

Then he'd strike out again, showing more anger and hatred than was right and wholesome for one boy to have. From experience I knew, he'd have to fight himself alone. At least, until all the energy wound up so tight within my brother would dissipate long enough, for him to remember who he was. Therefore, I went back to the cottage and told ma to leave Paul Francis Daniel here for the day. Insofar as he was ripping the shed apart, we'd have to go to market without him. She didn't agree with me or deny that which I had said was the truth. In reply, she told me to go back into the eating area, and wrap up the last of our *Pirta Oaten*[14], enabling us to have some breakfast along the way.

The road which led to Castlewarren's bi-monthly marketplace cut Feargus O'Connor's estate in two, like a slithering snake or a long, crooked branch from an oak tree. We crossed a bridge over the main stream. The stream and bridge no one knew the name of because Bailey Burke had decided such excellent fishing must be jealously guarded. Thus, it was off-limits to the village, except for those of us fetching drinking water. There was a sign posted just next to the entrance of the bridge. It was clearly written in the queen's own English, "Trout fishing—unlawful—punishable if caught". Paul Francis Daniel, when he would read the sign out loud would oftentimes intone the reflection, "I'll make a point of it—not to get caught then!" Which is probably why the only time we ever ate fresh, pink, trout meat was late at night. When me own ma was too tired to ask where the bloody fish came from in the first place. Still, the way she buried the bones in our backyard without waiting

---

14   bread made of flour and oatmeal

for the dawn to break, told us she had an inkling she knew where the trout came from.

Even without Paul Francis Daniel accompanying us, we looked forward to the enjoyments of market-day. Someone had once written on that same subject: "That from our poor, disheveled cabins we came, to take in the gossip and whisky and perhaps make small purchases. That in this way, the *croppies* had stolen a petty living from the jaws of a bog. That we had driven the red heather from a few square yards of moor, drained off the floods, and were now about to snatch the flying joy of a market-day from under the nose of a black and dismal destiny."

I guess that pretty much summed it up. Although, as far as this Irishman's concerned, I'd be the first to say back then I didn't care nor realize just where we hailed from. As soon as we crossed the "No-Name Stream" bridge, I'd start to look for my friends, John and Frankie Scullum. They still had their pa, and you could see them most market-days with their wagon loaded to the gills, full of current produce. Placed in wicker baskets were freshly picked vegetables, barley and lithing, several cows' head and feet while back in the corner of the cart, covered with a sheet were ten liters or more of black market *poteen*. Our locally-brewed drink had been distilled back in the hills, and brought skillfully if not altogether clandestinely to market. There, I've seen it exchanged for among other things a new bed and mattress. For the most part, the *poteen* was shared in the late afternoon. This occurred after the trading was finished amongst the men, and was a cumulative factor in deciding who could pull the wool over an Englishman's eyes faster. Don't let me forget as well, several ribald comments concerning the reproductive tendencies of a stud-letting bull. Or, more to the point that of the bull's concurrent rival...any warm-blooded Irishman. Apparently, or so I was told, after that much *poteen* had been drunk by the men doing the boasting, there was no distinction whatsoever, between a bull's virility and that of an Irishman. Excepting of course, the Irishman held a distinct advantage over the bull, in that he wouldn't accept a ring through his nose...unless you asked him politely first.

One thing which struck this Irish lad, was just how green the land surrounding Mr. Feargus O'Connor's house was. It was later explained to me that he kept neither goats, chickens or pigs to make a bloody, mud-strewn bog of his surrounding garden area. Without which, everything was kept un-pawed, intact and velvety green.

My brother used to ask, "Why does a man need so much land when he never comes to use it?"

I didn't think his question was inaccurate...just too impertinent for a bunch of *croppies* like us. We passed the Burton place where we started to collect other *croppie* neighbors making their way into the village as well. At last, from a quiet side road where the bigger boulders had all been pushed to one side, we hailed the Scullums. Now, Frankie and John Scullum were the outgoing type, anxious to give a glorious 'howdy-do' to me and anyone else they came across on one condition...that their father wasn't around. You see, Mr. Scullum was a man constantly concerned about something, or make that intensely worried about everything. Why it amazed me to no end how one man could hold so many worrisome thoughts in his head. Nevertheless, such was the case with Mr. Scullum. Not only did he spend an inordinate amount of time worrying for himself, but if he found you a bit too happy or not mournful enough, it would sure trigger a powerful force inside the man. Why he'd quick-like figure out something that'd be sure and take that smile right off your face. And even leave you wondering, why you hadn't been more concerned about next year's rainfall, or the apples which had come up seedless that spring over in Wexford County.

While his boys and I exchanged silent greetings, Mr. Scullum tipped his hat to me mother, and listened respectfully to her greetings of, "A glorious and top of the morning now, to one and all."

"Aye, and if that could only be so," came back the woeful reply of Mr. Scullum.

Me mother tapped "Job's" leather harness on one side of his flank to keep him moving, for our donkey had the notion that once a conversation started, he had the right to pull up, and listen in as well.

"Now what ails you, Mr. Scullum? Indeed, your cart looks to be right full with stores for to be a-tradin'?"

The man took off his soft, plaited hat to reveal thin, matted hair which hadn't seen a comb since Easter last. While his taciturn, round and unshaven face grappled with some smoldering emotion, "Aye, and if it isn't the missus, sure 'nough; she's come down with the ghastly croup and enough coughing to set the whole cottage a-shakin'. It must 'ave been shakin' a furlong or more, at least to me—I'm thinking."

"The croup? Why t'is nothing." Me ma bawled back, "Nothing that a good broth, with maybe some sheep's trotters thrown in, to bring the young woman 'round again."

"Aye, if it was only so." Mr. Scullum replied, undaunted it seemed to us over the querulous fact that sheep's trotters were indeed the answer for the croup. Or, perhaps more to the point, someone considered his wife still a young woman. "For no sooner have ye licked the fever, but that it doesn't descend right down into the poor woman's chest. And lord knows now, we're talking visits with the doctor and a half-shilling or more for medicine. Why I tell you, it's enough to drive a man to the poor house."

"As if we were not there already." This me ma sighed aloud as if she was repeating a prayer to a multitude of saints.

At length, Mr. Scullum turns to me mother all smiles and such. As if someone had just offered him a mince pie or a stick of Dublin chocolate, and puts forth the question, "Ah now, times are hard with ye, Mrs. Ruth? What could be the matter? Earthworms shot up into the horse beans again—no one willin' to let you rent a good plow horse out for this year's furrowin'?"

The man tried in vain to hide his abundant eagerness over our misfortune. Nevertheless, he reminded me of one of our dumb-witted villager's half-sad, half-excited state over witnessing a public punishment on the village green.

"As if we could afford it!" Me ma bawled back. She then turned to look mysteriously over her thick and curiously rounded shoulder, in case someone might be listening in, "It's the potatoes, I tell ya'—they've all been cursed!"

"Cursed ye say? Why that can't be. Sure and beholdin' to all which is holy, think woman—think! We're talking 'bout our daily bread now. It's all that we have to eat around here!"

For a brief instant it appeared Mr. Scullum was undecided, in the sense me mother's calamity was isolated and therefore a good thing. Or perhaps, what was probably more to the man's particular viewpoint; it was by rights normal that we all were about to share in such shameful misfortune.

"I tell ya, Mr. Scullum, by all that's sacred, I took a potato in me hand last night, and without so much as a tender squeeze, the blimey root shot all over me kitchen like a thickened soup. 'Ceptin' it had a bad smell about it, like the time our tomcat came home after a fight trailing most of his intestines behind him. T'awful smell I'm telling you, t'was troo-lie awful. Upon seeing such a shambles, I goes to the shed and sure enough if it wasn't the same with all the potatoes we've got. Then to make matters worse that indecent Bailey Burke comes 'round our place, carryin' on so. He's askin' after the very same thing I been telling you 'bout, and questionin' me, "If my potatoes are alright—nothing strange been happening with 'em?", he asks. That was before Paul Francis Daniel fetched him a kick in his side, so's the poor man can barely walk. But he tells us he's coming back on the morrow to see our potatoes with some sort of inspector. This he does, before he threatens to run us off Mr. O'Connor's land. As if we lived in a blessedly gloo-rious house on the gateway to the Kerry Sea. And everyone wanted our place for its partakin' view and the fishing rights. Ah, t'is no good I'm tellin' ya, no good a t'all."

I'd never heard so many worrisome ideas coming from our ma before. Except, perhaps, for the time she caught my sister Ann Horian glancing amorously at Mr. Fletcher's son, Gareth during the final blessing at Sunday mass, instead of the presiding priest. Still and all, and to be absolutely truthful about it, there was no way we could have turned young Gareth into buttermilk...at least to myself I'm thinking.

We made our way into market just at the western end of where Castlewarren takes up with a long, jaunting, milk-wagon, expressway road joining it to the neighborly county of Tipperary. The market place was to be found sandwiched in between two abandoned, gothic walls from some eroded abbey. Insofar as to say that without any kind of proper roof, the place with its ten meter in height, arching, monastic walls and cobble-stone floors was selected to protect everyone from the weather.

My brother used to say, "That unless the rain came down in ninety-degree horizontal sheets—the only elements we would be protected from would be the fog driven in from the moors. And those lice-infested Protestants, looking to take advantage of the Catholics once again!"

To our collective surprise, the market was empty or almost so. There was practically no one around, except for the Callaghan boys, looking as always to steal something. There was scatter-brained Joey Barton, who had a black Angus cow tethered to a fence post apparently for sale. However, when questioned as to its price, he searched blankly in either direction. It seemed to me, as if Joey was looking to find the price for his cow stitched on the bark of a tree. Or perhaps, the animal itself would decide what it was worth, and collect the payment before sauntering off with its new owner.

Mr. Scullum took one long look around the marketplace before muttering to our ma, it appeared to me overly satisfied at what he saw, "That's just fine now t'isn't it? We load and pack, making sure the only thing we've brought in is the freshest produce off the farm. Thus, when we do make it in to market, well now and be golly, there's no one here. I should have stayed home with Mary Jane's croup. You know she's not a young woman any more, to be left all alone like that. Yes, indeed that's what I should have done."

Upon completing his phrase he folded his arms, and stared malevolently at one of the Callaghan boys, displaying a prophetic certitude that an attack upon his eggs and horse beans wouldn't be long in coming.

Just then, a man wearing a black coat, a white vest with a burgundy tie, and seemingly to have come out of nowhere hailed all of us. With one hand, he beckoned for us all to approach him. He stepped up on a neglected, broken, wooden front axle which someone had left by the side of the road, using the branch of a nearby oak tree to steady himself. We being from the country and all, we walked a little closer to the man, but not close enough to put ourselves under his charm. This is because we were a cautious group of people, having heard from other folks down Dublin way, as well as other Irish cities that these wandering salesmen, by their verbal charm and sway, could put you under their ambitious spell. Then at a moment's notice, take you and sell you, as well as everything you possessed to the *Tinkers,* or Ireland's version of the gypsies.

To be truthful about it, there were only us, the Scullum's, the O'Grady's, one other family with black, sooty faces I didn't recognize and the Callaghan boys. These same Callaghan boys never seemed to have anything to do, but wait for a propitious chance to steal something. It seemed to me, like a foraging cat; its tail up in the air slowly moving back and forth while waiting for its prey to make some fortuitous mistake. As far as this Irishman's concerned, it appeared that if it wasn't properly nailed down, the Callaghan boys would go ahead and steal the object in question. Even if they had no use for it, just so they could stay in practice.

"The name's Sullivan—Thomas Merton Sullivan, and the reason I'm here is that I work for the Poor Law Commission."

Now, this Thomas Merton Sullivan while seemingly a grand orator, had heavy, ingrained wrinkles on both cheeks running all the way down to his flaccid chin. They were of a semi-circular pattern, as if they'd been put there by a hammer and chisel. He reminded me of a bloodhound, for his face sagged and wheezed as he spoke. As well, Mr. Sullivan had eyelids which seemed to have overcome both sockets in such a way that they were heavily wrinkled, and left little space for the man to see out of. This Sullivan fellow stuck both his hands into his white vest pockets, and then just as quickly removed them. It appeared to this Irishman, he did this because he wasn't quite sure as to whether or not the news he was to pronounce, would be accepted or rejected by those of us standing outside. Crowded together like orphans if you will, not far from the vestibule of the abandoned abbey.

"As I said I'm from the Poor law Commission and together, with your help, we'll all get through this calamity." The man proclaimed while removing his hands from their place in his vest before continuing, "I'm assuming the fact that of course you fine people want to get through this situation. Which of course you most certainly do—don't you?" He said this in a supercilious voice while peering out at us through eyes, heavy-lidded and somewhat blank.

Mr. Scullum, no doubt worried about Mrs. Scullum's croup, and its effect upon the rest of us, riposted this Mr. Sullivan, "You're darn, bloody right we want to get through this calamity—cough syrup at one shilling, six-pence the bottle is more than an honest man can pay."

Mr. Scullum, I suppose, couldn't help himself as he shot an uneasy glance over at the Callaghan boys, not at all sure if they would be offended or not, by his use of the word 'honest'.

"And you, Sir, are?" Thomas Merton Sullivan inquired, employing a condescending regard which seemed to ask if the man in front of him could understand the Queen's own English.

"Scullum's the name—Patrick Frederick Scullum with two l's, and if its calamities you might want—well, Stranger, you've come to the right place. Between flooding—topsoil that couldn't grow a weed, even if the archangel Michael himself came down from heaven to water the bloody plant now and again. What's more, we have this scourge of croup that's been affecting the whole village including me own Mary Jane. T'is enough to drive a man to the hanging tree, I tell you. What with the price of cough syrup and t'all—why we're all better off gulping down *poteen* three times a day. At least that way, we wouldn't feel anything, but damned good laughter while coughing ourselves to death."

Mr. Thomas Merton Sullivan held up his hand for silence. He took from his inner pocket a small writing tablet and writing stick, which he licked at once or twice, before asking, "Give that to me again. You say you've got an epidemic of croup here in Castlewarren?"

"T'is true, Sir, t'is true enough." This, Mr. Scullum insisted conversationally while he looked around at the rest of us, hoping for confirmation.

Again Sullivan held up his hand. "What if I were to tell you that what I'm talking 'bout doesn't concern Castlewarren, Tipperary, or even Wexford? Rather, it concerns folks just like you, all over Ireland, that's right—all over Ireland!"

At this point Mr. Scullum whistled aloud before declaring, "Why sweet mother McCree, you don't be telling me now that all of this blasted island has the croup now, does it? No wonder things are all jimmied and fouled up the way they are!" He scratched the stubble on his chin, once or twice in unmatched gratitude, before continuing, "Why no wonder the price of cough medicine is so expensive. The English have cornered the market on it, and won't let the rest of us poor sods have any—including me own Mary Jane!"

Joey Barton piped up his own contribution to the proceedings, still holding tightly onto his Angus cow, "Aye, t'is a shame on us all, for the love of mike. What are we to do in the face of such an outrage? The bloody country's running out of cough medicine. What are we to do? Someone 'ave pity on us—someone! Aye, the bloody shame of it t'all."

Then he went back to petting his cow. Joey's satisfied face bearing witness he had done all he could to incite a sale for her.

"Silence—fore and aft!" Mr. Thomas Merton Sullivan cried out like a captain aboard some foundering maritime vessel. The bottom half of his freshly awakened and now piercing eyes peered out from under thickly-folded eyelids. The man appeared confused, not sure if what he had just heard was true. Or indeed, if he had just witnessed the response to the compulsory argument which had been raging for months in Whitehall, England. This debate of course, concerned a mandatory, minimum education for the Irish. Especially the ones left alone out in the countryside, amidst ghosts of the Druids and the homespun faculties of *the little people.*

Cocking both arms above his pant's pockets like an irritated scarecrow, the man from the Poor Law Commission declared, "This is not about a run on Ireland's stock of cough medicine. Nor does it concern feeding the multitudes with a stew of shamrocks and holy water!"

At the mention of "stew and holy water", we, as a crowd, suddenly became conspiratorially quiet. I, for one, hoped the man was going to feed us.

Noting with some satisfaction that he'd finally won our attention, he jammed both his hands back in to his vest pockets. This the man did, satisfied he could finally go on unhindered by our redundant, *croppie* questioning. "People, there are reports all over Ireland that this year's potato crop has gone bad with the blight!"

Having heard this, my mother emitted a heavy sigh. She fell to her knees where she slowly and reverently made the sign of the cross three times.

Mr. Scullum couldn't resist cracking both his sons about their ears while stating to those of us too dumbfounded to speak, "Ya see, this is what comes from living the good life in Castlewarren. Ever since ye's had the choice 'tween gruel mush or *stirabout,* we've all taken on airs. Why t'is enough to make one wonder if we won't all be sucking our bleedin' thumbs one day, and proclaiming total allegiance to the British crown!—That's how high and mighty we've all become!"

There was a slight chirp from Joey Barton, asking if he couldn't have a bowl of *stirabout* right then and there. Joey explained, he was awfully hungry from holding his cow. He also added to those of us listening close-by, his cow apparently would take some as well.

Undaunted, Mr. Sullivan continued, "The English government has decided upon several measures to bring you and the rest of Ireland, immediate relief. We're in the process right now of bringing in corn from India to help feed you people, until we can get the potato crops turned around, and the blight arrested."

At the use of the word "arrested", the Callaghan boys took off at a fast-paced run towards the heather, without so much as a look back at the rest of us.

Barely concealing a grin, Mr. Scullum kept repeating the following phrase while slapping his hands together, as if he was celebrating the end of Lent, "I knew this would happen, knew it would happen—could have predicted it meself. The way everyone's running around, taking days off from the growing fields, slugging down the *poteen* as if it were water—t'is the end of our world.

T'is the end I tell you! You can't outwit the devil, we all have to pay his bloody invoice one day or 'nother—. The devil never forgets what you owe him. D'ya hear me, now—never!"

Me own mother asked me to translate for her to Mr. Sullivan the following question, "What then are we to do? How are we to feed ourselves?"

The agent from the Poor Law Commission straightened his burgundy tie, before hooking his thumbs back into his vest pockets. At last, he looked out at the rest of us as if we were a bunch of blind, teat-groping, puppy dogs, and couldn't think...much less take care of ourselves. "Besides the Indian corn we're currently importing, we'll be working closely with your Lord Tenant, Mr. Feargus O'Connor to make sure you'll be getting everything you need to get through this calamity."

"Aye, the Lord Tenant and his Free-Mason manager, Bailey Burke would just as soon see us off their land. The land, may I remind you which was taken from us by those pea-eyed bastards in London. The day they decided, Catholics ran a close second to moss and fungus in the natural order of things around here in county Kilkenny." This came from the man, who, including his children, were all black and sooty-looking, as if they made their respective beds from within the chimney flue.

"And I say we're trying to do all we can." The agent emphasized nervously.

Once again, this Mr. Thomas Merton Sullivan looked at us condescendingly. Indeed, as if we were going to starve to death, no matter what he said, or no matter what he and his cohorts decided. This included the promise of corn from India with all its peculiar, agnostic trimmings.

In frustration, the man from the Poor Law Commission added, "Look, if you're not satisfied people, some Irish folk similar to yourselves have already left for other countries; like Australia, Canada or the American states."

Joey Barton raised his shirt-sleeved hand high in the air, letting go for the moment the cow's tether. He lifted his hand, as if he intended upon asking a pertinent question. At length, apparently thinking better of it, he brought his hand slowly back down, reaching for the cow's tether. This he did while addressing his question directly to his cow, in such a way that we all could hear, "If we go to Australia, can we pass by me Uncle Stewart's farm in County Mayo? We always had a grand time there when we were *gossoons*—plenty of sweeties n' all."

Aye, besides starving the lot of us, they're trying to run us out of our own country—probably end up doing it too, the conniving Brits. Just like that the thought hit me.

I looked down past the arched gables of the crumbling monastery, out beyond the half-submerged, quarried foundations wading in the slow-moving river like ancient mastodons. I wondered fitfully, if we were truly half as stupid as the English gave us credit for. And if we were, why didn't we all become monks? Then we could take our precious time about writing long and winded poetry. In ornately decorated books, about how their English souls would be forever wallowing in hell, for what they were doing to us.

It took the better part of an hour to get "Job" turned around, and heading back towards home. Even so, he tried to bite me twice.

Chapter Five

It seemeth such a little way to me,
Across to that strange country, the beyond.
For it has grown to be the home of those
Of whom I am so fond.

And so, for me there is no death
It is the crossing with abated breath
A little strip of sea,
To find one's loved ones waiting on the shore
More beautiful, more precious than before.

Author unknown

Have you ever seen the beauty of an Irish maiden? One who has been brought up in the glorious, open air, deep in the unpretentious countryside, on fresh, organic food with nothing to tame her, but the rigorous solitude of disciplined farm life. I, myself, have witnessed the incomparable beauty of just such an Irish maiden since I was seventeen. And it has haunted me the rest of my natural life....

In fact, she made a point of it.

I'm still surprised about her visage after all these years. The way the colleen[15] carried herself, and what she wore. As I most certainly recall, there was a white kerchief bonnet which was tied just below her neck. This allowed her dark, mahogany-turning-to-sunset-red, braided pigtails to peak out from underneath the bonnet. These were all cleaned and shiny, and fixed about her neck and shoulders just so. In contrast to her braided and tidy pigtails, her forehead was a whirlwind of frothy and remorseless curls. Her face was round, linked together by fiercely red, thick eyebrows and seemingly without expression, except for her un-charming tendency to pull her lips together as if to pout. Her cheeks rode high on her face, and when combined with her ability to descend one eyebrow down with the other eyebrow cocked just so,

---

15   A young maiden

she resembled a school mistress about to mete out some punishment, for a lesson as yet unlearned. The day I met her, she was wearing a grey muslin, fully-sleeved dress completely buttoned up one side, and over it a white, full-length, cotton apron. Over the top of her dress, she wore a shoulder-covering, v-necked kerchief of the same material as the apron. She wasn't particularly thin, nor given to drooping fat like some of the women today, but seemingly of the right proportions. I'm no expert when it comes to women, nor do I propose to be. I only know what I like to look at. Thus, if I had my choice between something which is soft and pretty, or a grouchy, belching farm animal, I prefer something pleasant and feminine. On her feet, she wore wooden sabots the likes of which are more attributed to the northern, Dutch people than to *the children of the Gael*. Oh yes, there is one other thing before I forget. The singular, most remarkable aspect about this young girl, upon which all her other attributes appeared as merely passing whims, was the following; she wouldn't give me the time of day. Nor did she barely acknowledge my presence. As if I was some sort of underlying bacteria, best left alone until I was scrubbed clean, preferably sterilized, and thus made presentable.

It must have been two weeks since our winter crop of potatoes had gone sour. I was sent to *exchange* broth with the Scullums, now that Mrs. Scullum had decided her bout with the croup was over. She was up and about, full of energy, and had sent word that she had barley-broth, for which we could *exchange*. We were all constantly hungry, and for a bit of broth I was ordered to the Scullums to *exchange* our *kitchen* for theirs. For those of you unaware or unaccustomed to our ways, to *exchange kitchen* simply meant to trade. And by trading I mean; if we had a particular abundance of a certain soup or broth, we would send over a quart jar of our broth to a neighbor or kin. Thus, in the same emptied and returnable jar would receive whatever our neighbor or kin had to offer. In this way I was sent by me mother to the Scullums to receive their *kitchen*. It couldn't have come at a more opportune time, for we had begun to dig for bulbs of wild onion, as well as strawberry hay grass which grew at the beginning of the Northern foothills.

The day was a perfect one for making fog. The rainy drizzle was thin and airy, like a soft comforter, misty and falling so lightly you could barely feel the rain. It wasn't a biting cold, but just enough to match the one in my belly. The one that said the coldness was quizzically thick and brewing while something somewhere in Castlewarren had gone wrong, terribly wrong. I hadn't been out and rustling my way through the village since market-day. Therefore, I was surprised to see a number of cottages deserted. The thatch had disappeared, as if some giant wind had funneled in from somewhere, and blew the people and their roofs away. Indeed, leaving our little village in a disreputable state of having been forgotten, or completely discarded from Ireland's map. You could see a cluster of four or five cottages sitting side by side, yet there was only one with a fire burning. The others were missing their thatched roofs. They appeared bizarre-looking, in the sense they resembled cadaverous, home-styled, tool boxes or giant horse molars that someone had removed and left scattered about. Abandoned they were, yet still grouped together, a strange, and for this Irishman—a most alarming sight. As I trudged listlessly along the road, I came to realize there were more empty cottages in Castlewarren than there were occupied ones.

These thoughts coupled with the continual pain in my stomach and buzzing about me ears, led me astray and right into a female trap. This trap I might add, that Divine wisdom, needing only six days to create the heavens and the earth, has kept tinkering with since time began. Moreover, from what I've been told, just after the first Eve was created that somehow He, God, had been distracted away from His original design. Or to put it another way, the situation had gotten completely out of hand. As a result, it no longer was a divine prerogative, but rather, more of a feminine one. Because of this strange turn of events, His sublime creation turned out to become; consequently, emphatically...in an absolute sense, much more than He ever bargained for. Perhaps, it is as someone once suggested, since God in no possible way can error. That our heavenly father, in sensing the banality of the situation and believing it to be of such little importance, left one of the arch-angels to finish his creation of the first woman. This He did, while having already established a kind of celestial jurisprudence, continued His much warranted seventh-day of rest. At length, upon rising from his slumber—only then did God realize the creation of woman had gone perfunctorily amuck. However, at that point, it was far too late. The damage had been done and man's ignoble fate, as some would say...unfortunately sealed.

Later on, it was explained to me because of his infinite sense of justice, God put everything else aside. He decided upon the use of eternity to correct the basic blunder of his arch-angel. While at the same time, and due in no small way to His irreproachable sense of justice, declared married men need not apply to purgatory. That these same men, having already, through no fault of their own, served as it were, a certain, purgatorial apprenticeship via the married state. Therefore, it becomes a rhetorical question, my earlier inquiry, a sort of double-edged sword so to speak; "Have you ever witnessed the beauty of an Irish maiden...?"

I wasn't too far from the Scullum place that day, perhaps a half-mile or so from "No-Name Bridge and Stream". There I saw a dozen or so soldiers armed with rifles and an extended family milling about outside a tidy, white-washed cottage. In the bedraggled courtyard were saddled horses and barking dogs kicking up a fuss. At the same time, in and amidst these various groups, our elderly local priest, Father Kincaid, hatless, was chained to thick, wooden timbers which in turn were nailed to the front door of the cottage. He was trying to engage the soldiers in conversation. The priest stood there tall and erect, chained as it were against the front door. His stance (insofar as the chains would allow), appeared much like a boxer's; leaning forward and provocative as if he was taunting them, and couldn't get the soldiers to engage themselves or admit to something. Perhaps their colloquial attitude was understandable in that the soldiers were only half-facing the priest. In this way they kept talking in low voices amongst themselves, before turning to hear what Father Kincaid was saying. Almost as if they weren't quite sure as to how to proceed. There was one young man (not a soldier) kneeling down and asking for the priest's blessing. Father Kincaid's manacled hand rested heavily on the back of the young man's neck, for his reddish-blonde head was bowed in prayer. Some of the women were weeping while others were consoling the ones weeping. Most of the men looked stoic. At the same time separated from the group of adults were a *gossoon* and a young colleen. The four or five year old boy was wringing his eyes with the back of his hands while a puppy dog leaned on his thigh, and made licking movements. The girl next to him was on one knee, and cradling a black-spotted sheep dog as if she was saying goodbye.

I never wanted to stop, nor was I supposed to exactly. Nevertheless, something besides my brain told me to rest awhile. For where people were gathered together, there was sure to be something other than onion bulbs and ludicrous wild-heather weeds to calm down the clanging in my guts. To be honest as well, besides the attraction of uniformed, spiral-helmeted and armed soldiers, looking back after all these years, it wouldn't be completely candid on my part, not to say that fate did indeed play a hand that day....Aye, for mixed in and amongst the crowd that very foggy day, those mahogany-red pig-tails stood out long and clear, like a stand of freshly-cut timber. Just as I believe, I may have mentioned earlier; they have come to haunt me deliciously for the rest of my life.

People were leaving on a trip; even an uneducated *gossoon* like me could understand such a thing. For one thing, the thatch was still on the cottage roof, and not left as yet to the outside elements, as I'd seen everywhere else in our village. Upon approaching, I noticed there was an elderly, half-stooped woman with a young girl in a long hooded mantle next to her, crouching outside one of the open windows. The older woman kept looking in as if she'd forgotten something. Or indeed, what was probably closer to the truth was thinking about the lifetime she'd spent in that cottage.

As hungry as I was, my stomach still retched when I saw hanging by rope from the roof's main beam the carcasses of two stray dogs. The two dogs were gutted and cleaned and ready for the stew pot. Hanging them up was a half-inch hook slotted through each dog's neck. I knew things were bad. But the fact of the matter was; if we had all been reduced to eating dog meat, what with the hairless skin knotted and stretched across bones and erstwhile meat which couldn't provide nourishment for a pack of flies, indeed, things were a lot worse than I had previously imagined.

Just briefly, I wondered, why is it that a man who appears to have a lot more than the others, like Master Feargus O'Connor, can't or won't share with the rest of us? As a case in point, I'm not saying for example, Mr. Feargus O'Connor invites a bunch of *croppies* to his white-linen table for Yorkshire pudding with ladles of gravy to wash our *croppie* faces in. Still in all, and as far as this Irishman's concerned, at the very least he could have given us what he produced on his lands in Ireland. After all, he couldn't possibly have any use for them since he never came from London for his land's surplus, leaving it all to the management of his agent Bailey Burke. Moreover, that's the idea which amazed me and wouldn't leave me alone. Like a wasp that keeps hovering around, its buzz a formidable reminder, just barely out of arm's length, but still there making its presence felt; *why is it that one man must keep for himself an over-abundance of necessities while all around him people are in a most desperate state indeed?* Unless of course, starvation is to be treated like some old wives' tale. In other words, starvation in our village couldn't possibly exist for Master Feargus O'Connor since it had never actually happened to him.

The more I wrestled with this idea, the more illogical I felt. Until finally, not wishing to be identified as being daft in me senses, I put the strange idea away concluding that people in important posts of responsibility would do what was right. Moreover in time, I would come to understand and support the logic behind Mr. O'Connor and Bailey Burke's policy of collective and effusive hoarding.

Just outside the cottage and facing the road leaving Castlewarren was a draught horse and wooden trailer. There were already several, well-bundled people sitting on the wood-slatted sides of the trailer. One man wearing a knee-length, expensive-looking, yellow turncoat was handing packages up to the driver. The driver seemed very tired, and beneath his round brimmed, *croppie's* hat in a state of shock. Or, at the very least hard of hearing, for he kept placing the parcels in an oversized satchel without any change of expression about the man. All the while, his scraggly, lugubrious and bearded face, containing an unlit pipe, didn't say a word, nor for that matter showed any sign of life. Not even, when one of the packages fell from the man's hand who was helping to load, and fell across the driver's shin causing a painful, sharp, slapping crack to fill the air. Next to the horse and trailer stood Bailey Burke dressed up as if for a night on the town. His hands hovered around his white riding breeches while a new, black and glossy-looking, full-stemmed stovepipe hat stood low across his brow. His appearance suggested a certain formality, as if he couldn't bear to witness what was happening before him. He acted so mournful and despondent that even his riding whip swathed across at a measured half-beat as if tapping time at a funeral march. There was one man staring intently into Burke's face, and listening earnestly as if he couldn't afford to forget a single word Bailey Burke was saying.

The man I recognized as Mr. Maddox from our own parish, was red in the face, with very pale, watery, blue eyes which looked to this Irishman as if they hadn't been closed for sleep in weeks. At the same time, they seemed very much upset about something, for they danced about his face with focused intensity as if they weren't fully convinced about some aggravating situation. His grey hair was regally thin, but carefully combed back on either side of his head while his full lips were pursed together in a restraining posture. His brown, beltless pants hung low on his hips, and his outdoor jacket smelled of the highlands and hunting. The tone he was using with Burke wasn't neighborly in the least, and could certainly have been construed as menacing, if not for the fact that Mr. Maddox kept repeating, "If it's as you say Mr. Burke—"all for the best"."

Bailey Burke looked up from somewhere underneath that preposterous hat of his and confirmed in a dashing manner, "But of course Mr. Maddox, it seems strange now, but you just wait and see—once across the Atlantic Ocean you'll be telling yourself ol' Bailey Burke was right, and why didn't I take Feargus O'Connor's offer that much sooner. That's right, that's exactly what you'll be telling yourself—why I can smell that fried badger right now!" His cheeks whooshed in and out to such an extent I was barely able to make out half of what the man was trying to say.

You could sense from the look on Mr. Maddox's face that travelling the breadth of the Atlantic Ocean to feast on American fried badger was not on his list of priorities. In that regard, he pinched his face up in sort of a querulous half-circle before asking, "What if we all get scalped by the Indians?"

Just then, the old woman waddled over from the cottage window where it was now noticeable to one and all that she'd been weeping. The tassels from her bonnet were no longer attached under her sparsely whiskered chin, but left to drag across the small of her thick and rounded back as it thundered to a monstrous height before deflating, seemingly, as if each breath might be her last. She drew everyone's attention to her. For not only was it rare for a woman to speak in public, but even rarer in our little village that she might have something worth listening to.

"Mr. Bailey Burke, it is high time we leave Castlewarren, for Ireland's

Angelus of Doom has already struck its first note. Still 'n all, tell me Sir, this has really nothing at all to do with potatoes, does it?"

Her challenge initiated a quiet spell which descended upon us all. Slowly, the people standing there stopped their conversations, and turned to see what this woman could possibly have to say. In the sense that she was in her old age, and not given to speaking in public. Even the driver and the man in the yellow turncoat stopped their loading. The driver took the opportunity to take the unlit pipe from his mouth, and stare into the pipe's bowl as if looking therein he would find some explanation for was happening around him.

She drew in her cheeks, and floated the words across the crowded courtyard, seemingly, emitting a curse upon everyone there. *"Ne Temere"*[16], she hissed, before croaking even louder, *"Ne T-e-m-e-r-e,"* she repeated herself. As if in some sort of accusing trance the old lady continued, not changing her intonation or the inflection of her voice. Nevertheless, insisting by repetition what she was saying, in order that the meaning not be lost on those of us standing there, and witnessing such strange behavior. At last, she flicked a thick peasant finger at Father Kincaid while with a final accusing *"Ne Temere"*, she swooned to the ground. There she lay still, yet continued to breathe as if in some Druid-like, comatose state.

Bailey Burke saw his chance and seized upon it, "Aye, if it wasn't for the cankerous papists and their policy of *Ne Temere*—we could have all lived together in peace."

The man wearing the yellow turncoat, held up his hand calling attention to what he wanted to say, "Peace with the English isn't possible, Mr. Burke. Not when they come over here like a pack of wild dogs, and carry away everything of value."

The priest echoed forth from his chained pulpit, "Aye, and your dying English integrity riddled with worms. Why Bailey Burke, you'd a sold your mother just like you sold your faith, for a job and a place to hang that Protestant hat of yours. T'is a shame I tell you, a crying shame. Why, I never would have baptized you, had I known how you were going to turn out!"

Father Kincaid might have been the living, breathing symbol of Christ's redemption on earth....Nevertheless, he still had many a Lenten season to go, to claim anywhere near, something, resembling Christian charity and patience.

Burke lifted his voice to the heavens, "There 'n again, you've said it for everyone to hear; t'is the Catholics against the Protestants!" He rasped threateningly.

Father Kincaid interrupted Burke, wrangling his chained sleeves as if to

16 The cultural separation of the English and Irish until finally in 1908 the Catholic Church made if official by outlawing marriages of mixed faiths.

emphasize that he...indeed all of us, were in some sort of prison, "Home Rulers versus The Unionists!" He intoned venomously.

Bailey Burke half-grinned like a presumptuous cat who has cornered his prey, "Why don't you make it final, Father Kincaid and call it like it is in this part of Ireland; A Catholic creamery versus a Protestant one?" This said, he rocked back on his heels, Burke's victory all but won, or so it seemed.

Father Kincaid offered a defeated smile, before finally conceding rather ironically, "T'is easy enough, Bailey Burke to sort out the Catholic farmers from the Protestant ones, but what about their cattle? What are we to do with that nettlesome issue?"

Bailey Burke stopped rocking abruptly. In any case, that didn't help him to hide his confusion for very long. Also, by this time, the soldiers had put a halt to their discussion and were following the proceedings no longer amused at what they were witnessing. Indeed, one of them self-consciously readjusted his bayonet, looking as if it might, at some point, come into play.

In a deferential tone, with just the slightest hint of mockery the priest repeated himself, "Aye, the cattle Sir, for what are we to do when a Nationalist buys an 'Orange' cow?"

Without waiting for Burke to answer, Father Kincaid explained to the people standing there still using his ironic tone of voice, "An Orangeman's cow in a Nationalist Creamery would turn the butter as rancid a yellow as the shutters down at Orange Hall. Or is that 'Orange hell'?—Not to mention that the 'Orange' cattle arriving every year from America are heathens—."

I had followed the verbal exchange as best I could, and was askance over the disrespect displayed by Bailey Burke towards our local priest, chained as he was to a door. Moreover, in my anxiety I turned quickly, accidentally knocking over a young colleen. The one wearing a muslin frock and Dutch sabots, I believe I may have described earlier. I gave her my hand to help her up, but simple words could not do justice to the defiance with which she refused my gesture.

"Stay away from me, *Spalpeen*, lest we all come down with the fever." This she ejaculated, as she picked herself up off the ground, making no attempt to hide her repugnancy at me and my kind.

For my part, I could only stare, completely intimidated while making the seemingly exhaustive effort to close my slackened jaw. All the while thinking I had never seen anything as lovely as this colleen. Thereby conceding, she couldn't have been more correct in her judgment of me and my kind. I might not have been, as she had described me, a degenerate *Spalpeen*, still I was awfully damn close. My hair was cut by hand and with scissors which had been worn to a pathetic dullness by countless nights hacking at crudely thickened yarn. My black, matted hair mirrored the craggy, scalloped edges of the scissors. In that regard, resembling a haystack where a farmer had haphazardly burrowed into after too much *poteen*, wishing to avoid the wrath of the missus until he'd slept it off. There were darkened, dirt-filled lines on my forehead and cheeks that even after a weekly washing left countless blackheads. As well, I couldn't seem to shake a permeating animal smell which after so long seemed to be a part of me. This particular smell could only be described as character-enhancing, if one wished to socialize with slimy, musky, mountain sheep or stagnant, bog-burrowing pigs. I had never up to that moment really understood or had an inkling of just how disgraceful I was. This young lady made it a point to clear up any confusion I might have had as to my social status.

I withdrew my hand while at a loss as to what to say, echoed the words of my Uncle Kippy when he came to visit us, "Edward Wallace Ruth at your service Ma'am!"

"I'm not a "Ma'am", but a miss—a Miss Katherine Louisa Maddox," she scolded back.

The way she pronounced her name sounded like she was the reigning monarch of all Russia.

I didn't nor couldn't respond. Who could in the face of such authority and overflowing beauty? It was my state in life to accept whatever meager scraps she might throw my way.

I truly believe my sorrowful guise woke up the Christian woman in her. Because for just a momentary impulse her cold regard became one of pity. As if for a fleeting second, she remembered some hallowed Christian teaching reminding her to have pity on the poor and wretched, Aye...make that lots of pity. As she stood up, she gathered the pleats of her grey skirt about her as delicately as one might suppose an angel would have done. Then she smiled thinly at me, before condescendingly reminding me that we knew one another from Sunday's high mass.

I explained to her, "Me and me ma, and brother and sisters don't go to the holy service all that often anymore."

She appeared to be struggling with something warring inside herself. Her face tried vainly to hide a modicum of revulsion as she called to mind the Christian message of reaching out to the more unfortunate ones. Of which I, without intentionally seeking it, apparently was a prominent member.

"We are leaving for America," she told me.

She might just as well have pinched her nose with her fingers, for she couldn't mask her aversion to my barnyard-like smell.

"A-m-er-i-ca?" I repeated, wondering aloud, as if I had just been asked to recall from memory the book of Genesis.

"You don't need to say it like that." She repeated the word 'America' as I had pronounced it, as if I was making fun of her.

Of course, I wasn't making fun of her. I'd been taught since I was a *páiste*[17] not to make fun of the angels or their helpers. I wouldn't say she spoke kindly to me now, or had changed her tone of voice. Rather, she spoke less coldly as if out of some enlightened duty, or a promise to a death-bed ridden grandmother that she would try to be nice to the scum of this world. Regardless of what the reason was, it was obvious she was making the effort to be civil with me. Even though it was just as obvious, she thought of me as some scurvy-ridden scallion, fresh from the heather. The outlying heather, where I guess she imagined, I spent most of my time singing incantations to the Druids while frolicking with *the little people.*

Timidly, I asked this red-haired Cleopatra, "What are you to do in America?"

She spoke as if she was bestowing some monarchical grace on me, "I am to become a nurse."

She then turned, her mahogany-red braids swinging to and fro like frolicking church bells in opposite flight.

The words spilled out of my mouth, in a stuttering monotone, much to my dismay, "Perhaps, one—one—one day I will come to visit you."

It was at such a precise moment in time my world imploded. Indeed, for having made such a masterful stand with her obvious revulsion, she couldn't help herself I suppose when she told me, "If one day, you by chance should come to visit me don't forget to wipe your feet off—. Or shoes for that matter, should in the future you will be so fortunate as to own a pair."

Having said such a thing the colleen turned, picking up her skirt and shaking it as she headed towards the luggage cart. I might add, shaking it vigorously as if she had just found a pestilent amount of lice lying therein.

I followed the swaying movements of her skirt as she made her way to stand next to her pappy. There, her father encircled his arm around her while he asked about for a small glass of *poteen*. The highland brewed drink was passed around until all of the men had a glass.

One by one, the men made a toast as if we were all at a wake, a wake where no one had died.

"You might be leaving us," proposed one man hopefully, "Still, here's to a better life!"

"Now Maddox, you'll do well and all if you'll remember but one thing?"

This came from the man in the yellow turncoat who answered his own question, "There's New York harbor and then there's the American-brewed

17   child

80

whisky called bourbon. Don't confuse one with t'other and try to drink the lot of 'em."

This perceptibly changed the tone of what up until then had all the makings of a funeral march. As a result, the men started grinning and bustling each other about, slapping one another on the back or shoulder while taking long, appreciative draughts of the *poteen*.

"What'll it be then, Mr. Burke? Are we to be on our way or what?" With a hand on his hip, the forgotten for the moment sergeant-at-arms called out.

"No, not until you've cleared the doorway of that priest. He's the one causing all the trouble 'round here—it t'ain't the Maddoxs!"

Father Kincaid challenged him, "Why don't you come over here yourself, Burke, and try and clear me away from this door I'm chained to? This way I can show you the practical side of what is meant by *turning the other cheek!*"

Bailey Burke looked dismally from the priest to the group of soldiers, in a poor attempt to ask them to intervene.

The man in the yellow turncoat came up and stood next to the chained priest. He put his hand on the priest's shoulder while offering the following advice; "T'is no use Father, they've accepted it so should you. Let them go in peace."

Father Kincaid shook his head, and in a voice full of defeat added, "T'is a disgrace I tell you, the English putting a man out of his own home—out of his own home I tell you, can you believe it?"

In an irritated and defensive voice Bailey Burke whooshed out, his cheeks filling and emptying like sails caught on an empty lee shore, "T'was never his home, he was there with the permission of Mr. Feargus O'Connor. I tell ye, and everyone else here a-listenin'—as long as he paid his rent."

"Paid his rent? Why should he pay his rent when the land belonged to him in the first place?" Father Kincaid inquired despondently.

Once again Burke looked at the soldiers with an expression which said; 'Can't you men do something?'

Freeing himself from the binding chains, Father Kincaid, in a limping manner, stepped clear from the blocking timber struts. "Let it be known to everyone here." He beckoned with his finger at all of us, "Let it be known to everyone here that not until Ireland stands free of the British, can we stop this disgraceful nonsense of running people out of their homes."

For once the driver of the cart changed expressions. He took his pipe away from his mouth. Then using the same pipe to dramatically stab at the air, he asked the crowd, "With the English running us all out of our homes and off to other countries, pretty soon there won't be anyone left to make a stand against the English. Except for the English themselves. And we all know Beelzebub cannot be divided against himself—isn't that true, Father

Kincaid?—Just imagine, the English sitting around staring at one another, asking themselves, 'what are we to do? We've done packed up and shipped off the Irish, so there's no one now for us to treat like dirt and do our menial labor, except each other. So if that's the case—who wants to starve to death first?' Now wouldn't that be something?"

The priest started to chuckle. Then one or two of the other men joined in. After a fashion, most of the men were laughing and the *poteen* was being passed around again.

This thought didn't please Bailey Burke. He removed his tall black hat and pointed a finger at the priest while motioning to the sergeant-at-arms to do his duty. In turn, the sergeant dejectedly indicated the pipe-less driver as if to say; 'if there was only one we could probably do something about it. But look damn it all—they're all against you!'

I stole a glance at Miss Katherine Louisa Maddox. She was standing next to her father with her back at an angle to me. She would on occasion stand on her toes and whisper something in his ear. He would then nod his affirmation as if what she had to say...a young woman nonetheless...was something of note. I believe I overheard her mention to her father she planned on continuing with her poetry. That even if she was to live in America, her poetry would keep *the children of the Gael* alive for all of them and not forgotten. I noticed she brushed a curl which was dangling in front of her eyes. The way she did it, reaching up with one slender hand was magical to me. At length, as if she sensed she was being watched she turned to look my way. At first she smiled. Her green, with specks of robin-egg blue eyes lit up with a remarkable coquetry. Right before these very same eyes caught mine where they suddenly became fiercely cold and unforgiving. In a manner of speaking, as if I'd betrayed my limits and crossed some inner sanctum. I really didn't care, for her beauty had already enraptured me. Thus, her displeasure became in a sense bittersweet, to someone who had finally found feelings for someone else.

By this time, most of the soldiers had moved out onto the road while Mr. Maddox was putting his family's final belongings into the cart. I couldn't figure out why Bailey Burke was still there, but he was. Also, why I was still standing there, but I was.

Father Kincaid took a sip of the local brew. This he did before reminding the Maddoxs with a returning, playful glint in his eye that Lent would soon be upon us. Therefore, the American prairie bison or buffalo, if he remembered correctly from his Maynooth theology courses was considered meat. That being the case, it was to be avoided at all costs during the Lenten season under penalty of grievous sin.

In simple deference to the priest's status the cart driver asked, "T'is be meat and all—to be sure, but where on the American prairie can a man find fish to eat Father, especially during Lent?"

Father Kincaid looked cheerfully around at all of us before replying, "Have you given any redemptive thought at all to the seasoning, preparation and salt-curing of nourishing rattlesnake meat?"

This brought a collective chuckle as well as several nods that the priest had indeed put one over on everybody.

The man in the yellow turncoat turned a knowing eye on the priest while addressing the group, "Saint Patrick didn't chase the snakes from Ireland just so you wouldn't have to eat the crawling bastards. No my friends, he thought of everything. He figured if there were any snakes left behind; they'd be food for the Protestants when they came to take away our land!"

Bailey Burke reminded us all using that mealy-mouthed voice of his, "There was nothing here when we came."

"When *YOU* came?" The man in the yellow turncoat complained menacingly.

"Well, not exactly when I came but—." Burke tripped over his own words.

Bailey Burke on occasion wanted to be one of us. But forgot instead that he had already made his bed with the likes of our Lord Tenant Feargus O'Connor, and there was no getting around it.

"Listen Burke, your backbone wiggles more than one of those snakes. Aye, and just like a snake it's hard to tell whether it's your head or your ass that's talking!"

I should have seen it coming to get out of the way in time, but I didn't; frozen as I was by hunger and fright. Upset and smarting from their collective ridicule, Bailey Burke thrust his stovepipe hat onto his head, and made for his dapple grey mare trying to contain his anger. Sitting upon his horse, he was but a yard or so away when he noticed a peasant-looking runt standing in his way. This peasant-looking runt, unfortunately was me. It was precisely at such a moment, I realized, I was in grave danger. He reined in hard his dapple grey mare. I could see the bit slide against one side of the horse's grasping mouth, causing spittle to fly across me forehead. Bailey Burke's eye flashed more white than anything else as he strained to look down at me. There were red and blue veins spread across the underside of his eyes. So prominent were they that for a minute I was afraid they might burst and rupture onto my forehead, like the spittle from the mare. Reflexively, I put a hand across my face praying the mare knew when to stop.

His riding crop was pointed menacingly at me when Bailey Burke thundered out, "You boy—yes, you, Ruth there—that's right, you. We have some unfinished business the two of us, don't we?"

This he ejaculated while looking back at the Maddoxs, and their family and friends, as if to confirm he was still the man in charge around here.

Turning back to me Burke continued, "You'd best buy or steal your passages to America because pretty soon it'll be your turn. You're damned right, don't think you can steal a kick in Bailey Burke's ribs, run out the door, and pretend I'd forget about it. Cause I won't! Why we take *croppies* like you, and load'em into English cannon just to see how far we can blow you out, Boy!"

I started to say it wasn't me, but my brother, who had kicked him that day in our cottage. In any case, Bailey Burke wouldn't listen. Half-deaf as he was, the man only took it as a further sign of my Irish *croppie* insolence in the face of his authority, not to mention in front of all those dubious onlookers.

He instinctively touched his ribcage. "Now listen here *Croppie,* you papist Irish think you can do your dirty work, then run and hide whilst we forget about your disloyal shenanigans. But it ain't so, Boy. And you'd best bear that in mind, the next time you or one of your kin think you can pull something over on Bailey Burke, you papist ragamuffin!"

In his cumulative anger, Burke lifted his riding crop above his shoulder before bringing it down with such a force that not only did it open my cheek, it collapsed the side of my eye socket, giving it a droopy disfigurement which I wear to this day. He also knocked me to the ground which I didn't mind so much, but it was the corner of my eye and cheek that were giving me the real pain.

Bailey Burke stood astride his dapple grey horse, seemingly, like a general leading his army into battle. He yelled down at me, "You tell your mother to get her things ready. The eviction notice from Mr. O'Connor is on its way, and if the Poor Land Office couldn't help the Maddoxs, they sure in hell won't help you!"

At last, spurring his horse to a precocious gallop, he rode away. In his flight, the man kept a tight hand on his ludicrous stovepipe hat, becoming a gross disfigurement of a rider while leaving a trail of wet grass and dew churning into the air.

In turn, a most amazing thing happened. I was feeling about for my limbs and general ability to breathe and hopefully walk again, when someone came over and stood next to me. The uncertain, pale sunlight shimmied for just a second causing me to look up. It was Katherine Louisa Maddox and she was holding a basket. In the basket was a sack of warm biscuits of which she was kind enough to offer me one. Now I am not going to fault Miss Maddox for what happened next. After all, she had a long voyage ahead of her. What probably motivated the colleen more than anything, was the need to be as clean as possible when the British and American authorities came to inspect her hygiene. In that regard, I don't fault her at all for what happened. I held out my hand, but instead of putting the biscuit into my palm firmly, she dropped it in like a she-hawk nurturing her young. Immediately after letting go of the biscuit, she rapidly withdrew her hand. It appeared as if she was afraid of my dirt-streaked fingers, and whatever other filth must lie within. I shifted the biscuit from my palm to my fingers trying to discourage my urge to smell it, not for the biscuit's aroma, but rather for the young lady's. At length, I looked up to thank her, but she was already climbing back into the front part of the wagon. I could tell from where I was sitting, her father was nodding deeply to his daughter, confirming she had done the right thing.

I picked myself up shamefully, trying to avoid everyone's stare. At last, wanting no more of the Maddoxs, the men drinking *poteen* and telling stories, or dead, skinned-out housedogs hanging listlessly from half-inch hooks corded over the cottage's main beam, I walked out of the driveway and onto the main road. Then without looking back I started to run. This I always do whenever that sick feeling hits me, as it has a habit of doing, right in the bottom part of my stomach, like a dull ache or thud.

I was running at a good clip, more from nervous, pent-up energy than from anything else. In a manner of speaking I struggled, trying to make some sense of all the thoughts competing for attention in my brain. Which is when I felt something that I knew wasn't part of my clothing that day. Looking down, I noticed the biscuit she had given to me was still in my hand, where it laid bent in half, and crumbling around the edges. I stopped right there in the roadway, and brought the biscuit up next to my face, right in front of my nose so I could catch every scent. There it was, mingled in and amongst the sugar and baked oatmeal was her smell. The smell of one who had been brought up with the angels; of one who was always clean, of someone who smiled knowingly at her father, and discussed things with him, as if that was how life was supposed to be. A driver and his milk-wagon passed me on the road. The driver hollered down at me to be more careful; that I could get run over by his horse and trailer. I merely smiled back, having the distinct and thrilling feeling that somehow I was now above it all...indeed they could no longer catch nor harm me. In a relaxing way, I was safe and protected from whatever it was which was scaring the lot of us in Castlewarren, Ireland.

One thing came into my mind while I was running. Well, two actually, but the first one, my dream about Katherine Louisa Maddox was beyond dreaming. Still in all, I didn't feel so bad about that. How can you feel bad about something you knew with absolute certainty it wasn't to be had? It wasn't in the cards. The heavens weren't about to bless such an outlandish idea. That there was no way you could ever be with her. You see, that I knew and understood. I didn't have a problem with such an idea. The unattainable is still the unattainable, and I was level-headed enough to know what I could and couldn't have. Still, I was pretty damned sure I could do something about the other idea. The other idea was to put down on paper what I saw and heard around me; the fascinating theater of life. The act of writing didn't require one to get up at dawn to pull on scabby, reddened and sore, pulsating cow teats. Or, sit up all night if the animal was bawling and sick. No, one could write anytime of the day. It didn't appear to require much of anything, but what wonderment it could provide. I could write about Katherine Louisa Maddox, and what she looked and smelled like, maybe even her *children of the Gael* poetry. I could write about Father Kincaid and Bailey Burke, and our struggles with our stolen land. How Bailey Burke spoke and acted like he was English, even though he had been born and baptized right here in Castlewarren, with the rest of us. In short, I decided there were a lot of things to write about. As it so happens, and as far as this Irishman's concerned, I'd be lying like a gutless Protestant if I didn't come right out and say what I felt. That I wouldn't mind if by chance, it should happen just so, perhaps a little deviltry by trying me hand at writing poetry might come to serve me in good stead. Although, right at such a moment in time, how and why I couldn't possibly know. Nevertheless, if Katherine Louisa Maddox had mentioned something about poetry, that it was a good idea to be involved with, it certainly remained a subject to look into. If, for no other reason than I just might see her again through my poetry. Who could tell afterwards? If the poem was delightful enough, she might just offer me another biscuit. Now, that was certainly something to look into!

I put my hand to my face, and carefully munched the oatmeal biscuit with its resulting crumbs. I felt no shame in licking my hand, nor thereafter, inspecting it carefully to see if I'd missed any specks of sugar or oatmeal. Satisfied with myself, feeling only the thumping ache from my torn cheek and swollen eye socket, I turned into the well-kept lane leading to the Scullum's place. Aye, I was a contented young man the rest of that day; happy and secure in the knowledge that Mrs. Scullum and her debilitating croup were a thing of the past.

Chapter Six

We are journeying on to partake of the feast
Which a Father's hand has spread,
For we go from here to the Land of the East
When the world shall call us dead.

Our footsteps tend toward the rising sun,
Which never a cloud doth mar,
And Christ shall place when the race is run,
On our brow the morning star.

We shall lave our feet in Eternity's tide
And our pain shall be washed away,
For pain or care doth never abide
In the realm of his perfect Day.

What though our suffering hearts beat here,
Neath the surge of affliction's tears,
There never a care, nor never a tear
Shall be ours in the blessed years.

Our hearts are athirst for the wine of bliss,
We long to partake of the feast,
That is spread for the sorrowing hearts of this
Sad land, in the Land of the East.
—H.A. Manville

My mother decided my sisters Ann Horian and Susan would leave first. They would join relatives in a place called Maysville, Kentucky. I asked if there were Indians living in Kentucky. They told me of course there were, but they weren't the dangerous kind, content instead, to sit around drinking their own brand of *poteen*, and selling souvenir tomahawks. I was disappointed, for I imagined our own listless, *poteen*-swilling Irishmen, who leaned against their stone hedges and waited for any kid like myself to come along. This they did, knowing they could make us stand for hours, listening to their endless drivel about the old days in Ireland. They would ramble on about how everyone had respect for the adults back then, regardless of whether or not, they were lazy and contemptible.

I still dreamed of seeing heroic Indians on horseback stampeding into this campsite or another one. They'd be taking down man-eating bears as something to do when they were bored or between scalping parties. I played with the idea of finding out who the big Indian chief was in Maysville, Kentucky. Then I could ask him; perhaps, instead of fooling around, whipping up defenseless bears for fun, maybe for a change of pace would they mind coming to Castlewarren and scalping a few Englishmen? Insofar as that goes, they would probably need to spend a lot more time sharpening their tomahawks in between scalpings. For it is well documented, that an Englishman's skull is so thick, it comes very close indeed to mimicking the hardwood likeness, of one of the great oak trees which canvass "No-Name Bridge and Stream".

Just as he had intimidated he would, Bailey Burke showed up at our cottage maybe a week after the Maddoxs had left. He had papers that left him no choice he said, but to evict us from our home. The reason being he told us, was because our rent was in arrears, and apparently with so little to eat, or produce from the sterile land we had tried to cultivate—so were we.

His dapple grey mare brought Mr. Burke into our little sweeping alley where he dismounted, leaning over to clean one of his tan, knee-high boots off on the lower rung of our sitting bench. The one we used to sit outside on when the weather permitted it.

Without so much as a second thought, he ballyhooed out a lusty, "God save all here," as if he was bringing us freshly baked scones to go with our morning tea.

My brother and I were outside in the shed playing *half-stump flurry,* instead of doing what we'd been ordered to do by me mother that morning. Me brother, Paul Francis Daniel, still had over fifty centimeters of a half-circle to go, before his captured rat (with which me brother was trying to amputate his hind leg, using the blunt end of a potato spade) could wriggle to, and thus by the rules of our game, his freedom as well. My brother would abruptly lessen his pressure on the potato spade or shovel, only to see the brown rat scamper once again, for the wooden board's flat end. Taking his pleasure, Paul Francis Daniel would bring pressure to bear once again, and the rat would freeze in place, sniffing around hellishly while his hind leg continued to bleed. The game would continue like this for hours. Sometimes, he'd let the little bugger have all his *juice* back just to see what the rat would do. My brother and I never gave much thought to the liberating effects of having once made the other side of the circle, indeed, what was the use of freedom, if the rat in question was bleeding to death from a partially-severed hind leg. Paul Francis Daniel believed somehow, the rat had received an even break that day, for we had allowed him his freedom, severed leg and all, without interrogating the little bugger first. I wasn't aware of the word "interrogate", nor what it implied. So my elder brother (by three years) explained, with what for him was something approaching exemplary patience.

"Aye, it's something the Brits do to scare the lot of us."

Like someone stupid I repeated his statement, "To scare the lot of us— why?"

My brother skewered his eyes up into something resembling two peas in a half-open pod, "They hate the Irish, they always have. We are considered to be an inferior people to the mighty Brits. Which is why they frighten us, intimidate us, keep us off-balance, to make us scared. So's one day, they can run us off, out of Ireland, meaning they can finally take over."

"Aye, they want to starve themselves to death as well?" I answered back mulishly.

This didn't make much sense to me. Although, perhaps to a thick-headed Englishman, buttermilk with pitted, blackened potatoes three times a day contained a certain attraction....Who was I to say?

Paul Francis Daniel's patience was wearing thin, "No, they don't want to starve to death like us, you scallywag. The English know the land is fertile. Therefore, they want to run us off, so they can use more efficient tools and seed to grow things better, and more of it as well."

I was quite frankly dumbfounded, and I said as much, "Run "us" off? "Us" a bunch of *spalpeens*? Run us out of Ireland, so's they can take over—? In God's great mercy—from what I can see (I was remembering the militia at the Maddox's cottage) they've already taken over. Besides, why should they be scared of us?—A bunch of bog-wading, luckless *croppies*?"

With a wave of his hand he shook me off, "It's more than that little brother. It has something to do with there being two Christs. With one of the Christs, I believe it's the Orange one who lives in England, who doesn't want anything to do or share with his brother, the one we as Roman Catholics call Jesus. It has everything to do with the two Christ-brothers, as well as Adam and Eve and their ark, with all of them flamin' animals in it."

He then made some vulgarly caustic remark about the animals aboard the ark and their subsequent waste, causing the boat to smell like a stagnant pool over in one of the shallows off "No-Name Stream", we both knew of. Where for some reason, people left the scalloped heads of dead fish they had caught and cleaned, but didn't want to eat. My face skewered up at the odorous thought, causing my brother to laugh which he didn't do all that much anymore.

"Well then, why don't the Protestants stay put with their Orange Jesus over in England, while we stay on our side of the ocean, with his Catholic brother?"

Paul Francis Daniel clapped me hard on my back, seemingly to affirm what I had asked. This he did, before glancing rapidly over his shoulder. My brother looked quizzically, first at the corner of the shed, before staring at his now empty spade, for we'd both heard the rat's nauseating squeal. It came from somewhere over behind the sack of onion bulbs and one or two dozen potatoes, which as yet had not turned into a black and oxidizing, ponderous sludge.

"Because the Protestant Christ doesn't want his brother, Jesus to become so big and mighty that he can make it over to England and take over their farms, like they're trying to do to us here. Which is why the Orange Christ keeps telling us to be like meek, obedient lambs, to "turn the other cheek", to be brothers and not to fight. In short, to love peace so much that we'll keep on doing the English bidding without so much as a by-your-leave. This then, so's they can come over, and kick our Roman Catholic asses back into the bogs whenever they've a mind to do so."

Again we both heard the rodent's squeal, although this time it was much longer and painful.

I asked myself if my brother could be right? Thinking back, I remembered the Maddoxs with all their belongings packed into a wooden trailer. I seized on the manner in which, the pipe-smoking driver kept looking at us all in a bizarre fashion, as if he was being escorted to the gallows. I could still visualize the deeply-lined smirk attached to his face, as if he couldn't believe this was to be his reward for hearty, dawn to dusk labor, with an aching back to boot. It seemed a rather bitter and ironic price to pay in one's waning years. Could it be true, that the English had more of a say in it than the actual people who live on these bloody farms?

Aye, after a fashion I remembered Katherine Louisa Maddox. Something welled up inside of me, to confuse me while at the same time making me happy in a sad sort of way. I do know because of her I was damned glad to be alive...finally. Things didn't seem so bad as they appeared, or as they did before. Let the Orange Christ and his brother Jesus have it out. Hell, maybe the Roman Catholic Christ would beat the living snoot out of his brother, the Protestant one. In which case, we could all go back to our peaceful ways again; eating churlish vegetable roots, living in a freezing cottage in wintertime, a slap of *poteen* to take away the ache in our bellies and once again, having a bloody, grand time of it all.

"Did you hear that, Edward?"

I stumbled out of my dream. "What was that?" I replied somewhat vaguely.

"I think it's that scoundrel Bailey Burke coming back to give ma our papers."

"Our papers?" I was now scratching my arm, which I did whenever I wished to hide my stupidity.

"Aye, we're goners now."

"Goners—is it?" I was scratching, then investigating the area I'd just itched, as if I didn't understand the reason for my arm's redness. Or, perhaps more to the point, was using it as a reason not to face something I didn't wish to hear.

My brother explained it rather succinctly, "Aye, with those papers, we have a month to find a boat, to take us all to Kentucky, to make a new life as Americans."

Paul Francis Daniel let his hand fall lightly across the stubble of copper-colored whiskers which had just recently appeared on his chin. While he fixed me with a look that was somewhere between his; 'I'm about to thrash you look', and his sorrowful look that said, 'There's a damned, papist, fish bone stuck in me throat, give me a hand now, will you?'

"Tell me, Son—." This my brother initiated, using the tone of voice, I believe he thought our pappy would use, if he'd been present-like and accounted for. "Tell me this, Son; you're not in an all-too unhappy mood for taking this here voyage to the Americas, are ye?"

Afterwards, he eyed me queerly...unsettlingly so.

"Well, I'm not—I'm not saying I'm against it, seeing as our sisters are already gone. Also, from what I've heard, we've gotta heckuva better chance of finding something to hang onto over in the United States. Other than an empty pantry, full of memories that don't do nothin' to fill me belly!"

I looked around the shed already planning my escape route—for I knew my brother's temper.

"That's not what I'm asking about—." His voice took on a certain edge, making me anxious.

"Well what is it, Paul Francis? Speak your mind, instead of doing this city-smoking imitation of a hook-nosed colleen, who won't give you the time of day unless you buy her a meal. And asking all the while after real cream, as if your pockets were full of cigars and silver coin as well."

He answered back, "I'm saying that ever since you went a traipsing 'round the Maddoxs, and their daughter favored you with a great, big, oatmeal biscuit and the likes, you've been mooning around here like a cow in the middle of a damned, breech birth. One minute you're lowing around and moaning, as if your sides are about to burst, then the next minute laughing and carrying on. All the while, as if it was bloody spring time, and we's about to celebrate your ruddy birthday—."

I couldn't hold it in anymore. I felt my brother would understand my feelings and I told him as much. "That Katherine Louisa Maddox is a real colleen, Paul Francis Daniel, and I ain't a scared to say so neither! So's what if we gets to see her once we're in the United States, and I'm working and all, so, what of it? She gave me a biscuit didn't she—and a damned good one to boot, I might say!"

To my unabridged surprise, my brother clipped me sharply across the side of my face, using the cupped palm of his left hand. To add to it, there was no disguising the uncompromising air of disgust with which he treated me.

In that regard, he lectured me, "With a woman in your destitute life like *that one,* you might just as well spend the rest of your days queuing up with the other boys to see her. Or, better yet, clinging to some bloody, high-tide, water-raft, for you won't have a clue as to where your heading with her. Nor how long'll it'll be, before you're good and drowned."

T'is true—I'll admit it. I didn't know Dublin, the big city, like my brother did. Therefore, how could I possibly understand when he told me to turn my back on Katherine Louisa Maddox; the one, true, fresh breath of hope I'd known in quite some time. Unless of course, you count the time my dog "Blister" was gone for three days, and didn't he finally limp home, happy to see me, with a hunter's trap firmly ensconced on his back leg. Still in all, at least he made it back home. For the life of me, I couldn't accept my brother's relentless face slapping, as if I'd done something awful, and needed an in-house reprimand.

"Hey, stop it now—will you? You damned *croppie* fool—", while raising a protective arm. This Paul Francis Daniel, with his shortened fuse, took as a sign of war.

Underneath my raised arm, he threw a stealthy, short jab which crested my ribs, and found its mark in the distended underside of my belly. I sat down hard on the floor of our shed, searching somehow to breathe again.

"No," he screamed at me, "You stop it. You've got a mother and a brother and sisters to watch over you. We're all here, to take care of each other. You leave well enough alone—you hear me!—You don't need any colleen, especially her. She'll drown you in the end just like I've been saying. The only thing you'll ever need is your family!"

I was sitting on the floor of the shed, trying to determine who had let the spooky hurricane out of my brother, when we heard two things and at the same moment as well. The first one, was me ma calling us to come around the front where we needed to be. The other, was the languishing cry of a rat in painful duress. We both got up to answer our mother's call. I turned to me brother, and indicated the corner of the shed. We both watched as the rat tried his best to hobble up one side of the blistered, unpainted, wooden planking, where we stored our makeshift gardening tools. The rat would barely make some headway, before he'd slide back, slipping on his own blood with his dangling leg trailing behind him. This he did, pleated, in a most awkward position, the rat's head turning in every direction. And all the while, sniffing the air like some daft Druid priest, wondering as to what had become of us all.

Paul Francis Daniel turned to me while waving his hand behind him, as if the rat was of absolutely no concern to him. He sermonized, "No one, including the bloody, Catholic Christ gives a damn about us. So, unless you want to eat *the little darling*, I say let him find his own way out of the shed. And if his leg starts troubling him—then let'im limp out of here, just like the rest of us!"

In that manner, my brother started hobbling to the front of the cottage, as if he too was in pain, or was looking for someway out of this hopeless mess... just like the crippled rat.

We found me mother and Mr. Bailey Burke talking to one another, and commiserating like family members inside our cottage, hunched down by the barely glowing hearth. I instinctively touched the corner of my eye which hadn't quite healed, as I strained to follow their conversation.

"Oh, this is terrible, just terrible." Me mother was caught between wringing her thick farmer's hands over what the man was saying, and what I believed to be a better use of her resolute energy—wringing Bailey Burke's traitorous neck.

"Aye, Mrs. Ruth," Bailey Burke kept intoning, his face just as serious as if he was trying to judge the weight of a Parish Gowan prize pig. "She too, thought she could get a fair and clear hearing from the Poor Law official. But the man said he couldn't see the woman, not this close to Christmas and all. That she should have understood the man's responsibilities, and not come calling this close to the holy feast. So off the woman goes, another seven, if it wasn't more onto eight miles, back through the sleet and stormin' rain."

Ah, me poor mother was shuddering at what she imagined the poor, helpless woman had to endure. Moreover, as pure as her heart was, she still dared to say, "The man may have been a *dacent* person and all. Never let it be said that I judged someone too harshly, without taking the beam from me own eye. And whilst there may have been truth in what he had to say, still a Christian man from London no less, should never have let the poor woman dare the storm alone. With another seven miles of it as well, you say? Why I've never heard of such a thing, happening before, here in Ireland!"

Bailey Burke, using a rather incongruous, half-twisted, ironic look of sallow indulgence, which I believed he thought, may have resembled something close to pity, took up his story, "Not only does she brave the elements on the twenty-seventh, but the woman repeats it when she comes back to the Poor Law official's office on the sixth of January, believing he'll finally see her now that the holidays are quite finished; the feasting, the drinking and what not—."

My ears pricked up, and I believe I instinctively let out a sort of half-growl, very similar to what a wolf would do when they believe they've been trifled with. For I didn't appreciate Bailey Burke and his notions of feasting and what have you, when we were scrambling like a pack of rutting, out of control, Curragh bucks, to get something in the way of nourishment inside ourselves. Ironically, and like a man in some sort of demented pleasure, I remembered to myself; *still you passed on the maimed rat a short time ago didn't you?*

Bailey Burke turned around to look at me. It seemed he wasn't quite sure if he had heard the growl coming from me. Or, if it had come from somewhere outside and therefore close by, which could be dangerous. "Mrs. Ruth—", Burke started in, as if they were long-standing, intimate, family members; "Mrs. Ruth, well it just so happens, this fine Irish woman eventually ends up in a meeting with the Englishman, only to tell him that she buried her daughter Bridget without a coffin on the twenty-fourth, and her son Michael on January fifth, both dead from hunger."

Well then and upon hearing this, me poor mother gets to wringing her hands again. She starts muttering to the blank walls while casting about as if she was in need of air. It made for a bizarre sight; the vague, undulating light from the red-stringed, fired-up peat that continued to burn slowly while ma rocked herself back and forth. Amidst our matriarch and her wretched movement, the fire spat out its dying gasp. Slowly enough, to where it left long trails of wispy smoke while playing havoc with the cottage and the uneven-walled shadows within.

"I can't see where any of this has to do with us, Mr. Burke? Unless of course, you've a notion to send us scurrying out and about in the snow?" Ma pleaded.

"Now, now, Mrs. Ruth, we're not talking about sending anyone anywhere," he replied soothingly enough, caught up as he was in this intimate moment of friendship....

Hell, caught up as it were in his own damned Protestant indecisiveness and mischievous falsehoods, condemning us to what eventually happened.

My brother realizing the man's mistake, played on it instantly and with as little pity as he'd shown the rat. "If what you say is true; that no one's going anywhere, why are you here, Mr. Burke with a stack of papers which you're holding in your hand, for an Irishwoman to sign who can only speak Gaelic, and doesn't know how to read or write?"

To say that Bailey Burke froze up in silence would be a gross understatement. Please bear in mind that our land agent had turned his back on his village, on his Irish heritage including his faith, to make his bed with the English-backed, Scottish-rite, Free-Mason Protestants. In which case, someone with that amount of gall (Father Kincaid described Bailey Burke in a moment of deep, reflective, Christian intuition, "The man's plain stupid in thinking he can outwit the devil.") wasn't going to lay aside any plans he'd already made, just because my brother had called him out on something which all of us in the room (except for our mother) knew to be true. Nevertheless, for a long, drawn-out, Protestant-minute, Bailey Burke stood frozen in place. His black, bushy eyebrows became furrowed together in pointed thought. All the while his slack cheeks drew up together, like sails slowly filling when they pass some point of land to eventually meet the dominant sea breeze. It appeared he had reached some definitive decision, for his cheeks, like two bellows from a forge, exhaled in a lengthy manner, before flattening themselves concavely against the side of his face.

He told us while his hesitant eyes scoured the room, "No, I just don't want you and your sons to get false hopes up, like that lady did, waiting for the Poor Law Commission to do something. You live on more than a quarter of a statute acre; therefore there is no possible way you can qualify for aid according to the new laws."

Me mother asked hopefully, "Even if we give up the land and just kept the cottage?"

"Aye now, that wouldn't be good for anyone, would it now? And where would you plant your crops—on your deteriorating roof?"

Me mother played out her desperate, last, aching card, "Why then, we wouldn't plant any crops at t'all. Because, by giving up our land, and keeping just the cottage, we'd be below the minimum of a quarter of an acre, thereby qualifying for aid."

I could tell that Bailey Burke didn't like getting caught up in a discussion with a peasant farmer and a woman to boot, when he stated crisply enough, "It wouldn't be aid you'd be looking at then, but a central room at a work house, including everything which that entails——. For the love of mike, Woman, you don't want that for your boys now do you?"

At length, as if even he couldn't stomach the thought, Burke continued, shaking his head solemnly while uttering, "Aye, t'is nothing like a batch of cholera to bring people and friends together, well enough, isn't it Mrs. Ruth? Besides, your daughters have already left Ireland haven't they? Don't you want to join them?"

She wiped a thick arm across her brow before answering the man, "It won't be but two shakes of the cat's tail, before the two of them are married, and settled down with their own hearths. Now isn't that so, Mr. Burke, tell me now if I'm wrong, Sir?"

One could tell he didn't like the conversation. Furthermore, he didn't like us, and even less the idea of reporting back to our landowner, Feargus O'Connor that the Ruths were still his financial responsibility. This of course, was the plan of action as decided upon by the English government during the famine. Perhaps what was worse about this whole affair was that Feargus O'Connor would have to pay out a relatively important sum for the Ruths to sit around, like some sort of Catholic fungus, in an over-crowded workhouse. Who knows what might happen afterwards? They could be kept waiting in the workhouse, and getting indignantly angry perhaps. That's right, waiting for the day they could come back, and maybe in force as well, with possibly just the slightest sense of wanting to right some ill-perceived wrongs....No, no, this would never do.

Mr. O'Connor had been quite specific when he had made the statement in confidence to his manager Bailey Burke, "Let's eradicate the Irish pest just like we would treat any disease—in damned good, short order!"

At last, as if he remembered just exactly where he was, or perhaps more poignantly who he was, Bailey Burke stood up to his string-bean, conniving, full-engaging, slender height. The man looked down at the papers he was holding in his hand, then rather harshly at Paul Francis Daniel, before he extended the papers to my mother, and muttered something about we had a fortnight or so to clear out. Then me mother,—aye, me poor, broken-down mother, wearing one of the three dresses she owned; the one with faded, vertical stripes that warped away into slumping half-circles around her thickened waist, sang the call of the fallen Irish. Aye, it could have been the time in 1798, with Theobald Wolfe Tone waiting for the French to arrive, only to have disaster fall with unequivocal death at the end of a pike for insurrection. It could have been the gay, solid, and believing heartstrings of her youth, snapping in two when our pappy left her, without so much as an, 'I'll be back, now, don't you worry none....' But she'd finally had enough, you could tell. It was written all over her white, chalk-like face. The face which was puffy and slack with thin, blue, vein lines spinning in all directions, like the butchered stretch of a half-eaten, cow's brain, revealing she'd taken more than what any normal woman should and could endure. Her pale, watering, grey eyes looked frantically about the room as if something had loosened, given way, then finally broken in two, and she no longer remembered where she was. Her flitting eyes finally settled on a faded, denim work-shift that was hanging from the clothesline drawn tautly down the middle of the room. She continued to gaze at the work-shift, as if this drying piece of laundry was her compass. Indeed, ma was gone alright, for she'd taken more than her fair share of unmanageable dismay from this unforgiving world.

"Aye, we'll be out then. I've had it with these times. You said in a fortnight?" Ma asked despondently, her eyes never once leaving the denim work-shift hanging on a clothesline, stretched across our darkened sitting room.

Bailey Burke was staring at the walls—our walls, as if he was deciding which ones would stay and which ones would go. Probably to make a bloody grand parlor, in which he and his mates could sit around, sipping their imported whisky while admiring the thirteen point buck they'd brought down, amidst their morning of sport.

He called back over his shoulder, "You can even leave in three weeks time. I'll mention nothing to Mr. O'Connor, on that you have my word."

He walked over to the spindle, and put money on one of the carding racks. He tapped it righteously with his fist as he turned away. "This'll buy you passage from here to Liverpool then onto the United States of America, to join your daughters."

Apparently, he was quite touched by his generosity, for he kept looking back at the moneyed envelope, then to us, grinning that mealy-mouthed, Judas Iscariot grin of his. As if from the monies within it, we could now flirt with the idea of buying a mansion on the Thames. Even outfitting a privateer, with which we could sail directly to the Americas, loading up on rum and sugar from the West Indies as we travelled. This we could do while needlessly bypassing Liverpool and its havoc-filled quarantine station, now that we were suddenly and fortuitously rich.

My last vivid memory of Mr. Bailey Burke, is of the man just settling into the well-oiled saddle, on top of his dapple grey mare. He turned to us, his cheeks round and full, as if he had a sack of walnuts in each one.

Then he looked for and found my older brother to whom he lamented cynically enough, "It's too bad you can't come for dinner this evening, we're having you and your father's favorite; Curragh buck with all the trimmings—especially stewed for those of you getting ready to leave Castlewarren!"

Upon saying that, he spurred his dapple grey mare out of our entryway while his unrelenting cackle drifted back to us...a cackle which I could never forget. For it reminded me of someone, making sport out of people who could no longer defend themselves; the desperately lost and hopeless. How could anyone with a sense of decency, grind someone else down, using their own nothingness to do it as well? Still in all, this didn't stop Paul Francis Daniel from making an obscene gesture with his hand and arm. Even when my sainted mother saw him, for once, she didn't say or do anything. Like I said earlier, the poor woman had had enough.

As far as the rest goes, we were only to hear about it later; much later, when we were on the other side of the ocean. Such things, as we didn't then, nor would we ever have the right to hold land, to vote, to be elected, and practice law or our beloved religion. That as far as the English were concerned, we, the Irish, were nothing more than a bunch of "able-bodied paupers"...no more, no less. Indeed, as far as this Irishman's concerned, the Orange Christ had won and by a significant margin, I might add.

At the very least, which brought me untold hope; thankfully, and by the grace of God, we, 'Irish paupers' still had our Gaelic poetry, and I, my poetic lines still meant to be written about a certain Katherine Louisa Maddox.

Chapter Seven

Oh you brave Irish people,
Wherever you maybe
I pray stand a moment and listen to me
Your sons and brave daughters are now going away
And thousands are sailing to America

Oh, good luck to them now
And safe may they land
They are pushing their way
To a far distant strand
For here in old Ireland
No longer can stay
For thousands are sailing to America

Oh, the night before leaving
They're bidding goodbye
And it's early next morning
Their hearts give a sigh
They will kiss their dear mothers
And then they will say:
"Goodbye Father dear I'm now going away"

Oh, their friends and relatives and neighbours also
They're packing their trunks now ready to go,
When the tears from their eyes
It run down like rain
And the horses were prancing going off for the train.

It is now you will hear that very last cry
And a handkerchief waving and bidding goodbye
The old men tells them be sure to write
And watches the train till she goes out of sight.

It is God help the mother that rears up a child
It is now for the father he labours and toils
He tries to support them he works night and day
And when they are reared sure they will go away.
                                    Author unknown

I am not going to bother you with all the ramifications of our flight. Instead, let me be perfunctorily accurate by stating that in spite of his higher calling, Father Kincaid insisted on being chained to our rotting front door to protest our eviction. However, since mother wouldn't hear of it (the turn of events already having been decided as it were), and that being the case, the irascible priest decided on a chain of novenas to Saint Patrick. He included as well, a number of other inveterate saints, designed to rain bloody hell down on the English. My brother, in his close-hauled, cynical and endearing way, asked if it wouldn't be better for both God and us, to concentrate our collective spiritual energies on one or two of the aforementioned "bloody English". By whom, I believe he meant, to be directed towards certain *messieurs* Bailey Burke and Feargus O'Connor. According to our Father Kincaid, this wouldn't do. That it wasn't theologically sound, nor by any means charitable as well, to direct God's justice against certain individuals. The well-meaning Irish priest explained in good conscience, as well as in great detail that it wouldn't be proper to single out certain persons for God's wrath and punishment. On the other hand, he added;—if God decided He'd plummet the whole of England into the sea, without so much as a second thought about it....Well then, who was he, a simple rural priest, to second guess the hand of God. Father Kincaid was then heard to mutter poignantly, "And let the life boats be damned!"

Sure enough, the Scullums all came to say goodbye. Mrs. Scullum was kind enough to bring us a minced pie while her husband, never one to let such a moment as this go by, declared that this was all the devastating work of the devil. And hadn't he seen it all coming; the moment Mr. O'Riley had brought in the first handle-turning, gear-meshing, butter churner to our village, making us all into a bunch of lazy, not fit for anything, incorrigible heathens.

"Indeed," he proclaimed in his sagest tone of voice, "If the Ruths are to leave the village soil, they being one of the oldest families in Castlewarren and all—why it is only a matter of time, before the very earthworms themselves leave. Then let me ask you, who will be left to aerate the soil?"

I firmly believe we were all quite touched and sentimentally so, at being mentioned in the same breath as an earthworm by Mr. Scullum. At the mention of earthworms, the appallingly frail Mrs. Scullum looked apologetically at her minced pie, before handing it over to our ma. Upon which, a fight broke out between her sons Frank and Johnny as to whom was to get the biggest piece of pie. While Mrs. Scullum told the two of them the pie was for us, and begged the two boys to stop their fighting, me mother graciously handed the pie back to Mrs. Scullum. At which point, each of her sons helped themselves to a rather large piece of minced pie, before galloping off somewhere, back of the cottage to eat it. Thus, we left our little village of Castlewarren.

We traveled on foot to the marketplace. At the marketplace, we were able to find ourselves a small wagon and driver, who took us as far south as Cork. There, by his own Christian initiative, he found a couple who gave us another ride to the port of Cobh. From the port of Cobh, we took passage to Liverpool, England, on the steamer, named "Nimrod". The driver, whose last name was Brennan, who also never allowed the admittance to a Christian first name, told us through craggy-green and blackened teeth the following story. He also, could have left Ireland years ago, if his own wife hadn't departed their domestic home first. This the woman did, going back home to her mother, leaving this same Mr. Brennan in luxurious, bachelor-like peace. For which, he apparently had been ever so thankful, and would under no circumstances fiddle with. This included emigrating anywhere in the world, under the precarious chance he might run into the same Mrs. Brennan again. No, he told us, his cart and horse were all that he needed to be happy in this life. Still in all, should he feel the need to talk to something sweet and feminine again; why he would run up and visit his sister Georgina over in Carlow. His sister, besides being inevitably happy to see her brother, on occasion, enjoyed throwing hot soup at him. This she did, for no other reason than after listening to his brother-in-law, Georgina's husband had run off as well. This he did, unfortunately without the providence of leaving Georgina a horse and cart (like her brother's), to make up for the marvelous times they'd enjoyed together as husband and wife.

I wasn't given to much conversation during the three days required for our overland voyage. No, for once and without any chores at hand, I was completely caught up in the moment and my surroundings. Why it was absolutely fascinating with so many things to see and smell and wonder about. Looking back and to be meddling honest about it, I paid little heed to me mother's anxious and fretful regard, as she left the only thing her fifty-six years knew. Moreover, what was exceedingly worse for her was the underlying admission she would never see Ireland and its peoples, ever again. This had to be devastating for her. You see, I had no knowledge or comprehension of such a thing. Being only seventeen, I was completely unaware because of our choices we could and couldn't do certain things as a result. I was of the belief that should I desire to come back to 'the old sod'; why I would just climb on a boat, and reverse the process. This included in a moment of personal, light-hearted revelry, *stealing* back the minced pie from the Scullum boys upon my return. Thus for me, the time during our travels was beyond belief. It was a mystifying journey of continual wonderment, and I paid little heed to my mother's wails. It wasn't something I did through some appalling lack of charity, but simply because I couldn't grasp at what she must have been feeling. My one desire was to be able to write down some of the things I saw. However, as much as I desired it I couldn't, not having any formal training in the matter of reading or writing. My brother, on the other hand simply wouldn't leave me alone. His one burning goal was to see revenge meted out against a number of different parties. This included the venerable English, whom he declared responsible for forcing us from our home, as well as my father because he had never come back. All this occurred while the green and untilled, fertile countryside passed by on either side of the wagon.

"Come back to what," I asked him as if it was high time to turn the page, and forget once and for all the old man, wherever he might be.

"To his family, you harelip." This my brother quipped as if I should have known better.

I turned in the wagon to look at him, for he seemed to be changing before my very eyes. Paul Francis Daniel was still slim and lanky, with his hands forever stuck in his pockets, like some handicapped scarecrow left in the springtime field. Nevertheless, the boyish gleam had left his sluicing, grey eyes, and some dark, haunting glint appeared to have replaced it. His words were short and bitter. He would look at you while you were talking, continually pasting his red hair with the palm of his hand over one eye, as if he didn't believe in a word you were saying. He was only three years older than I, but he had dark, saucer-like streaks under both eyes as if he couldn't sleep at night. I shuddered at the possibilities of what could keep Paul Francis Daniel up late, and from his needed rest. The other thing I remarked about him was that my brother had sometime during the trip taken up with tobacco. He didn't have a pipe, but that he didn't spill out his tobacco leaf from a pouch onto thin paper strips. At length, with a certain, admirable, manual dexterity he would roll the whole compressed mess into long, cylindrical rolls, and finally to my utter amazement put fire to it, and inhale it into his chest. My brother explained to me, extolling the bluish air, this is what everyone did in Dublin. It wasn't the tobacco smoking that put me out nor his stale breath, like the confined dung-laden air of our shed which went with the smoking.... It was Paul Francis Daniel's general attitude toward everyone and everything that bothered me.

Like once during the trip when I pointed out to my brother, barely hiding my excitement over a water-wheel which reached nearly three meters overhead;

that actually through a series of well-engineered, interacting gears it could, by the use of running water, actually power a sawmill. Absolutely fascinating I thought to myself, and wanted my brother to share in my wonderment as well.

Why if he didn't look down at me to say, "Aye Edward, what's to us the water-wheel, or the sawmill for that great matter, for we's been born to extinction."

Aye, t'is true enough—that's what he told me, "We's been born to extinction."

This set me in arrears terribly, for I banged him on his shoulders while begging him to reconsider, "Life is just starting for the two of us, Paul Francis Daniel. We're on our way to a new land wrought with new things to see and do. No more passing round the hat like incapacitated *Tinkers*," I told him, trying to wring some sense into my brother. "We've got more than enough to look forward to, and if that shouldn't be enough to bring a smile to that unhappy face of yours, dear Brother—."

He answered me by shaking his head against my strange utterances, and lighting one of his tobacco sticks. Which he then extended to me, claiming it would help against hunger pains.

I continued to look around at the strange countryside and felt within myself somehow if I knew letters and how they went together, what a pleasure that would be. I would write about a sky which turned the color of an overripe, bursting pumpkin just before the sun left us, to make iridescent, illuminating allowances for the night. I would write about the young farmer and his wife, who permitted us the use of their barn just outside Dungarvan, where we gorged ourselves on the farm's brown pears and slept on freshly shagged, sweet-smelling hay.

What struck me the strongest, more so than anything else during our three day trip, was the smell of the sea. From the inlet bay which feeds the lough[18] at Waterford, the smell of iodine-enhanced, spirit-soaring cleanliness filled my nostrils. Aye, the deep, soothing tonic of the ocean's own forceful breeze, not so much for its coolness, but more so it's vivid aroma and undulating temperate delight. The saline gentleness set me insides afire, so that I was hungry and satisfied, sleepy and fretful, all at the same time. I had seen water in streams before, but nothing like the sea. No, nothing was quite like the sea. But who was I to share it with? My brother was meditating on destroying the entire race of Anglo-Saxons while my mother was somewhere else, the poor thing. Now, I'm not saying it would ever be possible, still, I'm not afraid to admit I wished with all my heart that Katherine Louisa Maddox was with me. For together I believe, we'd have experienced our Southern voyage like

18   A partially landlocked or protected bay

no other human beings had ever done since time began. Nor would ever after, I confided to myself.

We said goodbye to Ireland as we traveled about. To the people who took their living from the land, dressed as they were in baggy pants, three or four sweaters and coats piled sloppily onto one another, with the traditional, *croppie*-flattened, derby cap caught my eye and my spirit. They had decided to stay on, to make a *go* of it, in spite of the poor crops...not to mention the unpitying eye of the English. Indeed, as far as this Irishman's concerned, these people would not only keep their pain to themselves, but keep on tilling their land forever, or die trying. I also saw wayside shrines to the Virgin Mary, with candles sometimes still holding their flames. These candles appeared to me to be like countless angels, praying for any kind of succor, and more hope as well, until the expected help arrived. As such, our trip touched my heart in ways I didn't think possible. All the while, the wagon bounced over the gutted roads, and me mother continued to sway back and forth in her seat. She sat there, clutching her pitiful bag of belongings while looking all around her as a pigeon does. The poor woman had sometime back, taken to twitching her neck this way and that, illogically, without a clue as to where she was, or even how she'd gotten there in the first place. Once in awhile she would look at me, a glassy expression on her crumpled face, before she would turn away. Whatever she had wanted to tell me, became as we say in Gaelic, 'a ghost whisper'. Something that if repeated would make no sense, like a banshee howling out its jaded and unremitting discontentment, alone upon the moors.

I became used to seeing the kilometers of emptiness between villages and farmland left to return back, towards the Druids and prehistoric barrenness, instead of feeding our people. I was starting not to care, becoming more ambivalent about Ireland. Indeed, more excited about seeing a place which at the very least was still very much alive and bursting all about itself—the United States of America. With that in mind, I took one of the brown pears we'd picked and crunched it down, determined that on the other side of the sea, we'd feel once again the freedom the English had stolen from us.

Once during the trip, right after we had all evacuated the cart to relieve ourselves, Mr. Brennan asked of my brother, him being the oldest and all, what he thought we might do once we landed in America.

"I suppose we'll find a farm that we can all work on." My brother told him half-heartedly.

Mr. Brennan admonished him with a craggy finger and a leering, blackened-teeth smile, "T'won't do Laddie, t'won't do at all."

The driver readjusted his flat cap, ran a hand over his uncut whiskers as if what he was about to say was the solemn, gospel-like truth. "Ye fellers know that in Americ-a-a—", the way Mr. Brennan pronounced America it sounded just short of a crow in mortal agony. "Now in Americ-a-a, a feller can succeed at just about anything, given that he's got a certain aptitude for it and the drive or initi-a-tive, as the Yankees say—to do it—certain things which are full of promise and this here initi-a-tive. Call it what you will, ye see, ye young fellers, Americ-a-a is for newcomers like yourselves, willin' to seize and take full advantage of their initi-a-tive."

My brother and I shot a glance at one another, wondering how someone could have drunk so much *poteen,* without either one of us seeing it going down the man's throat.

"Now fellers, this is what I think you'se ought to do, seeing how's you got plenty of aptitude and this here initi-a-tive for it to boot—become bank-robbers! That's the damnedest idea of it all!—Become Irish-American bank-robbers!"

Mr. Brennan slapped his scrawny thigh and let out a whoop, as if he'd suddenly been named a Sabbath-day preacher against his will, and regrettably, he'd just laid his unbelieving eyes on his first miracle.

"That's it! I'm telling the both of you. There's no more gettin' down in the fuss of a farm and mucking the animals at dawn, or watching the crops give out before your very eyes. No sir, in Americ-a-a you rob a bank, and more'n likely you'll be congratulated, for showing some good ol' fashioned, Yankee initi-a-tive. You see, the "Yanks" they love all that initi-a-tive. Which is why they're all there in the first place. 'Cause the English didn't like no one showing so much initi-a-tive, so's they chased the lot of them out of England and over to Americ-a-a, where's they can show off their Yankee initi-a-tive without bothering the English about it any longer! Not only that—why with four or five hundred dollars to your name, ye's be taking some time off as well, get to see different places too, lots of spankin' new country. 'Ceptin' you might want to think 'bout maybe gettin' to changin' your name every once in awhile though, in order to be on the safe side. That so's no one can trace you, like the sheriff and all. Lot's of time off though—don't you be worryin' none about that now, kind of like 'tween harvest time and planting season again—. Yep, lots of time off, the way I figure it. No need to worry 'bout turning the soil over—ever again! And at the end, you'll be congratulated, and probably given a medal to boot, for showing so much damned-good Yankee initi-a-tive!"

Mr. Brennan clapped the horse's reins with renewed enthusiasm while looking back at my brother and me, curiously distraught it appeared that we were not as caught up in his 'Americ-a-a-n' plan as he had hoped.

It was the only time of the trip I remember my mother speaking. For she leaned over towards Mr. Brennan and asked the driver, "This bank-robbing work—does it pay well?"

The driver quivered the top of his upper lip back, much like a horse does to accept the bridle, and answered her, "Why that it does, Mrs. Ruth. That it surely does, it pays quite well. Why I've heard tell that if one becomes a successful bank-robber, it's only a matter of time before one gets invited to all the galas and bonafide fetes. So much so, it becomes irritating, like a headache. After that, it's not long before you're refusing their invitations, claiming your liver and newly acquired gout can't take anymore pigeon eggs and watered-down whisky. Now isn't that something!"

My mother must have been impressed. In that regard, she settled back against the wooden-planked, upright part of the bench. This she did, before folding her hands together while saying out loud a prayer of thankfulness to God, for giving us all the possibility of going to the United States of America, to become initiative-oriented bank-robbers.

It was in the village of Cork where I heard the bagpipes or "pipes" as they are reverently called for the very first time. As the milk cart rolled into the cobble-stoned, main street there he was...a magnificent bagpiper. The soldier was dressed from the ground up in plaid green and tan socks, wearing a kilt with a matching tartan thrown over one shoulder of a sumptuous, royal green coat with golden buttons that forced the coat to hug his hips. Expensively tailored, the coat's upper reaches and shoulders flared out to address the broad expanse of a soldier. The bagpiper's outfit was completed with a red pompon adorning a green beret. The piper's beret did not sit on his head, creased on a jaunty angle, like the ones I later saw worn by the French. No, the piper's beret almost looked sloppy and out of place, sitting like a sand-filled balloon right square in the middle of his head. As I mentioned, the beret appeared clumsily out of place and ill-fitting alongside the rest of his well-designed uniform. It was as if the musician had taken all morning to get his regimental outfit precisely upon him and in place; then upon leaving his barracks, immediately remembered he was without his beret. Thus, he ran back to retrieve it while at the same time throwing it ineffectually upon his head. In effect, as if he no longer had the time to see how it sat, or indeed what it must look like. The soldier was standing with his back to us facing an archaic, partially moss-covered, stone wall. He started intermittently sounding his pipes, allowing the notes to bounce off the wall as if he wished to pay particular attention to the inaugural tone of his bagpipes. There were two stems or cylinder-like reeds together, with off to one side and directly in front of the piper's nose was another reed, perhaps, two times the length of the accompanying ones. The three reeds were joined by a white tassel, with the sound-emanating bladder tucked under the piper's left arm, where he applied pressure using his elbow and forearm. There was something extremely placid and eerily haunting in the melody the soldier played. It seemed to call up or culminate in me the country I was leaving. I could easily have stayed there the rest of the day listening. As he changed his way of playing from disorganized tuning to a gorgeous melody, the entire moment became surrealistic—only because it made me think of my father. I don't know why, but I did. I hadn't really cared, nor thought that much about the 'old man'—ever. He had left Castlewarren before I'd been breeched, and that was all there was to it. However, I seemed to recall a distant memory of my father and his (was it coming back to me?) almost sacred love for the "pipes".

Nonetheless, or perhaps more to the point, the bagpiper's melody became for me a very frightening, intense moment, coming as it did, so suddenly and unannounced. I was not only scared for myself, but in addition to which, I also became afraid for the 'old man', the non-existent patriarch of our family. Something paralleled the tune the bagpiper had seized upon that grabbed my entrails and forcefully tore at them brutally, like nothing before nor since has ever done. It appeared to me my youthful manhood had been called into question, for I asked myself, unsure of the intimidating reply; *how could someone turn his back on his own flesh and blood, leaving his own loved ones to their mediocre resources...to fend for themselves inadequately, in a sense condemning them without a just cause? And if my pappy did it, me being part of him and all—WHEN WOULD I?*

Other than a frightened shiver, I didn't have an immediate moment to reflect further on what the bagpiper had unfairly called into the reticent mind of a seventeen year old *croppie*. We worked our way through the village of Cork where I became more than amazed at what I saw. There were streets leading in every direction with provocative signs calling my attention to things I'd never heard of. There were descriptive words on the signs, but I had to carefully ask Paul Francis Daniel what they meant. For once he seemed cheerful enough, until people started looking at us like we were unwanted, mongrels even. Then he turned his face into that of a sneer or at the very least a warning, to those city dwellers, who appeared to look down their noses at what the poor countryside had thrown up on their doorstep.

Once, upon looking up, I saw what I would give Miss Katherine Louisa Maddox if ever I had the chance. There was a red brick building, and in the windows of this building were wonderfully delicate, whitened tissues. These tissues were hung liltingly, in such a way that one could see partially through, past the openings when they fluttered just so, and into the living quarters. These window sills bore the delightful evidence of a woman's touch that much was certain. And what a touch! There were bowls filled with lovely budding flowers such as fragile red tulips, balancing delicately in the pretentious opening which the half-drawn window drapes had created. On one such window sill, there was a flower pot. Painted around the outskirts of the pot, on a background of glazed, white ceramic, was an orange and blue-colored swan swimming furtively across a turquoise-shaded lake. To think that a delicate creature had arranged all this, made me realize and ache to have a room (if it were possible even several rooms) wherein, Katherine Louisa Maddox might string together flowers all the day long. Even better, call into play yards and yards of airy linen; fashioning them into such a wonderful, delightful place to come home to that one might leave the planting fields early, feigning illness, just to come back to such distinctive balance and femininity.

We took passage for the short Irish Sea jaunt to Liverpool. Some call the port of Cobh; "The harbor of tears". Indeed, it may have been true for some. As far as this Irishman's concerned however, I saw it as a dream come true. We were on a boat, flaunting the incredible ocean. The white-doffed ocean swells, criss-crossed our wake, running in a southerly direction while stern-following frigate birds shrieked out their half-expectant, odiously-demanding cries. They kept on insisting so just to be heard, culling amongst each other for the ship's scraps of undesired and spent-aside food. I sat outside (our passage did not allow for inside berths), as close to the wind-shielding wheelhouse as I was allowed by a loathsome looking, corpulent, burlap-covered figure, who kept trying to fondle each woman as they passed by. At first, I thought the man was only having a bit of a tease with his wife. But when he did it to the next colleen who happened by, then another girl, even a *croppie* such as I, knew things weren't all that they appeared to be.

I stared into the wheelhouse, through a dusky and dirty window, feeling the ship rise and fall, then suddenly heel away, as if someone was having a bit of fun with the ground. But no, it was the ocean's swell confusing me and my senses. So much so that bile forced its way from me mouth and sent me stomach a quivering, finally emptying itself of its own accord. I wretched and watched as an eerie, elongated spire from a church in the port of Cobh separated itself from us while the ocean invaded our immediate surroundings. Eventually, the seas became more important while the land turned into our hollow-eyed background. One or two of the passengers were weeping. One even went so far as to wishing all the English to be damned. Still, I wasn't sure if the man finished by saying, 'To go and work the devil's own farm', or that 'working the devil's own farm was too good, for the likes of the English and their thievin' ways.'

The man beside him added in obsequious commiseration, "You've not the likes of workin' the devil's farm, if you're already in bed with the thievin' bloke."

Another man burped sharply, inhaled in a wheezing manner, then while maintaining a most admirable economy of words exclaimed, "I say, fook the lot of 'em."

This apparently made sense to most of the passengers clustered about, for one or two made clucking sounds as if to mark their agreement. While I for one marveled that the poignant salt air and compunctious distaste for the English could bring such unity to mankind.

To my friend the reader, beware; I do not wish to paint the picture of a sky-blue, calm, ocean passage with us bellowing out lusty sea-shanties. As if our arms were draped around one another while gulping down gobs of hearty-bodied, dark ale and enjoying the maritime view. Not on your life. We were for the most part scared and destitute *croppies*. Most of the men who I saw were drunk. Needing I suppose that liquid strength to get on board the *Nimrod,* trying to forget at least for the moment, they'd ever had a life, even if it was one marked by *a vale of tears.*

I'd be willing to bet, even my eventual admiration for Jefferson Davis and John Hunt Morgan that we were without exception, a starving mass of fools. We'd been duped by our English masters to accept the four or five English pounds they'd thrown our way (or thirty pieces of silver if you like), as well as the sea passage, to clear the land of our sorrowful and distempered countenances. I glanced around the soggy and bird-shit-streaked wheel house to take into account the rags these people were wearing. Rags, I believe that would have meant the white ash sapling should my sisters Susan or Ann Horian worn such garb outside in public, for anyone to see. Aye, I would have liked to say it brought pity to my heart, but it didn't...no, sadly enough it didn't. I was hungry and numb as we all were, with nary a thought to say to the one sitting next to me except perhaps, 'I had no idea the Irish Sea was so vast.'

There was a smell as well. It came at you all at once. As if someone had just opened the cob-webbed window after six months of cumbersome winter, and let the outside stench in brutally, and with an emanating force as well. I can't spell out what it was exactly. Over the years, the closest thing which bears any resemblance to that particular smell around the wheelhouse on such a day was bodily decay. Be it from a mouthful of rotting teeth, or a pus-filled, festering sore, or even an animal such as a dead rat, left outside on the warmest of summer days to decompose. But what was worse was that we sat there, wallowing in the fetid odor and accepted it. Realizing, it seems for the moment, there was nothing better, as well as accepting the fact rather ignominiously that we had no choice. It might be as some have written on the subject in later accounts that the Irish folk were no better than cattle, and were accustomed to such an animal-like existence. I don't believe in such daft talk. Although at that point in time, with waters running high and free from the scuppers, whetting most of our backsides on board the *Nimrod*, I would have been hard pressed to argue otherwise.

One or two of the lads put on brave faces and a show. And therein recounted how they were glad to be finally free of Killarney or Gouganebarra or Tipperary and their respective lands which had sprouted such debilitating misery at every turn. While the other one reminded him that the land at Killarney or Gouganebarra or Tipperary might have been a helluva lot more rewarding had he spent as much time working the wholesome soil, as he did enjoying himself in the local tavern. We didn't smile so much, as nod our heads at the effort to make everyone forget their troubles, at least for a brief spell.

I, in turn, would watch out for our mother, but I didn't like what she had become. She sat there disconsolately, unmoving, with her back against the foredeck wall. Her swollen limbs splayed out limply, as if she was giving birth or a dressed-out chicken; composing a rather grotesque and unnatural form. There were small holes everywhere on her rumpled clothing; ripped and torn they were, with half of her side covered in encrusted filth from our travels. Her head lolled from side to side as the ship mimicked the ocean swells. I didn't like what I saw, but I curiously enough remember that I took a morbid consolation in telling myself that we all felt and looked that way. I consciously put my mind to work dreaming of a nice, warm hearth and currants with toasted buns to spread the currants on. Then something startled me. I heard yelling which I very much wished not to hear. I made the sloppy effort to shut my ears up. Nevertheless, the incessant yelling continued, forcing me to wake up.

There was my brother, Paul Francis Daniel in an ape-like crouch, his arms in a broad-banded fighting posture, as if he were readying himself for a hurling match. The loathsome man, who had been fondling the women when we first came on board, stood over me ma, his legs on either side of her semi-conscious body. One of his arms was in her satchel while the other hand was putting something in his pocket. He also appeared to be panting convulsively, like a wolf following some unmarked trail. Paul Francis Daniel had caught him out in the open stealing from her. There wasn't anything that needed to be said; no accusations—no gibbering denial. There was no need for sentimental, British-induced, parliamentary conjecture including a possible what-might-have-been. Scorn, hatred and compelling force were the rules of thumb. It was a game we were all slowly learning to play for keeps. It all came down to the basic question of who would do what to whom. Who indeed dared to call to accounts the thief? The look on the parabolic thief's face was not in any way shape or form a look of guilt, but rather a look of a bold and daunting—so what? My brother initiated the proceedings—he had to, there had never been a choice. It was more instinct than anything else. Paul Francis Daniel landed a spirited left jab from behind the man on his left side. He then peppered him some more, after the thief turned to face him, moaning incoherently while slapping at my brother's fists. My brother then stepped back, away from what could be certainly construed as murderous forearms; also perhaps, in wondering what damage he might have caused. The thief croaked slightly as if he had felt a grazing discomfort, no more. Something dropped from his hand as he turned to face my brother. I saw it, and so did my brother. The son-of-a-bitch had wrested me ma's wedding band from her finger, where it spilled across the deck, and disappeared into one of the low-slung, galley-way scuppers. The man had a most fearful and intimidating look about him. For one thing, he was at least a foot taller than my brother, and bore a look of disdainful shock about him, as if he wasn't accustomed to such migraine and tawdry interruptions.

He thundered out, "How's that?" several times. Each time with increasing propensity, like a mountain bear chasing away a lazily buzzing horsefly, more irritated that he had to deal with something deemed, otherwise insignificant. His protruding eyeballs gaped out of sockets much too small, for such a distended and overbearing load. His gristly, darkened jaw worked back and forth in a musical cadence, as he measured the narrow distance needed to reach my brother. At the same time, Paul Francis Daniel stepped back, just out of the man's reach while continuing to invoke an array of balled-fisted punches, some falling, but mostly not. He was like an itinerant paddlewheel, throwing up a wall of punches that wouldn't allow his opponent any opening. His pestering defense reminded me of a relentless, heel-biting terrier after a much larger great dane. In fact, it seemed to me it would be only a matter of seconds before my brother would take to his knees and begin biting the thief...as if that were possible. My sibling's face reflected the grim circumstances, within which, he had found himself. Indeed, his impertinent, salty-air-reddened eyes flashed all about as if he had just witnessed two speeding trains crashing into one another, with absolutely no chance for any survivors. You could tell Paul Francis Daniel was searching frantically, for any kind of solution against this grotesque figure of a man. In the meantime, the challenged and now anxious thief put one heavily booted foot in front of the other, obnoxiously thumping the wooden foredeck in the process. He was coming full-bore, with an unmistakable, murderous intent after Paul Francis Daniel; make no mistake about that, not in the least. It appeared that those of us sitting there, unconsciously moved ourselves backwards a pace or two, to give the sputtering giant some room. Perhaps with a full meal under him, and enough rest, things might have turned out differently. Alas, but for right now my brother needed to get away from the thief; his young, despondent life depended upon it. With each turn of his paddlewheel-like thrusts, my brother took to slowing down, and not methodically either.

It looked like more of a deflated-balloon syndrome. Paul Francis Daniel began breathing faster and shallower; his distended, bony, chest cavern more a thing of pity than an object of wrath. He had to give up...there was no question about it. No one could maintain adrenalin-enhanced, fisticuff fighting without the necessary reserves. You could see he wouldn't make it. My brother's face gave out first. With a long, extended, pitiful sigh which bore a harrowing resemblance to a wounded wolf caught in a hunter's trap, he let his guard down. Then he sent his wobbling arms to rest, putting shaky hands on his frail and skeletal knees. He was finished, everyone could tell. It remained to be seen just what the loathsome thug would decide was adequate for his revenge. He could even take his time about deciding, surveying which way to attack; my brother was finished and 'in the tank' as we say. With one eye open the wheelhouse bully advanced. The man kept his other eye half-closed, like he was measuring, calculating just how much of a destructive force was needed to tie up this young, fagged-out buck once and for all.

Then it all went down in the blink of an eye.

He sneered as he closed the gap. The thief passed close enough to me to where I saw a large brown mole below his left eye with a thrust of hairs bursting from the middle of the mole. I don't know what made me think about it, or why his mole reminded me of a furry, bulls-eye center marked out on a tavern-walled dart board. Maybe that's why I let go—it was too tempting not to.

Nonetheless, to be perfectly honest about what happened next—I don't know why I did it (perhaps the dart board came into play), or how I found the nerve to execute it. I would like to call it a cold-blooded, lethal reaction; a perfectly well thought out response to protect my brother. Most probably it was plain stupidity on my part. Even Paul Francis Daniel was stunned. I knew him well enough that I could tell. I could also see he resented it; my help...to him it showed weakness on his part. That's how much of a stubborn, potato-brained *croppie* he was. To be that close to getting his thick head stove in, and him worrying about his pride, or his younger brother's concern, or whatever it was that he resented so much. I didn't care even two shakes because to me my brother was somehow lying. Either to me, or...perhaps what was even worse, he was lying to himself. In any case, I couldn't take the chance. His medieval idea of gutted, pitiful chivalry wouldn't allow it.

My fear and adrenalin levels increased sporadically, with fear most assuredly in the lead. It didn't matter, time wouldn't allow for any further reflection, for the thief was starting to step right over me. His colossal boots seemed to be like two runaway trains; scattering everything in their path. I shot a stiffened, righteously-coiled leg up into the air and into the thief's unprotected groin with all of my youthful force. This had a lot to do with stopping the bellowing, blustering, fuming giant, dead cold in his tracks. He toppled down instantly, meowing like a poisoned alley cat, reminding me of the time when Mr. Scullum once did the same. I believe it was several years back when Mr. Scullum took to following a *Tinker's* eldest daughter, for several days around Castlewarren, in a trance-like and amorous state. This continued until Mrs. Scullum found out about it, and felled her husband with the help of an eight-inch thick branch from a nearby oak tree. It took Mr. Scullum a day and a half to come to, and another day and half to remember just exactly who he was. Some villagers even went so far as to say that with Mrs. Scullum continuing to brandish the half-cracked oak branch next to their bed; by the time he woke up, Mr. Scullum started to apologize to his wife *even before he remembered who he was.*

The stopped-in-his-tracks thief gave up the ghost as quickly and quietly as Mr. Scullum had, not too surprisingly, by banging his head when he fell against an iron ship's clew. Fortunately, Paul Francis Daniel had recovered enough by now to make a *fair fight* of it. Indeed, he took to raining down kicks all over the unconscious shoulders, neck and by now bleeding head of the man who lay there on the wood-slatted deck. The seawater continued its course; scurrying in, washing away the blood, with each sluicing down-turn of the port side scuppers.

We went carelessly back to our dripping-wet places, sitting down once again amidst the humid slop. My brother with his unrelenting gaze, looked fully around at the other men sitting there. After awhile, and expecting no reproach, he went through the downed man's pockets. Professionally and thoroughly, he tossed back to each one of us and in our respective turn whatever he found. To my diminutive delight, I was tossed a green and blue-checked handkerchief. Allowing for the distasteful fact that it had been used, and therefore remained pasted together, nonetheless, I soaked the handkerchief in the water sloshing about the deck. Afterwards, I put it in my pocket, somehow feeling more civilized for having it.

The grey looking, half-bagged shepherd, sitting cross-legged next to me, held up for everyone to see, the piece of meat wrapped in newspaper my brother had tossed to him. He showed it off like he had just won the lottery. I didn't care one way or another about the shepherd's good fortune because the meat wasn't mine. My brother, having finished rifling the man's pockets, motioned with his head that we'd best be moving along, at least to the stern of the boat for awhile. It was too late for such a movement however. For at that moment, a tall man, wearing a salt and pepper jacket decided to appear. The man, adorned with a rusted and stained, black, policeman's helmet, like the ones the London police or "Bobbies" wear, came up to us slumping about on deck. Besides his unusual headpiece, he was sporting as well, a pair of goliath handlebar moustaches which sprouted up from his mouth, like furry, brown, bamboo shoots before reaching half-way to his ears. This outlandish and hairy individual started prodding each of us in turn, with his glossily varnished Irish shillelagh, pointing to the man lying on the deck, and asking us what we knew about him.

The shepherd with a guarded hand on his bulging pocket where he had put the enveloped meat pointed to the unconscious thief and reported, "The man wanted to jump overboard, saying he was homesick for the 'old sod', so's we had to stop him right good and quick, 'fore he hurt hisself."

The ship's policeman after letting out a low whistle, muttered to all of us in a loud whisper, "It's me thinking you stopped him pretty damn good."

"Not half as much as we would 'ave liked to." Paul Francis Daniel, never one to leave a lee shore quietly, shot back.

"Is that so?" Questioned the policeman, all of a sudden paying more attention to my brother than I would have liked.

In vain, I made a hand signal begging my brother to at least, for once, lay off baiting the ship's policeman...that we'd had enough fighting for one day.

"Well, Sir," my brother retorted cynically, "I suppose we could tell you he was fixin' to lead us all in prayers when God done strike him down—like he'd been sinnin', or done something awful bad."

A small man with a rounded hair cut which set off his red and white-skinned, sketchy, bald pate pointed a defying finger at me and declared, "He's the one that done it. Set him down right quick-like he did—like he was a roarin' magician with a pair of all made-to-lay-out, invisible pliers. I swears to it—."

The policeman with the tremendous moustache which looked to me like a matching pair of Spanish-leather Jingo boots pointed his shillelagh-billy-club at me, like a billiard cue while menacingly he demanded, "You—the punk there—you done put this man, O'Connell down? Are you the one—well, speak up, Boy?"

I desperately wanted to run. And had I known how to swim, I probably would have jumped over the side of the *Nimrod* and swam away. Instead, I sat there staring down at my bare feet, feeling for my *new* handkerchief in my pocket, and wishing with all my heart things could be different. At least if I was a seagull, I could then fly away, and forget all about this mess.

All of a sudden, the man the policeman had called O'Connell struggled with one arm to right his straddling body. At the same time, and with a mouth half-closed, seeping flecks of foam and blood, he started to make a sound. A sound which reminded me of my dog "Blister", his mouth all in a froth, when he took to gallivanting around Castlewarren with the other village dogs. Aye, the thief sounded just like the other mongrels, during that onerous time of year when it was near on high time to mate.

The policeman repeated himself, "Well then, you's the one who done it or not? Come on Boy, I'd be right willing to know?"

At length, as if to emphasize his great desire for my personal rendering of the fight, the policeman took to tapping the shillelagh in the palm of his other hand. This he did while peering out from under the brim of his rusted, English policeman's helmet with two great, big, white eyeballs flashing every which way. The policeman looked to this Irishman, to be like a black African man (like in a photograph I'd seen), peering out from his hidden jungle enclosure in the darkness while waiting for my response.

My brother made as if to get ready for another knock-down fist-fight, for he quickly struggled to his feet. Also, the way in which he went about wiping and flexing his fists behind his back, I took as a sure sign of impending disaster. A disaster in the sense that neither one of us stood a chance against this man and his Irish nightstick.

I didn't want any more trouble period. This I felt in addition to wanting to stop Paul Francis Daniel from whatever he had planned for the intruding policeman.

I stood up, hoping to at least impress the policeman that I was no longer the *spalpeen* boy he figured me for. Then with half my nose contracted upwards, in what I believed to be my tough, roust-about look told the man, "And what of it, Sir? He 'as trying to steal from me ma there, and all's we did was 'top him. That's all 'e did alright was to up and done 'top 'im!"

Before the policeman could respond, we heard a bizarre cry. We turned our collective attention to where the injured thief was trying to be heard. The man kept on moaning, in serious, deep pain while attempting to rise himself after a fashion.

Again the bleeding giant struggled to right himself from the ship's deck, getting one unsteady knee underneath his buttocks while purporting to rise. Then just as if we were beholding to take up sides again, as well as to our unabashed surprise, the policeman brought down with a not so negligible force his shillelagh club on the back of the struggling man's shoulders. The impact caused a sharp thud to sound out like a beaver's tail thumping a churning river log into place. The man called O'Connell collapsed suddenly causing his head to snap into the ship's clew once again. Except this time a thick flap of skin from the back of his head turned away, exposing a red tissue that I firmly believed wouldn't heal itself in any convenient time soon.

In disbelief, I snapped my head around to follow the policeman. In answer to our outraged shock, he shelved his shillelagh inside his wide leather belt. This he did prior to smoothing part of his gargantuan moustache back and to one side of his face, like a cat preening itself, before announcing to one and all, "I've been after Mick O'Connell since before we left the port of Cobh. Amongst other things, it seems he tried to board the *Nimrod* without a properly paid for passage, claiming in fact he was half-brother to Daniel O'Connell[19], and therefore entitled to it. In addition to which, he claims he's trying to enlist funds for his half-brother's, legal defense from none other than the king of France!"

Just then a low-slung horn blasted its decisive resonance across the water. The ship's blast scared me into losing half me wits, or so I thought at the time from such a deafening sound. The mustachioed policeman broke off from whatever he was going to say next, calling out to each one of us to pick up our bits and pieces, and make way for the gangplank. In effect, we had arrived in Liverpool.

I wondered to myself as I picked up my things, just exactly how much scupper-induced slosh one might have to endure in order to travel to America. That was before I remembered my *new,* blue-checked handkerchief and reminded myself; *you've never had a handkerchief before.* So things were already starting to look up in a way I never would have imagined, for this *spalpeen* from Castlewarren, Ireland.

---

19   An Irish patriot

Chapter Eight

Good night? Ah! No, the hour is ill
Which severs those it should unite,
Let us remain together still,
Then it will be goodnight.

Author unknown

There are two didactic essentials which remain in my memory about Liverpool, England. The first is the fact that the inner harbor moved about, including for the most part the captive sea as well, in a most truculent manner. The other one being that I lost sight of Paul Francis Daniel for the entire three days we were there. Why he left us, and where he laid his unhappy head remained a mystery to us for a very long time.

The *Nimrod* listed close onto her green moss and mosaic-like, seashell-studded, starboard quarter. While she waited for the incoming, high tide that allowed the gates of the floating docks to open, thus granting admittance to our passenger ship. It was as if the great hand of God was enjoying itself in a most fustian and *sans regarde* demeanor while we were obliged to submit to whatever the Almighty decided was to be our reticent fate.

A morning sea-air, full of pregnant sounds, including cries from the hovering gulls, wood pilings chaffing against boat fenders, barkers and waiting loved ones cut through the light fog. This fog, coupled with the wharf-side animation made it a circus-like atmosphere as we prepared to dock. The intrepid, light haziness, laden with a dozen briny and wharf-filled smells, reminded me of the morning bog air back home. The dense air that drifted down from the moors and lay heavy like a thickened mist over the fields. This it did until the sun made it a point to either chase the fog away, or leave it be. Thus, allowing us to wallow around in it, doing our chores, like ethereal figures, not exactly sure where we were.

There are vast rows of these *wet docks* on the Mersey estuary. Immense maritime fortresses, each forming a massive *U* which can only admit, as I mentioned earlier, ships at high tide. Once inside, the harbor master is the Alpha and the Omega of the Liverpool docks, enforcing a rigid harbor discipline which includes the belaying of any thrown debris into the waters. This of course commenced as soon as the *Nimrod* docked, and we were left to our demeaning and *croppie*-laden resourcefulness. The man with the handlebar moustaches and rusting policeman's helmet used his shillelagh to keep us at bay and in a haphazard line which at first we didn't understand. However, a well placed thrust from his Irish nightstick, and we soon found a semblance of orderliness, much like the sheep of our village at shearing time. Still in all, we stood at attention; a miserable lot if you will while a line of high-fashioned men and plume-flying, hatted women left their private cabins to descend the gangway. This they did, trying their best to avoid our collective and destitute stares. As we left the swaying *Nimrod,* my only concern was to get some food into our vacuous stomachs. Making our way down the gangway we were jostled back and forth by reason of the slow-moving gait of mother. She slipped and almost fell more than once, nevertheless, holding on each time with a surprisingly iron-like grasp to my arm. Moreover, I couldn't carry her. I did everything in my power to assist the rasping, embattled, grey-haired old woman who no longer knew what day it was. She scarcely remembered I was her son, and seemingly wanted nothing more than to sweep out her cottage, and catch up on some sewing which she couldn't seem to remember where she'd left it last.

In the throng of sailors and boats and people making their way to the wharf, I saw the man we'd caught stealing from me mother, the one the policeman called Mick O'Connell. He was on a litter with a thick, dark, pea-green blanket covering his immense girth—everything, but his thickly bandaged head. His head was turned to one side of the litter and was grey and ashen, except for the fire in his protruding eyes. They flashed this way and that, like a caged lion with no thought for anything but his freedom. Involuntarily, I shivered when I saw his look. Moreover, it may have been in some significant way that his eye caught mine. Deep down in the depths of that man's castigating and intense glance, I captured the same burning look which I remembered seeing in Bailey Burke's eye. His look reminded me of the one phrase in Gaelic my mother refused to say aloud; *tà fuath agam do dhuine* or 'hatred for your own kind'. Aye, t'is a sad and miserable affair, this continuing *envie* to take what isn't ours. Still in all, and as far as this Irishman's concerned, we waste an inordinate amount of time believing it can be done just the same.

In the surrounding dockside area and in contrast to the immaculate harbor, there was debris and filth scattered everywhere. There were more people than I'd ever seen in my life. This included well-dressed men and painted-faced women that I couldn't for the life of me imagine, what possible business they could be construing down there dockside. It was one of these men who thrust himself forward, before catching the sleeve of me brother's jacket. Although I couldn't hear what they were saying, he took him aside, and after several minutes with a wave to us, Paul Francis Daniel skipped into the crowd. This he did, without so much as a by-your-leave to me mother or myself. You would have thought they were life-long buddies, the way my brother took to the stranger by hanging with one hand onto his coat sleeve, to be led away from the *Nimrod* to who knows where. It has always amazed me how people of the same taste or leanings have a knack for sensing people of their own kind. Then once having found their own species don't hesitate to jump into the same barrel of rottenness, with a marked enthusiasm one would find, had they been invited out for an afternoon promenade on the seashore.

My eye caught the silver sparkle as a fishing lure fell into the waters. It flashed away from a juvenile hand, before breaking the surface, just as quickly, with what looked to be a white, lumpish, sturgeon fish. The sturgeon struggled, hanging on, for what appeared at least for the fish in question— dear life. The young *gossoon* released his fish from the hook. Before putting it into his basket, and seeing that I was watching, showed the fish to me with the grandest front teeth-missing smile anyone could possess. I returned his ouverture. Trotting his way over to where I was, the young boy called out to me using an accent which made it seem as if he was speaking and eating his words all at the same time. A most amazing feat it was. While at the same moment, and as if it were possible, his manner of lynching each syllable made the *gossoon's* speech almost impossible for me to understand.

Aye, it was the Queen's English to be sure, but spoken in such a way that I for one, started to use hand signals to answer the boy. It was much like the time the Scotsman came to Castlewarren looking for a new wife to work his farm. As I recall, upon his arrival, we were hard put to understand the Scotsman and his accent. Eventually, through the use of our hands and crude drawings, as well as the occasional English word that wasn't bitten right off in the middle, we came to an understanding. Aye, that we did; we were made to understand that only Irish women were hearty enough to do a man's share of work during the day, and stupid enough to fix him his meal at the end.

The young boy pointed to the fish in the basket, and inquired of me, "Hey, little man, would you like some of this fish—in a burgoo perhaps, with onions and a potato or two?"

When he mentioned something about a stew, my stomach took to jumping in a most peculiar manner. Almost as if it would climb right outside of my skin, and take to scaling and cooking the fish all by itself. Without so much as asking me, whether or not he could borrow my hands to do it as well. I glanced down at the young lad, who might have been half of my seventeen years. He had a rustic innocence about him with a flush of cranberry-red hair that cropped up from under his cap, and lopped down onto his forehead like the thickened mane of a plow horse. His cheeks were ruddy and full while his mouth tilted to one side of his face. Because of this, when speaking, his twisted mouth pushed the rest of his appearance into an oriental mask, like a Chinaman with his foot on fire. He was wearing baggy pants which ended at the knees with ankle-high, rubber, fishing boots and a slick oilskin that was three times too big for the likes of an eight-year old. So much so that when he spoke, he had to turn around in his oilskin, to face you directly. If not, his words disappeared up a sleeve, or out the back of his jacket.

"Aye", I told the boy, "A bit of stew, any kind of stew, would be just the thing! But there's me mother as well," I apprehensively reminded the lad.

Well now, and to our good fortune, if he doesn't tell me to bring mother along as well. After saying so, he immediately takes to shouting at everyone on the dock to move away, for we were all coming through like Mr. Feargus O 'Connor used to do when visiting his estates. There you see, with no more trouble about it than that, I grabbed me ma and took to following the young *gossoon*. All the while telling myself, the English aren't as bad as all that...if they're willing to feed us right off the boat...now are they?

We straggled along the two of us, mother and I, following the young fisherman. She kept calling out for an Uncle Padraic that I, up until then, had never heard of. Me mother would then stop and listen, seemingly certain to hear her uncle answer back. When he didn't, mother took to calling him every kind of name, some of which I'm thinking are not fit for Christian ears. This of course, was not of her character at all to use such language. Sometimes she looked over at me and came close to my side, almost flirtingly like an affectionate colleen would do. While other times, me mother tried to separate the distance from the two of us, easily and unnoticeably so, as if I wouldn't realize what she had planned. As I figured it anyway—so she could up and run away.

Once in a lucid moment, through gap-filled and decaying teeth, she asked me where under God's heaven Paul Francis Daniel was.

"I don't, Mother." I said absentmindedly, my eyes following the young boy. At the same time, I wondered hopefully if fish burgoo in Liverpool resembled more than just the watered down brine and carrot mash we papists ate during the Lenten season.

After spitting through the gap in her front teeth, and in an uncharacteristically venomous tone, she commiserated about my brother's absence, "Aye, you're all like your father—now aren't you? Not a one of you can sit still for a moment, but that you have to go gallivanting off like some Curragh-cornered buck, not happy until you're up to your own necks in trash and whatnot, giving no quarter until your rousting and bawdiness is finished. Then with the courage-making *poteen* still inside of yourselves, you crawl back home with your tail 'tween your legs. Crying out it seems, trying to make some sense of what you've done whilst plying those of us back at home with your regrets and tears over why you destroyed so much of what was yours, and only yours in the first place."

Afterwards, me ma took to instinctively washing her teeth and gums like a cat would, rubbing her tongue vigorously back and forth. She needed only to purr once in awhile for the image to be complete.

I looked away ashamed, not only for what had happened to her and the way she was acting, but also for the fact that so much of what she had just told me, was completely true.

Not more than a half-a-kilometer away, where an iron bridge kept sentry duty over a vast and plummeting *lough,* did we stop under an archway. This archway gave out onto a non-descript alleyway which had windows and doorways blowing out in every direction. While at the same time and strangely enough there was no one about. The only visible evidence to break up the monotony of the alleyway was a sign in the shape of a military shield. The sign was old and dust covered, although the words in big block headers: *Crowley's Sourdough bread—baked fresh twice a day* could still be read. The young lad stopped about a third of the way down the alley. Before rapping on a ground-floor level door which was hinged with thick shackles, and looked stout enough to hold back Mr. Scullum's plow horse. The door barely moved, but that a lady looked out. All I could see was her face, for she was hiding her body behind the door with a fan-shaped, white bonnet fastened under her chin. She peered strangely at us, took her bloody time about it too. This the woman did while mixing in equal portions, as she stared first at mother and then at me, expressionless, under the white bonnet or fanning night cap. It appeared to this Irishman that the lady must have been pretty or maybe even beautiful; something of that nature, once upon a time. For her facial structure was intriguing in that her powdered nose was thin and well aligned, splitting two high sitting cheekbones into a well-structured and regal face. Sadly enough, there was now flaccid skin hanging from these same cheeks while her left eyelid flashed this way and that; exhibiting a twitch that went off of its own free will, and frequently enough as well.

Let it twitch away, I told myself. *I was damned hungry, and wouldn't care if the lady in question went blind right then and there in front of us, as long as I got to put something into me own stomach first.*

At length, the woman behind the door inquired pugnaciously. At first, with an elastic and demanding voice which she abruptly changed, to something resembling courtesy, when she took notice of the boy and his fish, "What is it Andrew, what can Auntie Cecilia get for her little man?"

The faint smell of distilled gin began to seep out through the door's opening.

"Auntie, these fine folks would like something to eat. They've just arrived, and have had nothing to put in themselves since leaving Ireland."

Then in an aside that everyone could hear, the young *gossoon* added, "They were on the *Nimrod*."

The way he intoned *Nimrod* made it seem like we had something to offer. Even perhaps, that we were special or that these people had relatives back in the land of *Erin* and knew how we felt. Leaving our land abruptly as we did, coming over and all to Liverpool, without any acquaintances of any kind to count on for aid. Hopefully...there was an air to this lady that once upon a time, she had been just that—a lady—and would certainly understand our plight.

The thick house door receded several more inches while the woman, who the young lad called Auntie Cecilia, beckoned to us from within. Looking past Aunt Cecilia, I saw the interior of a parlor with a short-legged, fluffy-haired, patchy-looking, mongrel terrier asleep on a sofa. It was dark inside, and must have remained so regardless of the time of day. It appeared to this Irishman as if the darkness had spilled in from the alleyway or vice-versa. For there was no mistaking the depressing air which seemed to permeate the backstreets of this part of Liverpool. Inside the place, there were odds and ends of furniture stacked against each other, every which way. Indicating wherever we were, it must be or had been, a sort of lodgings for strangers at some point in time.

"Now then, what do you say to boiled sturgeon? With a few potatoes and carrots to help you both get over your exhausting trip, you poor souls? Now, I'm not promising you anything that could be taken back to Westminster, to be sure. Still, I'm thinking I might have in the pantry what it takes to make up a healthy and filling fish stew, for seafarers like the two of you."

I stammered back, "You are more than kind."

The lady peered back at me with a cold, questioning stare that seemed to change just as quickly to aborted kindness once she reached for the boy's catch, still slowly thrashing about in his basket.

I had to restrain mother from entering the dwelling (without having first received permission), for she had put on her market-day face and inquired of the woman behind the door, "Would it be too much to ask you to boil as well the hind quarters of that dog I see sitting over there with nothing to do?"

Me mother coyly brushed her stringy hair back from her face, as if what she had just asked was nothing more than what two ladies could certainly arrange between themselves. It was then she made as if to enter the apartment. As if she certainly understood boiling the dog and its connecting torso meant work for two people, and she was more than willing to lend a helping hand to accomplish this arduous task.

The lady of the house called the young boy Andrew over to her side and told him where to take us to wash up. I was excited at the prospect of eating, mother was too, for she started to weep and kept repeating in Gaelic, "T'is a fine and *dacent* woman we have in front of us. Fine and *dacent* I say—she is sure to be one of St. Patrick's own."

I made as if to cross over the threshold of their dwelling and enter the parlor. The woman with the bonnet produced an ivory-white and blue-veined hand that while not exactly slapping me across my chest, at the very least prevented me from moving any closer.

She called out firmly enough, "That'll be two pence for the wash-up and a shilling more for the meal."

She was quite pleasant about it that I won't deny.

I looked down at the boy called Andrew and back again at the woman of the house, not fully understanding what she wanted.

I tried to explain that we were just off the boat so we didn't know anyone, and her nephew, or at least I thought so at the time had invited us to share his fish.

She interrupted my confusion by telling me, "Don't go-round telling me you've got nothing on you to pay with! 'Cause if you don't it'll go down pretty rough alright, for you and your dog-eatin' mother!"

At which point, the woman called Aunt Cecilia swung open the door revealing a scene of disorder and mayhem that from our point of view outside the door, we couldn't have seen before. There, just behind the door, other furniture had been turned over, and there were even broken dishes on the ground and scattered food as well.

At last, the woman named Aunt Cecilia turned nasty, very much like one of the squalls which arrive unannounced in our Northern waters. She turned on us, threateningly, "If you can't pay then get the 'ell out of here, and go back to the quarantine house before I call the Bobbies—for trying to break in and steal what little my Andrew and I 'ave left. Now either pay up or be on your way—quick-like, before the Bobbies arrive, and the two of you 'ill catch the livin' 'ell for it."

Because the door was wide open now, mother (who hadn't paid any attention to our conversation) made as if to enter. As she passed close to the woman, she called out to me merrily enough, "Pay her two pence more, for I'm starving to have me a fresh egg."

I tugged at her shoulder, and with temerity told me mother, "We can't pay these people and you know that!"

She turned to look at me blankly enough while complaining bitterly, "Sure there is—it's under the hen sitting right over there."

Then she pointed to the dog, who by now and due in no small part to the noise we'd been making, was sitting up on the couch and scratching its hind flank. Either preparing itself to lay that infamous egg, or perhaps, even more logically given the situation, getting ready to jump into the stew pot of its own free will.

When Aunt Cecilia heard what she must have suspected all along that we had no money, made pushing motions with her hands while screaming, "Get ye away from here, away do y'hear the lousy Irish, don't got nothing but weevils and typhus, even the fleas leave well enough alone! You've made bleedin' careers out of suckin' the English dry; well you won't find charity 'ere no more—of that you can be sure."

She took turns calling out. Either for the police, wailing out loud we were common house thieves and had caught us breaking into her flat. Or, turning to the boy named Andrew and bewailing him to differentiate between the poor and desperate leaving the immigrant ships, and the poor and desperate who had money to pay for their meals.

I heard him ask in a muffled tone, "Auntie, how can you tell?"

She hissed back at him, "From now on before you bring them back 'ere, ask 'em first if dogs can lay eggs? That should pretty much tell you 'oose bleedin' side they're on—or whether or not they 'ave 'alf a brain in their head!"

We were turned away from the closing door while from overheard catcalls started ringing down from apartments that until then had been deathly quiet.

"The lousy Irish—praying and drinking is all you poor farmers know how to do!"

"Don't forget the twenty or so, screaming little brats they drag along with 'em!"

"Bunch of brooding sows!"

"Go back to the 'old sod', and stop contaminating the English!"

By now it had become a veritable symphony of insults, both guttural as well as cultural sideswipes aimed at the people of *Erin*. It wouldn't be until much later in this century that Charles Darwin would put ink to paper and publish his famous work on mankind's evolutionary origins. But for the moment, and in accordance with the inferences issuing from the apartments overhead, me mother and I were genetically, as well as intrinsically linked, to the frogs that lived in and amidst the muddy banks of the Mersey estuary.

We left the alleyway and made for the main street, which emitted a little more sunlight through the late morning fog onto the both of us. The light was certainly welcome, but what we weren't prepared for was the number of people who accosted us, claiming they knew our cousins Bridget and Michaelene from County Clare or the family from County Sligo....

"Ah, if it's not Sligo then it must be from Wexford—do you have family in Wexford?"

"We saw you at the Doyle's wedding two years before last. Come on, don't say you don't remember us? Look again, Mate!"

"You must be a *cooperman* from Donegal, the one who took last year's sweepstakes. Here now, how would you like some American-English lessons?"

Thus it went, on and on. Everyone wanted to help us...for nothing? We had offers to go to Australia and rub the bloody Aborigines' noses into the ground. Or, fix ourselves up in a lovely chateau on a charming French protectorate in Corsica—"did we possibly have bloodlines which could be traced back to Bonaparte's?"

I was only too happy to respond and tried my best to be helpful, "It could be you know," I answered. "Is he the one that could make puffs of smoke come out of his ears, doing card tricks while workin' his clay pipe down in County Cork? I've heard our people say this pipe-smoking magician named Johnny Bonaparte was a third or even second cousin of ours."

We were even asked if we wouldn't like to become slaves ourselves (in name only), and work tobacco plantations in a place called Virginia. That up until now, would selfishly allow only Negro people to enjoy such a regal and fortuitous existence.

Finally, a Catholic religious nun, wearing an enormous black and white starched wimple cornered us. She told us to leave this area at once, for it wasn't safe, and we were sure to be robbed or cheated. She had a delicate, youthful, almost impish face which appeared to me to be well-scrubbed and plainly beautiful. I'm speaking about those places where it wasn't hidden by the white cloth that covered her ears and neck. She had as well, very pink lips and gracefully rounded brown eyebrows which appeared out of place for someone wearing a religious habit. You could see however that underneath her chin and around her neck it was red and chapped from the wimple. She spoke to us in a manner which was both forceful and kind, as if she understood something about our condition.

"Sister, where can we go?" I asked, confused and hungry.

I even started wondering to myself whether or not it was worth it anymore. Also, the question came to mind; the nun said to leave, "for we would be robbed or cheated" of what? We had nothing. Except perhaps; my *new,* blue and green-checked handkerchief that I allowed needed to be washed.

"It is not a question of where, but rather you must; the quarantine house, legally everyone off the boat,"—she made every effort to hide her grimace but failed—"must report to the quarantine house. Unless, you have medical papers stating to the contrary you are free of infectious disease. Do you have papers to that effect?"

I didn't have time to answer. The nun seemingly knew our plight all along.

"Then come along it's not far from here."

She took off at a clipper ship's pace, her gigantic, black skirts billowing backwards and forwards in an effort to keep abreast of the other. The nun set a pace which would have plowed more than a few Castlewarren acres that day. At the same time she took from her black pocket, not as an afterthought, but as if she was used to doing such things, some fruit and hard tack which she then gave to the two of us. We took to eating it as fast as we could while me mother tried asking the Catholic nun in Gaelic, 'if she didn't by any chance have one or two freshly-laid eggs?'

We kept on following the Catholic nun while I became amazed by what I saw. There was everyone and everything spread out before us. Yet, the one question I kept asking myself was: *where do these people grow their food?* I tried, but for the life of me couldn't see any fields or rows of vegetables—anything which would suggest agricultural husbandry. It was very strange to my eyes. I would be lying to the reader, if I didn't say what exactly was on my mind. Indeed, as bizarre as it seemed to me at the time that there was no food being grown there, the people milling around, were even stranger to my eyes than the absence of farmland. The ones I saw were wearing looks that I'd never seen before on another human being's face. Except, maybe for the time old man Scullum, having finally realized that his wife had beaten him rather severely with a stout tree limb, took to frowning and moping about the farm. Aghast, that she would do such a thing to her very own loving husband. Insofar, as he freely admitted, womanizing with a *Tinker's* daughter merited a certain domestic punishment, but not to the staving-in of her own husband's skull. Thus, he continued to sulk his way around the farm. Still in all, that only lasted for three or four days. The time necessary for Mrs. Scullum to threaten him with worse, if he didn't wipe that look off his face and get back to his chores.

Just then, a man walked by. He stopped, turned to face us, before stammering out, "Well, if it isn't Mary Rose? It is you isn't it, Sister?"

He was out of place on such a busy street, for he was sunburned and healthy, even robust-looking. His hair was greased down or something of that nature. For it was shiny and wet in appearance, although very much orderly and in place while the man himself affected enormous affluence. His face, although not sinister, appeared creased and ineffectual as if he never let his guard down. Perhaps something had happened, and to make up for the resulting consequences he had become quite serious about everything, and searched for results rather than innocuous talk. The man, who the religious sister addressed as Roger, wore a beautiful three-piece suit with a tie which was fixed to his shirt by a chain and clasp. That to my querulous surprise, looked very much like a miniature, silver elephant.

"It is Clarice now, Roger—Sister Mary Clarice."

Although, I don't believe in the least the religious nun was ashamed by her religious vocation. Nevertheless, she would answer then put her head down, as if she didn't belong, or would rather not discuss certain subjects with this expensively-dressed Mr. Roger.

Perhaps to answer more imposingly I suppose, than from what he had intended, the affluent Mr. Roger asked, "I have some free time before me. What can I do to spend an hour or so with you and help—if indeed that is what you call—what you do?"

Again, with the black-veiled head slung down to her chest, she answered demurely, "These people need food and a bit of cleanliness before they find themselves at the quarantine house."

"Consider it done—Mary Rose—er, I mean Sister Clarice." The man answered quickly enough.

Completely out of turn while surprising everyone there, me mother turned to the man, warning him in our Irish tongue, "You might be a' warmin' to this gal and all, but let me tell you right now, she's done been spoken for by our Savior, God Himself."

Then as if to explain what she meant, mother turned to me and declared, "Is the man daft or what? Can't he see she's wearing a religious habit? This woman is married to God. She's not to be running-after, chirping around with mooning-eyes and such!"

I told Mr. Roger, our mother spoke only Gaelic, and then tried to translate what she had said, leaving out the part about him being daft and all. It just didn't sound right, calling the man crazy to his face. With a firm push from behind, me ma also bade me tell the man, she wasn't moving from this spot until she got herself a fresh egg.

At length, this Mr. Roger removed his hat, exhibiting a politely restrained as well as a hesitant smile, before courteously asking me if my mother and I would be his guests for supper. With a sincere yet comical look at the nun, he insisted she come along as well.

Upon which, me ma took to warning me, as if I also knew from someplace else, this wholesome Sister Mary Clarice, "You'd best be careful young man, for if you're off to separating what God hath joined together—then you'd best be prepared for one thundering-thunderbolt."

She took to chortling and laughing over her little joke. So much so that I couldn't tell if she was smiling any longer, or calling out for air to breathe.

We walked not far afterwards, perhaps four or five city blocks, before we came to a small street-corner shop. This shop had situated out in front, a glassed-in counter displaying all sorts of appetizing wares. There were pies and plates, with cuts of meat and green bits of salad, sticking out from underneath these same, savoring pieces of meat.

The proprietor inside at first called out to us, "Go away you two, before you know what's good for the both of you! We'll have no ragamuffins 'bout here—disturbing them clients who's payin'!"

When somewhat startled, he noticed the well-dressed man, called Roger by the Catholic nun, who made a sign with one hand, holding up some money as well. This he did, while at the same time, indicating he knew the two of us. That changed everything right then and there. The proprietor brought out several plates and laid them end to end on his countertop. All of which to my amazement, my mother refused to eat, pointing instead to a sealed jar on the counter, containing pickled eggs.

She was finally given one that she tasted in a refreshingly lady-like manner. While carefully holding the egg delicately balanced between two swollen peasant fingers, she tasted it. Unfortunately, in a not so lady-like manner, ma spat out what she had chewed protesting, "Ayeee! This tastes just like hill-brewed *poteen*! They must have put these eggs in the dregs of the *poteen*—. Besides, who else but the devil would eat such a bitter thing!"

Mother wasn't used to the vinegar and tangy taste of such English delicacies. Forgetting her astute manners for the moment, she then tore into a piece of lamb saying it was the best "dog" she had ever tasted.

While we ate in silence, the nun and the affluent man spoke, not hurriedly as one might expect from old friends, but rather in calm and accepting overtones. That the man epitomized whatever it was he was supposed to be I couldn't say. I only knew he was a gentleman, not only for the way he fed us, but also in the way he made the Catholic nun feel comfortable in her new life.

I didn't make a point of listening in, still, I couldn't help overhearing when Mr. Roger told her, "You're a very lucky woman, Mary Rose—." He laughed before adding, "No, I'm still going to continue to call you Mary

Rose, if only for remembering the brightest time of my life that you in part, inspired."

She didn't respond, but rather looked away as if she was recalling something distasteful, or at the very least, extremely nettlesome.

He then mentioned he was on his way to an English country named India.

Sister Clarice or Mary Rose (depending on who was talking to whom) asked him why he was going to India—on business? Her nose crinkled up slightly in anticipation of the man's answer.

"Yes, you could say that. However, it's of a personal nature."

She laughed modestly before inquiring timidly, "To find your lost soul?"

Immediately, he grinned back. "You think it's funny don't you?" Mr. Roger explained, "To have it all, but then not knowing why?"

The Catholic sister replied in a reserved tone of voice, "No one has it all, dear Roger."

The man bit into a large piece of yellow, egg-encrusted toast, before reiterating in a comely voice, "Anything but emptiness. I say anything but that."

"That's a strange remark coming from you." The nun repeated.

"What's even stranger is—it's the truth. And you know it is too." He displayed his open hands as if to show he wasn't hiding anything.

"I'm sorry, Roger dear, but if it's confession that you're after, you'll need to speak to a priest and not to me—an inconsequential Sacred-Heart nun."

"You're wrong there, Mary Rose, for once upon a time I did confess to you. But then again I guess you're right," he emphasized sadly, "You wouldn't listen to me that day either."

The nun couldn't help herself, but blushed red and full. Her eyebrows became knotted together in rigid concentration, as if she absolutely didn't want to consider what the man had just said. Or what was probably more to the point, as this Irishman understood it; time and distance had changed things between the two of them. Thus, the only thing that could be claimed by going back to their common beginnings was acute embarrassment, I'm thinking——at least for the nun.

She made to change the subject, "Come along, my friends I must take you to the quarantine house. It's not very far, but it's best to get you settled in as quickly as possible. Why with the number of outward-bound ships in the harbor, there's no telling whether or not you'll get a cot, especially with the clan of Scotsmen just in. To be honest about it, they act like they own the place! They might just as well put up a sign that says 'McGregor and Sons', the way they tell everyone what to do! So finish up and come along now."

Roger stood up, shaking toasted crumbs from his engaging suit, at the same time addressing me, "You say you're on your way to America, and may I be so bold as to inquire of your plans, which is to say—what you intend to do once you're there?"

Speaking for me mother and myself, I explained as best as I could my idea of farming on any kind of small plot, if need be in Indian country to feed ourselves. At which point Mr. Roger broke in, his tepid smile a mixture of satisfaction and regret. The satisfaction I assumed was for the help he was able to provide my mother and myself. The regret I saw, was wholly reserved for one Catholic nun. A nun, who, perhaps once upon a time was the credible answer to this man's purported emptiness.

"Well, it just so happens that I have a friend there, a legal and practicing dentist by the name of John Waylan. He is a dental surgeon who lives and works in the slave state of Kentucky. You mentioned earlier that your sisters were already there, living in Kentucky. Perhaps if you think it might be of some assistance to you, I will address a note on the bottom of my business card to him—you never know, if you get down John Waylan's way he might be able to help you, I do believe."

I gratefully accepted the man's business card, immediately scrutinizing it with the utmost diligence, all the while not having a clue as to what was written on it. For as I mentioned earlier, I didn't know letters and their written significance. I also didn't understand what Mr. Roger meant by the use of the term "slave state". However, I decided once I knew letters it would be a simple enough matter to find out the meaning of a "slave state". Although as far as this Irishman's concerned, I was darn near convinced that a "slave state" must be where the Indians, the Irish and the Negro folk got together and decided when and where to toss out of Kentucky all of the Bailey Burkes of this world. So they could all go on about their business, and have a bloody, good time about it too. Without the Bailey Burkes of this world breathing down your neck at every turn, threatening everyone with starvation if you don't hold court with their incoherent beliefs, or so much as look the other way.

I thanked the man called Roger for supper while me mother showed her appreciation by offering the man a rusted baby spoon she had taken from her belongings.

To my surprise he accepted the gift with a knowing smile, asking me to tell my mother, "You have given me something of infinite value."

I looked curiously at the rusted spoon with a certain reserve while telling myself at the same time: *the man's seeking affection from a religious nun. He goes around telling people he's empty inside then decides for himself to light out and travel about a place called "India" just so his bloody emptiness can go away...? Why doesn't he take to the hills, spill out whatever's bothering him to the little people with a pint or two of blessed poteen. Then come back nothing worse for wear, but that the head's clearer which should sure in hell get rid of whatever emptiness has been festering inside. So that you pretend you've got everything you need, but the only time you ever smile is when you're giving a beggar-man something to eat. Then in payment you take a rusted spoon and act like you've just crippled a Protestant. I daresay these English are a strange breed, indeed I do.*

My dear and kind, graying mother answered back in the only English phrase she knew, "You're a kind and *dacent* man, Sir—I tell ya' a very dacent man indeed."

At last turning to me, she quipped in Gaelic, "There's no question in my mind Mr. Roger's a *dacent* man—. Still in all, he needs to do something with those English eggs they've got bottled up all around here. They taste like they were laid by a daft hen in the withering drifts of a graveyard."

Chapter Nine

I turn thy leaves and one by one
The gems of Fancy glisten;
So real are the thoughts here wrought
In wonderment I listen.

Author unknown

Sister Mary Clarice was exactly right about the Scots. No sooner did we arrive at the quarantine house, even before exchanging any kind of greetings, we fell right into singing with the lot of them. And this continued almost non-stop for the entire three days that we were there. Well to be sure, I can't in all honesty say I fell into singing with the Scots, for I didn't know the words to any of their songs. In all honesty, I can say I sang with them in the sense I was pushed and manhandled from group to group, before being pulled, cuddled, thrown back and forth, with complementary, healthy smacks of acknowledgement given in-between. So much so, that in a very real sense I did end up singing right along with them. After three days of their 'highland uprising', I even ended up knowing the words to most of their songs as well.

It must have been the *poteen*. Although it wasn't like any I've ever tasted. It burned and burbled and set your insides to firing up something fierce. Still in all, one of the more introverted Scotsman (introverted under these circumstances meaning; he didn't start every sentence by saying "to hell with you, runt, if you can't sing..."), a man by the name of William Saticoy, told me I was too much of a "lighthearted pantywaist" to hold down even a thimbleful of what the Scots called, "our afternoon tea". Which had as much resemblance to brewed, afternoon tea, as a befuddled Englishman does, to even one of the stupidest Irishman God put on the face of this fine earth.

William Saticoy also claimed that after drinking this famous "Scottish tea"; "Well now," he pontificated outright, "To such a thing indeed—once

132

you've had a sip of this "tea"—you'll have hair on your chest so thick—you'll need a team of dray horses pulling disc harrows just to trim it!"

Seemingly on cue, someone would start up in a full baritone, and with arms locked around one another they would all get to singing once again;

> *What'll we say, Lads?*
> *What'll we say?*
> *To the bright and lazy sunny-boy,*
> *What'll we say Lads?*
> *What'll we say?*
>
> *To the lovely maid who comes a' knockin'*
> *What'll we say, Lads?*
> *What'll we say?*
>
> *To the master sergeant callin' to take up arms*
> *What'll we say Lads?*
> *What'll we say?*
>
> *To the grim reaper bearin' his forlorn scythe*
> *What'll we say Lads?*
> *What'll we say?*
>
> *Tell 'em we've no mind for what they're worth,*
> *They can all go to hell,*
> *We've got Scotch whisky and a'-plenty*
> *That's what we'll say Lads,*
> *That's what we'll say....*

Seemingly in unison and just as soon as the song was finished, the Scots would face one another, banging each other on their respective shoulders and backsides. All the while ballyhooing about what they would do once they arrived in the great big United States of America.

I suppose one should be excited about one's new home; the sailing trip, seeing a different country, Indians and wide, untamed plains. In addition, the adventures waiting to fall like so many slices of my sister, Ann Horian's, apple bread. Still in all, the way the Scotsmen told it, you'd think America was just sitting there, holding its youthful and collective breath, waiting for the Scots to show up. And not only for the Scotsmen to show up, but for them to correct everyman's ways with their thick-headed, brutish, stubborn and obnoxiously, penny–pinching ways.

In the years that followed, it was confirmed time and time again to me, so much so that I now know it to be the absolute truth. I've often heard people claim that the Jewish race is ostensibly cheap, but they are as eager philanthropists in comparison, as generous with their money as a bachelor in a tavern on the eve of his wedding, in contrast with the Scots.

Why to hear them say it, whenever they were called upon to pay for something—something they truly owed; they never had a heaven-sent nickel to their name. For many a time I heard more than one Scotsman claim, 'If only I had a quarter or so, I'd insist on paying, not only for myself, but for everyone here—and t'is the very truth about it now!' Before hammering his fist on the table to emphasize how sincere he was. This stunning performance always seemed to come just as soon as someone else at the table paid for the round.

They were forever on the brink of insolvency, and if somehow a Scotsman was found with a dollar on his person it was only because he had thirteen children to feed. In addition to which, if anything was left over after all that, then it must be passed on to his cousins, who claimed they hadn't had a decent meal since the Red Sea was parted by a certain countryman named Moses. Who, according to the Scotch, had himself descended from the heather leaving all his money to the Pharaoh, which is one of the reasons they were all so poor. The only thing which surpassed their miserliness was their supposed ability to be able to do just about anything, and that *anything* better than anyone else. In that one afternoon alone, I learned how the Scots had invented everything from celestial navigation to the invention of the American frontier banjo.

When questioned about it, one Scotsman replied, "Of course, we don't know how to play the banjo. If we did, we'd have no time for new discoveries!"

Afterwards, they'd be off banging each other on their respective backsides in agreement. All the time laughing to one another, and downing more Scottish whisky than I thought was possible, or existed for that matter.

Now then, if ever I hear another conversation that starts with the following phrase, 'You must realize as a matter of course, a Scotsman would know better and do it like this....'

I'll go ahead and shoot the man who says it, and any subsequent jail sentence be damned. For it'll be a justifiable homicide, with my lawyer arguing rightful cause by reason of insanity. Aye, the Scots can certainly make you crazy alright.

There was a tall man, with a strapping beer-keg of a chest wearing a red and black, plaid jacket standing right next to me. He was standing so close that he had to incline his neck and bearded head away from where I was, to be able to speak down to me. The tall man did this, enabling me to hear what he had to say, instead of trying to pick out his words, as if they had all come bursting forth, and at the same time as well, from a sack of dried muffins. Even so, I was ever thankful for this punitive distance, for the stark aroma of burnt, uncured, green tobacco seemed to permeate the air whenever this man spoke.

"The good thing about Scotch whisky, Lad, is that it'll just about do whatever you need to have done. And that includes cookin' and healin', and with just the right to-o-och about it—why it can even tuck you into your own damned bed at night!"

After saying this, he threw back his rotund, fluffy head and roared like a lion. So much so, one man of the group told him to be quiet. He further mentioned the English would be down and about, to maybe even throw the lot of us out of the quarantine house and back out onto the street, if we made too much of a noisy racket.

The bearded fellow roared again before explaining, "I doubt it, Laddie. The thing with the English is; they need forty or more of their own kind before they'll even make a peep at one of us. And since we're at least a dozen or so Scotsmen in this place, why the English would have to corral the entire Liverpool garrison and probably a few others as well, in order to rebuff whatever we'd have to say to them."

He then made a determined and disgruntled face, before going on to say, he alone, could account for at least a dozen Englishmen by himself. The way he grudgingly named *only* a dozen Englishmen, it seemed to me, he was acknowledging a considerable advantage to himself, should it come down to that.

I looked around the quarantine house and wondered how much of it was true.

The quarantine house itself was situated in a southwest corner of Liverpool. To arrive there, one had to follow two street urchins peddling vitriolic-looking seed cakes, a half-dozen soldiers that were so out of tune in their drunken overture, they appeared to sound rather like engorged parrots. In addition to all this, there appeared as well a defrocked preacher, who kept intoning the ocean to come and sweep him, as well as the other straying members of his congregation away forever, in atonement for their collective, impartial and apparently unmitigated way of sinning.

The quarantine house was a long mulish affair. Rectangular and stretching out long enough to hold over one hundred beds laid out end to end. With just enough space in between each one, to satisfy my sister's cat's need to squeeze into very tight spaces, and lie there forgotten for hours. There was a lone, stove pipe furnace down at the other end of the hall. The sides of the wall next to the furnace were charred a grainy black from the next-of-kin, unyielding heat. Normally during the day, there would be a large group of women gathered around the stove. They always seemed to be enjoying a good how-to-do while they kept a wary eye on a load of undergarments, drying out on the blackened metal. The walls of the quarantine house were of pinewood which had yellowed due to age, with darkened brown knots and disheartening messages left from travelers. These same weary travelers had spent the night, or several nights, and scrawled something into the wood before moving on. Some of the messages were full of hope while others betrayed a certain deception with the current state of affairs in this world.

One that was read out loud by my neighbor made me afraid because of the image it drew forth in my mind, for it read:

> *I am sailing away...*
> *far, far away to new worlds—*
> *Oh! That they may be right in that the world is round,*
> *and we end up not sailing, right straight over the crown!*

Another one bespoke of an enduring amour from a Ukrainian adventurer:

> *To Emily my darling—*
>
> *Let this departing kiss be but a reminder,*
> *of your unworthy yet devoted husband, Ilyaska*
> *Alas when you reach America please don't try to find me,*
> *for I'll be hiding out from your dominating clutches,*
> *in the hinterlands of that unmapped territory—Nebraska!*

Perhaps my favorite, was the one written in such a way, one had to remove the slip of a pillow at the head of the cot to read it:

> *To Ann-Marie wherever you are;*
>
> *You've disillusioned me*
> *Once too often,*
> *I bore your lack of attention*
> *Again, though not forgotten.*
>
> *I took it all in and kept faithful,*

so deep was my love for the maiden from Menchy.
Alas, I can no longer bear it,
For you ran away from my arms and dreams—
With a garlic-smelling, snail-munching, disgusting Frenchy!

And so on and so on. I enjoyed listening to some of the messages being read, for they seemed to express what we were feeling ourselves. Aye, a certain discouragement, due in part, to the loud and brutish smacks, the Scots doled out as if they had decided amongst themselves what was to be.

No sooner had I found two cots for me mother and myself, then a pair of knee-booted Scotsmen, with arms around each other's muscled shoulders, grasped, then lifted me over their heads right then and there, and in spite of my best efforts to resist.

"What would you say, Lad?" One of them asked me while at the same moment he examined his formidable forearm, as if what he was going to say was an afterthought, as casual as inquiring where the salt might be, "In helping us to overthrow the government and putting a Stuart back on the throne?"

Even though I barely understood half of what the man was saying, I knew it to be treacherous and full of impending danger. Nevertheless, the way the man plied his idea, it was with the same tone one would use to invoke a stroll around some rose-lined park, on a desultory Sunday afternoon...the overthrow of the English crown notwithstanding.

The other man turned to his companion and remarked, "He couldn't help you in any case—he's Irish."

There was no mistaking that his referral to my being from the *land of Erin* was comparable to filing a complaint against me, for untold crimes against humanity, simply for my being Irish.

As if he needed to explain his position, the man went on, "The Irish have been the bootlickers of the English for so long now, they have to ask their English masters for the right to pee. Even so, once the English have given their permission, the Irish still need another minute or so to figure things out. You understand, which leg to lift?—like the tail-less mongrels which they are."

For a farm boy from Castlewarren it was too fast and incomprehensible. The singing, the gestures, the belittlement, as I said, it was much too fast for me to digest anything, much less defend myself. So I listened and when I remembered to, closed my slackened jaw, so as to avoid looking too much like the English bootlickers the Scots proclaimed us to be.

Just then the door to the quarantine house opened, and in walked my brother, Paul Francis Daniel. To my surprise, standing next to him was the "Bobby"-helmeted, mustachioed policeman from our Irish Sea-crossing ship—the *Nimrod*.

I called out my brother's name, but either he couldn't hear from the loud singing emanating from just about every blasted corner of that hall, or he was pretending not to hear.

I called out again, and this time Paul Francis Daniel twisted his head slightly, as if straining to make something out of all that Scottish cacophony.

I crossed the hall, shaking myself free of the encircling arms of one Scotsman. The one who'd been advocating for the last half-hour or so just how "damned 'appy" certain American Indian tribes would be to join forces with the Scots, and chase the English out of America once and for all. And in the spirit of their movement, keeping as many English scalps as they could find time to take.

As I approached my brother, I could see he'd been fighting again. His ears and neck were purple and swollen, with the bottom skin of his left ear torn and in a tattered and still-bleeding state. His hair was wet and matted on one side from the blood, and both of his eyes were rimmed with a shaded, blackened crescent, as if he hadn't slept in the seventy-two hours or so since we'd last seen him.

The policeman from the *Nimrod* spoke up, "Aye, your brother Paulie here is what the Brits call "the devil incarnate". And with that unforgiving right hook of his, you figure him to be able to light up the sky on a moonless night."

My brother wiped his mouth off with his shirtsleeve, inclining his head my way as he did so. His face, other than showing signs of being tired, was blank, expressionless, but deep in those grey, Irish eyes of his, there was no denying the simmering of some long overdue and as yet undiminished hatred.

At last, and as if he had just talked himself out, my brother, who was never big on words to begin with concluded, "The Liverpool Irish are the most despicable mob on the face of this earth."

As if to confirm whatever had happened in the aftermath, the mustachioed policeman from the *Nimrod* added, "Aye, it's true. They figured your brother for an easy target. So they took to selling him everything from an Earl's silver coated tea service that need never be washed, to a governorship which included a three story manor on the banks of the Hudson River that something tells me doesn't exist."

The man took into account my confusion, and offered by means of an explanation, "Your brother took it personally when his compatriots here in Liverpool told him they knew about Castlewarren, and how just about everyone was running away, their tails caught between their hind legs; leaving the entire village to the English. "Them gutless cowards", they told him— "just like the Maddoxs."

At the mention of the Maddox's name, I drew a deep breath. It was our village all over again; destitute and without hope, thanks to the potato blight and the English. Except this time, there was a certain bobbing and pig-tailed colleen, a particular Katherine Louisa Maddox who came to mind, and with it hope. The same hope which before had told me the world may not be such a bad place after all. Then I distinctly remembered her handing me an oatmeal biscuit, her hand barely brushing against mine...no, not such a bad place after all.

"Let me introduce myself," the policeman from the *Nimrod* half-growled. "The name's Mortlock—Longfellow T. Mortlock. That's correct—," he went on to say as if to clarify things, "one of the County Donegal Mortlocks."

The way he insisted on "from County Donegal" almost redundantly, and was intended I suppose, to clear up any confusion we might have had as to the genealogical ambiguities of the Mortlock dynasty.

I asked the man, "Aren't you a policeman on the *Nimrod.*"

He answered back, "No Lad, just helping out my cousin Stirling Mortlock, the captain and part owner of the *Nimrod*. He needed a hand keeping the passengers at bay as you may recall, and as I'm considered a bit skillful with this here shillelagh of mine, I traded my *certain skills* for passage back. You see, I'm heading once again for the United States of America."

Taking into account our stubbornly confused faces, Longfellow Mortlock reiterated, "Heading back I tell you!"

Then he leaned against the wall, his shoulder twisting around until he found a half-rounded, comfortable niche he could slide his shoulder into, as one might throw out an anchor. Finally, the policeman touched at his swooping moustaches, first one side then the other. This he did as one might his wallet; knowing it to be there, yet still feeling for it all the same, just wanting to make sure it hadn't got lost or stolen.

"Oh yes, I've been all over, from Normandy in the north of France to the backwaters of Juarez. But there's no place for a liberty-breathing man like the cities and plains of the United States of America—.Take the smoked venison of buffalo country, down Oklahoma-way, why there ain't a more—"

Before he could finish, Longfellow Mortlock was pushed rather violently from behind. Nevertheless, in the time it takes for me to write this passage, his Irish night-stick, or shillelagh if you prefer, was up, posed and prepared to come crashing down on any and all attackers.

"Mortlock, damn it all, I thought it was you!" A red-bearded Scotsman sang out, his hair and crimson beard all in a scuttle, fanning out in full bloom like a well-filled jib sail before the trade winds.

In recognition, the man we now knew to be Longfellow Mortlock stammered back, "Sure 'n b-golly, and I don't believe me eyes. T'is one and the same; "Devil" McGoran, the only man tough enough to stand up to the Brits while telling his own people they could all go to hell, for not coming together with their pikes like Daniel O'Connell asked of 'em!"

The man called "Devil" pulled Longfellow Mortlock to one side, and started half-whispering loudly to his old friend. While I couldn't catch all of what they said, bits and pieces drifted back to me like leaves on a autumnal wind; "It wasn't as physical as all that....You've hit me harder in jest....He might be dead, then again maybe he ain't...still, the way he was bleedin' 'n all....The next time I'm guessing he'll think twice before pulling that much money out of his pocket, for all the world to see...."

While it was certainly wonderful to see these two friends reunited, I'd heard news that Katherine Louisa Maddox had come through Liverpool and was desperate for more. I culled my brother to one side of the dormitory-like room. After telling him how mother was, for which he appeared nowhere in the least bit concerned, I asked him about the Maddoxs, and if it was true what Mortlock had reported.

Paul Francis Daniel reflexively touched his torn earlobe, and shook his head.

"They came through alright."

"But we knew that anyway, Mortlock just told us." I confirmed back.

"Then why do you ask Brother, if you already knew they've been through Liverpool like the rest of us?"

He repeated what I had just said, in that sarcastic way of his that made me, too, want to belt him. Nevertheless, if you wanted information from my brother you had to dance with him in a manner of speaking. Dancing in this case meant letting my older brother lead. Then, when he had a mind to it, and he figured he'd stiffed you long enough for his own amusement, only then would he tell you what you wanted to know. Afterwards, it was up to you to figure out whether what he had said was true or not. Still, I was after a glimmer of anything concerning Katherine Louisa Maddox. It was either that or harping out sea shanties the rest of the evening, with a room full of whisky-enthused, loutish Scotsmen.

I repeated myself, "I mean, I know they've been through Liverpool alright, but-but how are they? Did they make it onto some ship bearing for the United States? Or is it to be Canada or the Australian territories? Which ship was it? Did anyone say where in the United States they were heading to? When will they be there?"

Paul Francis Daniel looked slowly around the room before answering me, "Well, if they did make it onto some ship like you say—then they made it by the skin of their teeth."

As usual, I had to beseech my brother to explain himself.

He launched into what may have been for him the longest speech of his life. Except for the time, he had to explain to Bailey Burke just what he was doing in Feargus O'Connor's pear orchards, with several well-laden sacks and an ingeniously-built sliding ladder. A ladder by the way that looked to have been constructed rather suspiciously, using cross members and wall studs from Feargus O'Connor's dismantled carriage house.

"You see Edward, one of our blessed fellow countrymen," my brother spat venomously before continuing, "had done sold Mr. Maddox sea passage berths to a place in America called Newfoundland, up Canada way. Told old man Maddox that he could save himself a few pounds by hiring a canoe and Iroquois Indian paddlers to take his family the rest of the way, once he got to Newfoundland. Seems that old man Maddox not only bought the tickets, but seemed to be considering settling down right there in Newfoundland, because the son-of-a-bitch, Liverpool-Irishman told him, "The soil of Newfoundland was the only place in the world where potatoes grew without the need for constant watering."

I stared at my brother, unabashedly showing my lack of comprehension while at the same time, desperately wishing I could have spoken with the man, who had sold the Maddoxs their sea passages himself. At which point, I took to scratching and staring at my arm, looking for all the world like a dumb *croppie* Irishman; which I more or less knew to be true.

My brother answered in the only way he knew how; brittle and to the point, "Of course you don't need no water in Newfoundland to irrigate the potatoes, because the soil's bloody frozen all the time!"

"And that's—that's where they're heading?" I was incredulous.

My plans of waltzing Katherine Louisa Maddox through bright and Marigold-packed fields, to right down the church's center aisle came to a crashing halt. It was replaced by the dour scene of an exhausted, young woman sloshing her way through ice fields, up to her booted knees in rancid potato slush while crying out my name to come and rescue her.

"I don't know for certain if that's where they are going. I asked the man who was boasting of having sold them the tickets, how he could do it to one of Erin's own, a fellow countryman no less, when this Judas of an Irishman told me it was none of my business, and to go away before he gave me what for—."

My brother didn't have to explain beyond that. I knew him too well. You tell my brother it was "none of his business"—that was bad enough, then you tell him to go away before you make trouble for him. Well, that was like exhibiting a certain red blanket to one smoldering bull. One didn't have to guess what my brother would do. His anger was legendary, as well as engraved in stone.

"So you gave him what for, huh?" I said this while trying to avoid looking at the torn lower-ear tissue hanging there at an angle. An angle of ear that may or may not have been recoverable by suturing.

Paul Francis Daniel looked down at his swollen fists, before replying matter-of-factly, "We got into it alright. Nobody sells rotten meat to somebody from Castlewarren. Especially to someone that one day you're gonna marry!"

He then laughed that laugh of his, caught up as it were, somewhere between the actual truth and downright meanness, just so he could get a reaction out of you. And to him, thinking, if he got you to show your feelings, somehow my brother had won. That it was a weakness and all, to show him or anyone else for that matter, how you felt. But then again, I'm a stupid wisp of a man. I bought into his trap like one of the mewing white deer of Mallow; becoming a glutton on the first thrusting sprigs of summer corn, and yet not knowing there was a hunter just abaft of it all, waiting there all patient and quiet-like to take you down.

I was caught unknowingly out in the open. Thus, I played right into my brother's hands, "I never said I'd marry her! What did you figure me out for? A simpering boob? That I've gone daft like one of *the little people?*"

"Maybe not daft little Brother, but when you refused to wash your grimy hand for a week after explaining how the *archangel* Katherine Louisa Maddox had just administered the last rites of the church, by allowing you to dabble on an oatmeal biscuit right out of her saintly hands—.Come on now, face up to it, just so, we're all wondering as well; why with your wealth and sprawling farmlands what colleen wouldn't jump at the chance to share your cottage and hearth. Why the woman would have to be daft indeed, not to pass up a chance at such princess-like happiness. I can see the colleen right now, Katherine Louisa Maddox Ruth spending her time bustling around the hearth, fixing the noon-day meal, and wondering the whole time how her bloody husband could take care of so many acres of farmland and countless animal stock, with his head half-way up his ass all the time!"

He let out a long and fluted sigh, like he was tired of speaking. Afterwards, he smiled that niggardly smile of his before calling out in rapid order for Longfellow Mortlock, Scotch whisky and some sutures and medicinal ointment to calm his aching ear.

I was turning over in my mind what my brother had told me. This came after helping me poor ma with some watered down, red bean and sour cabbage soup. A soup that she claimed needed only one or two peeled onions for the whole lot to be a fit meal for Candlemas.

After we had eaten, I found myself sitting down in one corner of the room, my hands draped over my knees, not too far from the blackened-pipe work stove that I couldn't seem to get a little warmth from. As well as within earshot of what apparently takes place most of the time, in a certain neighborhood not far from the shipyards of Glasgow in Scotland. This of course came from the womenfolk gathered around the stove. They appeared bent on blocking its warmth from me and the others. These same women spent most of their time speaking in hushed murmurs to each other about the virile as well as moral aptitudes of their men, in spite of the shameless hussies who frequented the shipyards after-hours. While following these proceedings at the stove one needed to ask; who was warming who? Indeed, if such an energy could be harnessed from the well-crafted and seemingly unexhausted tales of women.... I've been told by no less an authority on the subject than a bridge-building civil engineer that half the world's coal supplies could be conserved indefinitely, if somehow women the world over could all be taught to gossip in unison. He also mentioned that as far as their men coming home late from work and tanked to the gills with ale...that the subsequent eye-scratching and the inevitable female tongue-lashing could be envisioned as a sort of residual energy reserve, should the need arise.

I found myself half-listening to the tale of one Scotsman, as told by someone else I assumed to be his ingratiated wife. Of how her husband was so spendthrift, he would bury his weekly pay in the back garden. Eventually, when his wife needed the money for buying the house necessities, this Scotsman would claim he'd forgotten where he'd buried it. At length, causing such a domestic riot, the local Calvinist minister would have to intervene, and oftentimes buy groceries with his limited parish funds, just so the family could eat, thereby ensuing a semblance of domestic peace.

All this I listened to while I was caught up in my own desperate thoughts of one Katherine Louisa Maddox. This involved the pale uncertainty of once having arrived in America, I should find her there, eager and waiting to waltz down the aisle with me in spite of what my brother had said. Indeed, as my brother had reminded me; that most women boasting of a certain degree of intelligence were not in the market for back-home, buttermilk squalor from an immigrant Irishman. One that would rise early and work the day down to a blackening twilight, but didn't have the formal education to maintain a conversation with the village goat.

He's right, I told myself, *Katherine may be in love with you as you say, but to keep her in love I've got to know letters and how to write them. Not only that, but then I could read and write poetry to her, thus she would never want to leave, ever again.*

Unfortunately, I reminded myself: *it's going to be bloody hard getting things in order, if Katherine's in Newfoundland, or even worse riding in an Indian canoe somewhere in the boondocks of Canada, as an Indian's wife looking for more tillable tundra.*

Someone was standing close by. I could feel the wooden flooring flexing and the overpowering smell of sea brine and shirt-spilled whisky filled the placid, suffocating air. I looked up to see the half-hidden face of Longfellow Mortlock breathing sourly and rocking a bit, as if the floor was shifting. The man was quizzically peering down at me with the air of someone who'd been called away to a mourning, the wake of someone he'd barely known, yet he'd gone anyway if only for the sweet cakes and free-fill of home draught *poteen.*

"What seems to be troublin' you, my good man?" His gigantic moustaches moved hither, as well as up and down, seemingly, as if they had a life of their own. Indeed, for just the briefest of moments I got caught up in wondering if one couldn't use his bushy and cable-thick handlebar moustaches as a sort of weighing balance; placing a one pound sack of sugar on the one side with something equally substantial on the other moustache, to see if things didn't balance out. But no I'm thinking, without chains of some kind to adjust things around, it wouldn't work. In no small part, due to his overflowing handlebar moustaches, the rest of his face seemed peculiarly small and to resemble that of a Chinese squirrel. His cheeks were puffy and unaccountably full of acorns. Mortlock's eyes were dark while being inclined towards the Oriental; which is to say softly-lidded, and appeared to be continually adjusting themselves to the light. But the truth be told; it was those gargantuan, ore-smelting, rock-boulder-like mountains of moustaches that seemed to burst from either side of his lip like an avalanche or a brown, silt-encrusted river spilling over the side of a hill to end up as a run-away, hairy waterfall that marked this mister Longfellow Mortlock.

He stopped his rocking, or at least leaned forward long enough to tell me (only once or twice slurring his words), "Listen here now, if you don't want to be bothered that's alright with me. But I just wanted to let you know how your brother sure stood up for you, even when there was three of them wanting him to change his mind, and might quickly at that!"

I moved over motioning for him to sit down. He glanced at the stove and the stout-looking women gathered around it.

He winced once before whispering close to my ear, as if he'd known me all my life, "The good thing about being married to a woman from Scotland is; when our Maker comes for you on your last day on earth—you just go on ahead and walk into paradise like you belongs, without a mind to anyone. If you're asked or stopped about it, tell Him you were once upon a time married to a Scotswoman, and I'm telling you no matter what you've done, that no matter your crime or disdainful mark on this world, you won't be spending no time in purgatory—seeing's how you were once married to a Scotswoman. Now don't forget about telling the good Lord, cause it will surely save you a lot of discomfort in the afterlife—. For not only being married to a Scotswoman; covers 'a multitude of sins'.... Why with their crazy and half-cocked, jealous temper; it makes one damn careful before committing any more!"

This thought apparently amused him to no end, for he held his stomach with both hands like a belt, as it moved up and down in silent fits of mirth. He then motioned with a shaking finger to be quiet. That even though you and he both knew what he had just said was true and all, it was best to be quiet about such things. For there were others near-by who might disagree and you know.... Longfellow Mortlock took his crooked thumb and aimed it over his shoulder at the women nestled about the stove, as if they were the guilty party, which he had just got through stating that indeed they were exactly that...the guilty party that is.

He then changed the subject. "For someone on their way and for the first time to America, you don't seem to be burstin' with too much excitement about the place." Longfellow mentioned to me.

Suddenly, he cautioned me with a strange look and an agitated finger over his mouth that said don't answer just yet, no, not just yet. Then he took to one knee and hollered out for his friend, "Devil" McGoran to bring him the bottle of whisky, and make it quick-like if he knew what was good for him. That was some hollering indeed, if one wanted to be heard in that place with the Scots still singing and several children bawling out for their soup. Still in all, I'll be damned if his friend didn't bustle right through, his red beard and hair lighting up the room as he passed by, like a fiery, red-river morning sunrise, the day after the heavy rains have done cleared everything away.

"I don't know the country, the people, I've got a sick ma on me hands and a brother who disappears without so much as a by-your-bloody-leave—you're damned right I'm worried."

After saying this, I looked at both men like we were all somehow crazy to be in this damned quarantine house in the first place.

Longfellow Mortlock took his time, eyeing first myself, before switching his gaze back to "Devil" McGoran, who it appeared was a lot freer pulling on Mortlock's bottle of whisky than he was supposed to be about sharing it. Disjointedly, the man unfastened his policeman's helmet, set it down next to him on the floor, and began rubbing his scalp, groaning in a happy sort of way as he did so, like a grumpy bear satisfying an itch.

Then Longfellow told me, "You've got to understand one single thing above all else in that pea-brain of yours, Edward Ruth. And that is, in America these days, everyone's in a bloody huff and to do about this so called slave and free man question. In fact, if I were hard put to explain it I'd tell you this: for years now these buggers down south in Tennessee, and the Carolinas, Virginia, even Kentucky, have been using the African nigger to do his chores for him. Now I don't see no problem with that—it's just the way it is. Hell, look at the plight of the bloody Irish—our own people for god's sake; they's on their own land, they didn't get imported from nowhere now did they?—Still, they're being used as slaves for the English. Of course you don't see no one—*especially* those milk-toasts of emancipationists, over in the United States, moaning about it. It's the same starvin' situation, except this time over here in Ireland, the slaves by and large speak Gaelic. But some bellyaching, Northern, Protestant women, who've probably gotta collective crimp up their collective asses, have decided to make hell for their husbands and just about everyone else they come across. For the simple reason; they are, they have been, and sure n' hell will always be so damned unhappy with their lot in life, they make it a point to make everyone else just as bloody miserable as they are."

He thought long and carefully for a moment before adding, "The only difference is; they serve steaming warm crumpets and tea on nice linen in between moaning and complaining about it."

He then smiled to himself before confiding ironically, "I suppose it helps to make slavery more palatable—when it's served up on nice fancy tablecloths that is."

I asked probably more timidly than I should have, "What's the Northern women's concern with what the Southern people do? I mean why do they stick their noses into something that doesn't affect them?"

As I found out later insofar as he had a terrible habit of doing, "Devil" McGoran broke in at a gallop changing the subject, "I was married once to an Indian woman...fine gal too."

Longfellow Mortlock accused his friend, his twin moustaches bobbing up and down from the effort, "You were never married...you were living in sin the two of you, right from the get-go!"

McGoran shot back, obviously offended by his friend's remark, "We were not! We had a right proper ceremony and everything that goes with it. Far as I could tell, once her pappy cut out the buffalo's tongue and made us each eat a half, we was done hitched, man and wife—retching stomachs and all."

"It wasn't cooked in the least bit...you ate it raw?" I couldn't help asking.

"The tongue is eaten completely raw...that's how come you can tell if the marriage ceremony is a valid one or not," McGoran answered, eager to explain the Indian way of life.

I couldn't help it, my interest was piqued so I asked, "What became of her, then...your Indian wife that is, uh, Mr. McGoran?"

Although, I had a feeling marriage with a man surnamed "Devil" couldn't be all that promising, regardless of what part of the animal's digestive tract one ate to lend a defining benediction to the ceremony.

"We was in the Dakotas trapping that spring and fall, and when we got back she was gone. I saw her pappy and all, but he couldn't make me understand where she'd run off too, 'ceptin' I figured out by listening to some other members of the tribe that whoever she'd done take off with was a military man. Probably a stinkin' officer to boot, they'se the only ones who ain't got no morals 'bout taking another man's wife. That's all I know 'bout it, 'ceptin' one other thing."

He scratched at an area, way down in the thick of that red beard, before answering my unspoken question. "Devil" McGoran must have found whatever he was looking for because he heaved a great big sigh of relief, like he'd just discovered water in the desert.

Finally, he flung something that was slimy and black with a lot of miniature legs off the tip of his finger before reporting, "I ain't never going to eat buffalo tongue again until I'm good and ready. Marriage is a serious business, and if the two of you ain't good and serious about it—. Well, hell, I don't care what you roast over the fire now, it could be a pair of the juiciest buffalo steaks in the world. Still, the marriage ain't gonna 'mount to a hill of beans, until you're both good and ready for it, and that includes bathin' once in awhile."

"Devil" then turned his attention to me, "The way your brother done explained things, it seems like you're just about ready to get hitched and all, yourself." As if to confirm what he'd said earlier he added, "Here's hoping she ain't no Indian woman you've a mind to marry—they're a grimy lot!" He nodded his head as if to confirm that he knew what he was talking about.

"Devil" McGoran was serious enough when he asked it, so I went ahead and told him how I felt, "If the truth be known, the young lady in question thinks I'm a poor Irish lad who is a dirty scoundrel, and not fit for much of anything. Except maybe, to stable her horses and clean out the sty."

He shook his finger at me, "Your brother claims she gave you a bit of cake or cookie once? Now that's something, Lad!"

He took notice of my expression of denial before continuing, "Now, don't underestimate what's in a woman's heart. While she was giving you that piece of cookie or cake she was probably thinking to herself just what it would take to get you all cleaned up and presentable like...."

Longfellow cut in, anxious to add his part, "T'is true, she's out figuring alright just what it's going to take to get you all cleaned up, to be presentable and all, just like a firing squad does to take better aim alright. For if she's half the colleen that you've described her to be, why you can bet she's figuring on what it will take to get you all cleaned up, just so she can turn around and make your life hell-bound miserable from here on out. But since you're all spic and span behind the ears and wearing starched linen now, her neighbors will all be thinking, and probably telling her as well, she's doing her job as a Christian wife and all."

"Devil" broke in to inquire of his friend, "She's about "doing her job", you say? And just what would her job be about then, if I may ask?"

Longfellow Mortlock sighed deeply, acting as if what he was going to say was as clear as the sun on the back-bay at the O'Malley's castle in Westport. "Why to make your life a bleedin' hell, just so all her friends can then say what a lovely and God-fearing wife and woman she is. Hell, I thought everyone knew that."

I got to wondering what had happened to my question about the Northerners putting their noses into the Southerner's business, when "Devil" McGoran interrupted my thoughts with a red-bearded filled glee and a resounding, "I've got a little something here that will help our friend, Edward to gain the advantage."

That said, he rolled back his sleeve, and produced a short but stocky forearm with a faded tattoo of a slinky mermaid entwined around a maritime anchor, "You just go ahead and give her a taste of this thunder." At last, he brandished his forearm once or twice more before concluding, "Then we'll see who's up and about "doing their job," eh?"

This seemed to "Devil" to make perfect marital sense, for he emitted a confirming laugh that was a cross between a polite hiccup and a bear mauling someone in the underbrush.

As for me, I couldn't entertain the thought of myself ever being brutal to Katherine, no matter what she did—. One didn't discipline angels that way—or so I'm told...ever.

Just then, me ma took to coughing and spitting, so that I had to excuse myself to get up and take care of her. It was just as well, for she wasn't the only one suffering; I had a head so filled with the brewed-up, Scottish *poteen*-induced thoughts of my two learned companions that I couldn't decide if the ache in my head was due in no small way to the aspiring thought that maybe, just maybe, Katherine Louisa Maddox could be found to have some affection for me. And if she did, then maybe she would consent to, after all, spend the rest of her life making mine as miserable as Longfellow said she could, or more exactly just as I felt right then and there. The only thing left for me to do was to find her and quick-like, before her father decided to lay down the first crop of potatoes in the frozen tundra of Newfoundland.

You see, I didn't really care if Katherine Louisa Maddox made my life miserable. In fact, knowing her beauty and gentleness as I did now I must admit I was rather looking forward to it. I just didn't want to sit by doing nothing while she experienced misery in her new country. That somehow, was something I didn't wish to see. For you must understand, a poor *croppie* like myself is used to it, he learns to endure, to accept his lot in life. What he finds most difficult (including this Irishman) is to see pain in the ones he loves—because he's not sure if they can deal with it; if they will have the fortitude to countenance the physical and emotional poverty of life. He knows for himself it's not a problem, he wears it like an old cloak...you see it has been that way since the day he was born.

Chapter Ten

To hear the sweet Rolian Lyres
That breathe from out thy pages,
Telling of passions strange and deep,
That fired the buried ages.

Author unknown

We had been at sea for one week. Although the mid-Atlantic Ocean was foretold to be a horrible place for a lengthy crossing, I was caught up in a panoply of strange and wondrous delights, and therefore didn't care. The air of the Atlantic Ocean made me so hungry, I gave a serious thought or two about dicing up and stewing one or two of the ship's wooden belaying pins. Indeed, my hunger was constantly with me, yet it was not like before, a seemingly dull ache. Now it acted as an impetus, as an inducement to live, to run from the bow to the stern laughing all the while over nothing. To ask what their lives were about to my fellow shipmates, imitating the "rude tars" or seaman as they scrambled aloft amidst the ship's spars setting the sails, to learn all that I could about anything and everyone. And I had just the right teachers for it too; Longfellow Mortlock and "Devil" McGoran. These men had been everywhere, seen everything and weren't afraid to tell me about their experiences. Furthermore, what they didn't know, they made up as they went along, convinced I'm sure that it was better I had something based on pure conjecture on their part to follow, than nothing at all.

Longfellow Mortlock, upon learning of my desire for letters and their significance, took me in the mornings and most afternoons in his forecastle cabin to teach me reading and writing. He also took the time to introduce my thick Irish head to some of his favorite writers, such as Homer, Virgil, Shakespeare and eventually William Pelican, the author of such genuine classics as "Life among the Cheyenne" and "The Night Riders of New Mexico".

Aye, life was pretty ship-shape on board the *Sylph*, a five-hundred ton brig captained by a Mr. Limerick and his wife Allyson. The captain's wife told me, after we had been at sea a week or so, she always traveled with her husband nowadays, as he used to have a bad habit when he captained alone, of holing up on the island of Trinidad in Caribbean waters for several months, before hoisting the mainsail and coming home.

"That is to say," she went on by way of a sullen explanation, "Of holing up with some very palatable West Indies' rum and a Creole woman, who reputedly knew voodoo-like, west African sorcery, and thus wouldn't let the poor captain come home to his beloved Allyson—as much as he tried or wanted to. Now, he's converted himself and become respectable." She added in hopeful triumph.

Although in all truth, Mrs. Limerick never admitted what exactly her husband had converted himself to. Still in all, to this Irishman's ears, it all sounded as the woman had said, "respectable" enough.

I cannot say with any certainty if it was because of the presence on board of his wife, or the absence of a premeditated *sejour* in Trinidad that kept our Captain Limerick in a continual foul mood. But for whatever reason, he was and continued to be for the length of our voyage, like a boiling tempest at sea. Someone used the phrase that the captain was "provokingly taciturn", although his wife certainly wasn't. She made it her sacred duty to mete out our daily one pound of meal or bread to each and everyone of us on board the *Sylph*. Allyson Limerick also made it her self-appointed task, to ask us how we felt, every time she came across one of us above or below decks. For you see, English law in all its compelling wisdom did not require the carrying of a doctor on these "coffin ships", as they were soon to be called. Mrs. Limerick couldn't do enough for me mother, the poor soul, but that she would offer some of her own milk, so that me mother could wash her bread down with something other than shipped water from the lower deck. All this went on under her husband's watchful and frugal eye, for these proceedings he felt were unnecessary, and beyond the scope of the immigrant contract.

Allyson Limerick also found time to tell us stories of her life at sea. And, while I wasn't captivated or yearned to follow in her sea-going footsteps, still I caught myself wondering why she had left her Donegal home to travel with this man, and feast upon mackerel and gurnet when the volatile seas of the Atlantic Ocean weren't giving their brig the once over. I came to the conclusion it must have been one hell of a life, I tell you.

He left me well enough alone, and to be sure this Irishman made it a stringent point of giving the Captain's keel a wide berth. On the other hand if the truth be known, I felt completely safe with Longfellow Mortlock and "Devil" McGoran around as my tutors. I could tell they had taken a liking to me, for they were forever jostling me back and forth, and filling my shoulders and arms with punches that became blue, swollen and only hurt for a day or so.

Only once during the entire five week voyage did the captain catch me by myself. This he did not far from the companionway ladder, which I desperately wanted to use, as I had found a small cubicle in the forecastle, where I slept and could be alone.

"You thou—'Shakes'," (I have no idea why the captain insisted on calling me "Shakes") nevertheless, he called out to me with a commanding air that demanded immediate obedience.

"Aye, Sir", I answered back, trying to disguise the husky trembling in my voice.

I found myself staring into the face and eyes of a white-whiskered and ruddy appearance. A salt of a man, who either knew the bottle too well, or having once known it, couldn't or wouldn't see clear to put it behind him. His stark-white, unshaven whiskers rode high on his cheeks, and along with his beet-red eyes and rolling eyebrows gave Captain Limerick the look of an aquatic albino rabbit. He only needed to sit and sniff with his nose in an elevated position, basking in tall heather once in awhile, for the image to be complete.

He started after me something fierce. So much so that I feared he was either going to shake me frightfully, sneeze violently or have some sort of malaise right there on the ship's deck.

"I say thou, 'Shakes', do you know what it is to die?" Having put this frightening question to me, his whiskered cheeks blew up like twin balloons, as if they were about to launch something.

I didn't know how to respond. Even if I had, I didn't have the necessary intellectual capabilities to do so. That's because I still thought of myself as a blight upon the earth, with nothing of consequence to say to anyone, much less our estimable captain.

I guess he took my lack of a response as my solicitous and impertinent way of upsetting him. For he broached his eight-day stitch of whitened beard closer to my face and repeated his question, his thick and bedraggled, white-frazzled eyebrows moving in furrowing half-circles, confirming his disenchantment with me.

Knowing I must answer or say at least something, a multifarious list of thoughts came into my head. Still, I guess this Irishman took too long to answer, because the captain tilted his head angrily to one side, thereby exposing one scrutinizing eyeball that knew more red than any other color.

This then, I found staring down at me, not unlike someone staring down the length of a telescope shaft in the face of danger, which is to say—menacing and direct.

"We might just founder you know 'Shakes', then you'd not be so disrespectful, with your lungs half-full of water and your eyes about ready to bolt from their sockets, screaming out for unmerited mercy while bursting just so, from the never-ending pain."

At length, he looked at me for the first time, happily so; as if somehow, he had dampened whatever he had seen in me that originally he didn't like.

I sucked in my breath rapidly, before responding just as quickly out of fright, saying the first thing I could think of that might appease the man, "Founder Sir? I believe me ma and I ate it for Lent several winters past, but I can't recall having any further longing for that bone-filled and tasteless fish."

"That would be *flounder,* 'Shakes'—*flounder,* unless you're trying to prove you're a bit too smart for the captain—is that it, 'Shakes'? Are you trying to pass yourself off as smarter than the captain? Trick the captain, eh—'Shakes'...? Founder not flounder—damn it all!"

I tried my best to apologize, "I don't know the word "founder", Sir. I thought you meant the fish we had eaten for Lenten season—this many years past."

I believe the man thought I was purposely fooling him, for he exploded, his breath a trace of frosty air with shining, tiny, rivets of saliva hitting me about my face. The captain cried out, "Thou hast never tasted the unvanquished fury of God, nor in my righteous knowledge hast thou tasted his bitter vengeance."

In my innocent, *croppie*-like manner, I answered back truthfully enough (although looking back I certainly wished I hadn't), "Dear Captain Sir, if it will help you to sort these matters out; I have neither tasted God's fury nor His bitter vengeance. However, I once tasted a bowl of *stirabout* gruel which seemed to maintain a rather gristly, one week-old, sour bean flavor to it. I believe the sun's warmth did indeed turn it, Sir—the *stirabout* I mean."

Now obviously this youthful remembrance to *stirabout,* and comparing it to the Lord's solemn and apparently justifiable vengeance, as it applied to a seventeen-year old *croppie,* didn't in any shape or form help out the situation. Instead it rather—as they say—added coals to the fire, for the captain rolled up first one sleeve then the other, as if he was going to tan my hide from one end of his brig to the other.

But first he countered, his unblinking, red, saucer-like eyes not leaving my face for one second, "There we all are—two days out from Nova Scotia, and the ship can't move another inch with a block of undersea ice imbedded in our forward hull. And you, 'Shakes', you're finally on your knees begging forgiveness for this miserable and cursed life that up till now you've lived without a second thought, carrying on like a politician or a Lord tenant, never once giving a damn for the others." Captain Limerick sucked in his breath ferociously before continuing, "But all your praying and heavenly caterwauling won't help. No, it won't help thee now 'Shakes', you're as good as damned, at least until you turn to the Lord and confess yourself! For only then can a man go down with his ship to the depths below, carrying something like peace in his belly!"

In my fright, I reached out to take a hold of the companionway ladder convinced that the ship was about to sink at that moment, right under my eyes, with this crazy, preacher-like captain leading the way.

He added with a sinister grin, "If you're as good at confessing, as thou art at making a wreckage of your own life, up until now—then never mind foundering, Boy!—For I do declare—all is forgiven! I say all is forgiven! Now what say ye to this? After a good and sincere, soul-searching confession, and as a risen, new man we might just see free, the two of us, to turning south down towards Trinidad-way for a little revival and prayer-meeting! You know, to meet the devil, face to face! Well, what say ye to that? Huh—'Shakes' me-boy?"

At last, as if he had just caught himself doing something highly objectionable, he looked all around us, fearful-like, his nose and eyes barely making headway over the top of his thick pea-coat, as if he was afraid someone might be looking, or watching this strange turn of events.

Turning to me, he accused me both biblically and incoherently, "See, you've even got me doing it now. Thinking once again how you can trick me into going back to Trinidad, like the snake thou art. Why you're full of temptation—that's what you are. Now get behind me Satan...Satan?—I mean—'Shakes'—behind me...get behind me, Satan, er, 'Shakes'...I say outta the way now!" Then he started to raise an arm over me, in a most threatening manner.

We were interrupted by the captain's wife, who had her hands clasped together in front of her heaving bosom, and came between the two of us like the morning fog, relentless and clinging.

She murmured loudly into her husband's ear, "They've found a stowaway down in the hold. He's thin 'n shiverin' he is, shaking just like a leaf I'm tellin' ya, for I've seen 'im meself!"

The captain's wife must have foreseen the outcome, for she uttered the following warning, "Now don't do anything to hurt 'im Captain, he's nothing but a slip of a boy."

The captain mentioned something about quartering the boy's entrails, and letting the stern-following sharks have a go at them. Then he paused to look up at the heavens, muttering something about, "Not a crumb...not one crumb of our provisions will he get and charity be damned," before he stalked off to inspect the stowaway, and make a decision concerning the young lad and the rest of our voyage together.

The boy in question was brought before Captain Limerick. He was shoeless, wearing a green cap above his close-cropped black hair, with a great big, furled-reef cleft in the middle of his chin that could hold a marble or two, if only the boy would keep still for any length of time. At first glance he looked to me to be a black man or a Negro, for his face was indoctrinated every which way with oil and soot. He was wearing blackened, faded blue, baggy pilot trousers, the kind that mechanics often wear while they are working around machinery. There was nothing to hold the oversized trousers up but his hands, which he used in a jerking and twisting fashion. To such an extent that he could have been dancing all by himself out there on the foredeck, where he'd been hauled before the captain to answer for his palliated crime of being a stowaway.

Aye, he was a mere slip of a boy, but to escape the *An Gorta Mor* or "Great Hunger" as he called it in our Gaelic tongue, he had somehow bribed the watchman who was specifically paid to prohibit people from sneaking on board. He told the captain he didn't care, but that everyone called him, "Tom the fool". Yet, he knew the sea and boats and could fish some, if only "these blasted trousers would stay up long enough," allowing him to do so.

The captain poked his finger at him, before pointing it at the rest of us who had gathered there to watch the proceedings. This he did, finally, stabbing it in the direction of the vast ocean off the port-side bow, "Let it be as I say. Also, he is to have no food that is destined for the rest of us. It might seem like a hard line I am taking, but it cannot be avoided. We have just enough provisions for the one hundred and ten passengers making this voyage, and therefore, it cannot be helped."

The captain turned to steal a hard glance at his wife. A sure bet to this Irishman that Mrs. Limerick wouldn't mind sharing her lot with anyone in need, even if that meant "Tom the fool"—who just happened to be a stowaway.

I don't know what passed between the two of them, having no experience when it comes down to men and women communicating with one another, especially when nary a word is spoken. Still, it appeared to me as clear as if he had sung it out, right there on deck in front of everyone to hear; 'this is my brig and I'll not have a woman to meddling in its affairs—t'is clear and final!'

Only years later, after several months of married life, did I come to appreciate the maritime law of a captain's absolute and final authority. Still in all, the bounding high seas are one place for ironclad regulations while the implicit and emotional outburst of a newly-wedded wife, searching for her misplaced saucepan that I was using to mix mortar in...happens to be, quite another kettle of fish.

Our captain turned back to address Tom and the rest of us once more, "Nevertheless, if you can fish as you say you can, then trade with the others if they's a mind to doing it. On the other hand, let it be a clear warning to you and everyone else on board this brig, my brig;—anyone caught below decks with an eye towards breaking into our provisions will be keel-hauled on the spot, without so much as a second thought. That is all. Now, let's clear these decks so that the noon-sighting may be taken, and give us an idea of just where in the blazes we might be on this never-ending ocean!"

We were barely one week out of Liverpool, yet it seemed like our lives had always been this way. It would be of no particular advantage to state here in great detail, life aboard a five-hundred ton brig that was trying to avoid foundering (now that I knew it wasn't a papist fish) while crossing a conniving and manipulative ocean. This in a ship full of *croppies* and *skibbereens*, as well as the unflappable sailors or 'tars' that seemed more willing to toss you over the side of the brig and into the frigid water, then to give you the time of day.

Once I knew me ma was fed and cleaned up in the morning (although she'd taken to getting sores all around her ankles and lower thighs from her daily washings from a bucket of sea water), I'd skedaddle upwards to the cabin, the one Longfellow Mortlock shared with "Devil" McGoran. The cabin was a mere speck of a closet, holding two cots with one fastened above the other. There was as well, a small, wooden, writing surface chained to the wall so it could be stowed away to make more room, and the overhead bulkhead that wouldn't allow for my dog, "Blister" to stretch himself comfortably without hitting his head. If one of the two was sober enough, I would take a writing or reading lesson with whomever had touched less of the *poteen* the night before. Regardless of who was teaching me or explaining the current subject, a fight would inevitably break out between the two of them. This seemed to occur frequently, over some mute point that made no sense to this Irishman, such as Shylock's demand that the debt be paid and the pound of flesh excised.

"With a good, sharp, hunting knife I could take off however much I needed to, down to the last one hundredth of a gram." Having said this,

"Devil" McGoran went back to his whittling, as if what you were asking him to do was nothing more troubling than picking a rose.

Longfellow snarled back, "No one is that exact, which is the whole point of the story, and that includes you—you pompous old melon-head!"

Then Longfellow picked up the book and continued with our lesson on "The Merchant of Venice" while stroking his gigantic moustaches that seemed now to bear a striking resemblance to the ship's rusty anchor, in both color and form.

There was a rumbling below decks coming precisely from the cabin in which I now found myself. When "Devil" McGoran while scratching vigorously behind his left ear, which I had learned since coming on board to be a sure sign of trouble, told his roommate, "Belay that talk about me being a "melon-head", or you might find yourself wearing this whittling knife, as a permanent reminder that a McGoran backs down before no man."

Longfellow took to tapping his shillelagh lightly, and with exactly the same slow-measured, half-beat against the side of his leg, a sign that maybe a McGoran wasn't the only one whose honor had been trifled with.

I stepped into the icy moment by asking them both, after having fallen in love with Portia's line and what followed; "The quality of mercy is not strained.... If having served justice by allowing Shylock his pound of flesh wouldn't Portia by rights, become the very person she was condemning?"

"She's not condemning anything, Edward, but merely fulfilling the law." Longfellow stated, his teacher's eyes full of pride I suppose because of my question.

"I say run him through, what's one less Jew anyway?" "Devil" McGoran boasted.

"Today it may be "one less Jew", McGoran as you say—and tomorrow? The day after? Or, even before?—Maybe one less papist for Her Majesty and the English to worry about."

Having said this, Longfellow looked at me with a disdainful regard for his friend, as if "Devil" possessed the quantitative intelligence of one of the spawning gray whales that had been following the ship the last three or four days.

"Which is why we're on this fool's boat to begin with....The English have made Ireland their colony, and you, Irishmen their slaves—with barely a yelp from the whipped and castrated Irish—one way or t'other!" "Devil" reiterated, his blue eyes seemingly to belch forth fire.

"Speak for yourself, Mate—I am and have always been a free man." Longfellow reminded his friend, I must say calmly enough.

"You're Irish and more 'n a little daft. Why your people wouldn't stand up to the thievin' English is beyond me—t'is as simple as that." "Devil" challenged him.

"Well no-o-w, we can certainly see about "standing up for ourselves" like you say, 'ceptin' I won't be taking any flesh from around your heart...it'll be 'tween your ears where it won't be missed!" Then Longfellow stood up from his bunk, his shillelagh tapping his thigh at a much more emphatic pace.

I decided to do something, anything, before all hell broke loose between my two highly flammable teachers, in that tiny closet of a forecastle cabin.

"I'm starting up on deck, my head can't hold anymore lessons today," I told my two teachers. After which I paused, with one foot outside on the yawing companionway, and spoke back through the opening to the both of them, "As for the two of you; the quality of mercy may not be all that strained, still a good crack over your thick and stubborn heads might be just the thing to quiet the two of you down, and prevent you both from killing each other." Then I skipped up on deck to see what the other passengers were up and about.

As usual our emigrating brethren were gathered around the two open air fireplaces placed on either side of the foredeck, and as far away from the *sacred* afterdeck which was off-limits to us under pain of the stoppage of one day's ration of water. For the afterdeck was where Captain Limerick stumped about and glared at us collectively as if we were a herd of cattle, or worse, pagans without a notion of God, but what we had learned inside our rock-piled caves from the Druids, and whatever else we begrudged a peasant's mind to listen to.

The fire was contained in a large wooden case which was lined with bricks and shaped like an old fashioned settee, the coals being confined by two or three iron bars in front of each case. These fires were kept alive from morning until evening, surrounded by families making *stirabout* or morning cakes cooked upon hand-fashioned griddles.

There was Tom the stowaway, trading away some shiny, blue-scaled fish in exchange for a morning cake. The cake must have been hot to the touch for he kept shifting the cake from one hand to the other. All the time he kept blowing upon it while trying to maintain a bearing on his falling-down trousers with his one freed-up hand. It made for a comical picture; Tom scooting around the foredeck with one leg up in the air, his pants caught tight against the one raised leg so they couldn't fall down anymore until he shifted his weight. At which point things started to unravel at a heady pace, until the other leg came up forcing his pants to stay put while he shifted the hot cake to his free hand. This allowed Tom to grab quickly at his pants once more, with his newly liberated hand to save them from falling down, and the process would start all over again. Regardless of his best efforts, Tom's pants slid down little by little revealing a goodly portion of his Carpathian-colored buttocks.

One of the children whispered too loudly to his sibling that he could see Tom wasn't wearing any underwear under his britches. The mother hissed for him to mind his own business, before giving him the better part of a lively forearm that sent the *gossoon* rear end over teakettle down into the gunwales of the ship where he lay dazed for a bit. I watched him as he sat upright, thought better of it, then checked to see if his own underpants were still in place before hopping back up to make his way next to his siblings, and a long stretch away from his mother and her decisive forearm.

Some of the younger married adults bore up rather nicely, their arms encircling one another while they talked about their new home and what it would be like. This would go on until the ship settled rather dramatically into the pocket of a vagrant swell, only to be lifted up free and clear in an instant, and the liberated seawater suddenly splashing over the sides like a violent tropical rainfall. The seawater wet the young lovers, causing them to hold on to one another more tightly than before. This of course, seemed to be from my vantage point, a most welcome incursion into the monotony of our life aboard the *Sylph*. As I believe I may have mentioned earlier, the dynamics of people engaged in the art of romantic love has always intrigued me. Indeed, no more so then when there is nothing much else to watch or wonder about, leaving my mind free to wander about unhindered. I often wondered, as is my personality to do so, how would the new world receive us? These young couples so full of hope and courage, our small family the Ruth's, Longfellow Mortlock, "Devil" McGoran; could we make it over there, and with something more than just a blighted and soggy potato or a blackened eye to show for our efforts. Aye, in lying back on my makeshift cot at night I would say my prayers as I'd been taught for all of us. Asking for heavenly guidance in our new lives, with an eye towards Katherine Louisa Maddox, and what I would do or say, should I catch up with her one day in the captivating land they called The United States of America.

We were up on the *Sylph's* deck. I know it was a Tuesday, for I had just spent the better half of the morning writing and rewriting this enchanting day of the week, and receiving several *love taps* about my ears from "Devil" for my supposedly lackluster efforts. Or, was it "Devil's" ill-perceived conception that somehow, lately, I had been siding more often than not with Longfellow, who didn't hit me as frequently. And therefore, this was his chance to right some unaccounted for wrong on my part. In any case, I told my tutor I would go up on deck until the ringing in my ears had eased somewhat, and I could once again think in a correct and lucid manner.

The passengers on deck were caught up in the collective game of mockery with the stowaway nicknamed "Tom the fool". This seemed to occur on a daily basis right after the noon time meal when we had nothing better to do than to make fun of one of God's own. As if Tom didn't have enough problems of his own making, notably his limited intelligence, that we shouldn't use him for our uncharitable enjoyment as well. There he was skipping around the deck, with as usual one hand on his oversized pant's leg, to keep his trousers from falling down. When someone stole up beside Tom and captured his green hat which the thief then sent sailing away, over the railing and into the ocean. Tom started after his hat as soon as he realized it was no longer on the top of his head. The sight was both comical and pitiable at the same time. Tom let go of everything which meant of course, his trousers fell down to pile up somewhere around his ankles. At length, with his hands on his knees, Tom watched the futile sail of his hat into the Atlantic sea-chop. There stood poor old Tom, as naked as an empty cupboard, crouching down with a look of imbued complexity on his face. The crowd around him jeered and hooted, as full of toothless, facial expressions as one might find amongst a group of village idiots, at a funeral for one of their own kind.

Someone hollered out, "Pull up your pants Tom,—'fore you catch your death of a chill."

A sailor added his own thoughts on the same subject, "Aye, belay your britches there young *salt*, afore someone's liable to attach a line to you, and try to hoist away something that bulky and white!"

In the meantime, someone else sneaked up from behind him, and attached a rope to the bottom of Tom's jacket to make it look like a tail. This of course was what we had all been waiting for.

Once Tom had decided his hat was gone for good, he straightened himself up, and took to hopping up and down the length of the ship. He continued, looking out to sea, his one free hand straddling the gunwale while the other held up his pants. All the while, his roped-tail danced and jerked behind him, giving Tom a monkey or chimpanzee-like appearance which of course made us all laugh and do double-takes, as he bounced about the ship's deck.

Captain Limerick's wife was behind me watching this irreverent scene, and for awhile disappeared close by, to where she berthed with the captain. When she reappeared on deck, she was holding a red and white striped night cap which she proudly presented to Tom. This Tom took and straight away put on his head. Then as if he could no longer contain himself, he took to strutting about the deck in an ever-widening circle and showing off. He used his free hand, pointing often to his new, red and white-striped, night cap as if we hadn't noticed it, or seen what had been taking place. This of course highly amused those of us on deck, and probably would have continued long into the evening had not my brother grabbed me by the arm, and urged me to come and see our mother. I followed, half wondering if Tom with some verbal encouragement, couldn't be enticed to scale the main mast, thus imitating an ape in his natural environment. It goes without saying that the other passengers and I, indeed, would have enjoyed a laugh and funnier moments while waiting for our supper.

I guess it was her time to go, lucky for her. There wasn't much left of our mother underneath those filthy sheets. Her face was shrunken and not like her at all. It seemed as if someone had finally taken out of her mouth the rest of her teeth, for her cheeks were hollow and sunk back into the cavity of her mouth on both sides, like rotted railroad struts. Paul Francis Daniel said he'd found her that way, but thought that maybe she was asleep. We both knew she wasn't. We remarked how her hair had turned all white now, but that her eyebrows had mysteriously remained a darkened grey. She lay there, her legs tucked up underneath, bent or pulled back together, facing her chest. I guess my brother had closed her eyes for I hadn't. Someone I'd known and loved, and who had nourished me and protected me and told me what life might be about. Aye, it appeared to this Irishman as if someone had knocked the wind out of her. That someone had misplaced her broken spirit, mistakenly confiding it with *the little people* somewhere, so that it couldn't come back, wouldn't know how to come back, before finally deciding the old lady had had enough and she needn't come back. The lines around her mouth and on her forehead bespoke of a lifetime of trials and injustices. They were like sketchy hand-drawn maps of the highlands, encircling inconspicuous plots of land without any logic or linear form, and from following them one could tell she hadn't had an easy time of things.

I had been baptized into the one true religion, still I couldn't push the doubts from my mind that somehow we'd all been tricked, cajoled, manipulated. Indeed, besides the daily struggle to eat, the burning desire to try and keep body and soul together, the thought kept coming back to me; *what if God was an Englishman and didn't enjoy being merciful?* That being the shame of it all, they'd *stuck it* to *the children of the Gael* one more time—even in death. But no, reason took the better part of me and calmed me down. God was no Englishman, for just like someone with typhus or cholera—who would want to be one unless it was forced upon you? I reasoned, God probably hated them just like we did, probably more so. They'd been given their chance, and like a daft Curragh buck had made a bad go of it. Aye, kicking and stomping things so badly no one would know Ireland anymore, except as a place which specialized in blatant misery, unless one were English. Yes, that seemed to be about the size of it...unless one were English or in cahoots with the devil—why not? They'd spelled out disdain for anything Irish, and shoved it down our *croppie* throats from the word 'go'.

In any case, our ma was gone now, and more irrational thinking than I'd care to admit came storming up inside of me.

To make matters worse, my foolish brother dared to ask the obvious, "She didn't die alone—did she?" The look on his face was more irreverent and frantic than anything else.

I shot back, "Well, neither you or I, nor our sisters were with her at the end, wishing her a speedy and safe journey as far as I can see."

He pretended not to hear, "It's no good I'm telling you, she'll be around for forty days or more wailing like the banshees—that's what *the little people* say."

I especially hated it when my brother would bring up *the little people* and what they purportedly practiced or preached. I told him so as well. "Listen now, Paul Francis Daniel, ma's gone and they'll be no talk of *the little people*, d'ya hear me on this?"

But he wouldn't be shaken from proclaiming his blind epitaph, "She'll be around for forty days, wailing and grinding so, caught between the two worlds, you just wait and see."

"Wait and see—nothing—I'm going to tell the captain."

"Go on and do your duty, Edward. That won't stop the banshees from howling their insane cries, nor our mother trying to leave this place—. Don't you understand, damn it all, she died alone! Neither you or I were there to say goodbye, to make the final benediction—hear her final request—she'll be traveling about—a half and incomplete spirit just like the rest of them. And what's more there'll be hell to pay on the other side for her—because of it."

"I don't know what you're talking about." I told my brother.

"Aye, I think you do—and it's even sadder to say, had you not been spending so much time with the two town drunks learning to read and write, you might have been here at the end for ma."

"So that's how it goes?" I surmised quickly not hiding the bitterness I felt.

He went at me again, "You know as well as I if the spirit isn't liberated right away then it goes around and about, fearful-like, in torment, without any direction, like a cat that's lost its tail—searching and crying its awful laments, for forty days and nights in purgatory while it waits."

"Waits for what?" This time I asked trying to hide my interest.

Paul Francis Daniel crouched next to me as if he wanted to whisper to me. This I found rather ludicrous since we were alone below decks, the two of us anyway.

Still, the way he cautiously explained his fear, it was as if the room was already full of the spirit-world fighting over our dear mother's soul, "The forty days is a test, that she has to pass—she must pass, a test like the Christ-man had to endure in the desert alone for forty days. She'll be tempted alright."

Suddenly, his eyes got round and bright. The meager outside light seemed to play against his face, making the high circular spots of his chin and cheeks into shadows, dark and foreboding it was, turning his entire countenance into a ghoulish one. A face I could barely recognize as belonging to my brother.

He continued, "If she can't find her way out, or doesn't resist their temptations, then she'll be lost for all time—caught in the nether world, never knowing paradise and its rewards."

"That's what *the little people* say?" I replied disgustedly.

"That's what *the little people* say." My brother confirmed to me, ignoring my disbelief as he raised the sheet to cover our mother's lifeless face.

I didn't say another word. Instead, I left my brother and my mother's corpse to find Captain Limerick, convinced more than ever that if God wasn't an Englishman, He'd at least been horribly duped by the sitting members of the London parliament.

I found Captain Limerick, hatless, wearing a dirty, tidewater-green sweater which reeked of something akin to *poteen* in his cabin. The man was going over figures covering a piece of paper, and grumbling something about feeding us all *Portuguese men of war* should it eventually come down to that. The painted burnt-orange door was open, but I knocked anyway and hoped for the best.

He turned a vacant, red eye towards me, vexed I suppose, for this unannounced interruption. Then, apparently recognizing who I was, the captain absentmindedly let fly the pencil he'd been using, to where it fell down on the slatted wooden floor.

This he did before cornering me almost suspiciously in the way he asked, "What'll it be 'Shakes', has you changed your mind about helping me to work this ship down towards Trinidad-way, after we finish our run to New York?" He followed this by laughing to himself sordidly.

In answering for me, as if he was calculating for the both of us, he went on in a most effusive manner, "I'm guessing we'll have to unload at a rabbit's pace in New York, in order to make the trade winds—. Could be a fortnight or more, but we could make it, yes by golly, we could at that!"

He stopped suddenly in mid-sentence, issuing a furtive glance around the room as if someone he'd just as soon avoid might be within listening distance, overhearing the captain's newly-conceived plans. His ominous, glutinous, red eyes continued to search the room, looking from top to bottom, then back at me, as if to try and determine where reality stopped, and his dreams, of even I couldn't begin to guess at, started.

I looked at his arms and marveled that something so skinny could come from such robust shoulders. His whiskers maintained their propensity for being less than a week old while his purplish face and sagging mouth seemed all bunched together, even painfully so while he continued to touch his lips, like a man visibly athirst.

"No Sir, I mean Captain—I haven't changed my mind. I still cannot go with you to Trinidad, although it certainly sounds like a remarkable place."

Then out of fortuitous pity I asked, "—Uh, Captain, do they have potatoes there, in Trinidad?"

Captain Limerick's voice turned to a half-muffled shriek while he pulled nervously at his sweater. It appeared to this Irishman, the man was suddenly boiling hot inside of it. At the same time he answered me, "Potatoes? 'Shakes', potatoes? Why the only thing found growing on Trinidad soil is 'cane', 'Shakes', acres and acres of sugarcane. Now, why would you want to grow anything else over there, 'Shakes'? You got something against those fine people—the Creoles?"

The eye glaring at me, doubled up in size before seemingly to leap out of its precarious socket. The captain looked overly worked up, suddenly, about what I had just finished asking. "The Creoles have a hard enough time as it is just harvesting the 'cane! You go in, and throw something else in their soil for them to worry 'bout—. Well, they's about to lay down and die from being overworked. No, 'Shakes', you just let those good Creole folks alone—you understand? They's got to concentrate on the task at hand. They's a-busy enough, just harvesting the 'cane' and boiling it up just so; to make a batch of that delicious blue devil rum—.That's right Boy, that's just what they call it too—*blue devil rum*! I'm telling you 'Shakes', it just about puts a man right up on that mountaintop over yonder, discussing all them kingdoms of the world and other such delicate matters, why it surely does!"

I had no idea what the man was talking about. Although it was obvious to me, Captain Limerick must be highly educated, for he knew all about the Creoles and what they could or couldn't plant. Despite his high degree of education, I tried to avoid looking at the splash of white-whiskered gravy running down the front of his dirty, tidewater-green sweater.

Captain Limerick went off, murmuring to himself as if he was praying. All this time, he kept pushing his lips together. Just like a landed sea bass does after it's been gaffed; stretched out and flopping on the open deck, smacking its lips in against themselves, in between gasping for air needlessly, as if something wasn't quite right.

I could only stare impulsively as Mrs. Limerick halted outside the cabin. The woman looked at her husband punitively. Then she entered, changing her face to a soft sadness when she noticed me standing attentively, just inside the painted, burnt-orange doorway.

"What's this all about, Mervin—I mean, Captain Limerick?" She halted rather abruptly, right there in her footsteps, "And your sweater Sir, it smells as if it's been below decks these many weeks! And what is this young man doing here in the captain's cabin, what does he need? Mr.?—Mr.?"

I interrupted her, "'Shakes', Ma'am. My real name is Edward Ruth, but the captain likes to call me "Shakes"."

Mrs. Limerick put her doubled-up fists on her roundabout hips and glared at her husband.

She concluded, "I'm sure this man has a Christian name—in fact he just told you he has—"Edward"—why don't you use it? Is it so distasteful to you, Captain—by all that's holy! But that you've got to call this young man by a vulgar, non-baptized, roustabout nick-name."

"Now, Allyson my dear, don't start now." This the Captain said just above a whisper. No, make that more of a distinct-enough, slurring whisper.

"So t'is "Shakes" with you is it? Well, we wouldn't be calling in the fall harvest too soon now, would we, Captain? "Shakes" is it? My word!" Then she added disdainfully, changing the subject while sniffing the cabin's guilt-laden air, "Why I never! I know what it is—what you're up to! There's a bottle around here somewhere, and I mean to find it! I thought you were over that—healed in fact—been "saved again", you told me—promised me even! Oh, how true it is when it is written: "the wages of sin is death!" She remarked to the two of us with enough grit to turn us both into quaking school boys once again. Turning to me she added, "Don't be surprised, if at some point he approaches you, and asks you to be a deckhand when he puts this boat around heading south again to "convert the natives", as he likes to put it." "Convert the natives", she huffed out, "Don't be taken in, Edward with such ridiculous talk, for it's the devil's own backyard he's leading you to—! Why there's enough voodoo and heaven knows what else being practiced on that little slip of an island, to make the waterfront of Liverpool look like a mercy-mission by comparison!"

Then the captain's wife proceeded to turn things over in the cabin, although only half-heartedly so, as if she knew better. That if Captain Mervin Limerick had indeed been drinking, he was far too smart, sober or drunk to leave the bottle where it could be found.

"Now, now—Allyson, 'Shakes' er—I mean Mr. Ruth and I were just discussing in biblical terms (the way the captain pronounced biblical it came out 'bibli-coo-cool'), what it would be to refuse the devil, his own putrid tale of the kingdoms of this world and their false promises." The captain suddenly brightened up, as if he had just stumbled upon a vein of pure gold, "Yes, yes that's it exactly! Why we were just talking about Lucifer and his false promise of worship, against all the kingdoms of the world—and what we must do as devout believers to avoid—"

His wife jumped in at that point, abruptly cutting her husband off, which I had to admit had been up until then, a pretty slick *end around* as the *Yankees* might put it.

"And I don't suppose this kingdom, way up high on a mountaintop involving the sale of your truant soul, didn't have a sumptuous view of a certain island named Trindad, *n'est-ce pas,* Captain Limerick?"

Even I grimaced when she announced that.

"Trinidad?" Questioned the Captain, as if it was the first instance he'd ever heard of such a place.

Again, out came the "My word!" Taking her calculated time, Mrs. Limerick started to walk about the cabin, picking things up and mimicking her husband's "Trinidad?" "Trinidad?" As if she was a parrot, and that was all she could cull into her seed-sapping head.

Now all of a sudden, the cabin was becoming too small for the three of us; what with the captain struggling to stand up against his desk, and his wife wriggling her way past me, rowboat-hips and all. Then again; not only not arranging his personal effects any longer, but just pretending to pick things up while she looked hard and fast for a bottle, I presumed everyone in that airless cabin knew to be there, somewhere.

As if I suddenly remembered why I was there in the first place, I rubbed the cold from the tip of my nose and instinctively scratched my left arm. This I did prior to announcing in my most formal voice, "Captain Sir, I'm here to inform you of the passing away of my mother, this day, Sir. May she rest in peace."

The captain staggered blindly to his feet, like a fool, his arms outstretched at ninety-degree angles from his upper chest for assistance. He looked to his wife, his face and whitened hair askew. He appeared to me both fragile and fearful as if that were possible.

Pointing his fist upward at the ceiling of his cabin, and with a solicitous regard to his wife that said 'I told you so', he started in, "The Lord giveth and the Lord taketh away. What are we, but clumps of lay?—I mean lumps of clay—.Thus does the lay, er—clay say to its maker, 'I am only your servant, do to me as you wish-h-h'."

Having finished his appropriate remarks, the captain looked extremely satisfied with himself, for a second or two before emitting a giant hiccup.

Mrs. Limerick started to say something, thought better of it, then told her husband, "Come on Captain, let's sober you up. At the very least, we must give her a decent Christian burial with all hands."

He turned to look at his wife, his drunken face framed in the doorway, "Aye, a bit of cold water splashed about me ears, might just be the thing now. Wouldn't it be—just the thing—Allyson, my love."

At last, as if remembering that I was still there, Captain Limerick's face took on the downward countenance of a grieving clown as he remarked, "Listen-closely 'Shakes', I've had a bit of medical experience amongst other things on board this brig of mine. Let me get down my medical kit, including a good portion of laudanum, and let's take a second look at that mother of yours—you'll see—she'll be as right as rain by tomorrow morning, or my name isn't Mervin Limerick!"

We buried our ma, shoveling her over the side of the *Sylph* when we were but twenty-one days out of Liverpool and nine more days from New York, the tardiness being due to foul weather. When she hit the water she barely made a splash. My brother, Paul Francis Daniel wouldn't speak to me after her funeral for the remainder of the voyage. He stayed down below decks, and would only come up to restore himself when "Tom the fool" gave the clear signal there were no banshees up and about.

PART THREE

New York City-1852

Chapter Eleven

I revel through the haunting Past,
'Mid bowers so sere and olden.
The poets' pen lights up the scene,
And makes all fair and golden,

Far down the path by pen illumed
I tread in silent wonder.
And seem to hear, boom after boom,
The sound of martial thunder.

Author unknown

I am not nor have I ever been what one would call a talkative fellow. In fact, I seem to be caught up in having the reputation of being what some folks would call a 'dull spineless sort of chap', for my perceived inability to express my sententious and therefore attenuated thoughts. I do not hide from the fact that at certain times I am truly tongue-tied, with an acute embarrassment, due in no small way that while I feel I know what to say, at the same time am truly at a loss as to how to say it. That being the case, and with all due respect to you the reader, I will maintain what others have attributed to me as my personal case in point...that of a man who has little or nothing to say.

Still, I find it imperative to set these thoughts down, if for no other reason than history should be read correctly, and what is even more important *told* correctly. So that future generations should become enlightened by our failures. And not come to believe that chasing one another up and down beautiful, fertile, green valleys and across recently scorched fields pointing iron-belching rifles at one another, with every intent to remove some part of our enemy's anatomy or *hide* as it is expressed hereabouts, or belittling our fellow man to the point of enslaving him, is something to be aspired to. If that can be accomplished, then future generations should by all rights, avoid the snares and pitfalls that came to those of us who lived through the war of Northern aggression. This is why I have chosen to continue this unembellished tale of mine. If for no other reason, than to alert the Bailey Burkes or Philip Sheridans of this world that their postulating lack of compassion or myopic selfishness will no longer be tolerated.

I have every confidence in man's ability to correctly embrace the future, based on his experiences in the not so glorious and perhaps even tainted past. Which is why I find myself, happily entrusting these pitiful notes to the next generation of men and women, who couldn't possibly fall into the same trap that we did in my adopted country and given time frame of 1861. In our stupidity we continued, until countless deaths and perhaps even more to the tragic point; the unaccounted and hellish toll of the wounded for life, amputees, and families destroyed as a result. Or at the very least, set unhappily awry because of the narrow-minded clowns in the Northern government, calling the shots while enforcing their altogether misconceived doctrines.

I find myself thinking that I would rather be dead and buried up to my britches in mud, and in an unmarked grave alone in a marshy field somewhere, than to be sitting around my farm without my arms or the use of a leg while my wife does the work of her husband. Even if she isn't bitter about it which in most cases doesn't hold up. For although it might not show up right away, the bitterness comes in like a patch of weeds. That's how I see it anyway, just a few at a time, until all of a sudden the whole bloody ground is full of them. In the meantime, the real edible plants are choking, and she's decided to run off with another man, a whole man—someone mind you, who can do his share of the work. Someone she doesn't have to pity to love. And believe you me, I saw it happen that way to more than a few of my wounded mates. Yes, the Federal government didn't mind calling the shots, as if they had every God-given right to make a mess of things (which unfortunately, they believed they had every right). Furthermore, when all the fighting and warmongering was over, these same Northern clowns told everyone that we voted for them to do it. Not to fight themselves mind you, but just to tell others how to do it. Indeed, while they spent their time before the hearth, sipping mellowed, amber-colored whisky, slapping each other on their pompous backsides while proclaiming to one another in sagacious tones, the indignity of it all. Furthermore, I have read more than several newspapers, in which it was written in plain black and white newsprint that when pressed about it, these same politicians couldn't seem to recall what the indignity was all about in the first place. Other than the fact they were about to run out of their amber-colored whisky, if the South instigated their own coastal blockade like they were threatening to do....Now, running out of whisky (amber-colored or otherwise) *that* they pontificated was some kind of indignity, they wouldn't or couldn't allow. Without which, they maintained, they couldn't send anyone out to war, and then where would we all be?

This is why I chose to fight for the Confederate states when all was said and done. You see, the potato famine had left its indelible mark on me. They were the boys fighting for "Home Rule". The Northerners were just the bullying English trying to take over once again while making everyone's life miserable in the process. Except this time, and as far as this Irishman's concerned, we were able to take a shot back at the *English* (the Yankees)—and believe you me, I didn't miss too many either.

The thing that set my duff afire was the fact it was the same woeful situation we'd faced in Ireland. What with those cantankerous English, calling treason down against anyone, who dared to cry out for "Home Rule". At the same time, their "Yankee" cousins in America, wouldn't take no for an answer when it was explained to them on more than one occasion that slavery would be phased out. It was repeatedly argued to the emancipationists; to change the South's economic system would take time, and couldn't be done overnight like the Northerners wanted. Indeed, the whole Southern economic system would come crashing down around us, if we eliminated slavery right there on the spot like they wanted us to. Thereby, leaving everyone and everything in disarray, and in much the same situation we'd known back home in Ireland. In truth, we must be quite honest about this. It was a fact of modern nineteenth-century life in the United States; everyone knew it was just a matter of time before the South abolished slavery. But the Northern states wouldn't give the South any more time. Boy, talk about a basket full of *womperdeen* and jumping catfish.

Still, Lincoln and Sheridan were nice enough to send everyone off to war with new water canteens and boots on their feet. Also, with the promise of a shiny medal if they lost an arm or two while meddling in the Confederacy's affairs, as if they had every right to do so. So you can see, besides the medals and so forth, as if that wasn't enough to satisfy these very same men in power's lust for blood, the clincher being, the Northern clowns were voted in for everyone's collective state of health as well. As if economic famine and geo-political destitution were something to be aspired to. You've got to be kidding me! Now it has been my unfortunate, as well as eye-opening experience that these same clowns, who avail themselves of the great resources of this country, do so in order to advance some Paleolithic longing. This longing which they embrace, that may or may not have anything to do with what the fighting was supposed to be about in the first place. Rather, it is an excuse for selling arms to one another to blast someone's maverick neighbor to kingdom-come. Perhaps, even for a certain financial benefit for themselves as well. Aye, that doesn't much disturb them. And why should it? For they have been educated to think that way. Still in all, when I consider it, and cast about for reasons justifying such barbarity, I am completely convinced no future generation would be so stupid as not to recognize unchecked selfishness, clothed in abolitionist self-righteousness when it appears.

One has to wonder if there isn't a select group of men somewhere, who harbor in their inner thoughts, only to verbalize it boldly at their secretly-held meetings that since the rest of the world cannot think for itself, they have taken it upon themselves do it for the rest of the world, and at a fraction of the cost as well. These so-called liberated men or clowns at the top of things, or Free-Masons if you will, have decided the clock isn't just ticking in their favor anymore. But rather, they have engineered things to the point where there are now twenty-six hours in a day without telling anyone else of their plans. This they promulgate, as if the rest of us were too stupid to realize it—which is just the way these so called Masons or boys at the top like to think. They have decided to run things their way. In doing so, if the prevailing situation gets a little out of hand; well, there's an old boy's network in place, with roots deep enough to protect one another should things come down to that. You can call it what you will, but my gut feeling is there were a lot more of these good ol' boys, wearing Free-Mason smocks, looking to make a dollar out of the war, than trying to free the Negro man.

I've been told, these so called Free-Masons have been around forever. When I start to analyze it, yes, it makes sense that these men, have indeed, been around forever. For the sheep, decidedly, need someone to tell them what to believe and what to do with their time. How to interpret degrading immorality as evolution, all based on the august assumption that the sheep do not know what is good for them in the first place. Other than to shoot at one another when given half the chance. I've also been led to believe these Free-Masons were active in feeding this war to the American public. Now hold on, I'm not pretending to know everything about their secret rites and what goes on behind closed doors. However, based on the misery handed down to so many while a privileged few remained above it all, enjoying the hell out of their amber-colored whisky, one has to wonder when midnight will become ten o'clock in the evening, ten o'clock become eight in the evening and so on and so forth, until they get to their inimitable twenty-six hours in a day.

Luckily for us, we had Jefferson Davis and John Hunt Morgan to lead the way. Our President Davis had as little to do with the Free-Masons as vinegar does to honey, regardless of what those Northern degenerates purportedly said. They were both Southern gentlemen. Thus, in spite of what was formally written down by the federalist Northerners in their *skibereen* history books after the war was over, I would have followed Jefferson Davis and John Hunt Morgan to the death. If for no other reason, than they both went about fighting "Home Rule" like a couple of caged lions. Although this time, instead of a bitter London accent to it, this current version of "Home Rule", had all the taste of a draught-out and improperly-cured "Yankee" brew.

We arrived in New York City amidst tramp steamers and other "coffin ships" like ourselves. Upon debarking, we were immediately paralyzed by the vastness of this great American city. You could see it everywhere. This vastness was in the streets and in the shops, on the bridges and in the train stations, but it was mostly on their faces, and these faces belonged to the immigrants. It wasn't just the property of the Irish. You could see it on the faces of the Italians, the French, the Germans, on anyone who had arrived from the old world, and now were faced with a new life, with new parameters that their respective cultures hadn't allowed for—like I mentioned earlier a cultural vastness. A vastness that quickly became wild-eyed fright when the realization hit everyone, the old ways were vanishing, and if that was the case what was to happen to us, our being Irish, our being Italian...our German, our French ways? What were we to become? A vastness that bespoke of mopping floors and cleaning out toilets and offices with a certain immigrant laborer's dignity, trying to keep the family together until one day they came to mop you away. It was everywhere. We immigrants were alone now in our new country's vastness. One man's profit was another man's loss as we all scrambled to be on top of the heap, or at least not to suffocate too much from our place somewhere in the bottom of the pile. Each one wore it the best way he could, but you could still see it alright, one just had to look hard enough. Things were not the same as they'd been back in the mother country—no, not by a long shot.

My brother noticed it first. We were walking on some dirt-rutted street down by the East side, looking for half-spoiled and thus cheap food the shopkeepers set outside on trays for the likes of us, when he mentioned to me, "You know, 'Shakes' (yes, even my brother had adopted my new nickname), these people all have that rent-day look. When they know the rent's due, but they also realize they can't pay it—so they have to hide."

"Aye, I guess so, but how can so many of them have it, all at the same time as well?" I answered back.

He spoke like someone who knew; first pushing back his unmanageable crop of bushy, red hair that had taken on the strange resemblance to one of New York's towering buildings, in that it rose straight up in front of his face like a red, shimmering, brick wall.

"It's fear," he told me. "The fear of not making your ends meet, and therefore, the resounding shame in front of everyone, including the

Americans—that you don't have what it takes to make it in their country—. The fact is; since you can't make it, you don't belong here and then what? You keep on running. You keep on running, even though, it's constantly so close behind you that one day it will finally catch up to you. Then this fear you've been running from or trying to forget will have finally cornered you. Afterwards, it's all over. It'll be time to tally up the points to find out just how lopsided the final score really is. And I'm betting the score ain't exactly in your favor either. Are you so stupid you didn't see the same look on ma's face?"

He punched me lightly as soon as I asked it, "When she was alive or when she had died?" I was too excited with our new surroundings to care much for my brother's grubby insightfulness.

Still in all, I suppose my brother was right. There was anguish written all over these immigrants' faces (ours too, I suppose), like they would have wanted to run away alright, but to where and from whom? In any case, they were all running just the same, so it didn't really matter. It was just a question of when the white sheet would be pulled up over their anguished faces—for them, signaling their running was over. It was just sad in the sense...their inert running didn't seem to be taking them anywhere of consequence.

We had spent the better part of four days making our way from one section of the city to another. We stayed together the four of us; my brother and I as well as Longfellow Mortlock and "Devil" McGoran.

The last three nights we had slept down by a river. We tried to fish but couldn't catch anything. The days we spent crawling the streets while at the same time, trying to make some sense of it all...our new home that is. We took some delight in that based on my maritime schooling aboard the *Sylph,* I could now read the signs that said "No Irish need apply". I was thrilled with my success while my teachers were not. We were somewhere on the fourth day in America.

"Would you look at that?" Longfellow asked out loud.

"Look at what?" I answered back.

"*No Irish need apply.* We're not wanted on either side of the Atlantic.—If that don't beat all."

The way Longfellow Mortlock phrased what he was saying, it came out like he was one of those Shakespearean actors he pretended to be while reading the "Merchant of Venice" to us, back on board the *Sylph*. Insofar that his face got all twisted to one side, and his mouth became so small he could barely utter the words, so they seemed to come out like puffs of smoke from a pipe. Until then I had never seen him so disgusted. Except possibly for the time, the rather wide-hipped Scottish woman, in the Liverpool quarantine house, threatened him with her boiling hot tea kettle. This she did, for making supposedly improper advances upon her person, when he had inquired of her innocently enough, whether the highland air had made her skin that pink and glowing.

"I say we go and see the Irishman who greeted us off the boat. The one who told us he knew of good safe lodging for the four of us, with other Irish people living there as well." I said it, knowing they would remember the same man.

"And what?—Be crowded into a stinkin' dwelling that would make Dublin's stables a just reward in the afterlife?" Longfellow reflected accurately on his experience from a previous trip to the United States.

In fact, he had threatened just about everyone, including the fellow Irishman who had solicited us when the ship first docked that we could take care of one another, without their greedy help. And if anyone insisted otherwise, then he'd meet the thicker part of Longfellow's long wooden shillelagh to help him change his mind. In the meantime, Longfellow had specifically warned my brother and I to be on the lookout, for a group of unscrupulous Irishmen that he called "runners". For these "runners" enjoyed the reputation of luring the unsuspecting, debarking immigrants into lodgings that as he had already stated, "Made the Dublin stables—a just reward in the afterlife." Which is why I suppose, we had been crawling New York City for the last four days. There was something—I'm convinced—that Longfellow Mortlock wanted us to see or somehow feel for ourselves, before we went any further. As far as this Irishman's concerned, the more's the pity there wasn't a head of barley foam on all this urban vastness, for we could have blown it off, drank our fill, and still had some left over for the morrow.

We were sitting underneath a tree by some fast-flowing river. There was a makeshift fishing pole crammed down hard between two solid granite rocks. We were sharing a bitter brown beer between the four of us, as well as some bread and grey cheese that had non-uniform holes about it, when "Devil" suddenly announced to no one in particular, his bearded face mired down in peevish longing, "I'm going back to look for her."

Longfellow answered the Scotsman rapidly. For not only did he understand what he was saying, Longfellow also, was the only who could say it to "Devil" without getting his teeth busted loose for saying it, "You'll find her alright under the same old tree, stitching wampum belts and talking to a bear which may or may not be her fifth husband."

I glanced at my brother wondering who would explode first.

At length, and to our surprise, "Devil" McGoran said something which caused us all to laugh. Indeed, the Scotsman told us, "It may or may not be her fifth husband, but if he's got more fleas than I do, I'll just ask him to move over a place or two, so's I can sit down—fleas n'all, and reintroduce myself."

Longfellow retorted, "You won't need to reintroduce yourself my friend.

Your skinned-out buck smell will be all she'll need to place you in that Mohawk memory of hers."

I fished out of my pocket a tomato that still held together, and announced my plans for getting to Kentucky where my sisters were.

Longfellow pushed at his giant moustache handles. I remarked to myself; his moustaches didn't move much like normal hair, but more or less stayed in place like they were frozen solid.

Longfellow interrupted my thoughts by asking gravely, "And what'll you do there, 'Shakes'?"

I told him I hadn't given much thought to it, but it sure would be grand to see my sisters again.

"You'll get to see them one day, 'Shakes'."

The way he stated it, so much as a matter of fact, it definitely sounded like he had other plans for us.

Then my brother added his two bits, "I'd like to stay in New York for awhile, and see how the *Spalpeens* do things around here."

At which point, I added that I didn't mind staying in New York if we could have a bite or two of real food to eat in the meantime. Although, I was still keen on getting to Kentucky and my sister, Ann Horian's soda bread. Maybe if they could ship some of her bread to me from this place called Kentucky, I could hold out a while longer here in New York City. I don't honestly recall at what point my brain had slipped down to where my stomach was, but it definitely had. Thus, most of my thoughts were now being generated around belt level and gurgling at the same time as well.

At length, Longfellow explained in a firm but subdued voice, he knew of a place that helped people like us, especially, if we were what they called, 'good loyal fellows'.

I stammered back accusingly, "Well, why didn't you say so when we first got off the ship? Instead of showing us the cussed backside of New York City for the last four days. Hell, let's get over there now—I'm just about starving to death!"

Longfellow smiled that smile of his which more often than not rankled me, like he was too sure of himself, and consequently, whatever he had in mind we'd have to abide by without so much as an explanation. It suddenly dawned on me, that in fact, Katherine Louisa Maddox had been the same way; knowing in which direction she was headed and sure enough bloody stubborn-minded about it as well. Thus, what I had found admirable about that colleen, now rankled me with Longfellow, like I was a common cabin boy expected to follow orders. At first I thought about taking a stand with him, then thought better of it, when my stomach reminded me I was still famished way beyond my limits.

Following Longfellow's lead, we made our way to the corner of Nassau and Frankfort streets, to a place he called "The Hall" (later on we found out its true name: Tammany Hall). It was a non-descript building; square, painted grey with flecks of white imbedded in the walls, and corpulent like a hen guarding her eggs. Once inside however, we saw people swirling about like I'd never seen before. There were desks dolled out in a straight line, with people, in all manner of appearance, milling about these very same desks yapping about a mile a minute answering questions. Some I happily noticed were dressed as shabbily as ourselves. There was the aroma of stocking-strained, weak-brewed tea springing up from some far-flung corner of the room. It was just heady enough to make my insides jump from longing, and then just as quickly set me to dry, silent retching, as if I couldn't control my excitement any longer.

We were introduced to a man named John Morrisey. He was a beefy sort of fellow, who sported a sprig of yellow hair just aft of his lips and above his chin, like he'd shaved everywhere, but had forgotten that spot for several days on purpose. He was wearing Sunday-visiting clothes, with a bright mustard-colored vest that set off his green-checkered suit like the sunrise on Easter morning.

"Just off the boat, ya' say?" This John Morrisey intoned like he already knew the answer, based on our miserable *croppie* appearance.

Abruptly, he gave us a look that asked us to be patient for just one minute. This he did before turning to a much smaller man that I hadn't noticed at first. The smaller man spoke a language apart. To such an extent, that at first I imagined I was looking straight down at my first American Indian. Except for the fact, he was white of skin and owned a peculiarly horrific smell about his person.

Morrisey demanded of the smaller man rather coldly, "*Vous parlez Anglais, oui ou non?*"

The smaller man with a braided queue which stretched to half-way down his back just shook his head.

Once again, this John Morrisey fellow turned to us, as if he might need our collective advice about this irritating situation.

However, instead of saying anything directly to us, he half-muttered to himself, showing gapped teeth that surely must have known a brawl or two, "These Frenchmen,—the dirtiest sort of *wogs* I've ever seen. Besides that, if you help one then you'll soon have the whole *wogging* family down here, asking for help. What with their garlic-smelling, snot-driveling women claiming half their family is in Ireland as missionary priests or nuns. Hell, the only time they get excited, or even close to acting like they believe in something, is when they lop off the heads of one of their royalty!"

He pointed a fist that looked a lot like a battering ram at the puzzled Frenchman, before drawling out, "The-people-here-are-Irish. Irish—you-understand? That's-what-we-do; we-take-care-of-Erin's-own. Go-to-the-French quarters—there-you-can-find-help. *Comprenez-vous?"*

Possibly not understanding or for lack of a better English, the small man, who I now noticed had a pockmarked face that continued onto his neck, where red- infected welts disappeared behind his braided hair, took to doing a smart Irish-flavored jig. He crossed first, one leg before the other while his arms stood above his head like a fractured rainbow.

The pockmarked Frenchman shouted to everyone standing there watching this incredulous scene, *"Vive les Etats-Unis, et vive les Irlandais!"*

Whatever it was that he was saying didn't seem to have an effect on Morrisey. For he pushed the man towards the building's door, gently at first, then with more force after realizing the Frenchman wouldn't leave.

Morrisey kept repeating, "Go-find-Napoleon—Napoleon—. *Le quartier Français*, the French-quarters, go-to-the-French-quarters!"

Finally, in response to something the immigrant asked which I couldn't understand, Morrisey bellowed out, "How the hell should I know where it is? I ain't French—just follow the smell of garlic!"

At last, he pushed the man out into the street and came back to face us.

He looked back over his shoulder at the door, before asking us accusingly, "You're all Irishmen, I take it?"

We all said 'yes', except for "Devil" McGoran, who conceitedly claimed the only way he would be made to accept affinity as an Irishman, was to lessen his time in purgatory. At which point he added, his eyes furrowed together promoting a serious intellectual air, "But first, I'd like to see just how hot it really is."

Morrisey interrupted him, incredulously enough by reporting, "Listen Scotsman, Ireland isn't warm at all throughout the year, except on maybe one or two days in late August."

Then it was "Devil's" turn to interrupt, his Romanesque eyes all lit up gaily, "I was speaking about purgatory!"

"Well, I'll be damned....Then we can't help you, for this here *Hall* is for Erin's own."

The way this John Morrisey fellow eyed "Devil" while saying he had no place in the hall for the likes of a Scotsman, bespoke of someone who wasn't used to mincing his words. Nor for that matter taking a backseat to a cocky, immigrant Scotsman regardless of his impressive size.

"Devil" answered back calmly enough, "I'll be gone in the next day or so for to find my wife. Therefore don't mind me a wit."

John Morrisey didn't answer him after that. But one could sense that

Morrisey with the bright, mustard-colored vest and green-checkered suit was asking himself who could possibly call herself the wife of such a man, unless she didn't know any better herself, having just crawled her own way out of a bog somewhere.

Still in all, with much to his credit, Morrisey didn't hold it against "Devil" for not being Irish, for he told him to come along that he'd taken it upon himself to feed the lot of us, a thought which I heartily approved of.

We stopped halfway down Nassau Street at a place of eateries which I remember to this day as the most beautiful place upon this earth, Castlewarren notwithstanding. It was fronted with big glass plate windows like we'd seen in Liverpool. Still, these windows were a lot bigger and contained plates of food that I swore I would eat them all if given half the chance. These windows were set in amongst fading sulfur-colored walls while the flooring was of a green and white checkered pattern that felt rather slick to the foot.

We sat in a big, airy, thickly-cushioned booth, and right away I noticed everyone and I mean everyone in that eatery called each other "Mick", like we were all from the same neighborhood and had known each other forever.

It became;

"Hey Mick, how's ja' doing today?"

"Hey Mick, hav' ya' seen Sally and the girls?"

"Hey Mick, pass the *soda pop* along—will ya'—you're not the only one who's thirsty?"

This was followed by heaps of laughter from all around us. Except it wasn't soda pop we were drinking that day, but a delightful brown ale with a clinging, stout, stand-up taste to it. Aye, it seemed like the glass and I'd been friends for a heckuva long time, and would surely miss one another in the end. We ate something that Morrisey called a "pork-chop". Not only was it tasteful, but he told me I could have as much as I wanted. And all the while he kept spilling this brown ale into my glass liked we'd known each other since we were *wee bairns,* and still packing the linen so we wouldn't piss all over the place. Aye, it was a grand time all around us that day...a grand time indeed.

In the middle of sampling a sweet applesauce which Morrisey claimed would help me to eat at least three more of these "pork-chops", Morrisey wipes his face with his napkin and asks the lot of us, "Well now and again, what do you all know what to do?"

Then while waiting for a reply, he tore into a piece of meat that as far as this Irishman's concerned was big enough to have given fits to a fully-grown Curragh buck.

But before we could answer, he starts up again by telling us about a canal their digging, not too far away he tells us, right here in New York, called the Black River canal. He went on saying that help also is needed over in Jersey

City laying down railroad tracks. And all the while I'm pulling on my ale and thinking to myself, we've made it my boy, we've finally made it big!

All of a sudden with a finger that displayed more thick brown gravy than I'd ever seen in my life, Morrisey points with his finger at my eye, the one Bailey Burke had been kind enough to crush the corner of and inquires, "What happened to that eye of yours, Boy—it ain't no breech-birth either because it's still red n' all like it ain't finished healing. Who whipped who? Or did you get the better of things that day?" Then he looked at the rest of me, trying to size me up I guess.

My brother, Paul Francis Daniel answered in my place, "It wasn't no fight, so no one got whipped. It was the Lord tenant's manager done that with his riding whip, a man by the name of Bailey Burke."

I nodded in agreement, although what I really wanted to do was to lick the man's finger.

Morrisey inclined his head respectfully, as if he knew what we were talking about.

Just then a woman stopped at our table, wearing so much alfalfa-imbued fungus on her eyelids I couldn't possibly imagine how her eyes, with that much painted weight on them—stayed open. She was wearing a low-slung green dress that frightened me and a flowered bonnet that would have put several gardeners out of work.

Landing a flighty hand on Morrisey's shoulder the lady asked hopefully, "Mick—buy me a drink?"

This she said at first to Morrisey. Then when he didn't bother to reply, or even turn around to acknowledge her presence, the lady spun back, to look at the rest of our table as if her question might apply to us as well. At length, thinking better about it, she turned from us, calling out to someone further away with the same flirtatious question the same insoluble response.

The man from Tammany hall whisked ale from a pitcher into our five glasses, drank off his glass like he'd been out in the hot sun all day, then startled us by saying, "Dames—!"

Afterwards, he hesitated, as if the mere thought of what he was going to say would haunt him forever, and came back to what he had been asking before, "We've got work for you—the lot of you. You see, here in New York we take care of our own. And our own—," here he tapped lightly on the table with his fist to emphasize he really meant what he was saying, causing the table to jump up a good six inches from the ground, "are the Irish—Erin's own. So you see—." At this point he glanced around the table at all of us, exposing one fully-toothed corner of his mouth like he was a satiated, well-fed tiger of sorts.

He began again, "We gives you the work. We protects you from these

Lord tenant—finagling—*wog*-rats like this Burke fellow, and when it comes election time, then we comes a-callin', to remind you that *you're* one of our own."

As if to emphasize what he'd been talking about, he politely pushed the plate of pork-chops towards my brother and me. Even though we'd been finished for awhile, there were still six more pieces of grease-whitened pork-chop being offered.... At this point, it was enough to make me sick. Still, I wouldn't have minded stuffing several pork-chops into my pocket for later on.

Paul Francis Daniel eyed Morrisey like they were long-lost brothers and explained to him, "Aye, we need work alright, and if you're true and all about what you just said then let's have a go of things. I reckon I can pick and shovel as well as the next man, at least well enough to earn me board and all."

I puffed out my chest until I thought it would burst, wanting to be like my older brother, before adding my two bits, "That's right," I told Morrisey, "I reckon shoveling and digging is just about what we've damn near done mos' of our lives, and just about what we nees to do to see this new country of ours'n." Then I distinctly belched.

Although, I could barely make out most of what he said, I vaguely remember "Devil" telling me something to the effect; if I drank much more of that ale in my glass, the only shoveling and digging I'd be doing this day would be in my dreams, with my eyes closed back by the river, lying face down in the early spring grass.

Morrisey took into thoughtful consideration Longfellow and "Devil", as if he wanted to hear their side of things as well.

But before he could add another word, "Devil" McGoran answers, his deep, blue eyes as serious as if he was talking to the almighty Himself, "I've got nothing agin' diggin' nor swampin' around underneath the city, trying to lay railway or blastin' out holes n' such. But the truth is, I'm a Scotsman and need the open highland air."

In response, Longfellow Mortlock poked him in his side, and reminded us all sitting there, "Even if the highland air has a particular Mowhawk smell to it now!"

This made "Devil" laugh, his full red beard bobbing up and down like two fluffy, marmalade-colored cats fighting over the same fish. Longfellow added he wasn't going to stay around New York that much longer anyway, as he had some business to take care of. Although he wouldn't explain what his "business" was, but just kept pulling on his oversized moustaches, like they were a pair of cow's teats and eventually milk would issue forth.

At length, after listening to our bantering Morrisey stopped eating, wiped his mouth off, told the waiter we were finished, and pointedly tells me to stop drinking my ale. When I asked him why, he motioned for my brother and Longfellow to assist me in getting to my feet.

I continued to protest against their help claiming, "I can sand on me own freet, thank you mary much."

Morrisey grunted a hollow "thank you" to the waiter, who announced our lunch is being paid for by the proprietor of the eatery. After which, our host proclaimed, by way of a curt explanation, for having me stop my mere sipping of his watered-down ale, "Lunch is over Gentlemen—now let's get a move on—we've a parade to attend!"

He proceeded to take his jacket off right there in the eatery. Morrisey followed this by rolling up his sleeves, as if at the mere mention of the word "parade", we'd all best get ready for a good old-fashion donnybrook.

Chapter Twelve

We know when all is said,
We perish if we yield.
Author unknown

Indeed, I'm against claiming what happened that day at the parade was the main reason for me leaving New York City, and eventually getting down to Kentucky to visit my long forgotten sisters, and finally starting a life for myself. It might have been the drudgery of *coopering*, or of having lived several months in an Irish slum that didn't offer hope to anyone, unless you wanted to sell out to the boys at Tammany Hall. Which of course I couldn't do, me being too dumb and having too much of the countryside in me—bogs and all. It might have been the *drink* that finally drove me away. Aye, those hours my fellow workers and I spent *boozing* together, extolling our miserable lot in life to one another while clinging to a bottle. Heck, you would have thought it held the elixir of life within, the way we kept after it night after night. This we did without wanting to do too much to change our miserable lives (this I realized long afterwards). Still in all, it would have taken a clan of banshees to keep me in New York City after that St. Patrick's Day parade, even though for several months afterwards I stayed on out of fear or stupidity. Call it what you will, I'll admit to being a dumb Irishman and fighting over a rock as long as there's a breath of hope we can squeeze a potato from it.

As I recall, it was a St. Patrick's Day parade which had all the physical elements of Gaelic hurling[20]. You can add to that as well, the refined genteelness of a country free-for-all. Like the time Lord Feargus O'Connor announced the closing of the Castlewarren tavern, *except* during the Catholic season of Lent. This was paramount to inciting a near riot in our village. Now this may appear to the reader as something of a contradiction (the Irish assume contradiction

---

20   One of our very rigorous National sports

to be a defining measure, as well as commiserate with what kind of people we truly are). Still in all, our Lord tenant had his reasons. Lord Feargus announced the tavern would remain open *only* during Lent because with our Catholic abstinences occurring all at once and for forty days as well; we were just as likely to kill one another through sheer frustration before Lent came to term. Without coming right out and saying it, the man compared our village men folk to a pack of wild hounds, during a full bloodless moon, braying to our master to free us from our pens. In honest Christian charity, it must be remembered that Lord Feargus could never know the simplistic, spiritual joy of fasting as we did. Which is probably why, he endeavored to discipline his personal habits heroically, through a more rigid and monastic display of the gout illness. We assumed this to be the case, as our Lord tenant was forever praying to the Almighty how sincerely thankful he was, for his swollen and painful members. Indeed, Lord Feargus used to pray in the *holiest* of terms. These same terms I was led to believe, that only those locked-away in Dublin prison or stranded, destitute, ship-wrecked mariners employed.

Yes, a day perhaps, I would like to soon forget about, except for the fact it taught me something I'll always remember. That sooner or later you must pick sides and not waffle about it either once you make your decision. Then having made your decision, learn to use your fists as well as can be to defend what you've decided upon. Nevertheless, once the fisticuffs are finished, one can then go back to his unintentional waffling. If for no other reason than it helps pass the time while waiting for the physical swelling of one's various bruises (incurred during the above mentioned fisticuffs) to recede.

After lunch, and with my ale-soused brain rattling along at a most cumbersome speed, James Morrisey bade us come with him to New York City's finest Irish hour, or so he claimed—the running of the St. Patrick's Day parade. Morrisey also made it clear that with a little help from almighty God, the parade could happily result in the dismemberment of a large portion of New York's "Orange" or Protestant population. This all occurred while I wondered if I could make it back to the river alone and a carpet of grass, where I could sleep off some of the effects of the ale and a rather engaging headache. At the same time, I also questioned why everyone needed to take time out from their daily hatred of their fellow Protestant man to organize it in parade form. Thereby, insuring in effect, their collaborating dislike was duly observed by those lining the streets. Ultimately, I came to the conclusion; if we could just find some way to always have plenty of pork-chops and cold, dark ale on hand, it might help to diffuse things, and indeed, end up being a formidable answer to world peace.

My brother, his grey eyes ablaze, kept pestering John Morrisey to find out if there would be at least ten or twenty people there who didn't share our

Catholic "genteelness". All of a sudden, while I didn't care all that much for any more ale, and in particular wanted to be left alone; more to the point, it sounded from the way they were talking that the Catholic Christ was finally going to have a go at his brother the "Orange" one—and may the better man win. There was no mistaking that money-making bets from our point of view were being laid on the Catholic one, if for no other reason than He was one of our own and thus wouldn't back down to his brother, the "Orange" Christ.

"Now wouldn't that be grand—if everyone showed up," Morrisey claimed, his green coat thrown lazily over his broad shoulder, as if we were all off from work for the day and headed to a...to a...well glory be to God—a bloody parade.

He explained that it was the day for all "practicin' Irishmen" (this was Morrisey's way of distinguishing between the Catholics and the Protestants) to unite. One could tell by the way he drove his mouth up in a snakelike hiss after saying "practicin' Irishmen" that the Protestants needn't have worried, there would be room for all of them in hell, once the good and kindly St. Patrick came back to put a little order in all things Gaelic.

On our way over to Mulberry Street, Morrisey filled us in on several things; first off, the All-Irish 69th Army Regiment would lead the parade. Because he told us, if they didn't, things could break out in the ranks, and he cited some ancient Druid order of Hibernians as an example.

"Nope, it's best we keep focused on the Orangemen and not let things get out of hand like they did in '35." He confirmed.

Paul Francis Daniel demanded, "What happened in 1835?"

Morrisey answered in kind, "Some of the boys got antsy and wanted a go at the "forty thieves"[21]. And before you knew it, we were fighting amongst ourselves so fiercely that you had to wonder who was the real enemy? Luckily, our own Archbishop Hughes set things to right; "to stop fightin' amongst yourselves," he warned us and get after the "true enemy of the church". This we did afterwards, we took off after the "Prots", like we should have done in the first place, instead of wasting our energy on each other. Fortunately, for those of who fought that day, we still had several months to heal up before we got right back into it on July twelve, or what the "Prot's" like to call "Boyne Day". By Jeebers, the Fenians and even us don't like to be reminded too much of that. I'm telling you the Fenians see red when they see "Orange"."

He finished by at first burping incoherently, before laughing at his unintended joke.

I noticed when we were finally back at Tammany Hall, we were given Indian gear to put on. Thus I reasoned, *normal* Irishmen celebrate on St. Patrick's Day—dressed up as American Indians to honor their Gaelic past.

---

21 A term relative to the hierarchy at Tammany Hall

My cry for a blanket and a pillow went unheeded amongst the calls for feathered bonnets and moccasins, and more to the urban point, whisky, which seemed to disappear around the room like so much *fire-water*. Except this day, it was Irishmen dressed up like Native Americans who were drinking it all.

Morrisey explained that in truth he was an *Okemaw* or hunter, and that everyone involved with *The Hall* had Indian names bestowed upon them according to their function. A man who crossed the room wearing a great big headdress of eagle feathers was pointed out as being Fernando Wood, one of the thirteen *Sachems,* who actually ran things down at Tammany Hall.

We respectfully kept our silence, in front of so great a being or *Sachem* as I mentioned he was so named.

However, once this Fernando Wood had cleared his way to the other side of the room, my brother, being my brother and all, leaned over to me and intoned, "Perhaps, this Indian knows "Devil" McGoran's wife. Even if he doesn't, maybe he knows a female beaver or a raccoon who'd be interested in a long-term relationship. In this way, we could save "Devil" a lot of traveling miles, since he wouldn't know the difference anyway!"

I told my brother I didn't think it was that funny, and more to the point I told him I wasn't looking to fight anyone that day. Because I explained, if I took one punch to the stomach (after the lunch we'd just eaten), I'd be more likely to throw-up on my opponent than to do him any other serious harm.

All my brother would say in reply was, "Edward, you never were very patriotic."

I answered back, pointing out my braided Indian vest, "To whom; Ireland or the Iroquois nation?"

All around us, men that I understood were carpenters or iron-workers or brick-masons were donning various forms of Indian garb and speaking in low and dangerous tones. If there was a dominant theme making its way around the room that day, it was one of *us against them*. I understood *them* in this particular case to be just about everyone outside *The Hall*, except for priests and spouses. Even so, some of the spouses were invoked rather suspiciously. It was as if we were in our own little world at Tammany Hall and that was that. Everyone else was considered an outsider....Someone said it was easier this way—that physical presence defined everything. Either, once work was finished wherever that was, you came back to *The Hall* to eat or drink, even improve yourself through multiple instructional classes *The Hall* offered, or you lived and carried on outside *The Hall* and thus were treated differently... as an enemy.

A man next to me who was bald, except for the short ringlet of hair which stopped just above his ears, ears I might add, that might have been smooth once, but were now full of scar tissue like a rugby man or boxer, kept talking about how *the brotherhood of the hall* was going after the ice business. Accordingly, the last that he'd heard, they were pushing the ice to thirty cents the block which included delivery as well. Apparently, it was a price that up until now had been unheard of, for it set the men around me to grumbling something fierce.

Finally, a *Wiskinsky* or the doorkeeper to those outside of *The Hall* beckoned for us to leave. Indeed, the parade was about to get under way.

Just as I started to step through the door, the bald man who had cursed the execrable necessity of ice at thirty cents the block, stepped through at the same time I did, intentionally or unintentionally (I'm not sure which) blocking our respective paths.

He motioned me to go through first, then whispered to me as I did, "When ya' hit the bloke, make sure it's a *coup sec* just aft of his wind-pipe. That way he can't make a sound and alert the others."

The bald man added with a certain gleam to his eye that he knew more than he was letting onto, "It also looks funny the way their neck just kinds of lolls there for a second or two, before keeling over, like a rabbit's, once you've chopped 'em...!"

I nodded my confused agreement. Although and at the same time, I silently wondered to myself that with all this Indian garb on, why couldn't we all just find a teepee somewhere, and settle our differences over a damned-good peace pipe. Somehow, I knew it wasn't meant to be.

The 69th All-Irish Regiment was waiting and stamping impatiently outside. While I for one knew, as soon as I saw them that with these boys in front, we could whip the English anywhere they saw fit to fight. For not only were these men dressed in fine tan boots with matching shoulder belts that seemed to crackle when they marched, but the uniforms they were wearing had so many brass buttons and were creased so sharply, they could have paraded down the street all by themselves, with no bodies inside. So that's where the Irish men have come—to New York City—. For it was obvious to me, here was Ireland's best; as fine a group and as handsome a group of men as I'd ever seen. They were big and tough and rangy while looking like they could kill an English soldier just by staring at him long enough. Probably could have taken out the whole lot of them, by blowing their collective breath, if they had half a mind to do so.

T'is a true pity...and a pity it is now, to have seen so many of Ireland's finest over in America, instead of back home where they belonged and where they should have been. Nevertheless, as far as this Irishman's concerned, it was one of the proudest days of my life to see so many of our fine men together in one place, even if it wasn't back home in Ireland.

There were several barrel-chested men out in front and leading the regiment, wearing army tartan and green kilts that reached down to just above their knees, with tan and white crisscrossing socks and tassels that stretched the length of their calves. These my cauliflower-eared friend told me were called by their enemies, "The ladies from hell". For they were even tougher fighters than the regulars in the 69th, which is why they were given the honor of wearing these forest-green, plaid kilts into battle.

I asked him naively enough, "—Oh, and why the "ladies from hell" nickname?"

He sintered back his eyes and ears in a tight grin before explaining, "They're named that way because they refuse to wear any underwear. Thus during wartime, when they leave the trenches on a windy and blustery day to attack the enemy.... Well, you can almost imagine the disorder and eventual fear these men caused. From what I've been told, just about all hell would break loose—thus the nickname!"

The men from Tammany Hall fell in step behind the 69th Army Regiment. I guess we wore our feathers proudly enough. Although, to think of it now, it must have been something to see; a splendid, handsome, disciplined, regimental army followed by a group of pale-faced Indians, wearing baggy leather-pants, beaded chest-plates, feathered headdresses and stinking of whisky. Well now, and in any case, the crowd seemed to warm to us, for they kept calling out as we started off;

"Hey Chief fat-Katokas, wait'll you see the wilderness over in Brooklyn—"

"How much junk-jewelry did you sell Ireland for?"

"If it's a stew you want—wait'll you get to Five-Points!"

Some of the men started singing songs, but I couldn't, for I didn't know any of the words. While others called out to the bystanders to come and join the marching, especially taunting the women wearing clean clothes and more impressively, didn't have their hair all piled up on top of their heads, like ordinary Irish domestic help.

Taking into account the hundreds of people lining the street, I hollered at Paul Francis Daniel, "Fifteen or twenty huh?—It looks like half of Ireland's here!"

My brother just shrugged off what I had to say, as if he had finally found his element, and parading around, celebrating something Irish with a tomahawk in one hand was it.

I couldn't stop gawking. It seemed like the whole city was there. They were lined up six or seven people deep in most places, with some men lying back against the walls, lackadaisically, with nothing better to do or more to the point, as if they were waiting for something to happen.

I looked over at Longfellow Mortlock and "Devil" McGoran. They were waving to the crowd, and in response, several of the spectators were excitedly waving back.

I even heard one cry out, "Will 'ya look at that—a couple of *paddies* with nowhere to go. Why even the pigs threw them out!"

There was no getting around the fact, there was a certain hostile as well as a carnival-like atmosphere to the whole parade. I watched Morrisey and the fellow named Fernando Wood leave the line and walk closer to the crowd, where they would bow and heave candies in every direction, for the anticipating children to scramble after.

Behind us, and stepping out in more formal lines were derby-hatted men, there must have been one hundred at least. They were all dressed the same; with dashing, Sunday, three-piece suits and long, billowing, black overcoats. Most of them wore tri-color sashes that stretched over one shoulder and were green, white and yellow in color. Perhaps at the fourth or fifth line and equally distant apart, several of these derby-hatted men carried the American flag. Next to them, another marcher, bore up the Republic's flag while several men sported large signs that were easily read; "A Free and Independent Ireland", "Sent from Ourselves—The Last Cry will Be—A Cry for Freedom". It was all very entertaining and all, and had I not been feeling the effects of the ale (being still groggy and whatnot), I'm sure it would have been all the more stimulating. We marched past a large church somewhere between Mott and Mulberry streets that my neighbor said was St. Patrick's Cathedral. I'd never witnessed a church that big before. Indeed, if it was anything like Castlewarren, then I told myself that the local priest like Father Kincaid back home, must have a hard-enough time of things, keeping the animals, especially door-battering goats out during the winter months.

My brother, in a rare moment of enthusiasm barked at me, "It's even got the white deer of Mallow beat—I've never seen anything like this!"

Somewhere from inside the church came the rolling thunder of bells; lots of bells, then from all over the parade route hats came off slowly at first, then more and more, until there wasn't a man's covered head to be seen. Just like back home it was the Angelus, the noon-day prayer. Not everyone was intently praying however, for out of the corner of my eye I saw "Devil" reach carefully for something in the rear pocket of the man marching just ahead of him. He showed it to Longfellow, who worked his two handlebar moustaches up and down like two hairy oil derricks pumping up one side of his face then down the other. It was obvious to me he was telling "Devil" to desist from pilfering from the man marching in front of him. In something approaching timid acquiescence, "Devil" tapped his neighbor on the shoulder, and gave the man back his wallet. All the while, "Devil" continued making signs, as if the wallet had fallen out of the man's pocket by itself. The man marching in front, at first profusely thanked "Devil" for the *finding* of his wallet. He then started to put it back in his pant's pocket. Hesitating, he looked back over his shoulder at the red-bearded Indian marching behind him, thought better of it, and put his wallet inside his Indian vest where he continued to pat it several times while keeping a guarded eye on the *wallet-finder*, "Devil" McGoran.

About that time, a most sensational, yet strange group of marching men took up their places in the parade, perhaps a good fifty yards to our backs. The leader of this group was wearing a hat, shawl and skirt over his pants and vest all made out of grossly-thickened straw. You couldn't see what he looked like, for his huge straw hat was positioned so low over his face, one could only make out a mouth that pursed and relaxed its lips according to the beat he was playing on a walking drum. The drummer was followed by a fiddler and several accordion players, with a score of straw-outfitted men bringing up the rear. Apparently, these men were one of the crowd's favorite and easily recognizable, for upon the sight of these men, children and women took to squealing, "It's the little people, the little people...watch out everyone!"

One of the fiddlers took off heading straight for the crowd, and at such a pace that the people before him dissolved into two sections like the Red Sea before Moses, giggling and pleading in their feigned fright. He stood there alone as it were, captivating everyone within earshot. With a bent leg to support his fiddling posture, the musician played to the crowd, his wood-burnished fiddle sending up a tune to lighten even the heavens. The March sunlight caught him just so, making him standout. A darkened figure outlined against the weak and tepid, steely, afternoon sunlight, seemingly all alone except for his tune; one that brought a mystical silence over everyone if even for just a few enlightened seconds.

It was then a rock flew over us and hit Fernando Wood square on his upper back. He went down on one knee before straightening up, his face a bright scarlet of flushed-red, his hands were shaking from the suffered indignity.

There were cries of; "Go back to Tammany, you bunch of brigands!"

"There'll be no more graft from the likes of you!"

"Ireland didn't want you—and neither does New York!"

It was like a clap of lightning, a peal of thunder, and in two shakes of a wink, a carnival-like, Sunday-afternoon atmosphere turned to one of enmity and disaccord—. No, on second thought, better make that full-length, unleashed bitterness and religious hatred. It was as if everyone's self-fulfilling prophecy had come true; *us against them...and the sooner the better.* I didn't seem to mind it all that much, right then, when it all started, because for once I wasn't hungry, just sleepy. It just goes to show you how much man can tolerate with a pork-chop in his stomach. I have never seen a referenced study to prove it. Still as far as this Irishman's concerned, one day some clinical laboratory will undoubtedly demonstrate that peace on this earth between neighbors, countries, even Christian factions, what have you—will dramatically increase when man has a full belly. Until then it's best seen as a crap shoot.

I was pushed from behind by the short bald man, who had convinced me that unless we attacked first there'd be hell to pay. Already, there were scattered cries of, "Get after 'em,—come on don't wait on 'em another minute—get after 'em!"

"Attack who? Damn it all, I don't see any cowboys around!" I offered; half-choking, half-wondering if I could find my way back to the river on my own, without having to suffer through the formalities of a slugfest first.

Looking up, I saw what appeared to be stones being hurled through several windows of a nearby apartment building. Then I didn't need to wonder anymore, for one stone caught me fish to kettle right square on my nose and I started to bleed.

Not too far away a woman's voice screamed out, "Take your cholera and papist sorcery and go back to Ireland."

Then more stones followed.

At length, and right before we broke ranks a booming voice echoed forth, "He said multiply the loaves and fishes—not the miserable, starving, papist children you can't feed in the first place!"

Decaying fruit and rocks were filling the air all around us now while off just beyond the glittering lads of the 69th I heard a rifle shot...then another. Paul Francis Daniel rushed past me with "Devil" and Longfellow in tow. He called back to me, "Come on, we're out to break some "Prot's" bones, let's go-o-o-o...."

And somehow I was swept along, forgotten for the moment a blanket of grass and that sobering breeze lapping gently in from over the river, cooling men and tempestuous spirits.

Some incandescent woman broke from the crowd, ran up to me and bellowed out ironically enough, "Blessed are the peacemakers", before she let loose a basket of decaying fish in my face.

They had to be Protestants for they appeared evil and damned. One man hadn't shaved in days while wearing a look that made whosever husband he was more than likely, blind from fright, probably starting at day one of their marriage. The man, I swear, had deep sinister lines frozen in his face from cheek top to chin, in close to his nose, as if he was forever unhappy, and determined to be mean while making those close to him just as unhappy as he was. His greasy, alabaster hair came to a point billowing over his forehead where it formed a slithering *V* that outlined his depraved regard, like a troll guarding a bridge somewhere.

I don't even know how we came to face-off from one another.

Except we did, finding ourselves staring at each other, as he kept taunting me, "A rope, a rope, by which to hang the pope—a rope, a rope—."

His first punch rocketed in to my stomach, then a second one in rapid succession causing me to take a hesitant, sweltering crouch down on one knee. I searched rapidly for my wind or some breath which I desperately needed to help right myself. I felt confused and ashamed, for I hadn't had the decency to put up much of a fight. At which point, I saw above my head a shadow of two locked fists poised to come falling down on me from somewhere just next to a patch of distant clouds. I remember considering the thought for a brief second or two; *this can't be by anyone's stretch of the imagination a good thing—whatever happened to the peace pipe?* Afterwards, I braced for the inevitable, punishing and forthcoming shock. In a heartbeat, the man with the poised fists suddenly doubled over and fell so quietly to the street, you'd a thought he just had his three o'clock feeding, and had been put to bed by his tender mother.

I felt more than saw Longfellow's presence and his comforting words, "You 'kay, Laddie?"

Seeing that I was only breathing heavily, Longfellow laughed at me. As if my adversary and I had done nothing more than rough one another up in a make-believe play-fight, which hadn't been much to watch based on Longfellow's sardonic smile.

He shook his head in my direction and pointed to maybe fifty yards away. There, my brother seemed to be having the time of his life with a man who was twice his size, yet was inheriting the fury of my brother like an unleashed Midwestern twister.

More so than Longfellow Mortlock or "Devil" McGoran, Paul Francis Daniel seemed to take his time between measured punches. As if there was so much pleasure to be had he preferred extending the moment, thereby prolonging his opponent's suffering.

While in the same time frame he kept repeating, "So's you don't like "Home Rule" now, do ya'?"

Then—wham—a punch sent home...then another; his enjoyment was twisted and sinister. As I've said many times before, something had slipped in that poor lad's head the day our pappy left home. There in front of me, right there fighting it out on the streets of New York was all the sad evidence anyone would need to see my brother's out of adjustment inner-workings. Like the two-tongued cat, Mr. Jenkins claimed back home in Castlewarren was his departed Eleanor. Mr. Jenkins swore his wife had come back in the body of a cat, and continued her ways just like in their married life together; forever gossiping and dripping with stories about her neighbors and what went on within their parlor walls.

More so then watching the three of them joust about, with what must have been the dregs of New York's Protestant population, was the gay and unabashed way a Catholic priest kept stepping in and out of a fight with another frail man. This frail man looked for all practical purposes to be a hold-over from the first Puritan ship to come to these shores. They were both older men which probably explained why no blows ever actually landed. However, their hard core rhetoric certainly made up for any obnoxious blows unintentionally missed.

"If it's a Reformation you want, then that's what you'll get."

This said, the black-cassocked, swaying priest stepped into the vacant middle between the two of them throwing innocuous blows about that seemed to be there for the taking. Although none of them, as I said, ever actually landed on his opponent. The other man was taller and more aloof than the priest. His disdainful regard at the priest's pitiful boxing antics seemed a mere afterthought, visibly portraying an attitude there was nothing to be worried about. Still in all, like his opponent the priest, he sent a long and just as vacant roundhouse punch that for all practical appearances could just as easily have been dropped off at the local post office and mailed in. His bespectacled eyes glared down at his Catholic opponent, as if the priest presented all the annoying competitiveness of a house fly despite his vibrant buzzing around.

"It's not a "reformation" that we want, my good man. But that the *skibereen* Catholics go back to the bogs and wayside shrines where you belong. And let the governing of Ireland stay with those of us, who know how to do it best!"

Then the slow, air-churning, round-house punch would follow, allowing even a two-day old corpse plenty of time to get out of the way. I didn't begrudge either one of them anything, for it appeared to me the only thing to suffer come the end of the dispute would be their respective self-esteems.

Further down the broad avenue I caught up with my brother and "Devil" and Longfellow, who was singularly dismayed that someone would actually try to chew through one of his moustaches. It was late afternoon when we turned back towards Tammany Hall, all of us tired, except perhaps for my brother, who seemed unabashedly exhilarated by the whole affair. As if he'd been put back in his proper surroundings and couldn't hide his satisfaction. His grey-blue eyes danced about like a rooster at a cock fight, strutting this way and that, curious as to how many more opponents wanted to face him.

I don't know how or why a stately parade in downtown Manhattan could turn into a fist-fight every year, but somehow back then it did. Although now I've been informed, the parade has become a lot more respectable in that no one bites anymore. Also, the city fathers with a Catholic affinity have introduced a green colorant into the river, which has the Protestants more confused than ever before.

Maybe it was the dressing up of Irishmen in musty Indian clothing. Or the Ides of March that induced the premonition of springtime and gestational awakenings which brought to life the need to either kiss or punch someone. I'm more of the inclination that man cannot get along with himself, even if you spotted him, whatever it was he was desperately after in the first place. And therefore, incorrectly assumes his neighbor must want it as badly as he does. Or, maybe that's the root cause of it all, in order to give man his just due; he doesn't know exactly what he wants. Nevertheless, he's got himself all worked up over something, and completely convinced to such an extent, the only way he'll ever be happy is to make his neighbor just as miserable as he is. This he can do, by taking away whatever it is that his neighbor might have by any means necessary. And that includes straw hats, fiddles and an insatiable desire to parade his weary ass around in public.

After the parade and despite my better intentions, I didn't leave New York City right away. No, I took the job *wet-coopering* that James Morrisey from Tammany Hall offered me. I got myself a flat over in Mullen's Alley, and I even caroused some with the "Dead Rabbits"[22], taking down defunct names over at the various cemeteries to add to the voting lists. Time has a habit of slipping away from you regardless of what you're doing. But when you add a couple of drinking buddies like "Devil" McGoran and Longfellow Mortlock, as well as some more of the thirstier ones from Tammany Hall, to ease the evenings away....It becomes more and more painful to find yourself alone, in a bizarre closet of a room, following four flights of stairs. Inevitably realizing, the only thing you're gaining any meaningful experience with in the New World, is conjunctive depravity.

Still, that's the way it was in 1852, at least for awhile. Now to me, *coopering* isn't the best of occupations. But I do thank the Almighty, in the sense it taught me to use my hands, for something other than clawing in the dirt planting potatoes. We'd saw and lay up the wet oak planks in the morning, stretching the iron bands tighter and tighter, at exactly the right length, enabling the middle band to bell outward, just enough to keep the cask, water tight. This, us coopers would do, careful to avoid staving in the

---

22   A group from Tammany Hall that executed certain "directives" from the ruling members of the "Hall"

whole bloody operation when the cask was empty, without you know what in it. That's right. The only problem being, once the whole operation was packed and ready to go, was they put non-conformist whisky in it at the end. Now what's a man supposed to do, damn it all? With "Devil" and Longfellow around, even another cooper my age from the hall named Maxime Chaubert, a French-Irishman who claimed that with his ma being Irish-Catholic and his pa a temperance Quaker from Marseilles, France, he could never make up his mind about anything, and that included drinking. So he finally took the *enlightened* approach to drink with us every evening after work. This he did, Maxime claimed while continuing to think about what his decision should be. Maxime further added; this way, if he finally decided he was supposed to drink (from his mother's side), he wouldn't have to make up for any eventual lost time. On the other hand, if he wasn't supposed to drink (from his father's side), he promised to join a temperance league and chase us all back to Ireland, once he sobered up. The three of us didn't care one way or the other, but more often than not laughed about Maxime's indecisiveness. Looking back on it, we lived more or less like everyone else in those hearty times. Either spending our meaningless wages on forgetting our vacuous lives, or hanging back in the alleyway between us and the next apartment building over, convinced we were being punished for something, only Almighty God knew about. From the way things evolved, we eventually became hard-core roughnecks, and decidedly threw our weight around. Even if it was only within a fifteen by one hundred foot alley, between a dozen or so of us, with several colleens to lend an aloof feminine benediction to our banal, chest-beating activities.

Indeed, where we lived, and especially how we conducted ourselves had all the makings of a *clachan*[23], albeit an urban one. Looking up, we could see the steel scaffolds suspended from the sides of our apartment buildings. They stood out as cold, naked porches for those who wanted an evening out with the steamy night air of the surrounding slaughterhouses to breathe. Harking back on it now, I don't know how anyone could stand it, being caught that way...without any hope...without any creative virtue.... Why it was just like the great famine again, except the urge to rage against something or someone took the place of the empty, bloated stomach. The desolate desperation took a little bit longer to transfigure one's face. Yet make no mistake about it, back in those life sapping tenements, man's just as dead as if the potato crop went under all over again. You were alive alright, but you had lost your soul. Yes, that was it in a nutshell...we'd lost our life-giving souls...that's exactly how it was. And for everyone living there, in those tenements, it was the same...there was no difference between anyone, nor for that matter any way out. God help those unfortunate people!

23 A small village community

Some days when I was free, I'd go with Longfellow and visit my brother digging a canal over by Jersey. He and the gang he worked with looked like bearded, half-blind, pipe-drawing rats. They were always underground and half- underwater most days. They were a mean-fisted pack of men inseparable from their picks and shovels with muscles that were tight and braided like marine-corded, hemp rope. They must have been the toughest bunch of men who lived anywhere underground except for my brother. Paul Francis Daniel looked out of place, for he couldn't grow any hair over that red-freckled cast face of his. Although, his grey-blue eyes were more wide-awake now, fuller, with more brightness like they'd finally adjusted to the lack of light. When I'd show up with "Devil" or Longfellow, he'd come out of the pit like some mud-packed rodent. Indeed he so appeared, for even above ground he couldn't stop, but took to sniffing this way or that, like he wasn't comfortable being above ground anymore. Or, more to the point, like he'd been trapped and couldn't wait to be free again, down in the earth away from our stares. When my brother and his mates would look up to see who had come, they would only glare at you for awhile, like they couldn't distinguish figures in the light anymore, or more to the point didn't want to. To this Irishman, it appeared as if they were happier, with their faces packed down, next to the swampy bottom; a half-dozen, four by six inch wood shanks tottering close-by overhead, protecting them from having half the city street tumbling down on top of them. My brother never came right out and said it, but he would invariably gush a huge sigh of relief when we'd announce that we were leaving. This he would do, before slithering back down the excavated side with its protecting cross-members which were put there for safety reasons against flooding, but looked like they couldn't hold back a light drizzle of rain.

I'd been living like this for three or four months back in Mullen's Alley, *wet-coopering* and helping the Irish down at Tammany Hall to stay in political power. I had an extremely hard time with the local Americans. For one thing, they didn't seem to be able to understand me when I spoke. So I took to writing poetry and whatever else came into my head...the only problem being; from all the whisky we were drinking, I couldn't understand myself what I'd written. Which is why I'd inevitably tear up what I'd freshly composed before heading back to *The Hall*. At the very least, back at Tammany we all seemed to understand what we as Irish folk were all about...a crusty, genetically-deficient, torn and conquered race with a colossal chip on our shoulders that we couldn't seem to shake. Therefore, we continued to drink, and where this activity was concerned you might just as well strike from our vocabulary the word 'sipping'. For we drank hard and unequivocally, as if to make up for some deficiency, or to dig our collective grave so deep, our self-fulfilling prophecy that we were all a misguided and luckless race to begin with...might indeed come true.

It might have stayed that way for awhile. Except that one day, having received mail from my sister, Ann Horian, in which she mentioned she'd had news about Katherine Louisa Maddox. And wouldn't I be surprised to find out she was living in Dry Creek, Kentucky, not too far away from where my sister lived, and wasn't that something. Yes, to this bog-wading Irishman it was indeed something. Something that made me decide my time in New York City was at an end. Thinking back now while reminiscing along those very same lines, according to this Irishman and his cursory regard for anything logical, it couldn't have happened any other way.

By now, "Devil" McGoran had said his goodbyes, and along with Longfellow Mortlock they took off together for territories unknown. Although, I distinctly remember "Devil" reminiscing about a place where an Indian woman didn't answer back to her husband in a garbled language he couldn't understand. While at the same time, squirrel meat and bear fat made the cold winters a damned sight more comfortable than an empty flat and Mrs. Papineck's Tuesday night's baloney special.

My friend, Maxime Chaubert thought he might come with me to see some of his people in South Carolina. Maxime remembered that his distant family lived in some forgotten train-stop whistle of a town called Chester, South Carolina. I told him I would be happy for the company. He answered back he would be even happier if I would pay for his fare, thereby ensuring his company, as well as his conflicting happiness. I responded in kind that I couldn't. Indeed, I didn't have enough money available for the two of us. After listening to my friend and his insufferable logic, I couldn't decide whether Maxime did or didn't have the money to travel with me down south.

"Ah! What am I to do?" Maxime declared. "If I say only one thing—try to do only one thing—then the Irishman inside of me, my mother's side, admonishes me; why do you do such a thing? You must think, *réfléchir*, consider the situation from all angles! While the French side of me, from my papa, tells me to go ahead, live the adventure, so what if you break a few eggs while doing it. It is well worth the effort—*le tres bon omellete*—you will make for yourself in the end!"

All things considered, I myself, having no knowledge of a Frenchman's way of thinking and even less of his language, wasn't sure if my friend Maxime, as a matter of course, didn't have the money to travel with me, or was in desperate need of a French-cuisine omelet. In any case I traveled alone.

As I mentioned earlier, my brother didn't seem to be able to make it above ground and in the daylight hours anymore. "No, no",—he said demonstrably so, when I asked him to come with me. He told me to pass along his greetings to our sisters. That he might be along shortly, but then again he might not. So I took my leave of him and headed out of New York City, anxious to finally see my sisters, Ann Horian and Susan, and even more so, to meet up again with Katherine Louisa Maddox. Not for a moment realizing, she might not wish to see a *skibereen* immigrant from the land of Erin, like me, again.

Chapter Thirteen

There is no hope. I can but reap
The weeds I've sown for all my life,
Blinded with pride, I took the leap,—
Like one who speaketh in his sleep,
I called her wife.

Author unknown

There is a great man living in Kentucky, who steadfastly claims, as he has unequivocally stated on more than one occasion: "To have a God-given right to our allegiance." Not because, as some are quick to point out, this man has a need to order us around, as if we were dull-witted soldiers milling about, with only perfunctory thoughts dallying around inside our thick and uneducated heads. Nay, to be exact and honestly put, it is because as he stated, "Without your unquestioning allegiance and uncompromising Southern tenacity, the Yankee scoundrel will in a quick and cat-like fashion soon make minced meat out of the lot of us!"

This was prophetically stated by Captain John Hunt Morgan of the Lexington Rifles well in advance of the war of secession. Not only was it prophetic in terms of where as a country we were heading during those pernicious times, but needless to say, here was a man regardless of what the scallywags and bog-waders criticized him for, led us to victory after victory in his unorthodox fashion of making war. And may we all in a sense, be raiders like John Hunt Morgan to the end. Also, having served under the man, and having by necessity camped out in close quarters with Captain Morgan involving all which that entails, I can say as my mother would have quipped; "Aye, he was a *dacent* man he was, a kind and *dacent* man."

For the record, the above was emphatically pronounced by Captain Morgan (who didn't enjoy a stalwart reputation as a public speaker) while we were in Dry Creek, Kentucky. We were there watching an exhibition of the Lexington Rifles, as well as celebrating the twelfth anniversary of America's 1847 victory at Buena Vista, Mexico. Of which I am told, Captain Morgan and his brother Cal played significant roles.

To be truthful about it, I indeed heard the above while only listening half-heartedly to what the man had to say on that particular day. I wasn't at that point necessarily interested in anything Captain Morgan, or for that matter what any man had to say that weekend. The truth of the matter was, I happened to be in Dry Creek, Kentucky, wishing to pay a visit to a certain Katherine Louisa Maddox. In which event, I had been dragged along by Katherine, not really caring one way or the other, to watch, as these men paraded about dressed in stylish, burnt-green uniforms with side-lengthened gold stripes and bright, green, plume bearing—shako hats. It wasn't until much later, the destiny Captain John Morgan had inherited from the Hunts and Morgans, came to bear on my life in such an intimate and fascinating manner.

If the Free-Masons hadn't hog-tied Jeff Davis' hands with their supercilious emphasis on *the craft*, furthering their malarkey about a one-world government, and left "Morgan's Raiders" free to liberate Kentucky, we would have succeeded in confirming the confederacy of the Southern states. Nevertheless, we gave them a damned good run for their money...something I guess even that old fox, Ulysses S. Grant would have to admit.

This was not the first time I had been to Dry Creek to visit with Miss Maddox while trying to influence her favors my way. The first time was back in 1853, when I had initially reached Maysville from New York City to take up rooms with my sister, Ann Horian and her husband, Stewart Thompson. Now Maysville, Kentucky, sits on the Ohio River at the mouth of Limestone Creek. It is a most engaging town, except in the summer time, when the high heat and humidity rekindle a longing in me, for the incandescent, temperate, highland fog of Castlewarren. Nevertheless, I called Maysville home, even if it was only to be for a short while. Now then, and to be absolutely truthful about the affair, no sooner had I put my feet in the door of my sister's and brother-in-law's house, but I wrangled their ears raw asking to be taken to see Katherine Louisa Maddox. For I was convinced, she had either a perceptive, unrequited longing to see this Irishman again, or was baking *ad libitum,* and thus willing to give away more oatmeal cookies than she knew what to do with. Unfortunately for me, I was wrong on both counts.

As I seem to always be in want of repeating myself, let the reader be aware it is in no way a reflection of his own intellectual abilities. But rather, the inferiority attitude of one who has come to the written application of language rather late in life, and is not quite sure, if indeed, his message has been brought forward clearly, to the point necessary for mutual understanding. Back in 1853 I had been in Maysville but several weeks, when in response to my insistent requests to visit Dry Creek where the Maddoxs lived, my sister and her husband Stewart, if for no other reason than to restore a sense of quiet to their household, agreed to hitch up the horses and satisfy my desire to see my beloved Katherine once again. Besides, Dry Creek, Kentucky, was only five-five miles or so in distance away from Maysville; "a good stretch of the legs", as we would say back home in Ireland.

We arrived some two days later in time for the midday meal with the Maddoxs. They owned a surprisingly large farm. It was well tended, with sloping lawns that folded away next to impressive full-length bay windows, wherein the front parlor stood. The garish, white-washed bay windows were set off with blood-red brick, giving the whole ensemble a most imposing, as well as successful demeanor.

Although Mr. Maddox did not personally stop his working day to find out how I was, he didn't seem particularly rude to me, or for that matter especially sentimental about seeing me again. Nor did he find it in his head to laugh when I told him how the fellows at Tammany Hall had taken it to the Protestants on St. Patrick's Day.

"A coarse lot—eh?" Was his succinct response.

Then I caught myself wondering who exactly was he referring to—us or the Protestants?

Katherine's father hadn't changed all that much to my eyes. Although, he now sported a thin, absurdly so, miniscule moustache and he owned a small, oval, like a pear-shaped belly where there hadn't been one before. I also liked the fact he spoke a delightful English that I could readily understand, without straining a hog's ear the whole time he spoke.

On the other hand, Katherine Louisa Maddox not only appeared disdainful, but continued throughout our visit to be as rude and as unsympathetic as a man could imagine (I wondered indeed what had become of the oatmeal biscuits or cookies as they are called in America?).

She started in immediately after her truculent welcome. Then as if she couldn't figure out the message she wanted to get across, she more than made it clear during the rest of the day.

"God save all here," was what I said to her when we first met after such an extended passage of time. Heck, my salutation wasn't anything extraordinary. It's what *the children of the Gael* say and do when they see each other once again, that's all.

Apparently, this wasn't to Katherine's liking, for she did something with her nose that made it go sideways in a peculiar twist before chiding me, "Do stop it, Edward, you're not in the bogs anymore!"

Nevertheless, the way she took in my best Sunday suit pant's legs which contrived to stop well above my ankles, and my salt and pepper tie and vest, wrinkled and ill-fitting as they were, made it clear she thought me best back in Ireland taking care of the sheep once again.

I remember thinking, how can so much spite be uttered by one of God's creatures as beautiful as she was. I thought maybe her pappy had run off as ours had done, making her bitter and spiteful to everyone like my brother, Paul Francis Daniel. But her pappy hadn't run off. No, he was out in front of the house explaining to my brother-in-law the advantages of a new thresher-combine for his wheat crop. I guess it came as no surprise to anyone, including myself that I was the source of her irritation, a poor *croppie* to be sure. Still it seemed to this Irishman, a stunning contradiction that one so intimidatingly lovely, could be so hard put to say something nice and be gracious. After all, she was beautiful and possibly took comfort in that knowledge on a daily basis (probably while combing her hair in the morning and at night) while we *croppies* had only the saints to pray to for comfort. I came to the disheartening conclusion that I must have been a reminder to Katherine Louisa Maddox of something which caused the colleen an immense amount of discomfort. Aye, and wouldn't that be just like a woman...calling your name off the dance card, only to tell you her feet hurt. Indeed, she'd have to sit this dance out and would you mind getting her a small measure of sherry while she rested and discussed the weather with the handsome lieutenant, who just happened to be standing by.

One thing I immediately noticed was that Katherine had lost the last vestiges of the Irish country-girl. Where she had been listing towards plump before, all I can say about that instance is that it was gone for good; giving her not only a more mature, but also a more delicate and full-bloomed feminine balance. Which is all I care to say on that subject other than to mention—it was damned unsettling, I can tell you that. Her face had gone the way of the city women I'd seen back in New York, and had been daubed, colored, primped and prepared like a Sunday goose. Still, I wouldn't say she looked like a goose, not any goose that I'd ever seen anyway. I suppose the real litmus test was I'd never met a goose that I wanted to kiss as much as I did Katherine Louisa Maddox.

We hadn't spoken more than five minutes when we were called in for supper. Luckily for me; in any case, and from what I saw being served out on the table ...it wasn't goose.

Prior to going into the dining room, she told me that she was studying to become a medical nurse. Although, I certainly didn't understand it right at that moment when she added, "It's a profession that Protestant women are very adept at."

The clue confirmed itself later, when we were all seated around the table. Instead of making the sign of the cross like a good Catholic, Mr. Maddox simply said, "Let us pray...." After lowering his head, he mentioned something about a mountain called Sinai, and how the fatted calf was to be divided equally amongst us all. I hadn't heard such gibberish since the time Frankie Scullum claimed his Uncle Alfred had been turned into a toad by *the little people*. Frankie kept calling out for candies and such, claiming his uncle's sweet tooth was acting up on him down in the bogs, and wouldn't Frankie (and therefore his friends) be kind enough to do something about it.

I started to make the sign of the cross as we do before meals, but my sister shook her head, therefore I didn't. Instead, I took it out on the fricasseed dumplings that made their way around the table, figuring to myself as they passed my way; *with just a little more meat gravy, they could go ahead and keep their fatted calf.*

My sister and her husband Stewart talked about life in Kentucky while I listened and pretended I wasn't the shameful *skibereen* that I sure felt to be. The meal was animated enough, with everyone talking about President Buchanan, the union of federal states, slavery and a host of other subjects which made no sense to this Irishman. Therefore, I just nodded my head and kept on eating. Once in awhile, I stole a glance at Katherine, deciding that not only was she beautiful, but how could she manage to eat anything with her mouth puckered downward like it was, as if she still hadn't made up her mind to be happy that day or not.

At length, Mr. Maddox interrupted my appetite when he asked me what I was interested in doing right here in Kentucky.

"I don't rightly know, Sir. I did some coopering up north, maybe I'll look for that kind of work again." I said it more than a little self-consciously.

In response he told me, "Well, there'll be some fence-mending I'm sure on all the farms up your way, once the harvests are in the barns."

"Aye, Sir, that'll be grand," was all I could think of to say.

It seemed to this Irishman, I saw the confirmation of something in his eyes, a confirmation of what—I couldn't quite say for sure; although it seemed to reek of disappointment at something or someone.

After supper, Katherine accepted my invitation to walk outside for awhile. Although she made it clear, had she better things to do, like enjoy a lightning storm or a brush fire involving a nest of hornets, she would have sworn off our little walk.

We made our way down a graveled road that led to the reddish-orange colored barn. The barn was set back maybe two hundred yards from the house and just in front of an apple orchard. It was in just such a cozy setting that she calmly explained to me, as if I was a *croppie* in school for the first time, and the first thing I would need to learn would be to wash my filthy *croppie* hands, that yes, Katherine Louisa Maddox explained to me, they were no longer Catholics but Protestants.

"You mean like Bailey Burke?" Trying the best I could, still, I couldn't hide my surprise at such a treasonous declaration, even while fearing for her well-being.

"No," she replied while dabbing at the corner of her mouth as if to announce something as common as a winter rainstorm, "Bailey Burke converted to the Church of England while we are all Methodists now."

"This means you're all going to hell!" I blurted out instantaneously and without thinking, like a nervous reflex.

"Not until I get married first, to a real gentleman," this she admitted calmly enough, without so much as a reference to what I'd just said.

At length, she touched her hair by pushing on the top of it, then on the sides, finally she patted the part of her mahogany hair which brushed her shoulders. This she did, as if her hairstyle was all made of interchangeable parts, and one couldn't be trusted to stay in place, thereby betraying all the rest.

I thought back briefly to what my brother had said about there "being a Catholic Jesus and also an "Orange" one—his brother." Now I wondered if there wasn't another Jesus, living somewhere in America, who had possibly tricked everyone, including his two brothers, and taken off with the family heritage or something of that prejudicial nature.

When she saw my stunned face, she explained that with all the hatred directed against the Irish here in the United States, it couldn't be helped. That her pappy had told them, for their family to be successful and prosper in this new land, they had to be like everyone else and that included religion. She explained it was tough enough having to deal with a foreign culture, but when you threw in; "No popery, the Druids, and being taken for an Irish domestic at every turn," it was better she said to turn the page. Actually, I believe her exact and unforgiving phrase to be, "They can bury their Roman religion back in the bogs—from which it sprang."

To be honest, her statement conjured up mixed feelings inside of me. I couldn't fault her, as I hadn't given much thought either to where God was, or whose side He was on. It was just that we had been brought up the Catholic way in a most convincing manner, and that was it. Who was I to argue with the sainted Patrick; someone who'd driven the very snakes from Erin? Everyone else who wasn't Catholic was going to hell—inevitably, and too bad for them. Something vaguely scratched at me, as to where the truth was in all of this. Unfortunately for her and everyone else who did the same thing, you didn't switch allegiances like this, it was too damned easy to give in that way. We'd condemned Bailey Burke for changing sides, and well should we, nevertheless I felt bloody uncomfortable believing the woman I loved was on her way to hell (with or without her hair in place). Like I said it was damned confusing to this poor Irishman. Still in all, despite her heretical leanings, the woman was a delight, full of energy in her new life in America, direct in her thoughts, one of which was directed at me.

"And you, "Paddy"...? What is to become of you?"

For the time that it took for the sun to break through a lapse in the cloudy sky, I saw something of her inner self. Now it wasn't love, not by any stretch of the imagination, and I'm not fool enough to warrant that. No, to this Irishman I saw a person who seemed to care for someone else, that we had something to share, that she wasn't all cold and scary and mean. Nevertheless, her use of the word "Paddy" (what the Americans used to ridicule or mock an Irishman), more or less summed up what she thought of me.

"Well, what do you mean?" I couldn't hide from her my unacknowledged lack of ambition, unless looking ahead to the home-cooked evening meal accounts for something. Then I added apologetically, "I can read and write now."

"So much the better," she contended.

"Aye...." I answered back more sullenly than I'd intended.

"Why don't you do something with it, "Paddy"?"

I'm convinced she added the "Paddy" as an insult, meaning I wouldn't know what to do with myself, even if Michael the archangel decided to come down from heaven, take me by the hand, and become my personal tutor.

"Aye, that I will." I said it once again sullenly, as if recognizing for the first time it was my right to remain a *skibereen,* if I so chose to remain one.

Katherine stopped right in front of a tree laden with the first buds of the season.

"Then please don't come back until you do!"

With her buttoned, long-sleeved arms crossed in front of her bosom, she reminded me of an angel guarding Eden, and I was just about to be thrown out on my duff, because of some precarious infraction, such as a determined lack of ambition. This then, to spend the rest of my days earning my bread by the sweat of my brow. In other words, doing what I had been doing up until that very moment. The only difference being, I was now wearing new boots and owned a recently acquired penchant for dark ale.

"Do what?" I lamely replied.

I'm in no way stretching the truth when I solemnly swear I wanted a sip of whisky in the worst way right then. Katherine had backed me into a corner, challenging me in some subterranean way to stand up for her or back down. Either way, she was playing a game with me, a mocking game in which I hadn't the slightest idea of how to compete. But she knew, yes, she already knew I could never measure up. Heck, even I was pretty much convinced of that, which is why I wanted the whisky in the first place. Ultimately, this craving for whisky may have gone a long way towards showing everyone (including Katherine Louisa Maddox) that I'm wasn't completely stupid.

Her eyes flashed, more in disgust then as a challenge, "You come back and see me, when you've got something more to offer, besides fresh mud on your new boots and a *skibereen* attitude about life."

She turned and walked away, leaving me to quell by myself a desperate prayer for help, before self-pity should over take me once again. I wish I could declare and write down for the record the solemn vow which I made that I wouldn't see her again, until I had something to show for myself. Alas, I never made that vow to her or to anyone else, myself included that I recall. I only recognized the choice was mine and mine alone to make; to stay a poor *croppie* or to? Or to? To do what? The hell with it all...as if I knew my choices. Maybe that was it; only hell or God knew, but if they did, they weren't letting me in on their little secret. Still, something was bothering me inside, but I'll be damned if I knew what it was. Somehow, I honestly felt like I did as a *gossoon*. If I could just take off running for the highlands again; feel the cool highland air filling up my lungs, my legs churning up the various paths, out of breath and light-headed, not concentrating on any one thing, but rather on everything....Maybe then things would work out. That I'd be okay finally, like when our ma told us one time, she'd heard from *the little people* that maybe, just maybe—our pappy would be coming home....

When we got back to my sister's house in Maysville, I clawed through my belongings until I found what I was looking for; the address—the gentleman, Mr. Roger had given me while feeding my mother and I lunch back in Liverpool, England. It was the address of a Dr. John Waylan, and it said his office and place of residency were in Northern Kentucky, in a town called Covington. Which my sister explained, just happened to be a short stretch of the legs the other side of Dry Creek, where Katherine Louisa Maddox and her marked disdain for anything smelling of Irish lived. Maybe Ann Horian said this to motivate me. Because I found out eventually, a "short stretch of the legs" for my sister is well over a hundred miles. A trip requiring a team of oxen, and with all the fools and brigands about can't be done in less than a week. Unless you don't have a particular prejudice about getting shot at, robbed, or maybe just strung up at the end of a rope by the conniving locals because it just so happens "to be a helluva nice day". In any case, I would have gone anywhere and done anything, to improve my up until then, non-existent lot in life. And put me closer to Katherine Louisa Maddox...brigands and fools, notwithstanding.

I noticed on Mr. Roger's hand written note that Dr. John Waylan was a dentist. This said, thought about, and finally agreed upon, I packed my meager belongings and decided to pay this Dr. John Waylan a visit. To see if maybe, he couldn't get me out of a jam pulling teeth...or into one as the case may be.

I made it to Covington, Kentucky, by sure grit I believe. In any case, our driver constantly warned us to be on the lookout for Indians ("they get so drunk —they throws up all over you"), rustlers and some furry animal he continued calling "a bar". We pulled in late on a drizzly Saturday afternoon. Still, I wasn't sure where I was, even to the point of asking myself if I was still in America. There were more German people speaking German than one could shake a stick at. They were centered in and around the downtown market place, and going on and on about the local current events while purchasing the ingredients for the next day's—Sunday meal.

"Welcome to Campbell County, My Boy—what'll be your pleasure?"

This came from a man with throbbing double chins and a patch of hair missing from just over his left ear. I guess all the rest of him looked normal enough though.

"I'm looking for Dr. John Waylan," and showed the man my note as if to prove to him I could read by myself.

He appeared thoughtful for a moment or two before replying, "If you ain't got a toothache, I'd put off seeing the doctor until Tuesday—. No, make that Wednesday. Yeah, that'd just about do it—late Wednesday afternoon."

Then he looked at me to make sure I understood correctly, which of course I didn't.

Like an imbecile, once again, I showed him my paper that had been written by Mr. Roger back in Liverpool. The double-chinned man waved it aside, like it didn't belong there, and if I had any inclination or aptitude for normal reasoning, maybe I didn't belong there either.

"Well Sir, perhaps if you just give me directions to his place of residence, I can make my way there myself, and won't be a bother to you any more."

I took my time staring at his perforated scalp as I would anyone's infirmity; hoping he'd get sick of my staring and send me over to the good doctor's house without much more to say about anything, which is exactly what happened.

It was in fact three streets over and two streets east from Main and Sixth, or as I found out later *the Mainstrasse*. So called, because of the serious representation by the German population in Covington, Kentucky. I attended to the front knocker of a non-descript house with a tottering sign which read simply "Dr. John Waylan—Dentistry".

After knocking, I heard what appeared to be soft padding from somewhere within the house. Several minutes went by before the padding approached and the door opened. Without so much as a howdy-do, a middle-aged man beckoned me in. Then with one hand firmly ensconced upon my shoulder, he practically shoved me down a fraying blue-carpeted hallway where at the end I could see a medical office of sorts. Having never been in a dental office before, I had no idea what the job was actually concerned with, nor what exactly transpired there. I supposed that being the way of business in that profession, is why, without so much as a greeting, I was impolitely pushed by the man down the hallway. The pushing and shoving continued through a red-enameled door and into a soft grey chair which had a sloping recessed section to it. Once in the chair, I took into account its frayed stitching, allowing for a loose glut of animal feathers to seep through the stitching and that pivoted upon the man's touch. As well, I took a minute or so to scrutinize the man in front of me who was now whisking about humming to himself (still not having offered a greeting of any kind). This he continued to do while he straightened several silver-colored trays with small metal tooling which clanked this way and that upon his unsteady handling. The man was of medium height, wearing brown pants with dark suspenders and a long-sleeved, coffee-stained shirt with blue and white stripes. It was fastened above his elbows by two corsets. He was white-haired, balding and wearing paltry-thin spectacles that rode just above his nose. It was a Jewish, hawk-like nose with a prominent ridge that certainly helped to fasten his spectacles to his face and prevented any impertinent sliding thereabouts. Instead of shoes, he was wearing a brown-checkered pair of thick bedroom slippers, from which, on the inner soles, both were bursting through with worn-away seamless padding. I assumed that was why instead of walking about normally, Dr. Waylan sort of slid around from one place to another, as if not to lose anymore of the slippers' padding. This is also why whenever he moved, he instigated the impression of a ballroom dancer; a ballroom dancer that refused to leave his feet under any circumstances. Oh yes, the faint but penetrating smell of whisky seem to emanate from wherever the man was.

Motioning me to take my place in the chair, he spoke to me for the first time, his eyes bearing down on my mouth much like my dog "Blister" does after a hen cornered in the yard.

"Now, you just tell me Son, where the gosh-darn thing is hurting you, and I'll have it out in no time—. Or, at least before the sun sets—make that—either today or tomorrow's sunset!"

Having said the first thing since I was welcomed into his house, the doctor (I assume it was the doctor for we hadn't been formally introduced as yet) took to laughing, wheezing then laughing again, as if he had made a joke that just might be the damnedest, funniest thing anyone had told since the world began. He would look at me from time to time, his thick eyebrows moving up and down as if trying to make me understand that I had missed something of a humorous bent. He spoke with a lisp. Therefore, his exact wording was at first hard to understand, as I moved my forearm closer to my face to avoid the fine spray of spittle which whistled from the doctor's lips, whenever he pronounced a word that started with 'th'.

You could tell at first, he was trying to be politely restraining. Nevertheless, whenever I opened my mouth to introduce myself, he was there like a coiled leopard with a pronged instrument trying to breach my mouth in a moment's notice, without actually forcing his way in.

Finally, after this unstated thrust and parry went on for several minutes, he walked over to the sideboard, reached for a coffee mug, and took a deep draught of its contents. At last, the doctor turned to me with what could only be called simple exasperation.

He explained slowly, making a valiant effort to control his lisp, "I do not speak German. However you must understand, if I am to extract anything other than your gall-bladder you *must* open your mouth!"

That was enough of that, or so it seemed to me, for he took to sliding around the room in his falling-apart slippers, pausing every yard or so to repeat; "I can take out your gall-bladder—but not your teeth—ha...ha...ha ...ha...ha...ha."

I struggled to sit up, however as soon as I did so, he was right there, bobbing right then left, looking for an opening, anything that would allow him access to my seemingly uncooperative mouth .

I eventually took to slapping his hand down. Although, I used a little too much force I believe, for he began staring at his compromised hand then back at me with a look of marked bewilderment on his face. In any case, my action was justifiable, for the man was becoming an atrocious pest.

"Now see here, Doctor," and by way of explanation I immediately thrust out the small note of introduction which Mr. Roger had written that starving day back in Liverpool.

Without bothering to read it, the dentist, by way of reply, crossed his arms, closed his eyes and shook his head before repeating, "No, no and a final no! I've told the other Germans who've come in here asking the same blasted thing; that I won't work—now or ever—on horse or other animal flesh regardless of how much extra plowing your wife may have to do. Now...now— *guttenabben*—or whatever it is that means good afternoon to you—Sir!"

His spittle flew around him like a watery comet, as he turned to make his way back to his cupboard and his uncompromising coffee mug.

"Sir, I don't think you understand?" Again I proffered Mr. Roger's note which he finally accepted, putting it close to his spectacles before reading it aloud: *Now, in the event that the bearer of this note should find you in safe and reasonable health, financially within means, I, Roger Mrytle Heathcoat, do beseech you that every courtesy be shown this young Irish immigrant, one Edward Ruth, as he starts life anew in your country, including prospective employment.*

The dentist then turned to me as if we were both involved in a top-flight conspiracy and divulged this small conclusion, "Heathcoat?—The English aristocrat?—Never liked the man—wore false teeth made from whale bone, can you imagine that? And with a middle name like 'Mrytle'—whoever heard of a name like that anyway—sounds like 'turtle', for crying out loud."

With something approaching obvious disgust, he somehow, glided once again over to the side table, and slowly laid his pronged tool down. Almost wistfully at first, giving me the impression that in not being able to use it to remove any of my teeth, his day in fact, was ruined.

He turned and padded his way back to my chair, his mouth echoing the following, "Myrtle—turtle—Myrtle—turtle, huh! I'm surprised that ol' Roger Heathcoat wasn't wearing a lacquered carapace or shell the day he wrote this note!"

He tried to suppress a chuckle, but to no avail, "A shell, damn it all—Roger "the turtle" should have been wearing a shell...."

Then he clapped a hand to his side as if forbidding himself anymore tomfoolery with so many important matters, including my imminent business at hand.

"So you want to be a dentist, do you? By the way, what's your name anyway, Son?"

"The name's Edward, Sir,—Edward Ruth, just like Mr. Roger wrote on the paper—but most people hereabouts have taken to calling me "Shakes". And as far as being a dentist, Sir, well I hadn't much thought about it."

"In other words, you're just looking for work?" He stared at me long and carefully, "Any kind of work will do?"

A picture of Katherine Louisa Maddox crossed my mind in that instance. In my imagination, she was beautiful as always, with a charitable smile on her glowing face like the day she'd offered me that oatmeal biscuit. Suddenly, my mind turned to my last memory of her. Aye, when she had looked at me with unfeigned insolence, as if I had dared to crawl out of the bogs, to visit someone of her illustrative state in life. Me, being only a pauper, and not fit for much of anything, unless bootlicking was something to be aspired to.

Summoning up my courage, I blurted out without further hesitation,

"What I meant, Sir, was I hadn't much thought about anything, OTHER than being a dentist! You see it's been a life-long dream of mine to—to—(not really knowing what a dentist did exactly, I searched rapidly for something that would lend credence to my suddenly created life-long aspiration of being one) to put tools into people's mouths to help them—to help them along."

It was all I could think of to say at such a moment. At which point, I let out a long and exaggerated sigh, as if a huge weight on my shoulders had somehow dissipated. Why as a matter of fact, I felt so light-headed and happy, I would have let the good doctor remove one or two of my teeth...if only he'd asked.

"Now listen here, uh—Edward or 'Shakes' if you prefer," the older man slipped his thumbs underneath his suspenders where he proceeded to twist and thump them against his chest while speaking. He reminded me of a man from the government, who'd given a public talk to our village once before, back in Castlewarren.

He stretched and thumped his suspenders once or twice again, before proclaiming in somewhat of a winded manner, "It's more than just putting tools into people's mouths, to "help them along" as you say. Being a dentist is a life-long commitment. It's a noble profession wherein the mouth, tongue and palate are the only true friends you'll ever need. For you see, the good book was wrong in that regards 'Shakes', the true light of the body is not the eye, but a man's mouth!"

Instantly, he took notice of my sudden discomfort...not because of what the Bible purportedly said, but because I had no knowledge of what the Bible, in fact, had to say on the subject. Therefore, I had no idea what Dr. Waylan was talking about.

I believe he offered the following by way of an explanation, "Of course, back in those ancient times they didn't know dentistry like we do today. Which is probably why it was written that "the light of the body is the eye". However"—again a thump or two of his suspenders—"today we know that if a man's teeth are scrupulously sound, fundamentally antiseptic and without damning cavities then so is the man himself. This is probably one of the main reasons we find so many well-adjusted and spiritually-minded clerical men and women of various faiths today—with little or no noxious breath, along with healthy sets of gums and molars, as the case may be."

The good doctor, having found no fault himself, with his obviously well-corroborative logic, then neither could I. So I kept silent, pondering the correlation between the dental profession and its subsequent moral implications. Otherwise, he did go on, lingering if you will, for quite some time thereafter, mentioning something about the successive failures of the early millennium crusades. This in fact, Doctor Waylan continued to explain, was due in no small part, to a lack of practicing dentists in the Holy Land. However, at that point, I was no longer paying any concerted attention.

"In any case, I can turn you in to a competent dentist, there's no doubt about that." He eyed me querulously before continuing, "But make no mistake about this either; don't be wasting what I'm going to teach you on a pack of barnyard animals. No matter how much bratwurst and sauerkraut the locals promise you!"

And that is exactly how I indentured myself as a dental apprentice to Doctor John Waylan of Covington, Kentucky for a period of four years. My sisters, Ann Horian and Susan were needed as witnesses to sign the act of Indenture as required by the law, for anyone under the age of twenty-one in the state of Kentucky. This strange turn of events, took place in the year of our Lord—1854. Some of the act was written in Latin with a lot of *Anno Dominis* and what not, which I couldn't understand. However, the thing I retained above all else was that I was promised a monthly wage of fifty cents. This remunerative promise was to be distinctly apart, as well as above and beyond the "sufficient meat, drink, apparel, washing and lodging set forth in the act of indenture." For the very first time in my life I felt a certain worth as a person. And not just because I could plow fields during inclement weather, or keep my mouth from complaining when there was nothing to eat.

The indenture act also stated: *"At which time (for four years) he shall serve his master faithfully in all things which his said master shall require of him, appertaining to said profession or trade, or otherwise whatsoever, and that honestly, and obediently in all things as a dutiful apprentice ought to do, whether relating to his said profession or otherwise. And the said Dr. John Waylan, shall teach and instruct or cause to be taught and instructed under his direction the said apprentice, in the art, profession, trade and mystery of a surgeon dentist."*

Chapter Fourteen

Furl that banner; for 'tis weary
Bound its staff 'tis drooping dreary
Furl it, fold it, it is best;
For there's not a man to a wave it,
And there's not a sword to save it,
And there's not one left to lave it,
In the blood which heroes gave it,
And its foes now scorn and brave it,
Furl it, hide it, let it rest....

Author unknown

I ended up spending five years and nine months with Dr. John Waylan apprenticing to become a surgeon dentist. Although, the last three years I organized my time between the Ohio Dental College across the Ohio River in Cincinnati, and his office when school was not in session. It was a most fascinating mixture of learning and becoming inculcated with the United States and its hell-bent desire for implosion. Being from Ireland by way of Kentucky, I soon learned that what the potato was to Ireland, *King Cotton* was to the South. As a result, depending upon whom you were talking to, Kentucky was either unionist or secessionist, including, all which that implied. As far as this Irishman's concerned, this whole North versus South idea appeared a crap-shoot or a Chinese fire-drill. Take your pick—either way it was endless confusion one way or the other...with me right smack in the middle of it all.

Dr. John Waylan was not only a knowledgeable dentist, but he was also forthright in his pursuit of his profession. Indeed, the man seemed to be living with only one goal in mind; to extract any tooth which he believed was in subtle rebellion against the dental profession. His specific motto as a practitioner of his art, which as he explained to me one earth-shattering afternoon, included the ominous forewarning; "If you don't pull it out today while it is healthy—it will come back to haunt you tomorrow, when it isn't". I never understood the full gist of his enmity towards the palate and its neighboring enamel. However, it might have had something to do with the loss of his wife several years back, and prior to my apprenticeship.

Mrs. Waylan had been the victim of some monstrous mouth disease—an unexplainable cancer of sorts. This must have been why Doctor Waylan always took the unorthodox as well as vengeful view that every patient's mouth was somehow responsible for his wife's death. As a matter of fact, he would incise and amputate anything in a person's mouth which to him looked suspect. This oftentimes led to heated exchanges between his patients and the doctor. In which case, he tried to convince them, in the event they were afraid of his spirited surgery and its confusing results that starvation was the only other option in the patient's best interest. Therefore, it could only follow logically (as Doctor Waylan would explain) that whichever was the guilty tooth should by rights surrender itself up voluntarily, long before the patient could die outright from self-inflicted malnutrition.

I tried to bring some order into this man's office. For in truth, after his wife's death, Dr. Waylan became extremely absent-minded and myopic in his outlook on life. I truly believe he enjoyed our company together. In addition to which, I was extremely grateful for our mutual professional respect, and the fact he never once tried to intrude upon my bicuspids while I was in slumber with my mouth wide-open, and extremely vulnerable from snoring.

No one of the local citizenry that I can remember came to see him, unless the pain had become so acute it was all they could do to stand up. On the other hand, knowing the doctor and his lonely habit of indulging in drink, the German immigrants would show up in force. At the ready, were their full beer steins, like so many gavels, ready to tap out a Teutonic melody while Doctor Waylan yanked and cursed against so wily an opponent, in the interior of their mouths. The Germans didn't seem to mind that for every decaying tooth, four otherwise healthy ones were pulled out at the same time, just to be on the preventative side. They would leave the decomposing swivel chair, more often times than not, listing heavily to starboard, from the beer and nitrous-oxide gas. These German patients were comically careful, not to spill anything from their now empty beer steins (which they still believed to be full) while getting used to speaking with a freshly acquired lisp, due to the new-found gaps in their mouth where their sound teeth used to be.

It was into just such an atmosphere that I was thrust. I only wish I hadn't taken to drinking with the man...but unfortunately I did. Now a lot is to be said about an Irishman who drinks, and even more so is the case about a bird without wings that flies. Nevertheless, I'm not proud of it. Although by way of justification, it seems overindulging in drink is something which may indeed befall celibate men who are in sore need of company as I was.

I truly enjoyed the people who came to our office with their colorful personalities and adventurous stories. There was a lady by the name of Hendershot, who timidly curried and cajoled, refusing to explain what in fact was wrong with her, until we showed her what an abscess looked like in a medical book. Upon having decided that was indeed the perfect illness for her, she followed it up with an unusual request for a gypsy curse. Aye, a curse which would inflict the corresponding abscess upon her neighbor, whom she accused of flirting with her husband, who for the most part shoed Covington's horses. Doctor Waylan and I spent the better part of the afternoon convincing the poor woman we would do nothing of the kind. We explained as far as we could, that gypsy curses and their resulting effects were beyond the scope of a dentist's oath or practice. She finally left our office less than grateful about our constructive intercession, and more intent upon finding a snake-charmer who would.

There was a chief engineer from the L&N Railroad, who kept trying to sell us glass vials of black soot he had collected, from the exhaust manifold stack mounted on the train's engine. The man went so far as to claim, it was a natural preventative remedy against dental cavities. Indeed, his teeth were so black from the application of his soot, it was impossible to tell from our skeptical inspection, if contrary to what the man said, he still owned any properly cleaned teeth in his mouth at all. To his staunch credit however, he never let up for a moment, convinced that his remedy would absolutely prevent any sort of damage to a person's dental composure. By the same token, he did admit to us rather candidly, everything he now ate had an arbitrary coal dust taste to it. Besides the fact, his wife forbade him to smile in public, claiming as she put it, "When he smiles, it reminds one of the Bowling Green tunnel."

These stories could continue I would imagine for several more pages, but that's not to anyone's advantage. Except, perhaps, for the incident about the two brothers who were so close in affection for one another, that one offered to have his healthy tooth pulled just so his brother, the one with the diseased tooth, wouldn't be scandalized with pain alone. In this way, they would both be hurt and could suffer together, if only out of mutual brotherhood. In addition to this, if I remember correctly, Dr. Waylan so approved of their brotherly affection, he charged a reduced price for removing the two teeth, giving them a two for the price of one deal. This just goes to show the reader what kind of sympathetic man Dr. Waylan was.

As part of my indenture, I took classes at the Ohio College of Dental

Surgery. We were taught by professors that were as peculiar as they were instructive. One of whom was J. Taft D.D.S., who specialized in Operative Dentistry. He was a diminutive man with thin arms, who wore a sleeveless surgical tunic, as if he belonged in ancient Rome discussing politics. As well, and in keeping with his toga-like attire, Dr. Taft must have considered himself something of a Roman orator. In the sense, he was inclined to postulate for hours on the liberating effects of a frontal incision, where tissue inflammation and the lamentable loss of lubricating palate fluid, were to be our primordial concerns as dentists. More often than not, our seminar would end with a fellow student from the back echelons of the classroom where the light was dimmest, muttering to the rest of us, 'Et tu Brutus?' or something of that satirical nature.

There was as well, Dr. Geo Watt D.D.S. who taught us Chemistry and Metallurgy. He somehow tied it all in to the correct preserving and canning of fruits and vegetables which was the man's unmistakable hobby and passion. He would initially start the two hour class on a subject like gold fillings. Then suddenly change the subject, and go on for the rest of the allotted class time speaking about gooseberries and ripe currants, the proper mixture of sugar to boiled water and the application of sealing wax calling for equal parts; rosin, beeswax and tallow, especially for cans that had grooved rims. My neighbor in class, one Thomas Runn, would remind the other students and myself more than once, after class had ended that once established as practicing dentists, should business ever decline, we could always put up our own fruit and vegetables for the winter. In this way assuring ourselves of something to eat thanks to Dr. Watt. The rest of the courses were assured by J. Richardson, D.D.S., who instructed us in Mechanical Dentistry while Pathology and Therapeutics were taught to us by J. Byrd Smith, M.D.

Dr. J. Byrd Smith opened our collegiate eyes to the remedial effects of ginger syrup and aqua-camphor, without which, the good doctor practically assured us—life was no longer worth living. Doctor Smith claimed, he possessed test results which could prove that if as dentists, we gave our patients a two teaspoonful mixture of ginger syrup, camphor, catechu and opium after each operation they would live to be over one hundred years of age. Perhaps without any teeth to speak of, yet intact for all the world to see—the rosy, pink gums of a new born babe. Once again, from the back of the class someone inhumed the necessity of trying these tests on ourselves, in order to show that we as dentists practiced what we preached. Therefore, should the good doctor be kind enough to open the school's pharmacy and commence the partitioning of the ginger syrup and opium, we as a class could determine for ourselves whether or not rosy, pink gums were in fact attainable. Apparently, they were for I heard a lot more clamoring for practical test results after that... especially where the opium was concerned.

We studied as can be imagined a code of ethics for all practicing dentists which included the following points (it is interesting to note; someone from the dimly-lit section of our class, pointed out to the rest of us, it was a crying shame that our local politicians didn't have a code of ethics to follow as well—other than trying to outmaneuver and befuddle one another, as well as their constituents);

Section 1: His manner should be kind yet firm and every patient should receive the attention due to operations performed on living, sensitive tissue.

Section 2: It is not expected that the patient will possess a very extended or a very accurate knowledge of professional matters. The dentist should make due allowance for this, patiently explaining many things which may seem quite clear to himself, thus endeavoring to educate the public mind, so that it will properly appreciate the beneficent efforts of our profession.

Section 3: A member of the dental profession is bound to maintain its honor, and to labor earnestly to extend its sphere of usefulness.

Section 4: It is unprofessional to resort to public advertisements, cards, handbills, posters or signs, calling attention to peculiar styles of work, lowness of prices, special modes of operating, or to claim superiority over neighboring practitioners.

Section 5: When consulted by the patient of another practitioner, the dentist should guard against inquiries, or hints disparaging to the family dentist, or calculated to weaken the patient's confidence in him.

Section 6: When general rules shall have been adopted by members of the profession practicing in the same localities in relation to fees, it is unprofessional and dishonorable to depart from those rules except where variation of circumstances requires it. And it is ever to be regarded as unprofessional to warrant operations or work as an inducement to patronage.

Section 7: Dental surgery is a specialty in medical science. Physicians and dentists should bear this in mind. The dentist is professionally limited to diseases of the dental organs and mouth. With these he should be more familiar than the general practitioner is expected to be; and while he recognizes the superiority of the physician in regard to the diseases of the general system, the latter is under equal obligations to respect his higher attainment in his specialty.

Section 8: Dentists are frequent witnesses and at the same time the best judges of the impositions perpetrated by quacks; and it is their duty to enlighten and warn the public against them.

Section 9: The public has no right to tax the time and talents of the profession in examinations, prescriptions, or in any way, without proper remuneration.

This last section, section nine always got a healthy response from the members of the sitting class when it was read to us at the end of each term. And why not? We were being taught to exercise a dignified profession, and far be it for us to discredit other members of the same profession by accepting dishes of lentil bean soup or bushels of asparagus. This, Doctor Waylan was inclined to do in lieu of payment for working on the widow Shackelford's teeth. Or, the man from Keokuk, Iowa who had an insufferable time with one of his lower molars, and was transporting a wagon full of asparagus at the time he stopped in for emergency dental services.

As dentists we earned the reputation and I suppose rightly so, for our vacuous credibility in being one of the more exciting and innovative group of professionals that you'd ever want to meet. How else can one explain the dizzying excitement we all experienced when Dr. James Taylor (our professor for Dental Science), with a breathless recourse we had never seen on our professor's youthful face before, strode to his podium and with hard to control, unrestrained enthusiasm like a racehorse at the starting gate, let it be known to the class and perhaps as well to the medical world (in due time and when it would be ready to receive such incredulous news), the curative as well as miraculous effects of...hot water. In a trembling and solemn voice, trying hard to mask his delirium for this remarkable discovery, he remonstrated the following;

"It is now a known truth that more persons are today taking hot water for various ailments than any single drug in our pharmacopoeia. The benefits that result from the internal use of hot water must be due, in part, at least, if not wholly to the heat factor."

I suppose the good professor saw in our collective regard, our amazement at something which appeared on the surface so matter of fact to all of us, yet had somehow slipped under our high and mighty olfactory student noses.

As if noting our stupefaction, Doctor Taylor went on to explain the following; "The water must be taken in doses of from one goblet to one and a half. An ordinary goblet contains about ten ounces."

With a defining finger which seemed to shake at the sky, Professor Taylor continued; "It must be drunk hot and not warm, around 110 to 150 degrees. If necessary, fifteen minutes or more may be consumed in sipping a gobletful. Wooden cups prevent the water from cooling quickly. The water may be flavored with lemon, sugar, salt, ginger etcetera, if necessary, but it soon becomes very agreeable to the palate without such, after the patient has taken it for a short time. The dose must be taken one hour and a half before each meal with absolute punctuality, and one at bed time."

We learned that day and throughout the rest of the semester, if administered correctly (at least six months to get its full effects), hot water with a restrictive diet which did not allow for sweets, pastry, fresh bread in any form or fats would allow for the following;

a) A sense of warmth within the stomach will be produced, although eructations of gas from the stomach commonly occur within a few minutes after the first dose of hot water.

b) The skin soon shows the effect of the heat. A gentle glow, with a tendency to perspiration is developed rapidly. The circulation of the body appears to become more uniform.

c) The kidneys exhibit marked effects of this treatment early, and the pancreas and liver seem to be stimulated by the internal use of hot water. Flatulence and constipation are enumerated as things of the past.

d) This method of treatment has certainly one thing in its favor that few other remedies possess—it is harmless.

As a class we decided amongst ourselves; if we were to spend so much of our lecture time on *hot water* and its superlative effect on the human body, which as dentists we had little or no time at all for, we inevitably came to the daring conclusion that the Ohio School of Dentistry would leave no stone unturned, in its quest for turning out dental surgeons of a unique and unparalleled level of expertise.

As students, we made it a point to meet on Thursday afternoons down at the tavern, appropriately named *The Hofsbrau*. This we did without our professors, to read poetry as a group, discuss current events and drink more than our share of discounted green beer.

We all laughed together when one of our fellow students, his name was Gary Berdischevski, mimicked Dr. Watt's earlier symposium on the "double" or "grinding" tooth. For Gary stood up, hunching himself to one side as Dr. Watt was fond of doing, and began in a truculent voice imitating our professor with remarkable bravado, "Now see here everyone; a 'double or grinding tooth' which has no antagonizing surface to bite on, is gradually elongated and thrown out of the jaw.... On the other hand; pears, like peaches and quinces——." This is when we all laughed together, for it was so like Dr. Watt to say and do such a thing in class, "Should be put in cold water immediately after paring, to preserve the color of the fruit. Now did everyone understand that?"

Gary straightened himself up from his hunched position, and glared down at everyone as if he, like Doctor Watt, needed a confirmation from the rest of us that he'd been understood.

From the far end of the table came back the beer-induced opinion, "And on the seventh day while resting, having nothing better to do, God in order to prove his sense of humor created professors of dentistry!"

This of course set the table to rocking. This table-rocking inevitably spilled beer from the pitcher. Which of course, produced more catcalls and comic jabs about students and their stringent budgets, not allowing for the waste of such a precious commodity as beer and so on and so forth. We all had a grand time of it, and eagerly looked forward to these Thursday afternoons when we could relax as students and bid the week goodnight. This we did before heading home, or in my case, back to Covington and Dr. Waylan's office for the weekend. Besides our poetry, which we read and voraciously dissected, the principal theme resurrecting itself each week, with more and more volatile enthusiasm, was the one pitting the Northern states of our country versus the Southern ones. The debates were oftentimes heated over several totally different philosophies, exclusive of slavery. Those, who had come to the Ohio Dental College from the deep Southern states, like Alabama or Mississippi, claimed the Federalists or Northerners were jealous of the South's life style. Furthermore, in defending their Southern fellowship, they argued vehemently the North wanted to invade and do away with chivalry and honor and a strict moral code. A confirmed code indeed, having long since proved itself, which didn't allow Southern women to work in life-sapping sweat-shop factories, as they did up north in places like New

York City and Philadelphia. These Southerners claimed the Northerners were just using the slaves and the whole kettle of slavery, as an excuse to obliterate a way of life they found threatening. Because, it couldn't be exploited and sold like so much tonnage of iron or for that matter cotton. More than once, the case was argued that while Southern women were kept on a pedestal of sorts, their Northern counterparts defined high-societal living as a cross between domestic, tri-weekly headaches and trying to find a male over the age of twenty-one, who preferred listening to their drivel over what the Vanderbilts were doing, to a room full of cigar smoke, card-playing and good port. Not finding anyone to listen, these Northern women dusted off their temperance banners, changed some of the wording, and came after the South and slavery like so many locusts. Enraged these women became, intent upon destroying something, they in fact, knew nothing about.

The debates would rage on week after week, sometimes funny and sartorial as students have a reputation for. Otherwise, these debates became verbally violent, as if the Southern students had decided the "Yankees" reputedly knew what was best for everyone. Concerned or even fearful they were that the "Yanks" would impose their thinking on the South one way or the other. Everyone got caught up in the debate as the school semesters passed, including me. I didn't perhaps, have all the facts at my command like my fellow students. Nevertheless, to this Irishman, it smelled extremely close to what the English were doing with their iron-fisted imposition on the Irish. Which is to say, like it or not, things were going to be done a certain way—*a way* if you will that had a peculiar London stench to the whole affair. I still hadn't swallowed nor forgotten what we had suffered because of those English braggarts and their Irish cohorts like Bailey Burke. And I sincerely doubt that I ever will. Still in all, of one thing this Irishman was sure; I wouldn't stand for somebody bullying anyone else any longer. Indeed, I'd had my fill of it back home in Ireland while the remaining bad taste wouldn't let me forget. Furthermore, if Bailey Burke was now a "Yankee", and making his way about, his weevily mouth spurting out things like, 'It has to be done the Lord Tenant's way', or 'The choice isn't ours, but the Englishman's to make'. Regardless of the fact, they were our crops and our fine country Burke was talking about, nor for that matter he purportedly was a follower of the Orange Christ; I'd just as soon put a bullet next to his brain, and hope it wouldn't come out until it changed his way of thinking, once and for all.

I didn't mind expressing these feelings once in awhile. Speaking out when I had a mind to, in our informal Thursday afternoon meetings.—The *once in awhile*, being, when I'd drunk more than my share of immature beer, which must have come out of the vats just as soon as the vapor had turned to liquid.

Someone would ask, "Well 'Shakes', you don't say. It must have been pretty rough for you fellows back home in Ireland?"

You could tell the other students weren't used to me spouting off this way, for they would quickly fill my mug and motion to the others to be quiet, just in case I wished to continue. It was either interesting or comically appealing to them to hear me sound off like that—I wasn't sure which.

I took a sip of beer before continuing, "Aye, it was rough alright. My brother and I wouldn't think twice about knocking over a stray rat, so's 'n we'd all have supper that night."

Then the thought would come back to me how it really had been, and inevitably I'd start to tremble and shake. Especially, when I remembered the time they'd found the bodies of Mary and William Donahoe laid out on the little street alcove in front of the Poor Law Commissioner's office, with the forms they'd been asked to fill out to legally prove their hunger, shredded and stuffed in their mouths like so much food.

"Maybe if the forms had been printed on rice paper?—Huh boys?" I forced a sardonic laugh which wasn't me at all. Still, it caused every head at the table to turn my way, not really sure if Edward Ruth had just got through saying, what he'd just finished saying. Even I was more than a little surprised at what I'd just got through telling everyone. I was usually pretty adept at keeping inside what ailed me. But because of the beer, something fierce and intolerable had come out, probably, the closest thing to hate that I'd ever known or exhibited. For a brief moment, I thought of my brother, for he was exactly like that, a wound spring ready to explode. Afterwards the thought hit me, that maybe, just maybe, we're not as far off, my brother and I, as I'd previously believed. The idea or concept I might becoming more like Paul Francis Daniel scared me more than a little. After all, he was always in a rage over one thing or another, how could there ever be peace in the man's life? Then someone pushed my beer mug towards me. I drank it off, wondering if we couldn't, somehow, get the North and South of this country together to can peaches or quinces, and perhaps drink some beer at the same time. This indeed, might go a long way towards staying men's spirits. Hell, I didn't know, but it certainly seemed like a good idea at the time. Although looking back now, I can't help feeling it was a round-about-way to avoid setting the world on fire.

Someone, I'm sure, to change what had become a morbid and distilled April afternoon, tapped heartily on the table with his glass and extolled one of our dental aphorisms, "Decay of the teeth is never restored by nature."

This I knew, was not pronounced in the interest of furthering our education. Yet, rather as a bone thrown to the dogs, to see what someone would say as a flippant remark, so we could all get to laughing again.

It wasn't long in coming, "Unless of course your head's stuck so far up your long-winded *ying-yang*—that no one cares."

What he said got a great chuckle from the entire table, except for me. For I hadn't seen the dental term "ying-yang" in any one of my medical textbooks, and didn't understand what it meant.

This was followed up from somewhere else around the table, "Luckily for us, in which case we'd all be out of business!"

I presumed once again, he wasn't referring to anyone's particular "ying-yang", but rather to the aforementioned decaying of one's teeth.

We all laughed about that last remark and settled back to doing what we did best—being students and getting ready for the weekend. Nevertheless, when I had sobered up and was back in Covington, I made it a point to ask Dr. Waylan to find out what he thought about the whole secessionist affair. He was more than a little adamant and convinced someone was playing a dirty trick on the other.

"If our minister of defense in Washington, Mr. Jeff Davis, believes that the states are sovereign and came into the union voluntarily, therefore they have the right to leave voluntarily, then I say go with what Jeff Davis believes. After all, he's from Mississippi, schooled at West Point like the others, he knows damn well how those "Yankees" think and what they're after. You've got those abolitionists hollering and caterwauling like so many tomcats on a back-alley fence over slavery. Yet, it was them that started the whole, make-no-sense-to-me business in the first place, going to Africa to get them slaves and all. Now that they've made their money, they've all turned high and mighty and what have you. That's right, disgusted with the Southern folks trying to make an honest living on a farm, needing all the help they can get. While the same damned folk that started this salty business in the first place, sit in their front row, where-everyone-can-see-'em pews on Sunday, donating to the basket with their money made from importing slaves. And caterwauling that the bible says this and the bible says that. I tell ya', ol' Jeff Davis understands the bible just as they do. And he's come right out and says it, for everyone to know that the bible is in favor of slaves—. Says it's written, right there for all the world to see—somewheres in Corinthians; 'you gotta treat 'em right, feed 'em, house 'em, give 'em the whip, especially when they sass back, 'n everything else', like it says in the holy book. Well, if God almighty ain't ashamed of it—then neither am I says ol' Jeff Davis, and I for one gotta believe that man!"

I don't believe I ever saw Dr. Waylan get so worked up. Except for the time, they'd run out of whatever it was, he was used to putting in his coffee cup every afternoon, down at the mercantile emporium.

During this time I wrote to Katherine Louisa Maddox, and most of the time would receive a response. Even, if it took six to eight months to hear back from the *busy* woman. Maybe it was because the country was inexorably heading to war, thus we all needed time to think. And therefore we couldn't write as fast as before. She was both surprised and encouraging to learn I was to become a dental surgeon. A profession, in which she confirmed, was a much better one than being a *cooper*. If for no other reason, than being in a humid, oak-wood barrel most of the day, would eventually lead to lesions of the skin. A condition, she insisted, that would wreak havoc on fine Irish table linen.

In a follow-up letter, I naively explained that a *cooper* wasn't actually to be found, working inside a barrel all the day long. When she finally answered my letter (ten months later), it was with an undeniably cynical tone. As if now that she understood, and could thank me for the illuminating explanation; that since being a cooper one didn't actually live in his oak barrel—somehow, the world was a much better place in which to live. And therefore it could continue spinning as before—on its vertical axis.

I took this as a possible point in my favor. In so far, as without the intrusion of any kind of noticeable skin lesions, I became bolder in my approach. Indeed, I even asked if I might be able to visit her and her family once again in Maysville, Kentucky.

However, she never once said yes until several years had passed. Her rare letters were charming, and of a heartfelt nature, as if she was writing to an undertaker about something which was entirely disagreeable, and as further from her heart as a fish would be to a sparrow. Because of my thick Irish head, I didn't take no for an answer, but kept writing to her even when I didn't hear back from Katherine Louisa Maddox, for months at a time.

It was only when I was close to graduation did she consent to have me visit. A visit that inadvertently introduced me to Captain John Hunt Morgan of the "Lexington Rifles". A man, who I was to soon find out, set about doing everything at twice the speed of ordinary men, as if the day wasn't long enough to accomplish everything which needed to be accomplished. The man was a whirlwind in boots and a knee-length, grey, army coat. Thus, because of Kathleen Louisa Maddox, I was fortunate enough to meet the man who did so much for our country, regardless of what the blackguards say. At the same time, and when he had a chance to, made a point of bringing young couples together, couples that otherwise might never have seen the light of day.

Chapter Fifteen

Take that banner down 'tis tattered,
Broken is its staff and shattered,
And the valiant hosts are scattered,
Over whom it floated high;
Oh, 'tis hard for us to fold it:
Hard to think there's none to hold it,
Hard that those who once unrolled it,
Now must furl it with a sigh.

Author unknown

"Oh, just look at the Captain Morgan. Have you ever seen a more engaging man, Edward?" This Katherine invoked, all lit up, as if she had just taken bread from the oven, for she was flushed and red with excitement.

I added kindly enough, "If this is typical of the Southern command, then I am confident they may have no fear of the "Yankee" tyrant."

In the instant that followed, she laid her hand upon mine softly, like a kitten's paw, before whispering hauntingly much to my discomfort, "Oh, to be an officer's wife Edward, always alone and waiting—waiting for the news of the war, at any moment, from any wounded, dirty and bleeding, hungry straggler who comes to your door with news of the battle—always wondering."

In spite of her pernicious wondering, the way she told her tale was as if there was indeed, something strikingly enviable in all of this. Perhaps even of anointed martyrdom while waiting upon the inevitable and hungry straggler to bring news from the front.

She then blew a strand of hair from her face, as if all that wondering had made her tired. Or even worse, had burnt the imaginary bread she should have been taking out of the oven, for when her officer-husband came home from the war. It struck me as strange that a woman could get so worked up

227

about her being alone, with her bread burning and hair out of place. While it seemed so much more logical, to be worried about how much longer her husband would be holed up in a cheerless trench, with very little to eat, and men of a different faction anxious to put as many bullet holes in his body as they could, without losing any sleep over the matter.

We were in Dry Creek, Kentucky, on a masterly-clear October morning, and the "Lexington Rifles" with their commander, Captain John Hunt Morgan were parading about, putting on a fine show. All the while, Morgan and his men continued celebrating the twelfth anniversary of the grand defeat of the Mexican General Santa Anna, and his army at Buena Vista, Mexico.

Katherine Louisa Maddox and I, found ourselves outside Dry Creek's city limits and next to the livery stables, on a long stretch of good old Kentucky bluegrass. The area was decorated with makeshift Republican bunting, and set out with tables and foodstuffs for when the military pageantry was finished. Someone had conspicuously placed the American flag behind the makeshift bleachers where we were sitting, as if to remind everyone there that Kentucky would remain in the union, regardless of what Captain John Morgan and the "Lexington Rifles" had to say about it.

After a fine and meticulous parade, followed by a glittering and shiny presentation of arms with the sunlight, like undaunted lightning, snapping off everything metallic and shiny, we all stopped to take refreshments and listen to Captain Morgan, prior to the start of the shooting contest.

The man took a hold of the podium as if he was going to shake it to death. The captain was not a short man, perhaps leaning towards the six foot range or just below it, yet he was girth-round solid. He too, wore the same as his fellow "Lexington Rifles"; dressed in a green uniform, bearing a gold stripe down each side. Otherwise, one could easily tell he was an officer, or more to the point *the* commanding officer, for he had a bearing unlike any solder or master tradesman I'd ever met. Although he wore the same uniform as the others, except for the white trousers and gold epaulettes on his jacket, it wasn't until he gave you the full brunt of those clouded amethyst eyes, did one forget everything, save that powerful head and his hard, unswerving regard. Only then did one take into account they were in the presence of one who commands; the result of his command and solemn responsibility being life or death to many, or perhaps for the unluckier ones a qualified missing in action.

The women all claimed he was cleverly handsome, for he grinned easily and had a cheerful "howdy-do" for just about everyone who came into contact with the captain. His beard was well-trimmed and of the full-goatee style. Lending perhaps, much of the spin and dash which would later send "Yankee" pickets scouring for shelter, if they so much as heard the wind pick up. Believing it of course, to be one of "Morgan's Raiders" or perhaps the legendary man himself, come to take their life with a silent unmerciful knife. His knee-high, well-polished, black, leather boots and silver spurs bespoke of a man always saddled up and ready for the next bivouac, whether behind enemy lines or even in downtown Richmond, for a night of cards and amusements.

"We are not to be misled by a fancy table and the fine things that go on it." This Captain Morgan informed us while pointing to the display of food which stood before everyone. "We are not to be misled by all this grandeur—that hard times may indeed be right in front of us or at best, just around the corner. Still—," this he thundered out, "The "Lexington Rifles" and Captain John Morgan are ready. Ready for what?—At this moment in time, we do not know exactly....Nevertheless, no matter what they throw at us, I can promise you, we will be ready!"

At which point in his speech, I was convinced Katherine was going to swoon, for she put an arm to her face as if she was all a burr from the extremely mild October heat. And yet, I'm convinced, she surely would have fainted had only Captain Morgan been next to her, willing to pick her up bodily and carry her away to a place of solicitous shade.

"We will leave the men in Washington to decide our fate. And may God above assist them in their decision making—for it cannot be an easy task! Yet, whichever way the current may take us, be rest assured, the "Lexington Rifles" will not flinch from its duty. We will defend you and your hearths—to the last man!"

Having said this, he swept down from the podium, and with a decisive voice and undulating sweep of his arm, saluted and dismissed the "Rifles" to take their leave for the rest of the afternoon.

"What a remarkable man!" Katherine exclaimed, to no one that I could see standing nearby. Otherwise, I had the feeling, if the Southern states, should it come down to that, could somehow be defended by sweetly kissing the commanding officer on his lips.... Then the ladies, Katherine included, would be standing in line, rousting amongst themselves, eager to defend the Confederacy and their lips against any Northern invasion.

Captain Morgan made his way down from the speaker's platform and burst past us, as if the war was already amongst us and only he knew of it. Still, he stopped briefly, before stooping low in front of Katherine Louis Maddox while believing me to be her husband, I suppose, took my hand in what was one of the firmest handshakes I'd ever felt. His goatee broke out in an obsequious smile, as if he needed only an order from us, and he would be the first in line to do our bidding.

"May I have the honor, Madame?" He was so self-effacing, one wondered if we shouldn't order an ice or lemonade from the man, just to give him something to do.

He then turned to me without waiting for Katherine to answer, "Why aren't you in the "Rifles", Sir? You're young, healthy and unless I'm no taker of men, willing to chase those "Yankees" back to their hypocritical, Puritan homes and hearths. Where they can wail away at the unwarranted injustices God has placed on this green and fertile earth of ours. One of which is to grow food down our way, and stop from turning the earth into a briar of smoke and industrial burnings that allows for nothing healthy, including the evil ones up north and in power to keep on breathing once again!—Captain John Morgan at your orders, Ma'am—Sir." This was followed by an informal salute of his hand, touching briefly his Shako hat.

At length, he patted his muscular upper chest in an exuberant fashion with both his hands, as if to show us he couldn't get enough of Kentucky's sweet, unpolluted, very, un-Northern-like air.

Without missing a beat, Katherine introduced herself in a most lady-like and engaging fashion, with her back straight as a ramrod, before turning to me and my presentation. While barely keeping her disgust at bay, she coldly introduced me as an acquaintance from Ireland. It was left to me to add, we were both from the same village. Whereas Katherine allowed that she had been born and raised there, but now could barely remember the looks of the place. Insofar, as she found the fashion shops and emporiums of Cleveland, so much more entertaining and sophisticated. Captain Morgan took every word in, breathless and concentrated, as if Katherine had just divulged the Federalist's initial plan for invading the Southern states. When she was finished, he blinked his cloudy amethyst eyes slowly, like a camera's shutter, as if he wanted to remember indefinitely what she had to say. In case, at some future point in time, he might have need of it once more.

Turning my way, Captain Morgan looked at me rather decisively, up and down, before finally asking me, "Have you ever been to the Galt House over in Louisville?"

I answered, "No Captain, I don't believe I've ever been there."

He answered back, "A game of cards is what we make up over there, Friend. And if you've half a mind to join us, why we're there just about every Thursday through Sunday on the first weekend of the month."

When I was about to say how I'd be honored to meet with him over cards, he spoke up, as if he'd suddenly remembered something awfully important, something that couldn't wait for me and what I might have to say. I found out later the man was exactly like that. Why, if you couldn't say what needed to be said right there and in a brief amount of time; then Captain Morgan would cut you off, on the spot, and end up saying what he had to say and what you were probably going to say as well. As if he already knew ahead of time what you were likely to want to tell him, yet he couldn't afford anymore of his precious time.

"Why of course you'd be honored, playing cards with a bunch of scallywags and roamin' cheats like me and my men. Probably take all our money at the same time, too. Just so you could tell everyone in Louisville, afterwards, what a damned fool Captain Morgan is."

This caused him to laugh. As if the mere thought of losing at anything to anyone, even more so to an uprooted Irishman like myself, was about as comical and ludicrous as one could imagine.

Then he straddled a shiny, black boot up on a tree stump and looked at me levelly, straight into my eyes before telling me, "Edward Ruth, if you hadn't known it before I'm telling you right now, you can learn a lot about a man when you've been up all night with him, playing "bully-twist" or "six-cards running". And either you or your opponent are down to your last salt nickel, and your red-rimmed eyes won't hide the fact that you're bluffing 'n all. That's right; t'is like a window into a man's soul, I'm telling you. A 'window', Boy—you can tell a lot about anyone this way. 'Course the only, real, sure-fire way you can find out about a man's inner workins'—what he's got inside himself—his gut-down courage if you will; is to have some mortifying enemy come screaming down upon 'im in some dug-out trench, real early in the mornin', 'fore he's woke up, all good n'ready to split his guts wide-open in a heartbeat. He ain't had time to reload and it's just you against him—bayonets at the ready, you got what I'm saying, Mr. Ruth? That's when you can really tell what kind of fiber makes up a man. Well, since all that ain't practical, the next best thing is cards—you followin' me, Boy? A man can bluff and prattle-on all he wants, still at some point, either in the trenches or playing cards at a table until five or six in the mornin', a man's gotta lay his *hand of cards* down and show everyone at that table what he's got inside—. Is he bluffin' us all or what? A 'window', Boy—I'm tellin' you, a real 'window'!"

At last, realizing Katherine was listening in, and appeared to be fainting once again from all the "bayonets at the ready", he abruptly stopped and apologized.

"'Course Ma'am, I ain't saying it's to come down to all that and whatever else will be. 'Sides begging your delicate lady's presence, all I'm saying is that you want to go into battle with tested men beside you, and not a bunch of sizzlin', stir-fry panty-waists! Good-looking in their uniforms, but not too much in the way of real courage inside, when it comes down to it—that's all. Once again, pardon me Ma'am, for my sometimes vulgar ways. I do swear sometimes, I forget where the battle field ends and good Christian manners should take over once more, that I do indeed declare!"

Finally, with a touch of his forefinger to his hat, he pushed between the two of us, and went stalking off by himself. All the while, hollering for a plate of beef, boiled potatoes and some stew sauce, as if he'd just been single-handedly fighting the Mexican army. And couldn't a man finally get something to eat after all that effort?

"Well, I must say." Katherine sighed once again, more deeply than I cared to admit.

Aye the way she said it, was as if she'd just been run over by a freight train and couldn't figure out what indeed had happened. Or perhaps, what was even more baffling to this Irishman; for someone who had just been run over by the aforementioned freight train...she certainly seemed to have enjoyed it.

I fumbled out something about the man being a good leader and all.

When Katherine just looked at me, her green with specks of robin-egg, blue eyes a mirror of disgust, and remarked while shifting her stiffly-hooped skirts about her waist, "Edward, the only battle you'll ever know, is over someone's bucked and incorrigible front teeth!"

That having been said, she lifted up her skirts and moved off, away from me, as if she had been forced to visit the prize livestock entry at the state fair, and now couldn't wait to get away from its penned-up, stench-ridden smell.

I spent the rest of that day and the next day, Sunday, with Katherine and her family. Still in all, it was clear to me that we were no longer writing in the same ledger, nor had anything in common with our basic interests. I had to remind myself with a healthy dose of self-pity; that in fact, we had never once had anything together in common. Except for my unabashed affection, for what the Irish countryside could make up in a woman and a crumbling oatmeal cookie.

To be honest about it, Katherine made it a point of virtually hiding from me for the rest of the weekend, as if I reminded her of something she so desperately wanted to forget. Her mother, as if to show how much she understood what I was going through, made every effort to treat me differently. As if I was the head butler or the ancient family gardener, and she wanted to repay me for my long-standing service and unfettered loyalty. Thus, Mrs. Maddox made sure I had fresh eggs in the morning that I was served first at meals, even to the newly starched towels for my morning wash-up which she left next to my bed. To my surprise, even Mr. Maddox had decided to put aside our differences. Upon learning of my imminent graduation from the Ohio College of Dental Surgery, he at first congratulated me, then as one professional man to another made it a point of asking me to investigate the swollen lower jaw of his carriage horse. Putting aside for the moment everything I'd learned about the Ohio Dental school's policy on remuneration for a doctor's time and study, and while I reminded myself this only applied to the human population and not to farm animals, I politely told Mr. Maddox it wouldn't present any problem whatsoever. Insofar, as I was staying in the barn's solitary sleeping room anyway, which was only separated from the carriage horse's box by the tack room and wood pile. In keeping with his newly-found generosity, Mr. Maddox was most appreciative. He kept on repeating his debt to me several times, when as a matter of course, I told him that his favorite carriage horse had been the victim of a bee-sting. In which case, should he in the future, harness him far enough away from the fragrant honey-dew blossoms which seemed to proliferate around the barn area, his horse's jaw would soon return to its normal size.

Some years ago I had lost interest in my Catholic faith, indeed if I ever had any to begin with. Therefore, it was without any conscientious self-recrimination, I accepted the Maddox's invitation to worship with them on Sunday at their Methodist church.

The Methodist church in downtown Dry Creek, Kentucky, was simply called St. Mark's Methodist church of Dry Creek. It was a finely-varnished, dark wood and even darker brick building with several imposing stained-glass windows overhead. These windows portrayed a rather formidable, as well as muscular angel, leading the way with a bright fiery torch in one hand while with the other one throwing a rather wimpy-looking, as well as completely naked man and woman out of paradise. Besides each other, they were also holding on to a half-eaten apple, from which I understood it to mean, the angel as a last and pitiful change of heart had fed the naked couple, prior to showing them the door.

The Methodist minister, by the name of Reverend Lippincott Hoover, was a fine speaker with a fluffy, black beard that hung ominously from his lower jaw, and a trembling right hand which continuously pointed to heaven, as if he knew the place intimately. More to the point, if I was to understand his sermon correctly, all we had to do were to keep God's laws, and we would all get along just fine. Upon turning and studying everyone's face in the congregation, Katherine's included, I decided they all knew something which I didn't. Therefore I concluded, when I had the chance, I too, would find out what precisely God's laws were, so I could own the same smug and self-assured look they all wore.

According to the rambling Reverend Hoover, someone apparently was in deep trouble, for they had forgotten to keep God's laws (although why anyone would tamper with the Almighty was beyond me), a man by the name of John Brown. Everyone in the assembly stirred something frightful, when the Reverend Hoover reminded his parishioners that keeping God's laws meant staying out of the Southern states. And more to the point, the state of Virginia, where this man John Brown had made a mess of things, taking over the United States armory and calling for an immediate uprising by all the Negro slaves.

He lambasted the individual responsible, this John Brown, claiming he had once before taken the devil's entourage to Kansas to provoke rebellion against God's word. The Reverend Hoover continued to remind us, in both instances, this man was wrong; emphatically, dogmatically, in just about every way a man could be...this John Brown was wrong!

Two thoughts came to my mind at that point during the Reverend Hoover's homily; one—the Orange Christ and the Catholic Christ were having another go at each other over here in America. While the other, perhaps, more disturbing thought occurred to me rather distastefully while I stared at the stained glass window seemingly floating above my head. Indeed, if it were up to me, expulsed from paradise by a fiery angel, naked men and women notwithstanding, I'd swear off apples forever.

Reverend Hoover rambled on, "We have learned that a dark angel from the north, this man called John Brown, in stark and unabridged rebellion against the Bible and all that we hold dear and sacred, has decided to create havoc down in Virginia at the confluence of the Potomac and Shenandoah Rivers at a place called Harper's Ferry. If it hadn't been for the sagaciousness of our own Colonel Robert E. Lee with Lieutenant Jeb Stuart as officers handling the riot, why who's to say what massacre might have occurred? This is another example of the American Peace Society and the "Secret Six" deciding to take matters into their own hands, for which God—and make no mistake about this, all of you—will indeed punish them!"

Then he shook his head in a most somber manner and let it hang there for a moment, his fluffy, black beard resting limply upon his sleeve. It was as if he realized a change had come over the country, and that there could be no turning back from it now, this unfortunate and sinister change. The assembly, at that point was invited to pray.

Afterwards, we spoke with one another outside the church on the grass next to several well-trimmed red-berried hedges. We ate from squares of runny apricot-cobbler and drank tea, everyone offering their view of what had recently happened at Harper's Ferry.

A man by the name of Files helped himself to some apricot-cobbler, before sententiously complaining, "To a man they were wrong—you can't take the law into your own hands!"

To this, Katherine's father protested vehemently while glaring at the rest of us, as if somehow, we were all responsible for the goings-on down in Virginia.

Mr. Files while licking his fingers, explained to our little group, "People, who before, were willing to discuss things, wait for reasoning to surface, are now calling for cold-blooded murder on both sides to solve the problem and that's what scares me. It cannot be done that way—!"

Katherine's father spoke up, his face animated with anger, "It'll be done that way if people see it as the only solution possible. If a man comes to rob me, I'm not going to stay up half the night trying to explain to him why he shouldn't rob me, I'm going to fill his face with enough buckshot that he'll decide right then and there not to rob me, regardless of his former personal feelings on the matter."

This seemed to be the general consensus among the men in our group, for one or two kept mentioning the words; "buckshot", "just let 'em try it", and "when I get through with 'im, the thief won't be able to sit down for a week", grinning ignominiously and sipping their tea, as if one didn't go without the other.

I asked Katherine her thoughts on the matter. And she was as frank and purposeful as she had been the day before.

"I cannot see why they don't let Captain Morgan go in there and restore order. Why he could make those men see reason, even before dismounting from his horse."

Her father disagreed, "That's just it Katherine, those men don't want reason, or someone to explain the repercussions of their act. They're a group of high-strung, volatile men who only understand the consequences of a rope tightened around their slave-stealing necks!"

Katherine implored her parent, "Father, didn't we just come out of a religious service where the Reverend Hooper called for everyone to turn the other cheek?"

"He most certainly did not—he preached nothing of the kind!" Her father objected, turning to the rest of us to see who would agree with him.

Mr. Files wiped the cobbler sauce from his chin before interrupting, "I'm all for what the Reverend Hoover had to say about "turning the other cheek"—to me that makes biblical sense." Then he hesitated for a careful moment, as if he wasn't quite sure that we would follow what came next, before concluding,"—as long as the cheek in question isn't a black one!"

After finishing, he snapped his hawk-like eyes at all of us, as if we were all fools not to agree.

Some things come along that make a man stop and think. In the weeks that followed, I heard about and read enough about the happenings at Harper's Ferry myself, to know that trouble was brewing and imminently so, just like the controversy of "Home Rule" back home in Ireland. Except when all the trite and pandering excuses had been played out, there was no controversy at

Peter L. Crawley

all. It was just a bunch of selfish men trying to pull something over on the rest of us to line their pockets and the rest of us be damned. It seemed to me the fuss would never go away, until the Orange Christ or his brother, the Catholic one had succeeded, come out on top once and for all. Afterwards, we could all align ourselves behind the victor and be done with it. There wasn't any two ways about it or so I thought.

What happened after that forced my hand.

My sister, Ann Horian received a letter from our brother, Paul Francis Daniel, in which he wrote he had joined up in the Federal Army, the Union one, specifically the All-Irish 69th Regiment, forming out of New York City. I'm convinced my brother didn't settle on the Union Army for philosophical reasons. But rather, they were the closest unit that would allow my brother to kill someone without incurring any legal repercussions. Knowing what Katherine thought about the "Lexington Rifles" and in particular a certain Captain John Morgan, I made an agreement with Doctor Waylan to get myself over to Louisville and the infamous Galt House to offer my services to Captain Morgan.

Doctor Waylan told me in so many words that I had to graduate from college first, finish my apprenticeship with him, then God-willing, go and meet with this Morgan fellow.

All this I did in a respectable and timely manner. Indeed, and at the same time while remembering one or two effusive lectures, from the Ohio College of Dental Surgery, I even learned to can a few whortleberries after a fashion.

At last, having accomplished what Doctor Waylan had asked of me, it was finally my time to meet my destiny, down in Louisville, with someone who firmly believed you never stood pat on a hand of cards or in the game of life, for that matter.

There was a fire lit in the big lobby. The burgundy-colored carpets echoed past soft crème-tinted banisters and discreet love-seated alcoves where couples chatted amiably. In contrast to this grandiose and formal setting, I ended up on the second floor of the Galt House where raucous male voices and high female-pitched giggling caused me to reflect; that's probably why the Northern states in America and "Home Rule" in Ireland couldn't succeed. For there were far too many people caught up in erratic self-indulgence and not enough in resolute dedication to succeeding at something; be it "Home Rule", routing the Southern confederacy, or something as simple as taking care of one's own family. Just at that moment, two over-sized, half-split, bay doors swung open and a middle-aged fellow with a dangerously dressed young lady on his arm spilt out into the hallway. She appeared to be drunk while he wasn't.

The young lady in question was trying to pry something clumsily from his vest pocket while at the same time, he kept repeating, "No, no, she'll be able to tell right away—."

This he stammered out, clumsily clutching her half-dressed, milk-colored shoulder for fear she might run away. They brushed past me, her tightly-wound dress rustling with the woman's hurried step, like the sound of a snake held prisoner in a burlap sack.

I could see past this harmonious couple into the room they had vacated. In which there was a table with neck-clothed men without their jackets on, several opened whisky bottles, and more money piled in the middle of the table than I thought existed. There was a stand-up piano in the corner of the gaming room. The musician playing the piano was bald as a fiddle with long, extended, stick-like arms that moved together elliptically in an exaggerated, rolling motion, like a free-falling ocean wave. It seemed to me, he kept playing the same song over and over again, as if no one was really paying any attention. However, I was wrong, for every so often someone would encourage the musician, "Come on, play something else, damn it all!" Upon hearing this command, the stick-figured pianist would start the exact same tune he'd been playing the last hour or so, right from the beginning, once again. This apparently satisfied everyone there because no one yelled out anything anymore about the music being the same as before. But instead, went back to playing cards like before, with some of the players nodding their heads to the tune of the piano, seemingly like it was the first time they'd heard such a tune.

In the middle of this group of men I saw Captain John Morgan sitting and playing. He was studying his hand of cards as if his life depended upon it. Every once in awhile he would peer up from his cards and look at the others, as if he was trying to determine who could possibly beat him. Also, it seemed to me; if he harnessed the rather formidable energy behind his intense staring, with what cards they might be garnering to beat him with. He was dressed up in his Confederate States of America uniform. His uniform was breath-taking to behold. In that it consisted of a fully-sleeved, light, butternut-colored coat which hung way below his hips. As well, there were pairs of gold buttons running up both sides of this coat, fastened at the neck with military epaulettes signifying his officer's rank on both sides of the coat's stand-up collar. His hair was in place and his trimmed, yet full and bursting goatee, appeared carefully waxed and gently sweeping back from his pursed and reflective mouth. His eyes were of a cloudy blue and appeared dull, lifeless, as if they had nothing to say, or more to the card-playing-point—nothing to give away for that matter. This was only a ruse however. I had seen them differently back in Maysville, Kentucky, with Katherine Louisa Maddox. When his eyes mirrored his personal intensity, flashing about, as they tried to take in everything, construe everything, even trying to understand everything. That was back in Maysville, Kentucky, and not tonight at Second and Main Street in downtown Louisville, where the Galt House stood. The captain himself had explained to me before that to win at cards meant emptying yourself. To become in a sense, lifeless, so that nowhere in anything you did, could your opponent pick up a clue, as to where you stood, or what possible motive you could have for betting the way you did. Indeed, his only habit which seemed to give away any sign of life or personal discomfort or irreconcilable agitation, was when Captain Morgan would allow his left hand to drift up to his face, and in vivid, brush-like strokes silently paint the corners of his goatee, before falling back to rearrange his cards again.

"Come on, Captain, are you in or aren't you?" One of the men at the table inquired.

Therein, Captain John Morgan drew his cigarillo to his mouth and puffed several times, before answering like a cat which is slowly playing with its prey. "Well, if I'm in the hand then you Sir, obviously are not!"

"How's that, Captain?" The man asked, albeit less belligerently than before.

Captain Morgan answered him chidingly, "You already owe me half of this evening's gaming debts—it is not my custom to turn a man's wife or his children out into the street!"

"I have always paid my losses," the other man answered icily.

His neighbor; a slouching, sweating man sitting next to him, who had already folded his cards and placed them on the table, indicating he was out of that hand, bellowed fitfully after the pianist, "Play something else, for the love of mike—can't you?"

Wherein the musician dutifully recommenced the exact same song. This appeared to placate the man, for he took to whistling the tune to himself, oblivious to the rest of the men sitting there, as if he'd never heard it before that evening.

John Morgan looked slowly around the table, before settling once again on the man sitting across from him, who it appeared, was heavily in debt to the Captain that evening.

Then he growled out in such a way which made everyone at the table stop what they were saying or doing, to listen-in to what Captain Morgan imbibed, "I say clearly and publicly in front of everyone here present as witnesses— *before* we call each other out at fifty paces like a couple of homesick military plebes; you may lose to me all that you will, Sir—still, that won't cover half the debt of what I owe to you, Horace Ready, *for-having-introduced-me-to-your-most-charming-sister-Mattie!*"

Everyone at the table went from a serious and castigating air to one of uncontrolled laughter with Captain Morgan leading the way. Cries of "here, here" and "he got you on that one, Horace" filled the room. Even the bald pianist seemed to forget himself for the moment. For his music stopped, until someone reprimanded him, "Are we at a wake or what? Here, here more music, my good fellow—and play that one about the South Carolina cottonwoods again!"

It was an illustrious evening to be sure, and even more so when the Captain spied me standing there, not knowing what to do with myself. He looked me over just once, I'm guessing to be sure that he remembered me. He especially looked closely at my left eye, the one that had been severely crushed by Bailey Burke. I guess it was like a birthmark, for those folks trying to remember if they'd seen me before, at some point in time in their lives. Before I knew it, he was right beside me, plying me into a chair, and making me sip some of his whisky right from his very own glass. As if I too, had introduced him to the girl named "Mattie", and he would be forever in my debt.

"You're the Irishman—." He confirmed to no one. Still, the way he said it—seemed to me to be more for my sake—as if to remind myself, or at least not to forget who I really was.

"Aye, we met in Maysville, a year or so ago, right around the time of Harper's Ferry—. Edward—Edward Ruth it is, Sir, but my friends all seem to call me 'Shakes'."

"Well, 'Shakes', now that you've determined just who you are and where you have been recently, permit me to tell you what I've been up to since we last met."

He spoke to me in confidence as if we'd known each other our entire lives. Captain Morgan divulged a litany of his upcoming plans and projects, some that seemed to me too far-fetched and ambitious to be true. To my utter astonishment, he told me he worked with a fellow named "Lightning Ellsworth", who could patch into a telegraph line, and relay messages to the Federals in a cryptic signature so typical of their own that the Federal Army would then follow his bidding, and without questioning it, go out and dynamite one of their own bridges they had just finished reconstructing. Then Captain Morgan would slap himself all over in gleeful confirmation, at length standing up, anxious to go, as if all he needed now was to jump on his horse for all this to happen.

Realizing no telegraph wires were to be cut that evening, he sat back down, brush-stroking his goatee at a more subdued pace. He waved off an invitation to come back to the table and resume the card game.

Looking at me carefully, he asked me as one would a deceitful adolescent, one who had gone around the corner to play kickball, rather than the disagreeable chore he'd been assigned to do at home.

It seemed to me that Morgan wanted to take a hold of my shoulders and throttle me to illustrate his displeasure with something I'd done, for he asked me, "'Shakes', why aren't you with us? You may be Irish-born and all, but you're an American now. You've got to make a stand, Son, a firm decision—why we all have to at some point in our lives. Damn them and damn your weakness! It's time to strike back at those English cowards!"

As if he understood my confusion he went on to explain, "Be it Northern Federals or English aristocrats—it's all the same. They've both made it a point to tell us how we should live our lives. Not only that, but make subservient fools out of us all in the process."

I didn't answer right away, but appeared dumbfounded trying to remember to close my mouth from the complete amazement written on my face. I had never listened to someone before who was so convinced that he was absolutely right in everything he had to say.

Then he changed his authoritative tone to a more congenial one, less harsh, like a boxer searching for an opening as he tried to reason with me, "It's that woman isn't it? The one I met that day back in Maysville? The two of you are to be married—that's how it is, I'd be willing to bet on it! She doesn't want you to leave her cuddly side for one single day, or come back wounded—huh?"

He immediately answered his own question, "Why no! Back in Maysville, she mentioned you're just an acquaintance from the old country, Ireland—that's all. At least, that's what I seem to recall her saying."

Afterwards, he looked at me rather oddly, as if he suddenly remembered and now understood.

Taking into account my sudden consternation, he encouraged the truth from me like an irascible older brother who wouldn't take no for an answer, "So—it's the other way around is it? You've a hankering for that headstrong Irish lass. Can't say's I blame you, a real beauty if I do recall; the way her hair bounced all around that fair neck of hers." At length, he clapped his hands together as if to confirm an idea he had chanced upon. "What better way to show her what you're made of, 'Shakes'—come with us. "Morgan's Raiders", they're starting to call me and my men now, and we'll show that woman—what was her name again?"

I interrupted in a weak voice to tell him that her name was Kath—but he cut me off crisply as was his want, "I'm of the belief that back home in Ireland she saw you as one of those scurrilous fellows. You realize don't you, everything she hates about the place, and no longer wants to be reminded of.

Why you could do everything she asks of you, and it would never be enough. I'm telling you—you remind her too much of where she came from, and what that beautiful woman is still trying to forget! Why come with us, Edward, er, I mean—'Shakes', we'll fill you up with some good, down-home, Southern chow—fill you out right too, maybe add a muscle or two to that lean frame of yours, so she won't recognize you anymore."

As I am in the habit of doing, I started to explain and over-intellectualize my history with Katherine when he stopped me, curtly, almost rudely like he didn't have time for any more of my eternal, "panty-waisted, wrangling", as he liked to call it.

"Listen to me carefully now, 'Shakes'—." You could tell it was all he could do to refrain himself from giving me a formal order, "This Katherine— damn it all—any woman quite frankly, wants to respect her beau, her future husband. If you go around pandering to her, listening and paying attention to all her self-indulgent, panty-waisted ways—even if she's sincere...." He took a sip from *our* whisky glass before continuing, "Then again, what woman isn't—? You won't be fit for duty—any duty and that includes her love for you. You see deep down, 'Shakes', she wants—heck, they all do—a man they can respect. Who won't necessarily take their guff, just because it comes flying out of their mouths the first thing in the morning along with their hotcakes. Sure, you can listen to 'em howling about this or complaining about that, but deep down they want to know their limits—just how far they can go. Hell, if you let a woman—any woman say and think and do whatever they feel, it won't be a civil war between the states any longer, but the final and absolute apocalypse raining down on the rest of us!"

Then as if to realize he'd spoken harder than he intended to, he added as an apologetic afterthought, "That goes for Horace's sister Mattie, as well."

He pointed a finger at the man sitting there, still playing cards at the table. Although he now appeared to be winning, for the one he called Horace kept slopping the whisky into his competitors' glasses and urging them, "Not to quit now, Gentlemen—why Tuesday's still three days away!"

I didn't know what to think. It was all so confusing to me. In a sense I kind of liked it that way, for I could take my time about musing this way or that until hopefully, the decision would just up and pass me by. I knew that about myself. But seeing how Paul Francis Daniel had joined the army up north, and things were coming to a head down the Captain's way, with some of the states having already filed for secession, also, that I was done and finished with school. In addition to which, the bloody, Federal-English-Union boys weren't going to let the Southern states leave peacefully; once again telling everybody what to do and how to do it. And now that I recall, Katherine in fact, didn't have the time of day for me. Although to her credit, her father seemed to realize my inherent value when I relieved the bee-induced swelling on his suffering carriage horse. Therefore, I did the only thing which seemed wisest to me at that moment in time. I pulled slowly on my whisky, and wondered about St. Mark's Methodist church back in Dry Creek, the Reverend Lippincott Hoover and his stained glass window. In particular, trying to determine if Eve wouldn't catch a serious case of influenza, by leaving paradise without clothing of any consequence on her person.

Captain John Morgan interrupted my thoughts by putting a stiff, rugged hand on my shoulder, and told me solemnly, "Sometimes, a man gets a wake-up call in his life and he doesn't know why."

I jumped rather significantly in fright from the Captain's hand, for it had disrupted my altruistic thoughts.

I asked him reflexively, at the same time looking anxiously all around the room, "My goodness—are we at war already?"

He looked at me furtively for an instant, almost with disdain, like he was evaluating me....Measuring me up for something, but he wouldn't say anymore about what he wanted. Instead, he launched into an explanation about what Jefferson Davis was saying and doing to bring the conflict to a speedy conclusion. As far as I could tell, John Morgan had but two recurrent themes in his life; his eloquent respect and unbounded admiration for Jefferson Davis. And what he could do to help Mr. Davis get those damned, pole-cat, Union boys, including Lincoln and McClellan, off the fledgling Southern back.

You could see the whisky was starting to get the better of him, for more than once he held his finger to his lips, giving the sign of quiet, followed up by, "'Shakes'—."—Except, it came out more like "Sha-a-a-k-e-e,—I can tell, and believe you me I've got the experience to know such things—you'd make a fine Irish rebel."

Then he added in typical Morgan fashion what appeared to be a comical afterthought, "'Shakes', we'd best be more careful in how we light up our cigars tonight. Lest the dynamite we're to be using on the bridges blows up our way, taking the better part of our rear-ends and therefore our cerebral wherewithal, to execute our surprise plans—away."

Inevitably, he took to guffawing all by himself, in such a manner that the others stopped their card-playing to ask what it was which had made Captain Morgan laugh so hard. At length, as if he'd made a vulgar remark or a social gaff, he put his glass back on the table to try and sit quietly, something which for him was quite impossible to do. Nevertheless, he made the effort to sit completely still, with an amused air about him while putting his finger to his face motioning for quiet. At the same time Morgan kept eyeing the amber liquid in his glass, as if it too was dynamite and needed to be protected at all costs.

We sat there staring at one another, taking turns sipping from the same glass, as if it was a contest—. Which in fact (now that I know the man better), it most definitely was.

Eyeing the swirling, imported whisky Captain Morgan told me, "They say the Irish can hold their liquor—while I'll be damned put out to see if an Irishman can stay up with me."

And so it went for the next several hours until long into the night. Our drinking became interspersed with tales of Jefferson Davis, the Mexican campaign and how soon the anticipated ground swell in Kentucky would finally burst, and "the hallowed bluegrass state finally see the light and come over to our side!"

Things finally came to a close early the next morning, and not as some may anticipate because this Irishman couldn't keep up with Captain John Hunt Morgan's drinking. But rather due to the mayhem caused while we were reliving the battle of Buena Vista, when suddenly the room's sofa which had been turned upside-down and converted to resemble Zachary Taylor's artillery collapsed. The sofa fell abruptly and pointedly, thereby, provoking a rather significant hole in the hotel room's floor and consequently the ceiling of the room underneath ours. This invoked great concern with the Galt House manager who forcefully asked us to leave despite Captain Morgan's acerbic request, "Without rounding up the Mexican prisoners of war first?"

We ended up outside, on the corner of Main Street and Second, at around six in the morning, with our arms linked around one another for support as the ground was swaying something fierce. Captain Morgan and I sent word to the Mexican General Santa Anna that under no circumstances were terms to be given. That only an unconditional surrender and the laying down of all hostile arms would be acceptable. Other than that, the war would continue with Santa Anna to be held solely responsible for the resulting carnage. At last, the ground gave way before us, and we both fell down, our arms still holding on to each other, laughing impetuously as we did so.

Oh yes, there was one other thing which happened that early dawn. While waiting for the Mexican General's attended response, I was mustered into the Confederate Army. Or more specifically, "The Lexington Rifles", with John Hunt Morgan, who swore to me that august morning that he'd never been a Free and Accepted Mason, commanding.

PART FOUR

The War Years

Chapter Sixteen

September-1861

Furl that banner-furl it sadly
Once ten thousand hailed it gladly
And ten thousand wildly madly,
Swore it would forever wave;
Swore that foeman's sword could never
Hearts like theirs entwined dissever
Till that flag would float forever
O'er their freedom or their grave.

Author unknown

"Hawks are about." The coded phrase came to us in the form of a hand-written note from a Southern sympathizer, United States Senator John C. Breckinridge. His note signified we had to leave Kentucky immediately or accept the consequences which meant facing Northern muskets. Nonetheless, Captain Morgan being the far-sighted man that he was did not mean to leave his home empty-handed. We were instructed to meet at the Lexington armory; there he would disclose his plan. Until then, everything was to be kept bottle-tight and as secretive as possible. When we arrived, we found what Morgan had planned was as audacious as the man himself. Captain Morgan welcomed the seventy-five of us in to the armory and closed the door. He slapped some of us on the back, others he bear-hugged until they couldn't breathe while to others he mentioned a word or two about, "So it's to be like it was in Mexico—. Well then, and by all means, let's get onto it!"

He kicked over a wooden crate in which he could stand on in order to be heard.

"Fellows and members of "The Lexington Rifles", all of you have been following the situation. The Unionists from Camp Robinson have recently arrived in our city and intend to stay. The state assembly has declared in favor of the Union. Jeff Davis needs us now, every one of us—now—tonight! But we aren't leaving empty-handed!"

Then he slapped his hands together with incriminating glee, as if the Christmas duckling had just been served out, and he was the one nominated to carve it up just so.

"Men of "The Rifles", we'll leave alright and do our soldiering elsewhere for Jeff Davis if he'll have this motley, but courageous band of Kentuckians! But what's a soldier without arms? We're not worth anything to President Davis as we stand now—without weapons of any kind."

He then proceeded to take in the wooden crates of rifles carefully stacked up, greased and oiled that our pro-Southern Governor Magoffin had given the State Guard, of which the Lexington Rifles were a proud part.

"What good is a soldier if he doesn't have the wherewithal to fight?" He asked blankly of everyone there.

It was pretty obvious to us all now what Captain Morgan was proposing; that we leave the city, and borrow for a time being, what the Captain had decided was laying neatly stacked up in the armory, and by rights and his calculations ours to take.

He declared, "Now then, here is what I need y'all to do."

Even though he must have been up half the night trying to figure out a plan which would enable us to escape clean away with the rifles, the man was something to behold. Captain Morgan was freshly-shaven except for his goatee. As well, he appeared impeccably dressed in a black suit with matching vest and flamboyant white handkerchief, setting off a blue-colored neckerchief, and wearing a smile that seemed to say he'd been waiting all his life for this moment. It seemed hard pressed to believe this enthusiasm for battle came from a man who two months before had lost his wife. True, she had been bed-ridden for quite some time. Still, the man had recently lost his wife, and here he was a grieving widower organizing traitorous activity against the United States of America, like we were all headed out on a morning turkey-shoot.

Captain Morgan didn't waste much time worrying about things anyway, or so I learned over the following weeks. He called out quickly and in an electric voice that pretended not to harbor any misgivings nor doubt for that matter, as to what our course of action must be. We were ordered to fall into parade rank and practice our marching inside the armory and its window-barred, dusty interior with as much movement and noise as was thought possible. Not to antagonize the man that's exactly what we did, even executing a rather sloppy display of the manual-of-arms, and an insipient inspection of our muskets, which brought down the Captain's wrath upon us all. It happened while, he with ten or so of the others, were unloading our reclaimed rifles from their crates, and stacking them into hay wagons while replacing the empty rifle crates with bricks. During all of this, the captain was a whirlwind of direction, precise movement, and bellowing orders, as if it was possible for someone to be in several places at once. While at the same time, he seemed to be aware of what everyone else was doing, or at least supposed to be doing. This is what brought his ire down upon us all, starting with me.

Captain Morgan called out angrily, "Hey you there, the Irishman— 'Shakes', what the hell's the meaning of all of this?"

I hadn't been with the Lexington Rifles all that long, and was still having trouble keeping in step and my rifle from raking across my shoulder, causing a severe bruise after every march. I saluted him as best I could while trying to concentrate on what the man was after.

He smiled first to himself. Then as a father would to a son who had never done any of the thinking for the family, he chided us, "If the boys from the Home Guard come sniffing around and see us marching like you're marching right now—like a bunch of pantywaists—why even those stupid Unionist bullies would know something's up! You see men, we've got to make it look like we're really training and not just sitting around stealing rifles from the armory. You do understand the technical difference don't you, between pantywaist-marching and real-soldiering?"

Then those cloudy, amethyst eyes of the captain furrowed themselves into little slits, as he intimidated to those of us standing there, "And if you don't know what I'm speaking about, try concentrating on the difference between living free with the other Confederate states, and being trussed up to hang from an oak tree in the middle of Lexington for piracy and treason. While all your friends and neighbors gather 'round to watch you, as your eyes burst out and your face slackens and turns purple, as you slowly twist in the wind—."

Afterwards, he looked directly at me, asking me with his furrowed eyes if I could now understand and follow a simple order.

In return, I gave him by best not-to-worry sign while I wondered what time we'd break for supper.

So we gathered up our muskets and continued to march. Albeit somewhat quicker and more handsomely, as if we finally meant what we were doing. I mentioned to the man marching next to me, a former gunslinger from Missouri that Captain Morgan seemed tireless.

He agreed with me, "He'll need that energy—hell, we'll all need that energy when it comes right down to it in the months ahead. Now, don't you worry nothin' about it right now, 'Shakes'. You go on ahead and take your ease. Like I been telling you, don't worry about a thing. 'Cause when the time comes, and you've got hot Yankee lead trying to beat a tattoo up your front quarters and down your backside, you'll find all the energy you'll need, tryin' to avoid them bullets, just like the Captain tonight!"

I had a lot of time that night to ponder on what the man had to say. With Morgan in command, we sent the brick-loaded crates, labeled "Arms from Captain Morgan, State Armory, Frankfort", down to the railroad depot while the rest of us stole quietly from the armory, out back to the Versailles Road, with the guns concealed amongst the hay in several wagons.

I figured that once the truth was known, we'd all be in for a shellacking from the Home Guard ruffians. Therefore, the best thing for all of us was to continue discreetly on down the Versailles Road, heading towards Bowling Green, and the much more accomodating Confederate lines.

Nevertheless, Captain Morgan was Captain Morgan.

Which is why, without so much as a glance over his shoulder, as to what might be attempting to come out after him, he told us right there on the Versailles Road, during a balmy yet unforgettable September night, "Well Boys, how's to a little supper now—I'm just about starvin' to death?"

And he turned his horse around in a vicious manner heading *back* towards Lexington, and to my utter astonishment—the very unsympathetic Home Guard.

The gunslinger from Missouri, taking into account my glazed look of amazement, at the captain's forthright audacity, turned to me to ask, "You don't want to miss out on all the fun, now do you, 'Shakes'?"

I had come to the conclusion somewhat earlier that evening; there was a lot more "fun" to be had nearer the Confederate lines than back in Lexington, close to any sturdy oak trees. But then again, I hadn't given the order to steal rifles right from under the Unionists' noses.

Heading back in towards the city, my horse threw a shoe and took a bad fall.

Still in all, this only caused the men of my company to laugh uproariously at my mishap, and one of them even made the caustic remark, "Not such a bad evening after all, eh Cap'n Morgan? We got us our rifles back and almost lost ourselves an authentic Irish rebel—all on the same night."

Captain Morgan didn't answer. Instead, he smiled that close-to-the-vest ironic smile of his while he kept riding up in the lead. As was his habit, Morgan kept his head cocked like a half-asleep hunting dog in front of the hearth; always keeping an ear about, 'cause you just didn't know when trouble was about to break, or from what direction either.

You see, looking back after a raid or two, and riding with the then Captain Morgan (before he got into serious mischief and became a General), you could tell when the man was settled or unsettled. If he was darn sure the scouts were serious about keeping their noses to the trail and not half-drunk...that the

Federals, reportedly weren't up and about in the close vicinity of where we were heading...that things were going to be "hominy for awhile" as he liked to call it, why he'd settle back on his black mare, "Bess", lower his head and take to planning that evening's entertainment. On the other hand, and what I saw more often than not, was a man just about frozen on his saddle, attentive to everything, suspicious of the least bit of sound like the time that woodsman from the Cumberland mountains tried to take his ear off with a squirrel gun. Except the Captain just didn't feel right during the day, and would stop and start "Bess" every so often without any rhyme or reason to it, as if he didn't want anyone nearby to get a bead on him. And he proved to be correct on his hunch that day as well as on more than one occasion afterwards. And if you don't believe me just ask his ear.

I'm not exactly sure what kind of pleasure the Captain got, from being holed up in the middle of Lexington while the Union regiment from the fairgrounds turned the town upside-down looking for him, once they discovered the rifles were missing. But that in a very real sense was Captain Morgan—playing it as wide open as possible without getting caught. Then having a good laugh over those who went around scratching their heads while wondering where the heck he'd gone off to. And how could he have slipped away without anyone knowing about it nor having seen the man, like some sort of galloping ghost.

We heard later that the Federals seized his property. Thereby, leaving him without much of anything, except as the newspaper, *The Atlanta Commonwealth* wrote; "Houseless, wifeless, with little to live, love, fight or die for, but the new republic."

The next day we rendezvoused at sun down, picking up our rifles out on the Versailles Road. Thus we said goodbye, leaving Lexington, Kentucky; lock, stock and barrel to the Unionists, minus some "trifle weaponry"—a gift from the governor.

Following our break from the city, we still had to get ourselves and our rifles down south to friendlier lines. Consequently and as a matter of tactical strategy, we fooled the Kentucky Home Guard for two days and nights until we reached the outskirts of Bowling Green. Sometimes we'd stop and ask for directions, which road to take, and if the Guard was about. It seemed most of the time the people were favorable to us and proved it, by leaving us with food to eat. I especially learned to enjoy stewed possum with all the trimmings, as we made our way further south.

Although somewhere, just about a half-day's march south from Bardstown, we heard for the first time what was to become a most familiar phrase as the war and our raiding continued, "For the love of God never breathe my name."

We had just left a thickly-wooded ravine next to a creek of sorts, when I heard Captain Morgan asking a crippled woodsman we'd ventured upon, if it was safe to use the road leading down past the mill we could see, off in the distance.

That's when I heard that phrase. An unforgettable phrase, which seemed to conjure up all the unfettered and sleep-postponing remembrances of that war of Northern aggression.

For the hunched-back woodsman told Morgan, "Go on, you can use that road alright, for the Northerners left these parts yesterday around noontime. But for the love of God, Sir, please, never breathe my name or that I told you so."

The man would help us as an informer, but God help him if he got caught. It continues to haunt me...what he told us...his courage in doing so, and how he trembled when he said it until this very day.

Then we fell in with the others just outside Bowling Green.

Now, if you've ever bivouacked you'll probably understand easily enough (although you'll probably won't want to remember), the monotony and ritualistic-like existence of camp life. For me it was boring as hell. First off, I don't excel at cards. Secondly, sentry duty reminds me too much of shepherding, like I did when I was younger, back in the shallow hills and damp trails of Castlewarren, Ireland. You wait and wait for the time and your shift to pass, unless someone who looks important happens to come by. In which case, you have to look busy doing nothing or you get yelled at because you look too much like you're waiting—that's the army for you. Mix that in with the campfire smoke which seemed to settle over all of us, thus getting into all our clothing leaving its eternal, burnt, frying-pan smell, and the unhealthy living of too many men bundled together in close quarters. Why when one got sick we all came down with whatever ailed the first man. Add to that the stringy diet of hard tack and boiled whatever, all served up and coming again at you on the morrow—the same bloody meal. The thing that disheartened me the most was my blackened finger nails. They were like that from day one and stayed that way most of the time until Appomattox. No matter how hard I tried to keep them cleaned, remembering as a young dentist should that clean hands and cleaner fingernails were our professional badge of honor.

Luckily for me I was with Captain Morgan. For he didn't take much to camp life either, being more of the type of fellow that didn't calculate all that well like some of the other captains or reminisce much about; 'if I only had this or that many more men or guns or horses, we could attack the enemy here or there—if only—'. Rather, he took stock of what was available in terms of our companies' strength, and would then let fly like a ball of fur with whatever he had at his disposal to wreak havoc behind the Yankee lines. Indeed, this was Morgan's gift to the cause; raiding behind enemy lines and all that went along with which that type of opposition entailed. This included intercepting strategic telegraph messages *before* cutting the lines, blowing up supply depots, railroad tracks, in fact, anything that mirrored the French devised system of guerilla warfare.

As I recall we hadn't even mustered in (the Captain claimed it was only a formality for those pantywaists who had attended the Citadel or The Virginia Military Institute), before Captain Morgan gathered the lot of us one afternoon after our bean soup lunch with baked cornbread, and said we should make ready to ride in a day or two at the latest. Morgan insisted he wasn't going to sit around camp everyday while we turned into "pantywaists", and ended up not being fit for much of anything except being drunkards. For he'd heard somewhere that one of us already had set up a small still outside camp and had started brewing corn mash. This probably irritated the man even worse; to have drunken pantywaists as cavalrymen—that had to be unthinkable for a man of Captain Morgan's uncompromising standards. I suspect that given the fact we hadn't mustered in or been formally sworn to any kind of oath was in some way done intentionally. That it put Captain Morgan and the rest of us outside the conventional laws of war. And although at the time none of us realized it, had we been taken prisoner we would be considered as spies and dealt with accordingly. Which I believe confirms Morgan's continual flirting with an ill-conceived and ill-timed death wish. I refer to the paradoxical suggestion it was ill-conceived and ill-timed for the simple reason that his death wish involved his men, including me, without our approval, and therefore assuredly ill-conceived. And ill-timed; because most of us weren't ready to be hung as spies just yet. Heck, we hadn't even finished paying off our gambling debts, still lingering, from those mischievous nights at the Galt House in downtown Louisville.

In the meantime, men were coming in every day and in force as well to join our celebrated cause. They would throw up their tent in the nearest vacant spot, holler for the commanding officer in charge, and then almost immediately take to bawling for the things nearest their hearts—what time was chow served up? Where were the Texans and their wild card games hiding out, and when could one take to skinnin' some blasted Yankee "hide". This meant of course that there was no order to anything, daily living became haphazard and ill-meaning discipline settled in, which meant the inevitable, clan-festered bickering between the Southern states ensued.

I was fortunate to have my tent next to a young private by the name of

Nathan Bedford Forrest, who was as entertaining a man as I've ever met. His tales of backwoods hunting in the Carolinas made many an evening passable while we waited. It is only in consideration of what he later achieved do I mention that I was fortunate enough to have met the man when he was only a private. He was certainly in every respect what my mother would have called, "A *dacent* man!"

I also met a most influential person in my life, our chaplain, who happened to be a French Jesuit Catholic priest. His name was Father Alcime Stanislaus, and while he spent most of his time with the ambulatory hospital, still, his tent wore a painted cross on the outside with a sign next to the opening which read: *Bienvenue—confessions, confusion and conversions every Saturday afternoon.* Indeed, the man inside the tent wore a priest's cassock, as well as a profound dignity which I didn't start to consider until much later when I sobered up as a man, and wanted to understand a little bit more about why things are the way they are.

In spite of the lingering dirt, camp life and getting yelled at by dumpy sergeants who thought they were doing their job, it became one of the happiest mornings of my life while shaving, the third day outside my tent and having almost finished, I heard a voice arguing about the edibleness of our morning's breakfast.

A stark and maddeningly familiar voice threatened someone, "Why this stuff makes *stirabout* look like me mother's steak and kidney pie, my friend. Hell, even the Scots won't touch your breakfast! And believe you me if it's free they'll eat it even if comes from the rubbish pile—that bunch of Scottish good for nothings—."

I couldn't believe my ears, but that it wasn't "Devil" McGoran raising a not-too-subtle fuss over his breakfast. Putting the razor down, I called out his name and ran to where I thought he must be; two tent rows over and past a stretch of worn grass by the central mess tent.

It was "Devil" alright and not too far away Longfellow Mortlock was there as well, his legs up on a camp chair, still wearing his pitted with rust, faintly-black, policeman's helmet. Although now, it was tilted back off his head at a relaxed angle while the man himself was poking cautiously at his breakfast, like it was half-alive and might up and bite back at any moment. I hollered out as best as I could, and took to alternately hugging and stepping back to see my old friends.

"Devil" McGoran hadn't changed all that much. Still in all, it was hard to see anything of his face behind his bushy, red beard except for his shiny eyes which closed and opened, as his fanned-out, full beard shook up and down with genuine happiness to see me once again.

He kept pushing Longfellow in the ribs and repeating, "Well now, if it ain't the Irishman-turned-rebel. Well glory-be, t'ain't it so now!"

In fact, he insisted to the point that Longfellow slapped his fist away and had to tell "Devil" to calm down, that the war hadn't started down our way just yet.

On the other hand, Longfellow Mortlock had more creased lines on his elongated forehead, making him look older then when I'd last seen him. However, his handlebar moustaches as if it were possible, were even bigger and fuller than before. In fact, he reminded me of a grandfather walrus that had trouble speaking, as if the weight of his moustaches prohibited any extensive opening of his mouth. Thus his words came out garbled and barely articulated, as if he had been drinking, or worse for all of us back then—not drinking at all. Still he was a big man, and carried himself like he did back on the deck of the *Nimrod*; his shillelagh in one hand that took to a very drawn out tapping against the other hand unless he got excited, and then the tapping increased which generally meant a handful of varnished Irish timber for any provocateur in the nearby vicinity.

Longfellow Mortlock put down his plate and beckoned me to a place where the three of us could talk privately. I looked around at all the tents surrounding us. There were soldiers everywhere. Some of them were inside their tents, lounging about, with some of the others, outside, eating breakfast or chewing tobacco, smoking their pipes and continually calling out to one another with an array of remarks. It appeared to this Irishman, that none of these remarks were particularly heart-warming and most of them pointedly insulting, as men will do even amongst friends while bivouacking and away from their womenfolk.

We walked away from the camp and found a stand of birch that shaded us from the Indian summer sun where we could talk. I tried as best I could to fill in my friends as to what I had been up to, including dental surgeon school in the time that had elapsed, since we had left one another in New York City.

They both nodded trying to follow what I'd told them. Longfellow took to slowly tapping his Irish war club against his thigh while "Devil" grabbed a thick branch of birch, and started to whittle what looked to me to be the imposing silhouette of a woman. I guess that seemed as good a place as any to ask them where'd they been, and what they'd been up to since we'd last seen each other.

"Did you ever find your Indian wife?" I asked, half-wondering if "Devil" would even remember he'd had one.

"The Mohawk one, 'Shakes'?" He half-grumbled at me, obviously not liking the question.

"Was she Mohawk? I don't remember exactly now. Yes, but it seems to me you mentioned something about her being from the Mohawk tribe."

He scratched his red beard in particular disgust before answering, "Aye, I found her alright. 'Ceptin' her pappy done chased me off the reservation, 'fores I had a chance to make up with "Fox-wind"—that was her name you know. Too bad for me though, by the time I found out what my wife's name was she had already left, or so her pappy done told me."

Longfellow stepped in long enough to make a very caustic and pointed remark about how his ex-wife's name should have been "Down-wind" instead of "Fox-wind". His remark apparently had something to do with their tribal custom of waiting for spring before properly bathing themselves.

I claimed I didn't know anything about his wife, including her Indian name, which "Devil" then pronounced rather carefully, at first, in the Mohawk tongue. In such a way, it reminded me of someone trying to speak with two week old, dry cornbread stuffed to the gills of their mouth. I wanted to ask why the Indian maiden's father had run "Devil" off the reservation without a second thought. However, just then, "Devil" held up to the sunlight a scraggly, pincer-bearing, black bug which he'd found somewhere in the depths of his unwashed, red beard.

At that point, I decided I sort of knew the answer.

So instead, I asked, "Well then, how did you two hook-up again?"

This time it was Longfellow who surprised me. "We met when both of us volunteered for the Union Army back in New York City. We done seen your brother there too!"

"You both were in the Union Army?" I repeated more than a little surprised.

I tried vigorously to remember the Southern Army's punishment for aiding and abetting Northern spies. However, upon further consideration of my two lost companions, I calculated they couldn't possibly be spies. They just weren't sneaky or conniving enough, unless a second stack of buttered and griddled, buckwheat hotcakes was at stake, then perhaps.

Longfellow noted my discomfort and needled me gently in the side with his shillelagh, which still made me lose my breath for an instant or more, before answering, "It was only for a couple of days which is when we done saw Paul Francis your brother."

"Devil" cut in abruptly enough, "Whew boy—I'm tellin' you, those Northern sergeants are real sticklers for rock-solid, never no-mind, hell-bent-for-leather army discipline. We's had to march a certain way and hold our damned muskets another. Hell, they weren't going to make soldiers out of us, but damned near walking-statues—just as easy for the Southern boys to shoot as a wounded pigeon, the dog does play with out in the yard. So's we done take our enlistment bounty and high-tails it out of there to somewhere's else where you can shoot the enemy without having to ask the sergeant's permission every time you pull the trigger, or want to use the latrine for that matter. Sure 'nough, of course we told Paul Francis to come with us, but he didn't want to. Said his outfit was all-Irish—the sixty-second or sixty-third, something like that, I can't remember now. Still in all, he was pleased as punch that he was fighting with an All-Irish company, and they especially wanted to show Lincoln and the rest of those Northern commanders, including McClellan, they could fight just as well as any true-blooded Yankee. Aye, so that's a fact, he didn't want to leave and come away with us."

Longfellow explained half in jest, "It was the Sixty-Ninth Brigade that your brother joined up with, and they's got a formal motto which "Devil" and I sort of borrowed for our own—in Gaelic of course—'*faugh a ballagh*', which means—'clear the way'—."

At this point "Devil" took over, only too happy to translate. Although it was quite obvious, this is what Longfellow had intended to do all along. "Devil" explained, "'Shakes', it means 'clear the way'. Which is exactly what Longfellow and me have done; we 'cleared the way' out of that damned-Yankee, disciplined bee-hive and marching about like a bunch of ninnies instead of fighting. And comes down here, where the Southerners know how to square things up, are a bit more relaxed about the whole damned affair and what's more—."

This time Longfellow returned the favor, "What's more is this; if the Southern cooks don't clear up this here discrepancy about what kind of food to give this army—. We might just take their enlistment bounty and finds us another, even better army that looks to be relaxed about things, don't march too much neither, and can cook something other than what we'd throw into the rivers and streams back home, to fatten up the damned trout 'fore cattin' 'em."

He looked to "Devil" for approval. However, our friend had gone back to his whittling, and had damned near carved the better half of a woman, to where I was becoming embarrassed to look at that switch of birch tree.

"Looks to me that both you and "Devil" better get used to the cooking 'round here, and quick enough too. Because by the looks of things, the two of you are fast running out of armies to join up with." I laughed, shaking my head at my two friends.

"What about you 'Shakes', you ever get hitched up with that colleen you were so crazy over that you couldn't get your mind to thinkin' 'bout nothin' else?" Longfellow half-grinned, teasingly for the most part, or so it seemed to me.

Before I could answer "Devil" shot back, "If you ask me, your better off taking your chances with run-away, britch-snappin', fool horses than that style of gal. Heck, she'd truss you all up in Sunday meeting clothes and have you asking her bosom-buddy friends things like, 'Can I be of some service, young lady?' Or, 'May I inquire as to the state of your health, Madame?' In others words, stuff they got no right to ask you to say in the first place. 'Ceptin' it makes them happy to see their beau go off half-cocked and crazy, from so many rules and genteel regulations."

He took his time about taking a big breath before continuing, "If you ask me, go ahead and marry the bloody princess—you heard me alright—marry the almighty princess—then—cold-cock her one on your weddin' night. That's right; go's ahead I say and lay her out one good. Then when she wakes up and sees her busted nose or maybe missin' a tooth or two, she won't be so high and mighty. Or what's even mo' better for everyone concerned; you done busted her one so hard she'd have lost all her memory. After that, you could just about feed her any story you could think to make up, and she'd have all but forgotten who she was, and that her sole mission in life was to make your's as miserable as possible. Aye, that's what I'd do alright!"

At length, he held up his whittled female birch branch as if he wanted the stick figurine to say whether what he'd just got through saying was true or not.

All I could offer in return was a feeble, "Maybe you're right."

I went on to explain that the few times I'd seen Katherine, she'd been quite clear in her rebuff, and therefore I'd more or less made up my mind to forget all about her.

Longfellow prodded me once again knowingly with his piece of short Irish timber before adding softly, "It's a good thing, Laddie that you've finally made up your mind. Still n' all while watchin' your face just now, it appears to me; t'is your heart that might need some more convincing!"

"Devil" added salt to my wounds when he said with his big red beard bristling to and fro, "'Course you wouldn't need to do any of what I just told you to an Injun woman, cause first-off, you wouldn't have to because she knows her place well enough an secondly—."

Longfellow interrupted, pointing an ungrateful thumb at "Devil" while speaking out of turn, "And secondly, if you busted her one or "cold-cocked her" like our friend here just said to do, she'd more n' likely take you apart like a mountain cougar gone half-mad, 'fore you even got a chance to say you was sorry."

"Why couldn't you just win your wife in a card game like I've heard about in the hill country or *barrancas* of Mexico? They do that all the time down south I'm told. Then she couldn't say a word because you done won her fair and square, and paid for as well?" I asked hopefully.

Longfellow chimed in winking as he did so, "Aye, your right 'Shakes', it works well enough for a while I'm told. Until one night, when you gets to complaining for the one hundredth time about her gringo-burning, Mexican spiced- to-fire-breathin' frijoles that's got your insides all in arrears, and she answers you back with, 'Well, what did you expect *Amigo*? You won me with a pair of pitiful sevens—what did you expect; almond-buttered, sautéed trout and crab cakes bathed in a French crème de menthe?!!"

We were downright laughing alright when Basil Duke, Captain Morgan's second-in-command came riding up to tell us that Morgan wanted to see me and as well, I'd better get a move on, for he'd been calling after me since right before breakfast.

"Breakfast?" "Devil" snorted after the man had left, "First try feeding it to the Scots, if it don't kill one of those lucky bastards, hell I'll eat it. At least 'till we gets to raiding somewhere, and I get me some fresh milk and maybe a pound or two of smoked bacon. Yeah, then we'll truly be at war!"

On the way back to camp I asked after my brother. But neither one could tell me much, other than the fact, Paul Francis Daniel couldn't be happier, seeing how they'd finally authorized him to fight and kill legally—a thought which suddenly sickened me as we approached Morgan's tent.

We found Captain Morgan writing furiously on his makeshift camp desk. There was nowhere to knock so we called out and entered his tent. After several moments, he stopped his writing before looking up. At first, he stared at me stiffly with his piercing amethyst eyes. Before they got even rounder and fuller when he first took sight of Longfellow Mortlock, still wearing his policeman's helmet, and "Devil" McGoran who wouldn't meet the Captain's gaze because "Devil" couldn't seem to take his eyes off the half-finished plate of food the Captain had moved to one side of his desk.

Morgan looked around and asked the room, "Who are these two and what the devil are they doing here? I specifically called for the Irish rebel, the one with the busted eye, the one everyone calls 'Shakes'." This Morgan said, before casting a disparaging glance at Basil Duke.

I stepped forward to explain, "These are friends of mine, Sir."

At which point I introduced Longfellow and "Devil", trying as best I could to leave out the part of their innocuous stay in the Union Army.

Captain Morgan pushed his chair back from his desk before asking, "Friends of yours, huh?"

Even in that September heat, he looked just as crisp as if he'd been freshly bathed at the Galt House after a fine and lazy nap.

"Yes, Sir," I answered stiffly.

Captain Morgan waved off my formality with a flip of his hand, before we all took a seat—on the floor of his tent, for there were no more chairs.

"We don't do nor do we want to do things, like those bootlickers of Lincoln's do things up north."

Upon hearing that, the three of us cast a perceptibly wary glance at one another. "Devil" even coughed suspiciously once or twice. It must have been something reasonably suspicious, enough for Morgan to look at the three of us probingly. It seemed like he knew we were up to something, but he couldn't come out and ask us right then, knowing we'd just been introduced to him.

"Still, I won't have pantywaists among the cavalry!" He thundered out to no one in particular, as if to remind us why we were there.

Duke added in a soothing tone, "No pantywaists. It would never do, Sir—pantywaists in the cavalry—what with all those saddle sores and foot blisters from new boots—."

Duke said this in a way to try and calm Captain Morgan down. Nevertheless, as if he knew he was being patronized, Morgan shot him a look that might have frozen a younger man

I found out later that Basil Duke was in fact, Morgan's brother -in-law, being married to Morgan's sister Tommy (yes, that's correct, her name is indeed Tommy). With that being the case, I found myself wondering about what "Devil" had related earlier. And in particular, who gave the orders out in the Duke's parlor. Or, had Basil Duke already cold-cocked Morgan's sister once or twice, and therefore knew how to handle his brother-in-law as well.

Captain Morgan looked rather ungraciously once again at Duke before announcing, "Let's saddle up the men for four in the morning. Is that clear to everyone, or do you fellows need more beauty sleep?"

Having said this, he eyed rather severely both Longfellow and particularly "Devil", who at that moment was picking the rest of breakfast from his beard, daring anyone to say something. From his no-nonsense attitude, it appeared to this Irishman, our Captain needed to show his two new volunteers once and for all who was in charge, in case there was any doubt in either one of their minds.

He appeared to cheer up when no one challenged or answered back to him. Still in all, he directly addressed Longfellow while pointing at his policeman's helmet. For Longfellow wore it quite low on his forehead, barely showing his eyes. Something we all knew the Captain didn't appreciate, as he liked to look everyone right in their eyes prior to hollering at them.

Morgan rebuffed Longfellow, "I'm telling you Son, right now, that head gear ain't military or Confederate uniform in the least little bit."

Longfellow lovingly took off his almost completely rusted helmet, turned it around slowly with one hand, before responding in kind, "Well, Captain Sir, it might not look like part of a soldier's uniform—that I admit. But just the same, and with all due respect, Captain, I ain't met a bullet yet that had to knock first before entering with one of those Confederate-issued cloth hats. Why one of your Confederate hats looks like it couldn't stop a *ticked-off* rain moth from attacking, even if it wanted to! On the other hand, with this here iron hat of mine, a bullet has to think twice about deciding just where it plans to come in from out of the cold."

Morgan smiled before repeating to himself, "A "ticked-off rain moth", Soldier, did I hear you correctly?"

Again he chuckled to himself.

He paused to stroke his goatee prior to confirming, "Your darned right about that Soldier, now that I think about it. Maybe we ought to issue everyone your kind of helmet—be a darn sight more protective if you ask me. Take note of that Duke, right away now, won't you? See if you can't find any surplus helmets somewhere like this man's wearing."

Turning to Longfellow he finished his thought, "Well, here in "The Raiders" we do things a bit differently, so it doesn't really bother me that you're slightly out of uniform."

He banged on his camp desk to emphasize his next impulsive order, "Still, I don't want it to be said that we go around looking like a bunch of silver-helmeted pantywaists—that's something I won't stand for!"

Basil Duke intoned sharply, somewhat ironically, "Captain Morgan, his helmet is much too rusted and outright stained to be considered appropriate headgear for a regiment of cavalry-pantywaists in the least little bit!"

Looking at first more confused, than I believe relieved, at what Basil Duke had tried to console him with, and finally focusing his attention at us sitting on the floor of his tent, Morgan asked the three of us, "Gentlemen, what do y'all say to a little visit down Bacon Creek way? They say the woodwork's finished and the Yanks are just about to lay new tracks down."

"Devil" raised his hand high in the air, as if he was a schoolboy and wished to speak out of turn, "If it's got anything to do with "Bacon" you can count me in!"

You could tell the Captain was about to instruct everyone there as to army discipline and the correct way to address an officer when spoken to, but he didn't. Instead, he heaved an exasperated sigh and looked skyward as if accepting the fact he had to make do with the likes of us as soldiers. Perhaps we were not militarily reprimanded just then, due in no small part to the fact that "Devil" had closed his eyes and appeared to be dozing off.

Almost forlornly, Captain Morgan announced to his brother-in-law, "We'll take twenty men including these three here. You pick the rest, then tell everyone to draw rations for three days and sixty rounds of ammunition from ordnance."

The next day, somewhere in the middle of the night we left for Bacon Creek. It appeared to this Irishman, we were all happy to be saying goodbye, for the time being at least; to angry rain moths, panty-waisted cavalrymen and to bivouacking with all its social amenities.

Chapter Seventeen

Furl it, for the hands that grasped it,
And the hand that fondly clasped it,
Cold and dead are lying low;
And the banner, it is trailing
While around it sounds the wailing
Of its people in their woe;
For though conquered they adore it
Love the cold, hands that bore it,
Weep for those who fell before it,
Pardon those who trailed and tore it,
And oh, wildly they deplore it:
Now to furl and fold it so.

Author unknown

Captain John Hunt Morgan wasn't kidding when he said we were to be ready to leave at four in the morning. Basil Duke, his second-in-command had us in the saddle and lined up in pairs five minutes before the hour. Deep on that Kentucky plain there was an abrupt end to the pervasive silence inhabiting our camp even at four in the morning. It had absolutely nothing to do with our horses and their restless stamping movements, or the sound of bits and bridles being shifted about. In fact, from that day on it seemed everything was different to what I had been used to. The silence was louder, the smells around us headier, and the racing of my brain could no longer be stilled or tolerated for that matter. Which I believe is the reason I drank as much *poteen* as I did back then. These were the newly discovered sounds and smells of raiding behind enemy lines. These new sounds were most distinct and disturbing, like when one is working with machinery that has intricately moving, meshing gears with sliding, spinning belts and you're subconsciously aware that a mistake or a false movement which could cause you physical harm is omnipresent. It brought one quickly to an all-hours, every day, searing concentration, fomenting a certain amount of inherent tension. From that day on until the end of hostilities we were always on edge, even if we didn't acknowledge it as such. This pervasive nervousness, as I mentioned was always there. It subtly underlined our existence while pushing you to do things that once you did it, you couldn't recognize your act as being something you would do under normal circumstances.

Captain Morgan approached us at a lathering trot from the north, as if he'd already been up much earlier than us. Which of course he had been; scouting the enemy lines, putting together the route that we were to take, and now he had to impatiently wait for the rest of his cavalry to get started. In any case, he didn't care to hide his temporary, restless impatience from us, or to explain matters (now that I recall), to us either.

Instead, he kept calling to practically each one of us by name, asking if we'd slept enough and in anticipation of our cursory reply told us, "Don't worry men, the war will be over in three weeks time, mark my word on it. Then you can sleep all you want—until doomsday if you like!"

He laughed like he meant it too. At length, he turned "Bess" around, and we started off, paired up in a loosely-held line with Captain Morgan out ahead and Basil Duke riding between the captain and us. It was too dark at first to notice who was riding beside me. But as things got lighter, and the forest and its surroundings woke up with a cacophony of wind-driven rhythms, critter yells and intermittent yet distinct animal movements, I took notice of the man riding next to me. It was the Jesuit priest, Father Alcime Stanislaus. He was no longer in his priestly cassock, but rode and looked like one of us, except he had a wooden cross, absent of any crucified figure, which he wore on a leather cord around his neck. As well, the Catholic priest did not carry any firearms that I could see. He noticed me at the same time, but only nodded his head briefly in my direction. Instead of a soldier's hat, the man wore a dark-blue French *chapeau* with a distinct sloping crest, although weather beaten, with a small cloth bill such as I have seen men wear in the merchant marine.

We rode for several hours like this, even after the sun was up, until Morgan told us to water the horses and get something to eat ourselves. Immediately, one of my comrades took to passing some *poteen* around, and I, like most everyone else it appeared to me, took a deep and hearty swig of the vaporous stuff. As time went on, we found by drinking this delectable *applejack*[24] in the morning, we could sway in the saddle right comfortably so and for most of the day as well. We weren't as likely to buck up at the first sound of a musket being fired, or an acorn falling to the ground for that matter. Aye, it was a right glorious position to be in; riding and enjoying the countryside albeit somewhat drunk. Otherwise, neither Basil Duke nor

---

24   American poteen

Morgan would tell us where we were headed to exactly, although we knew about the train and its ironworks somewhere up ahead.

Even though it was coming onto autumn in Kentucky, we couldn't tell all that well, for it remained a lingering Indian summer. The heat and humidity seemed to stick to all of us, yet all we could do was ride on in the infernal muck. You could feel your horse shake and course itself every so often, as if it too was trying to forget where we were, or rid himself of that stifling and molten, damp, late-summer air.

Captain Morgan, on the other hand, would be up and down the lines probably every hour or so sticking in a good word, keeping our morale up by letting us know just how quickly he thought the war would be over. Most likely he told us by the time we'd get back, as the Northerner had no stomach for this conflict, and didn't trust their own Yankee women enough to leave them alone for any length of time.

We were pretty confident and as I mentioned a little drunk as we kept on riding, hoping we could find us some Yankees and shoot them, just to see if their blood was as "yeller" as the Captain said it was.

It must have been ten in the morning that first day, and the word came down from Duke that something or someone had been sighted. We walked our mounts off the road and into thickets, as efficiently as possible while at the same time, we watched as Morgan footed a hill alone to get a better view. He came back down and only very briefly mentioned there were sixty or seventy Union soldiers coming right our way. After this, we all watched as our Captain withdrew into the brush and waited along with the rest of us. The rising chatter of men and the tramp of the column grew louder as they approached. Somewhere about forty yards or so in front of us, they halted. I watched as Morgan became tense, as if he, somehow, had sensed that we'd been spotted. Or at the very least, the Yankees knew of our presence thereabouts, and an immediate decision must be reached. We looked at one another silently and anxiously, wondering if the war wasn't to be inaugurated right then and there in a point-blank range shootout. A horse from the Union side whinnied nervously. We waited; our hearts pounding away like so many thumping, oil-bursting pistons. Captain Morgan didn't miss a beat however, but stepped rakishly right out in the middle of the road alone. He already had his revolver in the firing position, and discharged a shot which went right through the head of the officer riding out in front of the column. The way he did it was extraordinary as well. It looked to us as if he was firing his revolver into a tree stump for practice. Indeed, the way Morgan fired was unusual, exhibiting an aloofness that one would display had he arrived late to a formal dinner, and wasn't quite sure where he should sit, but had the audacity of character not to admit it.

As soon as the Union man fell, a short, amateurish, disorganized scuffle broke out with misdirected bullets winging their way harmlessly into the foliage which protected us from the Yankees' view. But to have lost their commanding officer and with little war experience up to that point, the Yankees turned en masse to gallop in a pell-mell fashion back down the same road from which they'd come. Occasionally, a Yankee would turn in his saddle, crying out for someone to protect their unprotected flanks, just in case we had decided to pursue them.

I spurred my horse into flight with the others and slowed down when they did. Yet, I couldn't forget the sight of the Union officer lying face up in the dusty road. The front of his uniform was stretched taut over his rigid body, part of his shirt invested with seeping blood while his head and neck were tilted backwards in a skewered position, out of sync with a man's normal physical bearing.

To be truthful about it...I couldn't believe my eyes. *Didn't this man have a family? What would they say now? What could they say now?*

How was this man's family to take care of themselves after his death? This thought, somehow, disturbed me much more than seeing the physically-awkward disfigurement of the soldier.

Someone behind me called out, strangely enough vocalizing my doubts, "Ah well, you know, they'll get along alright after a fashion."

I turned on my horse to look behind me to see who had offered such a speculative and distorted point of view. It was the gunslinger from Missouri, and he was smiling through gapped teeth after saying such a blatant lie.

What did he mean "after a fashion"? Still in all, I didn't believe it. I mean, I'd been there myself before, and knew from experience that a family just didn't pick themselves up by their boot-straps because someone else said they could.

That was ridiculous and a poor excuse to forget about these people. It started to dawn on me the real stakes of war. It was right there alright, still in front of my eyes with more than a score of bottle-neck flies on its bloody face, and the rest adorned in striped and frayed blue-nothingness.

The shock on my face must have been pretty evident, for Father Stanislaus rode up to me and asked me if I was okay.

I don't remember what I said; only that he replied in turn, "This war isn't for you."

I instinctively thought of my brother while pointing back down the road towards the dead Yankee soldier, and answered the priest with uninvited surliness, "I don't believe it was for him either, Father."

The Catholic priest didn't respond in the least, but rode back to give the Union soldier the last rites of the Catholic faith with a thread-bare, purple stole thrown over his shoulders. I guess he prayed in Latin, but he could have been praying in Gaelic for all I cared, to me it was one more man who had died. And not to give anything away, yet I sincerely wondered if the Catholic Jesus or the Orange Jesus could hear his prayers over the din we'd created, by shooting at one another so indiscriminately.

We continued on our way after the short skirmish. But it took me a long while to forget what I'd seen. And thus, be able to sleep through the night, without dreaming of that officer, lying face up on the road while his family grieved out that man's wake, for the rest of their lives.

Later on that morning, I turned to Father Stanislaus and asked him as if he was the one responsible, "Do any of the political men making decisions for this conflict leave their paneled offices and speech-making to come down and actually fight with the rest of us?"

Father Stanislaus looked almost sick before answering in a heavy French accent, "No, no I don't believe so. It seems they are much too important to risk their lives at such an endeavor."

Was it me or did he seem to put forth an ironic smile while saying it?

The French priest had very light skin with patches of red veins like thinly-sliced strawberries garnishing his cheeks. On top of his high forehead his hair was white where it did grow, and he appeared to be wearing a mask of perpetual disenchantment that only made his puffy face puffier, and perhaps more thoughtful or in total disagreement with his surroundings, I wasn't sure which. His eyes bore a strange resemblance to my mother's in that they were untroubled yet sad. I don't remember what color they were. Just as I can't seem to make up my mind whether the man was continually smiling behind his thickly-bristled, grey-turning-to-white moustache, or was he just gritting his teeth, determined to win some race and wouldn't give up until he had.

I repeated my question. I'll admit, insolently enough because I wasn't satisfied with the priest's answer, "Why don't those men in government come down here and see things as they are—what we see?"

He smiled weakly before replying, "Because they know. They're not stupid as you would believe them to be, they already know."

I was more perplexed from the priest's answer than I was prior to asking my question.

It seemed to me the parallels between the English absentee landlords and their American counterparts extraordinary. What if these men in power could feel the same hunger we felt from a putrefying potato crop or could feel a bullet or two slam into their pampered and pudgy bodies? Would it help at all to bring men to the negotiating table quicker? One had the feeling if the politicians (on both sides) weren't there next to the rest of us during the shooting and blood—letting-carryings-on there was a damned-good, calculated reason for it. And it had absolutely nothing to do with looking out for our unequivocal welfare. But rather, a lot of meaningless dribble about how all men are created equal—up to a point. Still in all, I guess what the politicians really meant was that as far as starvation and bleeding to death are concerned; there were a few of us created a lot more equal to the task than some of the others.

Deliberately or not, Captain Morgan chose another road to continue on, perhaps a good half-mile from where we'd last seen the Union Army. The sun was high overhead when we decided to stop and feed ourselves. I left my horse to graze, and wandered over to where Longfellow and "Devil" were sitting down next to several scraggly juniper bushes. They were together, discussing the morning's events as if they had read the whole affair from a newspaper while sipping creamy, sugared-to-the-hilt, imported coffee.

"Devil" spoke, his mouth full of hardtack, "I'm telling you if Morgan wants to win the war, than he'd best understand not to let the enemy go wandering off, back the same way they came, when he's got 'em surrounded."

Longfellow corrected his friend, "Morgan didn't have the blokes surrounded. I don't think he even knew their numbers. 'Sides we's here to disturb the enemy—raiding, cutting up telegraph lines, just shooting the works *without* taking prisoners which are just going to slow us down—'sides eating up all our chow!"

Disgustedly, "Devil" threw down his hardtack until it bounced back up and he was able to catch it with one hand, "I for one, would only be too happy to share this Scotsman's delight with any pitiable soul, prisoners included that considers it worthy of eating!"

Longfellow looked out past his virtuosic handlebar moustaches and asked me if this Morgan fellow was either a fool or a Free-Mason, to be riding around behind enemy lines, without a thought as to his or our collective well-being.

"A Free-Mason? What do those people have to do with the war?" I wanted to know.

Longfellow answered while stitching up one moustache so he could spit, "Listen to me 'Shakes', someone's bound to be making a nice cozy profit off this here war by selling rifles, and all the rest of the boondoggling material that goes with it. And these here Masons got themselves a swell little brotherhood that ain't divided by no Mason-Dixon line either, if you get my drift. So's they just might be calculating on this here war to be going on for quite some time. At least until all the cozy profits are in."

I made it a point to ask the Captain whether or not he was a Free-Mason.

However, the time didn't seem appropriate just then, for he was studying a map with his brother-in-law, Basil Duke, and muttering something about the real guerillas were not at all from France, but were in fact the Spaniards who had successfully defended their soil against Napoleon.

I could hear Captain Morgan repeatedly emphasize to Basil Duke the importance of speed, "I'm convinced, Basil, if we can strike and then be off quickly, we can effectively hold down eight to ten times our number; simply because, the Yanks don't have the ability to know where we will attack next. Therefore, they must secure a variety of defensive positions just in case we attack from any number of sites. In the meantime, with a vigilant and effective scouting force we can decide where the enemy is weakest and move against him there."

He didn't bother asking Duke for confirmation because to the Captain his argument was so solid who in their right mind would dare to contradict him? Instead, turning to me, standing there without anything to do except for my woeful staring, he ordered, "Tell the men to saddle up—we're burning daylight!"

As I mentioned earlier, it wasn't the moment to ask our leader if he was in favor of a prolonged armed conflict just so that he and his Masonic brothers could fill their pockets. Besides I reckoned to myself; *how could Captain Morgan be a Mason...had he bothered to ask the Union officer if he was a free and in good standing Mason, before putting a bullet in his head that morning? Somehow nothing made sense to me anymore.*

We turned out of the thicket and onto the road that would take us on up to Bacon Creek. We bounced along for several hours, everyone paying heed to their own thoughts. Finally, out of boredom I asked the priest riding next to me why he had left France.

"The *Spirit* moved me to leave." Was how he answered my question.

I couldn't tell if he was making fun of me or what; "The *Spirit* moved me"? *What, for the love of mike, was that supposed to mean?*

He pushed at his French sailor's cap, to where it sat up a little higher on his forehead enabling me to see his face. Almost as if, he wanted me to know that he wasn't poking fun at me in the least. It looked to me like his fair skin was taking a severe beating in the Southern heat. He was sweating pretty much like someone not at all acclimated to this section of the country and its weather. He possessed a short, well-trimmed moustache that confirmed in my mind's eye; the man resembled either a sweating, pouch-faced beaver or a sweating, pouch-faced squirrel—take your pick. I, for one, wished he had stayed back with the others at our main camp. Instead of bringing his unsettling answers, along with his high-and-mighty attitude out here, where there was no place for it...damned lousy Frenchman!

The road Morgan had picked to avoid the Yankees was in fact no road at all, but just an untenable, gut-wrenching, rock strewn access-way to the high country where timber was being felled. That being said, the road withered and died away while we punched on through the forest, a monumental thirst continuing to mount in our throats. Some of the men knew that Bacon Creek stood a good fifty miles from where our main camp had been, just outside Bowling Green. Therefore, we more or less had it calculated to be a solid two-day ride.

We kept on riding through the heat and humidity, discussing our situation while believing that the conflict wouldn't last more than the three weeks Morgan had predicted earlier. If for no other reason, than this accursed heat, which no one, especially the Northern army could fight in. We continued on, slashing through thickets with wild-hickory which would slap at your knees and the flanks of your horse, causing some tears and lacerations. Indeed, once the saltiness of running sweat reached that area, it became a source of stinging madness to both rider and beast. We plunged on like this, without any definite trail marked out, until long after the sun had gone down.

At long last, Morgan rode down the line and told us to halt. He added, as if we couldn't figure it out for ourselves, we would pitch camp there that night.

"Devil" grumbled something about, "Why bother pitchin' camp now, Sir, the night's bloody well over any way?"

Captain Morgan replied kindly enough, "You men need your rest. But I promise you we'll be after the Yanks as soon as the dawn throws off its nightly shadow. Now how's that for you, Soldier?"

Then Morgan looked at "Devil", curiously enough, as if he wasn't quite sure how this *volunteer* had made his way into "Morgan's Raiders".

At length, turning to me, Morgan ordered, "'Shakes', you come with me. I saw a pen of turkeys not too far from a farmhouse back a-ways. I'll be willin' to bet you the owner has Southern sympathies, and is obligin' to let us have a few turkeys in the name of Confederate freedom."

This is just what the Captain and I did. We helped ourselves to three penned-in, nice and fat, red and brown turkeys. This we did prior to writing out a Confederate debit note to the irate farmer, who claimed he hadn't made up his mind just yet, as to whose side he was on.

Captain Morgan, unruffled as to the farmer's attitude responded in kind, "That being the case my good man, you're not invited to our feast tonight!"

This of course, provoked the farmer to great remonstrance against the Confederate states, claiming upon further reflection that his turkeys, had of late, shown a rather marked interest in the Northern cause. And now, wouldn't Morgan be so kind as to put back the birds from where he had stolen them.

Our captain rose to the challenge, "Now see here my good fellow, this turkey I'm holding in my hands, has pronounced himself decidedly in favor of the Confederacy. Therefore, if you'll be good enough to step back and let this bird have his say."

At which point, the Captain took a hold of the bird's neck with his gloved hand. He proceeded to shake the turkey with enough force that the turkey not only tried to take to the air, but emitted such a deafening cry that the animals in other parts of the farm took up the bird's forlorn shriek. Thus, before we knew it, the whole place became alive; with such braying, lowing and mewing, producing an ethereal sound that made even Morgan look thunderstruck.

The farmer, not lacking in a sort of *I have won* attitude, held out his arms for the turkey that Morgan was still slowly choking.

Captain Morgan answered the farmer far too courteously while reaching for his rifle, "Since your turkeys have settled in favor of the North—. Well then, we'll just have to cook them a little longer than usual—. At least, until the taint of unabridged treason has been boiled off!"

He then turned his big black mare "Bess" around, and headed back to our camp. There was a turkey strung over each side of his pommel while I held the third one upside down by the fore claws, unable to avoid an horrific avalanche of pecks by the bird, against my leg, causing me no small discomfort until I arrived back with the others.

Upon appearing back in camp, Captain Morgan told me to take several of the men, to clean the birds, then to make them as he called it, "Edible—hell, an Irish dentist-turned-rebel, can do that much now can't he?"

Showing that at least for once, Captain Morgan could become irascible with hunger at the end of a long day, just like any normal man.

The next day, we set off early for Bacon Creek. We made it a point to give Cave City a wide berth, for our scouts had come back reporting a large garrison of Union troops in that area. We rode on pretty much as we had the day before, taking *applejack* quietly on the side, right after breakfast, so that we more or less stayed silent in the saddle. You must understand; the roll of the horse can be a lullaby of sorts, and since our horses knew enough to follow the one In front, most of us could catnap along the way. I made it a point to take stock of my friends when it came time for watering our mounts. As usual, Longfellow and "Devil" were in a deep discussion, this time the talk was all about slavery.

"Well no-o-ow, if they can do it to the black man why not the Scots? They're just as lazy, if not more so." "Devil" wanted to know, motioning for me to sit down next to him.

He continued in his *enlightened* reasoning about man and his ambiguous origins, "Go ahead I say and give the African some rest. We'll just bring in a boatload of Scotsmen to take over their chores for awhile. Bloody 'ell, you can't please 'em anyway, so goes ahead I say and give in to their natural cussedness."

Longfellow couldn't see any reason for making the Scots into slaves and said so, "Listen here, McGoran, we couldn't have what you're suggesting because the Scots are a reasonable thinking people and the African isn't, it's been proven!"

You could tell "Devil" was stunned by such a remark, "That the Scots are capable of high-minded thought? All that tells me is that you've never been up in the highlands with 'em, when they're lost. "A reasonable thinkin' people" is it n-o-o-ow? Why, they'd set fire to one of their own kind, just to light their path to get down out of the highlands again. I'm tellin' you, once back home, they'd be asking each other why little Brian was so black—has he been neglecting his bathin' again?"

He looked over at me, then winked, as if it was only too obvious—the truth of what he was saying.

I didn't know much about the Scots, but stressed that I'd be a happy man to see one or two Englishman working the plantations, just like the Negro man did.

"Devil" came on while pulling a drink from his canteen, "The Scots, the English, maybe even a Mohawk father-in-law—they could all take their turns, that's fine by me!"

Longfellow concluded, his pair of moustaches bristling about, "It sounds to me that you'd make slaves out of just about anyone you don't like?"

For once "Devil" feigned hurt, as if his friend had truly insulted him, "Only for a little while—until they recognized the error of their ways?" He finalized hopefully.

It was then Captain Morgan started hollering for us to get a move on, insisting we weren't too far from Bacon Creek.

It turned out to be true.

We made camp that day in a stretch of woodland which smelled an awful lot like stagnant mildew and waited for nightfall. Morgan and his scouts left us in the early afternoon. They came back with a glowing report about an hour before dusk that the construction crew, along with their guides from the 19th Pennsylvania Infantry and the First Wisconsin Regiment had left the site, and it was ours for the taking.

We blackened our faces at night and rode out. Captain Morgan led us to a scalloped mountain side where frontal hill excavation and aggregate crushing had only recently been halted. There, clinging to the side of the mountain and spread out over a half-mile radius, were seven, forlorn-looking, train trestles. They burst upwards, like spindly, wooden and steel skeletons, their feet buried in a small river or creek, supporting a bridge with newly-laid train tracks. We arrived at the site, and Morgan ordered us to heap stubble and wood onto the bridge. At his signal, torches were applied and the ensuing flames leapt high into the chilly, early fall, somber night air. The flames turned our small group of men into a scene of distended figurines; grotesque and eerie to look at, with the undulating light from the fire illuminating them in such a frightful way. Everyone's movement acclaimed slow-moving shadows and half-hidden, fomenting gestures, enveloped in a bizarre, half-light of scintillating fire and smoke. Those brazen, reddish-orange flames turned in against themselves, before eventually, shooting up into the night sky with a loud crackling and hissing. Before finally, they erupted forth, in a shimmer of white and slivered crystals that popped hermetically about us, as they disappeared into the blackened air. Four of the seven train track uprights, were destroyed immediately while the others were left to smolder in the middle of the creek.

After watching the cavalcade of embers for awhile, Captain Morgan ordered us to mount up that our business at Bacon Creek was finished. We didn't turn south as I would have imagined. However, instead, we turned back towards Cave City and the Union garrison that maybe, just maybe, would no longer be expecting us. We continued like this for another day and a half, stealing from farmers when the need arose. Yet, having learned our lesson from the first turkey farmer, Morgan would hear the prospective donor out first, to determine where his sympathies lay. If the farmer was pro-Union then Morgan would make a grand display of throwing on the blue Union Army over-coat he had stolen somewhere, prior to claiming he was a special courier for the Union General, Don Carlos Buell operating in that area. If the farmer in question was for the Confederacy; then just by announcing who he was, Captain Morgan could pretty much lay claim to whatever supplies he needed, and that the nearby farm could provide.

We continued on like this until we reached Cave City. There we bivouacked three to four miles from where the Union Army was billeted. As far as this Irishman's concerned, it seemed that no matter where we were (including this foray), we always camped in spiny, vine-like underbrush amidst moss-covered, swampy-looking trees, lost somewhere between heaven and hell. Where no one would think to go or expect to find us either. By that I mean, we weren't camping next to a charming, tranquil lake, where, we all threw our fishing lines in the water, smoked cigars and passed the time of day telling incredulous stories while waiting for the fish to bite. No, where we were, not far from Cave City, the air was foul from rotting vegetation and dead animal flesh, the ground damp and full of slithering snakes. Or, so it seemed to this Irishman, who had never up until then seen a snake in his life. Therefore, seeing the one snake quite literally scared the *bejeebers* out of me. We ate our meals cold, for no campfires were permitted or incipient laughter now that I recall; for we were preparing to engage ourselves in battle with an enemy far superior in numbers. Morgan took the following day to scout, to determine our line of approach, as well as to talk to anyone, who besides insisting, "For the love of God, do not breathe my name to anyone", would also tell us the strength of the Union troops, including, hopefully, who was in charge.

When Captain Morgan rejoined us, back at camp, just as evening broke, he was swollen up with anticipation, a raging fire in those amethyst eyes. He had that winning-hand-at-cards-smile of his which told us the situation looked decently in our favor, for it appeared no one was expecting us.

He gathered our little group together to explain he had come across Union scouts, and that he, Morgan, had been assured by them (while pretending to be once again the special courier for General Buell) that the wily, slippery-faced Captain Morgan had been chased back to the Confederate lines. In fact, like the weak-kneed, chicken-boned fighter who he was, after being caught in an ambush trying to burn "several logs" close to the train tracks up around Bacon Creek. There was absolutely no mention by the scouts of any serious damage done to any of the trestles, or that the tracks themselves were in any way out of commission. In any case they jested, based on their heroic pursuit; no one and they meant *no one* would be hearing from John Morgan and his raiders for a very, very, long time.

This sat fine with us for we looked at each other, confidently nodding our heads, serene in the knowledge that with our captain around we would more than likely, always be one step ahead of the enemy.

We were ordered to eat something and get a little rest as the *evening's entertainment* promised to be at least folkloric, if not down right exciting.

That night around ten o'clock we rode through a placid swamp where fireflies seemed to abound. We traversed untilled fields and steep creek banks that were hard to climb because of all the uneven, flat and circular, cascading rocks that seemed to lie in our path. These rocks gave the horses fits because they couldn't get a good hold or *bite* on mother earth to navigate the boldly inclined creek banks. In the back of my mind was the thrashing snake someone had shot that afternoon. And the question to a man who had been brought up on an island which didn't know such intrepid beasts; that if one snake was around where were his aunts and uncles, cousins and friends? I wasn't myself the whole time we were there and even less so when we were ordered to dismount and take to our stomachs the rest of the way.

We tied the horses back, away from an untilled, lumpy field. Then we lit out the last three hundred yards or so by crawling through the brush close on to midnight, to where we could actually hear the Union pickets talking and chuckling amongst themselves. Upon arriving, as before any battle we were engaged in, I had to endure what was for me the hardest thing to do, other than fighting off the depressing thoughts which seemed to infest my lively mind...we waited. And when we were finished waiting...we waited some more. We looked at one another silently...curious as to what was to follow. Longfellow and "Devil" were stretched out right beside me. Although they weren't twitching their necks in every direction like I was. But sat eyeing each other knowingly, prior to glancing my way as if they knew something I didn't...as if they were watching over me. I don't know what the captain had in mind. Why we didn't just stand up and get to shooting at people. Yet, still we waited until my stomach started to cramp up on me. I watched with the others and continued to impress my being to calm down while we waited. Eventually I guess, I finally saw and understood what the others already knew way up in that faithless, unblinking night sky. We were waiting for the moon to go down behind a cloud, all of us careful not to breathe too loudly.

At last the moon left us, finding its cloudy solace hidden from our view, before Morgan signaled to us, and our quiet world erupted in a demonstrative panic. We fired from our knees aiming low to the ground for maximum effect. Immediately the cries and moans of wounded men rose from in front of us not fifty yards from where we kneeled. You could, by straining your eyes to see, barely make out men writhing on the ground. One of them screamed like a banshee and held up his fractured arm to the moonlight, as if to see more clearly what had happened, also to confirm his innate trepidation. We fired off one more round as per our orders, before relaxing our muskets and fixing the safety catch like an orchestra mentoring a concluding, *sans-tempo*, empty beat. This time however, instead of crawling back we ran for the horses and lit out like stampeding bulls no longer afraid of being discovered, or for that matter slithering into vile snakes on the untilled ground.

Back at camp a restless Captain Morgan, instead of being overjoyed about our showing, smiled grimly and concluded we'd done enough. We had accomplished what we had set out to do, therefore, we should head back to Bowling Green at once and so we did. You have to understand, the man didn't care all that much about our victory once the fight was over. It was in the preparation and execution that Morgan found his *on-the-edge* fulfillment. Once it was over that was it for him. He needed to start right in to plan for his next outing. The one that would take his adrenalin rush to the next level...a level which could never be satisfied. Still in all, that didn't stop the man from trying.

We followed the scouts out into the night. As well as we could we bundled ourselves up against the frosty air, as for the first time everyone could feel that autumn had come a-calling. Indeed, the early, pre-dawn air had a cutting, sobering, chilly bite to it.

Some of the troops were laughing, some were silent. Me, I chose to bide my tongue and ride on, keeping my thoughts to myself.

Perhaps around six in the morning when just the slightest hint that the night was over, with a pinkish gleam from the east announcing all was new again in this world we halted. My horse was snorting something fierce and kept snapping his neck up and down as if to say, 'that's enough'. Father Stanislaus reached out his hand to control my horse. I didn't like it because it was definitely something I could do on my own.

Then he asked me quietly, "Where are your parents?"

I mentioned something to the effect that they were where they should be.

"Fair enough," he confirmed. Before he apologized, saying he shouldn't have asked me something when it wasn't any of his business to begin with.

I'm not clear as to exactly why I said it, but I told the French Jesuit somewhat bitterly, "You say *the spirit* told you to leave France. Well, I would never have left Ireland, spirit or no spirit, unless we were slowly starving ourselves to death and couldn't do anything about it. Which was exactly right, for now my family is in ruins."

I think he wanted to say something. However, as he had just apologized for intruding into my affairs he stayed silent. Nevertheless, he continued talking to someone, for his lips moved and occasionally I could barely distinguish words coming from his lips. It was uncomfortable to me because his attitude suggested *the little people* and of knowing things that I could not be a part of. Aye, things like the nether world of the Druids, and death and spirits hovering about outside our sphere of reality. Like I said, these things I knew nothing whatsoever about, except that it was an affair for the old people. Especially, loosely-tongued widows and the absent-minded elders who were not normal anymore. The ones that went around mumbling to themselves while searching for five-legged black cats that they claimed were an elder sister or a mischievous uncle, who had once upon a time drowned himself.

I found Longfellow and "Devil" back down at the rear. They were speaking with Basil Duke and wanted to know why must we turn back towards Bowling Green when the Union Army was so close by.

Duke explained, "Captain Morgan's mission is to disrupt the enemy and not one of engagement. Besides we are almost out of supplies."

"Devil" scratched deep in his beard before asking, "You ain't been a politician once before have you, Fella? For all of your sweet-talkin' and infernal caterwauling 'bout 'disruptin' and engagement', you could just about make us all swallow a rattlesnake or two. Maybe all at the same time, and somehow make us all believe it was the right thing to do too—to make us all smokin'-healthy! Now ain't that just about right!"

You could tell Basil Duke didn't know what to make of this red-bearded Scotsman, who was forever criticizing his own people and just about everyone else as well, when he had a chance to dwell on the matter.

Still, he listened closely when "Devil" elucidated in a mischievous voice, "T'is all about arms and trading 'em—ain't it though? While we can free slaves in some states, but not in the others—. Negotiate about a man's liberty and states' rights in Missouri and Kansas and the Oregon territory while keeping a tight lid on things back home—. A pretty neat little brotherhood which stands together real tight when all is said and done—. If you ask me n-o-o-ow, Mr. Duke, ain't it so?"

Basil Duke looked concernedly at Longfellow then back at me before asking "Devil", "Are you fighting for Confederate freedom, Boy? Or are you out here because no prison will have your kind? Answer me straight, Boy!"

"Devil" took to tearing at his earlobe or scratching it something fierce. In any case it was a bad sign, and both Longfellow and I knew it.

Longfellow pointed a finger at "Devil" as if to account for his attitude, "He ain't used to military life and discipline just yet, Captain. This boy is what you might call a renegade Scotsman—you see, he don't fit in with just everyone...."

"Devil" then answered in his own inimitable way, "When we was up north and in Lincoln's army—it only took a couple of days before we could tell we wuz fightin' on the wrong side. I declare I heard the—"

Duke stopped "Devil" cold, "Listen Boy, did I just hear you correctly? Did you just say you fought in the Northern Army 'fore comin' down here? Is that what you just said—Boy?"

There was no disguising the frayed ugliness that had come over Basil Duke.

I felt it was my turn to try and clear things up—and as quickly as possible too, setting aside some of the facts—facts I believed Basil Duke didn't need to hear, "No, Mr. Duke, Mr. McGoran was never in the Union Army. Except for the time, he went to see my brother upon my instructions is all. My brother, Paul Francis Daniel Ruth is in the All-Irish 69th Regiment out of New York City," I declared proudly.

You could tell it took all of a minute or so for this to sink in with Captain Duke.

He then asked me trying to hide his confusion, "Your brother fights in the Union Army—is that it, 'Shakes'?"

I nodded that it was so.

Basil Duke shook his head vigorously, as if he was trying to free something from his inner ear, "Well for the love of mike, why does everyone call him "Devil"? I mean, who wants a 'devil' in their regiment?"

Only McGoran was qualified to answer the man's question and so he did, "Me own mother—bless her soul, gave me that name when she found me a cross, too difficult to bear for one woman. She told me that if I ever ran across Lucifer it wouldn't be a fair fight, and that I should take pity on the poor bloke!"

"So that's how someone gets to be called 'Devil'?" This Basil Duke inquired of no one in particular as he mounted his horse and turned his mount's head back toward the front of the line.

We looked at one another carefully, wondering as well, if one of us hadn't spoken too much about what needn't be anyone's concern in these difficult times.

"Devil" jerked a thumb towards the position Duke had taken up, next to Captain Morgan, to whom he was talking slowly while pointing a gloved finger back at us, "I don't rightly know what's eating that man? I swear I thought that was the whole point of this here American democracy—one could fight with whomever he wanted to, just so long as the man was sincere in his beliefs?"

"Being sincere in your beliefs does not mean joining up with whatever army has the better chow." This I quipped while blinking one eye at Longfellow.

Longfellow tapped his friend on the shoulder in passing while edging his horse to a trot, "You can be as sincere in your beliefs as you want to be; hip, hip, hooray and all that stuff—. I tell you right now in all seriousness; if you don't want to end up before a firing squad, for being a common horse thief or worse yet a spy, you better make damn sure of one thing...."

You could tell the way "Devil" spat in the road, he wasn't going to like or perhaps understand even Longfellow's answer to his own question.

But we all listened anyway, our tired and bowed heads heading back to Bowling Green, Kentucky after six and a half days of clandestine war, when Longfellow pronounced with recognizable certitude, "Make sure Gentlemen, if you don't want to be treated as a common criminal or even a spy, your side wins the war! Because if it don't, our politicians and head-honchoed officers start to point the finger, looking for someone to take the blame—. And it's always pointed at bottom-rung soldiers like us!"

We arrived back in camp early the next morning. We were too exhausted to even remove our boots or answer questions from some of the others, as to what our raid behind enemy lines had been like. I took care of my horse like any good cavalryman. Then went to sleep, wondering about such things as Union and Confederate turkeys, what "Devil" must have been like as a child, and if I was really cut out to be a soldier.

Chapter Eighteen

"Furl that banner, softly, slowly
Treat it gently-T'is holy-
For it droops above the dead;
Touch it not; unfold it never;
Let it droop there furled forever,
Here its people's hopes are dead"
Author unknown

This business of going on out and raiding wherever and whenever became our state in life, our *raison d'être* if you will, also our reason to escape. You have to understand, not only after our army's great victory at the first Bull Run, but even in the midst of setbacks involving the Confederacy, we could still get out and raid—create havoc, put fear into the Northern Army. We were reckless and fearless while riding with a much heralded chivalric abandon. And because of this, we paid perhaps, too much heed to our victories, or for that matter, not enough to our losses as we should have. In a very real sense we became part of a war within the great war. We did what we pleased, or rather, what Captain Morgan wished to do regardless of what was occurring all around us. This continued long after General Johnston's defensive position collapsed and we were forced to retreat into Alabama.

I guess it was sometime prior to Shiloh but still in the early part of 1862 Morgan saw fit to move his headquarters to Murfreesboro, Tennessee, an agricultural village a stone's throw away from the Cumberland River and Nashville. An interesting point in all of this and very much in keeping with Morgan's flaunting image—was that Murfreesboro was still in the hands of the Union Army.

It wasn't for any strategic military reason we moved, insofar that we as a unit could figure out. But rather to be closer to the East Main Street home of Colonel Charles Ready, who besides being a political figure during those lofty times had four daughters. One of his daughters was named Mattie, of whom Morgan was supposedly keen on.

Our group, which by now was being called by everyone thereabouts, "Morgan's Raiders", was outside the realm of army regulations and discipline. However, in order to maintain this distinction, as well as the Southern Army's peculiar homage for local heroes, Morgan had to keep us continually out on the road and raiding, or watch as we were absorbed by the Southern command. Something that was inconceivable to a man like Morgan, who couldn't live in the ritualistic drudgery and bureaucratic wasteland which was normal army life. Therefore, Jefferson Davis and the others in command let Morgan be—as long as he kept bringing home victories, albeit sometimes insignificant ones at best. Still, I don't believe Captain Morgan saw it that way. In other words, I truly believe it was in the excitement of outwitting a superior force, being trapped and seeing his way to freedom that therein lay the great quality of the man, as well as the unchecked seeds for his eventual downfall. In fact, had Captain Morgan (soon to be named General) been forced by the army's hierarchy to submit his often individualistic plans to the general consensus of what was best for the Confederacy, he would not have put himself into the ultimate situation that cost him his life. By the same token, his military arrogance, tactical skills and bravado I believe, would have been seriously jeopardized by an officer's post within the ranks of the regular Confederate Army. To understand Morgan is to understand the jaguar's need to prowl uninhibited and attack the opponent's exposed underbelly at any moment, without the need for preconceived notions or a *West Point way* of doing things, as Morgan was want to criticize.

No matter; for we continued to raid and raid so impressively that the Union Army's Major Sidell was seriously and provocatively questioned by a Union commission conducting an investigation on the war in middle Tennessee, as to the strength of a report that Morgan could be in two places at the same time. Major Sidell vigorously denied the accusation while looking furtively over his shoulder as he did so.

Captain Morgan called us together one night and told us to draw the normal amount of rations and ammunition from ordnance for a one week's raid behind the enemy's lines. This time, our goal was to try and kidnap a Union general to exchange for General Simon Buckner, taken prisoner at the battle of Fort Donelson.

I don't know why it was, but it seemed that every time we set out it was raining and humid. Almost as if the Almighty wanted to make it as hard upon us as was possible, so that we would turn back I suppose. The next thing we felt after the rain let up was the blanching sun and that was worse, for now the searing humidity ate into our bones and made arthritic skeletons out of most of us. What surprised me the most, looking back, was that I don't remember anyone really complaining very much about the weather and its conditions. Which is to say, we generally were happier out on the road, and preferred raiding with its inevitable surprises to being back in camp and its unrelenting boredom.

With the sun came the red dust; the fine red dust that made a point of clinging to everything while turning the entire column into a uniform, earthen-adobe color. To prove that we were used to it, I took to singing "The Rocky Road to Dublin", and rode on oblivious as usual to what was happening around us.

Before getting to Nashville two things happened. We found and burned five hundred bales of Yankee cotton which were left unattended next to a rail siding. Then almost immediately afterwards and by surprise, we stumbled upon a Federal cavalry detachment doing *siesta duty,* alongside one of the large creeks that feed off the Cumberland River. We engaged them in a heated skirmish with Longfellow Mortlock in the lead (for he was the first to spot them) crying out like some ravaged fool, "Death to the Sassenachs!" It was as good a war cry as any as far as I could tell. Indeed, the other side of the creek was only thirty yards away. Therefore, I could see clearly the look on some of their Yankee faces when Longfellow, his handlebar moustaches like two giant anvils whistling about his convoluted face, took to screaming his hellish cry and firing solo bursts from his musket. The Yankee soldiers impulsively began looking around at each other, fearful-like, as if to confirm the erstwhile figure that Longfellow presented. At length, they scrambled back up the creek bank, to bundle up in twos and threes, scared to be alone or so it seemed, in case Longfellow Mortlock could somehow traverse that creek and engulf the lot of them. While at the same time taking cover themselves, enabling a volley of their quickly rammed-home bullets to be fired back at us.

We followed their lead and staggered about in an ungainly fashion to hide behind the various trees—oak and ash I believe; their gigantic, twisted roots seeping down into the river, affording us a myriad of perches within which we could fire our muskets while enjoying a minimum of protection. Both armies were stretched out this way on both sides of the creek, perhaps for seventy-five yards or so in either direction. Looking across the creek, I saw clumps of Yankees in their blue-clad uniforms. Most had their sleeves rolled up revealing sweaty, white undershirts, with their short-brimmed hats in some cases, keeping bloodied head bandages in place, firing back at us. Some were standing and some were kneeling. Their shooting, like ours on the opposite side of the creek was indiscriminate and pell-mell at best. It continued without any fundamental idea of where to aim, but more of a panicked swarm of bullets that would by necessity keep us penned down for awhile, at least until they could figure out their next move. As a result, once or twice I saw a Yankee soldier throw away his musket in disgust, for it had overheated and could no longer be brought to bear upon us. With Morgan leading his charges we kept up a steady round of fire, blasting away like so many daft statues bent upon shooting anything which moved. As if to show us how it was done, Morgan waded out alone into the slow-moving river and took out personally a half-dozen Yankees, before they closed ranks and became harder to shoot than squirrels in wintertime. From behind a tree one Yankee fell. Or more to the point crumpled in his tracks, his head lunged down towards the river while his dead hand still engulfed his rifle's trigger in a firm grasp, as if he wanted to take aim and shoot a fish under the water. No one made a move to help him or see if anything could be done. He was left to lie half-straddled against the crumbling, pumpkin-colored, dirt bank of the creek alongside a giant grey boulder, the only object preventing him from sliding head-first down into the water.

On our side of the tree-shadowed tributary we lost in the first five minutes of the battle the gunslinger from Missouri. I never knew his name. He went down quiet-like as if he was in prayer, falling at first to his knees then collapsing entirely. His head ended up nestled between two overgrown tree roots with his back arched upwards in a rigid, spasmodic flex that could no longer relax.

Basil Duke stayed on his horse and kept patrolling behind us. The man took to waving his sword in a menacing fashion, indicating the direction of our enemy in a determined effort to get us into the creek itself and after those vermin-infested, sleepy-eyed Yankees.

The skirmish lasted no longer than twenty-five minutes. Yet, once it was over it took twice as long for the ringing in my ears to stop.

Little by little, the Unionists took to mounting their horses and riding away haphazardly in a confused retreat. As was his custom, Father Stanislaus said prayers for the dead on both sides of the creek. I could see the Jesuit priest, his hand steadying his purple stole about his neck while he made his way from corpse to corpse, pausing over each one to anoint them with some kind of oil and to say prayers for their souls. It was a forlorn and disturbing sight. Especially, since I didn't really speak to the man anymore. His vision of our lifestyle had become too detached for me, as if he didn't care that much or worse—anything at all about what went on around us. Aye, I didn't like the way the priest acted because he appeared to me to be aloof and callous, even though as I mentioned, we rarely spoke to one another.

"Devil" made some wiseacre remark about the priest, "What in bloody 'ell, can he do? They're dead—and that's about the size of it—they ain't comin' back far as I can tell! He should 'ave been blessin' the poor bastards while they were 'till enough alive to get outta the way—not when they've just upped and bought the farm!"

"Let him be "Devil", he's just doing his job like we're trying to do ours." I shot back.

"Devil" became excited, "No, he ain't! He's over there givin' those bleedin' Yanks the last bloody rites of the church, and he ain't got no right to do such a thing—they's our sworn enemies!"

I threw up my hands while looking at Longfellow, "You know we're all going to die one day. And when it happens, I want a man of the cloth praying over me. At the same time, I'm thinking it won't matter to me at that point whether he's Yankee or Confederate."

I remembered my mother and her cold ocean splash into the depths of the Atlantic with a bible-spewing, drunken Captain to pray over her. My whole body inadvertently shivered.

Longfellow said something that stung me, even though I don't believe it was aimed at me specifically, "Perhaps, it would be much better if we all prayed prior to shooting at one another, than to argue about it once a man's gone."

Just then Captain Morgan came riding up as animated as I've ever seen him.

"Boys," he beckoned to us, "I truly believe we've come upon more Yankee nests around these parts than even Basil Duke here believed. This isn't over by a long shot. Still, we need to keep our eyes open all the time even when we're asleep—. Those Yanks are slippery fellows. And you'd all better know that, before we get caught up in their nets and have to explain to some dumb Yankee colonel why he shouldn't hang the lot of us!"

Upon Morgan's orders we broke out our stolen Union overcoats, struggled into them and rode eagerly away, passing through farms while keeping close to the back road country that lined the outskirts of Nashville.

We put our spurs to the flank as we approached the lunatic asylum, six miles southeast of Nashville. We stopped every wagon, every detachment that we saw fit to do so. It was always the same; upon seeing us in our Union overcoats the wagon train would stop unsuspecting, assuming we were there to check passes.

Morgan commanded them, "Cut your traces."

Inevitably, the lead wagon would rebel claiming that Morgan's orders towards them as a Union officer were clearly beyond his scope of authority.

Morgan would then draw his pistol, and finally the wagon people would realize they'd been duped and by none other than John Hunt Morgan himself. At this point we had more than eighty prisoners but still no general.

Exasperated, Morgan ordered the troop to be broken up into multiple detachments and sent out to find and capture a Union general.

"And where in bloody 'ell are we supposed to find a Yankee general? They don't grow on trees 'round here—near enough as I can tell."

As usual, "Devil's" idea of fighting the war included the hot baths down around Sparta, Tennessee, with a copiously good, picnic lunch thrown in that would allow for lots of malingering.

It had been a warm and exciting day and I was tired of all this verbal jousting, "If Morgan claims he's got the inside intelligence which says there's a general round a-bouts, in these parts, then there's got to be one. Make no mistake about it—we've just got to find him that's all."

This I told to "Devil" who just glared, unsatisfied with me, as if to say 'Show me your general, then?'

There was a farmhouse not far up ahead, for we could see the weather-beaten, wood-shingled roof and low-slung terrace windows. This had been basically Morgan's orders; to sift through this place until we found what we were looking for—a real live, Yankee general. Therefore, we turned our mounts toward the run-down, paint-peeling, farm house to see if maybe a slobbering, big-bellied, pampered, Yankee general hadn't taken over the place for his command while the rest of us fought off mosquitoes and trail sores.

Captain Morgan told us to find a Union general so we looked. However, he never bothered explaining how to capture one if we did find him, for they were a very peculiar breed of men these haughty Union generals. Oftentimes, refusing to work alone, and with staff officers and foot solders around that were inevitably armed to the teeth and of a peculiarly contumacious disposition. That was Morgan's way and undoubtedly one of the reasons for his success; attention to the details of carrying out orders was left more often than not to his men.

"Bring him to me trussed up in his night clothes and cap for all I care," Morgan told us.

Still, we had to find one first.

The farmhouse in question sat up on a knoll. It had been fenced in and the surrounding brush haphazardly cleared out to a half-mile from the house and in every direction as well. As we rode up I noticed the actual farmland had recently been tilled which I thought unusual for that time of year. There were scattered sycamore trees planted in a haphazard fashion about the place, leaving their silver-tinted leaves to play havoc in the afternoon breeze, swirling about every which way before hitting the ground. The farmhouse itself was relatively new and looked sturdy enough. However, it desperately needed new paint for the wooden boards showed grey poking out behind peeling, scalloped, mud-brown paint, as if a man hadn't been through to do his chores in quite some time. Indeed, this was not uncommon for many places during this period where the cause of war had drained many a man from his farm.

As we rode up and dismounted, we took notice of a short, close-hauled, chubby Negro woman wearing a faded, blue and white paisley shift on the front porch. Her head was covered with a red bandana and the woman appeared to be wailing away, trying to clean several thick house rugs three times her size while at the same time, calling on the good Lord for some assistance in the matter.

She seemed convinced there were some shenanigans being played by the rugs and right under her nose as well, for she kept talking to the rugs as if they were living persons, "You'se done think what I wouldn't see—is that it? Say no mo' to ol' worn-out, you-do-too-much-around-here's-anyways-Bunnie. Why you set 'a dirty, ol', ungrateful rugs, tha's what you is—you just watch what ol' Bunnie done gonna give you—tha's right—what I's gonna give you! The done and said whuppin' of your life. And don't be thinkin' now, I might be just about changin' my mine neither!"

This was followed by a *wap, wap, wap* with a long-handled butter churner. Then the dust flew up and in every direction as well, like a Missouri born and bred tornado.

"You done best come clean with me—y'all—right here's on this porch— in the now, 'as before I done strike you down—."

Wap, wap, wap....

"Lordy, lordy , lordy, My han-some goodness, what says the good Lord 'bout all this here and you folks so full a dirt and disrespect. Why I never done see such disgrace and filth comin' from nobody 'fore I done set my eyes on y'all. Now I done 'nows why Miss Bunnie ain't never had no chillem! Why they wouldn' wanna lissen to me neither wiv you folks around to set some kind a bad example! Still never a mind, you gonna gets what's a comin' your way and I ain't gonna hold back nothin' now—you here me? Never 'fore mind the rod n' than you's done an' spoil the child—I do declare!"

As we stepped onto the railing she answered her own question, glowering daringly at the house rugs indeed while thumping them mightily with the butter-churner, "Oh, you' darn and filthy rugs, look'n here all of yous'n listen closely; I do declare you is dust alright, though it ain't my fault, and unto dust you aln't gonna return."

Wap, wap, wap....

When the Negro woman heard our boots and saw us in our Union Army overcoats, her eyes became big and round. They appeared more white than anything else with a small dot of brown in the middle, much like what happens to a raccoon when it's trapped and can't run anywhere—thick and saucer-like with anxiety and fear.

She dropped her cleaning stick like it was molten lead.

Then alternatively glancing over her shoulder at us and back to the house began crying out, "Missy, Missy come quick and soon too, it's them soldiers and I do believes they got news of Mr. Roberts. Missy, Missy come quick, it's all 'bout Mr. Roberts and when he'll be 'bout to comes home! Oh, ma lordy—.Oh, ma lordy me, is too much'n for one Bunnie to take care of, too much'n indeed!"

Finally, she practically pushed us down a petite, violet-wallpapered hallway and inside a parlor room. All the while, the Negro housemaid continued fussing incessantly after her "Missy", who I correctly assumed to be the lady of the house, as if we all were in the midst of a rampaging, out-of-control, house fire. Once inside the parlor, the Negro woman kept on wringing her hands and alternatively calling out for her "Missy" while glancing outside where she had left her house rugs. Probably convinced they were up to their incorrigible, dust-clinging shenanigans once again. After taking in the room, I thought I was in the midst of a military museum. There were crossed sabers decorating the four walls and lithographs of the Scottish Highlanders, oil paintings of battle scenes in which cannon blew ramparts to pieces, and sure-footed horses drew military caissons, along with several glass cases containing medals. In fact, upon viewing the medal cases, the thought crossed my mind that with what was inside those cases we could decorate the entire Confederate Army for bravery and still have some medals left over, for the next war coming through. In contrast to the walls, the room was bare except for two overstuffed blue chairs with white doilies on the arms and an old granddad rocker which set back just in front of the chimney. The rocker seemed out of place with the rest of the room which was remarkably clean and tidy. For the rocker was chipped, well-worn on the rockers and armrests, without a lick of varnish on its wooden frame, and left to look into a fireless hearth as if one in waiting.

From somewhere in the back of the house came a woman's voice, "What is it, Bunnie? What are you making such a fuss about?"

Then we heard footsteps approaching.

The woman entered the parlor holding two blue tea cups. She was wearing an elegant evening dress fastened above the neck in the high collar fashion of the day. The dress was burgundy-red and had shiny yellow or gold pleats running lengthwise down each side. These pleats opened and closed like an accordion with each step the lady took as she entered the room. Her reddish-mahogany hair was fastened delicately in an Irish bun (I believe the women call this type of fashion), from high above her neck to her head in such a way that she looked rather like old-school royalty. Still in all, her face was young and tender with just a trace of, for lack of a better word; despondence, as if some calamity had touched her recently and she hadn't quite gotten over it, just yet. To be sure, there was a lovely sweetness about her, a still-life, pale beauty if you will. Nevertheless, there was something else as well, and I'm not qualified as a lowly writer who came to the knowledge of words too late in life to really say what it was. Could it be that her beauty was at the same time gripping yet painful? I suppose with any woman it would be hard to describe. Yet this one in particular, froze me in my place, right there in the parlor, for reasons we will consider later. As well, her formal dress and apprehensive appearance suggested she was waiting in the immediacy for someone, or at the very least news of that person.

As she walked into the room the woman kept looking back and forth at the two blue and gold-rimmed tea cups she held in each hand. Both cups depicted painted white scenes from a fox-hunt on a solid blue background. Otherwise, the scenes on one cup appeared poorly sketched or inadequately glazed, as if the furnace hadn't cooked the enamel properly, and therefore, had indelibly smudged the image. This must have been the cause of her consternation, for she kept staring from one cup to the other in comparison of the two. At last, she gave up and set the cups down next to one another. This she did, placing the cups on one of the white doilies of the blue chair closest to her, as if she recognized her duty to welcome strangers in her home took precedence over her smudged tea set.

All of a sudden when I recognized the woman, it wasn't important to me what her tea set looked like or anything else for that matter. I felt extremely lucky for my own sake that it wasn't me holding the fox-hunting tea cups. Because, I surely would have dropped them right then and there and shattered everything to pieces, seeing as it was, this lady of the house standing there before my unbelieving eyes, was none other than Katherine Louisa Maddox.

She looked at Longfellow, "Devil" and myself strangely enough. Katherine hovered for a full second on my week-old, grimy, blackened beard and even longer on my crooked eye socket.

The very same eye socket Bailey Burke had been considerate enough to crush while at the same time Katherine addressed her maid, "Bunnie, we don't go around blasting our lungs from here to Dublin screaming, 'Missy, Missy', a lady announces company quietly, genteel-like after a fashion. Why you'd a thought the guns were firing over Fort Sumter again. Just think of what Mr. Roberts would have to say about such a commotion, indeed." Lowering her voice to simulate a man's baritone Katherine intoned, "'This house must be kept sentinel-quiet, like a military barracks after *lights out* enabling me to plan our position—and that's an order!', is what he would say."

The Negro housemaid bent her head as if she was offering contrition and answered, "Yes, Ma'am, Bunnie done wrong."

Meanwhile, in her embarrassment, the housekeeper took to rolling her head and looking at everything on the walls as if for the first time, blinking her sad eyes methodically in the process.

Taking into consideration our Union overcoats, Katherine breathed deeply and asked us the following, slowly, as if anticipating our response, "Have you come with news of my husband, Captain Robert Singletary of the Fourth Kentucky Cavalry; Lieutenant Colonel John Parkhurst commanding?"

None of us answered her.

Her voice still carried a formidable trace of Ireland, and in particular of our village of Castlewarren. For me, it was a joy to behold, as well as to listen to.

As feelings were reawakened in me, feelings that I thought had long been silenced, I wanted to respond, '*Yes, Ma'am, he's in a ditch somewhere up to his eye-teeth in bayonets so he can't come home!*' But I didn't. Instead I started to scratch my arm like I do whenever I feel embarrassed or at a loss for words. I also didn't wish to see the woman in front of me hurt in any way. At that point in time and in her own parlor no less, Katherine Louisa Maddox appeared extremely vulnerable. I convinced myself it was because she was the wife of a no-good Yankee captain.

At length, she asked me directly like a well-trained hunting hound onto the scent, "And you Sir, do you know my husband?"

"No, Mrs. Singletary, I don't know the Captain, your husband."

I answered truthfully while choking over my words. Then I scratched my arm some more until by all rights I should have drawn blood.

For the longest time her eyes came to rest on my crushed eye socket before dancing quickly over my face, neck and shoulders, seemingly trying to push past my week-old beard. Suddenly appearing faint, Katherine sat down much too quickly in one of the chairs, almost knocking the tea cups off from their place on the white doily. Her skirts billowed out from under her like wilting balloons, causing a most unladylike sound. This in effect made Bunnie, her housemaid, cover her ears in fright while "Devil" and Longfellow smirked at one another knowingly.

The room stayed quiet with everyone wondering and waiting.

Upon recovering herself, Katherine ordered Bunnie, "Take these good soldiers out to the kitchen and feed them. Feed them well, Bunnie, for they know only too well the hardships of these times, fighting those Confederate turncoats."

"Yes'm, I'll feed 'em alright by the larder of the great Almighty—I'll stuff 'em just like I woudda Christmas goose I will, stuff 'em so's they can't hardly walk outta here when they's got to be goin'. Yes, Mizz Roberts, I'll surely feed'em."

Bunnie looked at us with a bashful glance before leaving the parlor. She sauntered from the room waddling like a hen does, at the same time motioning to us, impatient for her straggling chicks to follow.

As I reached the spot where Katherine was sitting, she laid a gentle yet restraining hand on my arm, and inquired in a way that touched me to my soul, "T'is you Edward Ruth, is it not?"

I nodded perfunctorily and started to continue on my way towards the back of the house. At the same time I took to scratching my arm in an overly aggressive manner while searching for Bunnie and the kitchen.

She asked timidly which was unlike the lady at all to speak to me in such a way, "Please stay for a moment and tell me what you have done with yourself since we last saw one another?"

The way Katherine said it, was the closest I ever heard the woman flirt with the idea of begging something from me.

Upon hearing this, even though he was several feet closer to the kitchen than I was, Longfellow stopped. He glanced first at Katherine then at me in a reprobate way. As if he didn't approve of us knowing each other, much less speaking to one another, before he shook his head in disbelief and left the room.

She bade me take off my Union overcoat and sit down. Which I did, being careful not to soil with my dirty elbows the white doilies that armed each blue chair. Unfortunately, when Katherine saw my cotton-grey Confederate uniform with half of the front brass buttons missing and a dirty undershirt sticking through she gasped. At first, I thought she was shocked at my filthiness. However, as it turned out I had forgotten what continental flavor our overcoats were.

The woman stuttered as she spoke, as if she couldn't believe what she was seeing, "C-c-can it be true, Edward Ruth, what I am beholding right here in front of me, in this very same parlor with my very own eyes? You're fighting for the South but masquerading in my house—the house of a captain in the United States Army—as a Union soldier?"

The way she said it she might just as well have accused me of the most perverse crime imaginable.

Self-consciously, and needing time to organize my thoughts, I looked carefully around the room.

I took to inspecting the glass cases containing all those medals, before responding with a deep, thought-provoking, set-her-back-on-her-heels sort of challenge, "What war did someone win on their own to get all those medals?"

"Don't you dare try and change the subject!"

"What are you talking about? I'm not changing any subject!"

"You know quite well what I mean, Edward. The North constructed, promoted and protected the American *United States,* only to have the South behave like an ungrateful child. Yes, that's exactly right; pouting and whimpering because it couldn't have its way. Instead, calling for its inheritance from the North so the Confederacy could go on its selfish way alone and squander its heritage like the prodigal son once did. Is that what you are fighting for? And is that why you must hide yourself in a Union overcoat like some sort of treasonous defector?—You should be ashamed of yourself, Edward Ruth!"

I must say, I've always been amazed how quickly that woman could regain her haughtiness, especially, when only minutes before I'd been feeling deeply sorry for her, with her adopted ingratiating frailty.

"What is it to you?" I answered back. "You're from Ireland just like me."

"My husband happens to be a high-ranking officer in the United States Cavalry, and as such, we both have beliefs about what is right and what is wrong for this country of ours."

She proceeded to flip her well-coiffured head up and down. Much like a young, ebullient gelding might have done; quite unsure of himself, therefore, anxious and fretful before the race should start.

Either she believed in what she said, or she'd been given no choice about the matter.

In any case I answered her, perhaps somewhat out of turn, "You didn't seem so politically self-righteous or consistent with your current beliefs, back, when you were trying to flirt with "the prodigal son", in the form of one Captain Morgan—and make him your beau!"

"How dare you?" She cried back.

I didn't like how she was making me feel inside so I changed the subject. "Katherine, don't you see its *Home Rule* again, it's just happening in another country. Otherwise, it's still the same thing. The only reason the North ever extended a helping hand to the South is so they could economically control and sap the South of whatever products they can't manufacture themselves including cotton. Everything else is secondary. The North wants to control things and have the last word down here just like the English did, and it'll be a day of famine once again before I'll stop protecting the little man."

"Even if the little man happens to be a *black* one?" She shot back.

"As long as he's not a *black* Englishman!"

"It's immoral Edward! The South is immoral, with its hypocritical attitude on slavery." She crossed her hands in her lap defiantly.

"It's no more immoral than you changing sides?"

"What do you mean "changing sides"?" This she practically hissed at me.

"Don't fool yourself," I accused her, "You use such an innate and cunning probity to weave your sorcery—that you believe us all somehow to be fools."

"Oh, so now you're blaming your trials on my supposed witchcraft." She laughed impishly, full of unfeigned silliness, remarkably like an adolescent schoolgirl.

"In a manner of speaking!" I confirmed her vacant remark.

She shifted in her chair to arrange the pleats of her fashionable evening gown.

Turning, she confirmed to me, "While this supposed witch in front of you is most definitely married now; at the very least, I am forthright about it as I have always been with you. And don't have to stoop to magical illusions, such as wearing the enemy's overcoat to dupe those of us who used to trust you." Intuitively, she brushed away what seemed to be a tear as if I had truly hurt the woman.

I decided to change the subject once again—importunately I might add, "The States themselves should decide what's best for each one. I believe they call it "States' sovereignty", and it's not for the real "turncoats" or "Lincoln's hirelings" as Captain Morgan calls them to decide for the rest of us, and that includes slavery."

"And when did this come about, this sudden change of heart; for I don't recall much slavery in Ireland?"

"There are different types of slavery, Katherine. But to be sure, it didn't happen overnight, this "change of heart" as you put it. I guess it must have happened when I saw you, all in a goggle, over Captain Morgan back in Kentucky." This I announced a lot more impetuously than I meant to.

She laughed at the apparent ridiculousness of my suggestion, ""A goggle" over Captain Morgan?—I admit Edward, he appeared attractive at some point I suppose—it might have been his uniform. Weren't they called the 'Lexington Roughnecks' or 'Ruffians', something of that order? No, no wait—they were called the "Rifles", yes, that was their name—"The Lexington Rifles"!"

She repeated to herself while clapping her hands together rapidly like a young girl would, happy that she remembered their name. "Still, I hardly think "a goggles" is the proper term for what I saw in the man."

"Or, what I saw in you?" I challenged her.

"What you saw in me? Why—why you have no right—Edward Ruth! Don't you dare go any further!"

"You're right. It's only what I had hoped to see in you—believed to have seen in you." I added.

Fitfully, I sat back in my chair suddenly angry with her, yet more so with myself for having gotten involved with such a nettlesome woman.

Katherine suddenly leaned forward out of her own chair before lecturing me, "And just what did you see in me, Edward? A wench wringing a meager existence from a potato patch while the love of my life keeps me bare foot and a docile idiot, so he can have the time of his life ballyhooing down at the tavern with the rest of his mates? Then come home to level me with one of his drunken blows should I so much as speak out of turn. Do you really believe I would accept such a life?"

"No, but a little integrity would be nice."

"Who are you to call into question my integrity?—How dare you, Edward Ruth?" Her tone of voice was expediently insulting, as if I was very much below her station in this life, and she wished to remind me of that.

Then I, in like manner, started to get flustered by this woman, so I rebuked her, "You turn however and wherever the wind blows you if only for the sake of having someone who will take care of your whims, like the spoiled woman you pretend not to be. If it's worth your while not to be Catholic then you'll become Methodist, not because of any deep conviction inside yourself, but rather because it's more convenient for you and your quest for becoming someone other than who you really are. If you thought Captain Morgan could further your cause, showed the least bit of interest in your flirting ways, then you'd support him and the Confederacy until something better comes along—."

She interrupted me furiously, "You're more than a *skibereen* Edward Ruth, you're a disgrace to Ireland *as well as* to your new homeland!"

I sighed out of a morbid sadness within, "No Katherine, I saw how you looked at Captain Morgan that day—there's no denying it even though you try. You were caught up with the man and his charm whether you want to believe it or not."

Finally, I finished scratching my arm and laid my hidden feelings out in the open, "I was hoping that by joining up with Captain Morgan and his army, you wouldn't think me the *poor croppie* which you've always considered me to be. Perhaps even more—who can say?"

I felt more and more like the begging Irish scab which she took me to be. Impulsively, I tried to close up my shirt where the buttons were gone. This time I noticed there really was blood on my arm from all my unconscious scratching.

She touched at her hair instinctively before answering defensively, "Look Edward, I don't know what you're talking about. A *skibereen* is a *skibereen*; you can't change that for that's who you are. I told you once before to make something of yourself—. You're a dentist now. Why don't you practice dentistry, rather than running around the countryside with that marauder Morgan, who doesn't have the courage to fight out in the open in a fair fight during the day, but instead, murders men at night whilst they are asleep?"

In response I offered weakly, "And you; what about *Ne Temere*? Do you think that will go away? You were born in our culture and in the faith—what about that—does it mean so little to you, like a commodity, which you trade on market-day, to get something better? Stay the line—your Irish inheritance—stay the line, Katherine; who you were born to be, before you wake up one day and can't make sense of—nor remember who you are anymore."

Her face reddened as she questioned me angrily, "Edward Ruth, I don't recall you being so enamored by our,—er, your Catholic faith—. As I remember it, you're not even a practicing Catholic—or have you changed? My family and I used to go to mass back home more often than yours did. Why don't you start to practice your faith with some regularity instead of throwing it back at me, as if I didn't know where you came from? You're from Castlewarren, Edward, just like I am. But our roads never crossed, neither in our village nor here in America. For we seem to want the same things you and I, yet we only disagree as to how to achieve them. Nevertheless, you have the arrogant idea that you have cornered the market on integrity? Certainly not you, Edward Ruth. Certainly not you!"

This last part she cried out as if I somehow had violated some inner-sanctum and now the lady was in complete shock.

All of this must have startled Katherine's maid, for Bunnie called out from somewhere back of the house, "Missum Roberts, you gonna be's alright, everthin's the matter?"

"You leave us alone now, Bunnie. I got carried away is all. Now you go on back and take care of the soldiers like I asked." Katherine called out in the direction of the kitchen.

"Yes'm," from the rear of the house echoed Bunnie's reply.

Katherine dabbed at her eye with her dress sleeve, before turning to look at me, displeased that I had dared to remind her of her forgotten past.

I realized later I shouldn't have said it. Maybe it was the heat, the "applejack" we'd all been drinking heavily of late, of living out on the edge, of fighting these last couple of months without any tangible break of sorts. But I said it anyway, and I still to this day don't deny it....I can't deny it. Although, I wish now with all my heart I hadn't opened my big mouth.

For what came out caught her completely off guard, seemingly to cause Katherine insurmountable pain, "Some women, Mrs. Singletary, are condemned out of hand by the so-called righteous folk because they get paid for exactly the same thing you're doing; *services rendered.*"

"What did you just say?" Her face had turned chalky white with anger and her pale, scarlet lips trembled.

"You won't play with my feelings any longer!"

"Any feelings I have for you are exactly the same as the day I saw a little beggar-boy back in Castlewarren and I gave him an oatmeal cookie—. His ingrained poverty piqued my curiosity, as well as my Christian education of helping the downtrodden—no more, no less."

"In that case, I hope your husband, Captain *whatever his name is*, does come back to you and you continue to be happy together. Even though you aren't barefoot and planting potatoes any longer—." I spat the next sentence out, "Nonetheless, it still smells of *services rendered*. Why don't you take one of those medals down off the wall and wear it? For *services rendered* far beyond the call of duty—or integrity for that matter."

She let fly with the back of her hand aimed at my face. It caught me flat against my cheek with a dry and snapping sound like a brittle twig breaking in two. Her fingers lingered just enough on my face to drag one or two of her nails into my beard. Yet I didn't feel any pain, none whatsoever, only something warm and wet which trickled down my cheek.

Reaching down defiantly, I deliberately extended my right hand to where my belt hitched up my trousers, before I too, let fly a cuff that stopped...just short of? I don't know where because...because I just couldn't. It wouldn't have been the correct thing to do, and besides I was too ashamed of what we had both become to one another.

I didn't bother looking back, but impulsively ran out to my horse without waiting for the others.

While spurring my mount to a gallop, I heard her voice wailing and moaning like a banshee does, alone at night, screaming out its blistering misery somewhere distant and abandoned, out on the haunted moors, "EDWARD RUTH, COME BACK HERE THIS INSTANT—EDWARD, DO YOU HEAR ME? I ORDER YOU TO GET BACK HERE RIGHT NOW, THIS VERY INSTANT!"

Then, finally, I heard drifting away from somewhere behind me near the giant sycamore trees, "Edward, please come back—please."

At last there was silence...thankfully.

Riding away, my mind tumbled into pieces all around me. Thoughts of *Home Rule* (including the heartache)...*Ne Temere* justice...what an idiot I was for saying the things I had just got through saying...."Morgan's Raiders"...the

Orange Jesus versus the Catholic one all fought for possession of my thoughts. It wasn't that simple anymore, indeed if it ever had been. I was confused and angry, but damned if that woman would ever call me a *skibereen* again. At least I had made up my mind about that.

They told me later that I was unbelievable hell to live with for the next several days. I neither cared about anything nor would I listen to anyone. In fact, I had even decided I wouldn't go back to Morgan's camp right away. I needed some time. Something wasn't right and I needed time to think, to sort out some sort of crossroads I had come to. As well, I suppose, when it all comes down to it—what to do next.

It was all due to my own selfish initiative—what we turned to after that—what with "Devil" and Longfellow Mortlock sticking around solely to keep an eye on me. That's all they could do, I was wild and full of fire. The farmers thought at first we were renegade Union men out for a good time. It didn't help our disguise any when "Devil" proposed to one bewildered farmer that he'd take in trade a stout carriage horse and a fine livery wagon back in Richmond for a gold-inlaid antique mirror. This mirror he claimed was used by Marie Antoinette when she was supposedly betrothed to a Scottish prince, before she made her fatal mistake and married the King of France instead. Still in all, gold mirror or no gold mirror, the farmer was curious to know what business Union soldiers had back in Richmond, amidst the enemy. Mostly at gunpoint we stole hams and turkeys, fresh bread, fresh milk and cheese, as well as any "applejack" the farmhouse could provide. I'd slip a bullet out of its chamber without the farmer knowing it. And if he complained too much about our thievery, I would say here's a receipt from Lincoln, before clicking over the empty chamber while pointing it at the farmer's head.

We ended up by a river. It was perfect for us. A heavy fog shrouded the river and its surrounding valleys in a thick mist, screening from view everything more than a few feet away. We ate and slept and ate some more.

"That was her wasn't it?" Longfellow asked one day, skeptical that I was perhaps sociable at last, his thick moustaches glistening with bacon fat.

I nodded my head. "In any case she's married so that's it. And to a son-of-a-bitch Union officer too!"

"Take it from me, 'Shakes', she ain't happy 'bout it." He added with some satisfaction.

"Longfellow," inquired "Devil", "How can you be so sure she ain't happy? There's lots of folks miserable and happily married, I see's 'em all the time!"

Longfellow shook his head in denial, "Yeah, just so you know; the Negro housemaid Bunnie done told me when we was eating that the Captain is a mean and impersonal, petty you-know-what; said he treats Katherine like an enlisted man. Probably have her out marchin' n' all if he could! He's a lot older than she is too!"

Devil answered cautiously, "Aye, it may be as you say. The house seemed awfully stern and military-cold for having a majestic woman such as that one living there. Even so, she still holds her head high that one, like she don't want anyone to know she's been sufferin'. *IF* like you say in what matters between a man and a woman, the Captain ain't been treatin' her just right."

"She's married fellows!" I protested.

"It doesn't matter—she ain't for the likes of you anyway!" They both muttered in unison.

It seemed to me, my friends didn't care one way or the other for my feelings. They continued their almost evangelical comparison of Katherine and what would have been my fate. I might add, right within earshot as well.

"That one's a thoroughbred, 'Shakes',—no good for the likes of you." Longfellow cautioned me like an overly patient, older brother.

"Devil" jumped in, "He's right, 'Shakes'. Take it from me, what you need is a packhorse not a thoroughbred—they can climb with a load all day long if necessary and without complaining even once! Why a packhorse you gets to give 'em the whip once in awhile too. You know, just to show 'em who's in charge—all day long if you've got the mind and strong enough arm for it."

Then he eyed curiously enough his red-haired forearm as if he knew what he was talking about.

At length, he took a moment to think to himself before adding, "Either that or an injun woman; they's too dumb to talk back, 'sides they's used to beatings even if they're Mohawk or Iroquois." Sagaciously he added, "Course if you've a mind to take 'em to count and wail 'em a bit, I wouldn't be turning my back on 'em any time soon while you's is sleeping at night. 'Cause you might not see the morning once they get finished with you—. They's hard and dirty alright, but I forgot to mention—above all—they's a revengeful lot! Probably got something to do with eating all that gamey, bear-paw meat they're all so fond of."

"We're from the same village in Ireland." I tried to defend my feelings.

Longfellow tried equally to explain his, "Look it here, 'Shakes', it ain't my intention to hurt your feelings or get you angry none, but damn it all that kind of woman, it's their nature, country Irish or otherwise—."

I looked up to see where he was leading me.

"You see, they's been trained otherwise, them *thoroughbred* gals. Why I believe it's a natural fact of life that when they say 'yes' to something they really mean 'no'. And when they say 'no' they truly mean 'yes'. Your darn right; those *thoroughbred* women have been educated different-like from the rest of us. They's got a whole 'nother *pro-spective.*" He smiled in affirmation of what he was saying before repeating himself, "That's just what it is too—a whole 'nother *pro-spective.* They's a breed apart—ain't nothing you can do about it anyhows! 'Cept to forgettin' 'em! And quick-like too if you favor sleepin' at night!"

Apparently this was a subject that both of my friends had thought a great deal about.

"Devil" challenged me, "You was always saying you wanted to write poetry and such beautiful things which challenge the soul. Well, now's the time to write poetry when you's hurtin', hurtin' real bad inside too." He thought about it for an instant before adding, "Why that's wonderful!"

He took to tugging at the hairs of his unkempt red beard and staring wildly about, maybe looking for inspiration in the tall, green-backed reeds that dotted the shoals of the river.

Indeed, he must have found his inspiration for he started to describe, "Write about a jilted rose that's done up and died, its petals like the brown mud of the Mississippi."

Without any further prodding he threw out his arms like an actor does before reciting the following;
"This rose of mine,
Lies here, tattered on a log
Her love...no longer true
Is now, the house of a frog....
You see how the rose done got trod over or maybe became the house of a frog down on the muddy banks? Then one day you gets to read this here poem to her and won't she just change her mind with all that emotion bubbling over. It'll be a hallucinatin' miracle, the way she'll come runnin' back to you—you'll see." "Devil" sat back, a satisfied grin showing through his beard.

"Why not mention something about the swimming hog that's maybe got webbed feet while you're at, as if you knew what a woman cares about?", challenged Longfellow, a disgusted look creeping across his face.

A storm swept through "Devil's" eyes as well while he tugged at his ear, a sure sign that trouble was brewing. "A 'hog with duck's feet' and why the bloody hell not?" He intimidated. "I'm sure one of your female *acquaintances* Mortlock, would just about come to tears if you told her that things had changed and she was just as sweet as a tootin' hog. But she shouldn't go and trip over herself with those gorgeous webbed feet of hers now—for you couldn't live without her if she got hurt."

"Devil" practically squealed with laughter at what he thought had bested his friend.

Sure enough, it wasn't too long before the both of them were circling each other like a couple of bulls, in and out of the fog-lined river bank, sometimes splashing one another. Neither one, it seemed to me, anxious to throw the first punch, afraid of what might happen perhaps, stuffed as they were to *the gills* with so much farm produce inside.

We ended up straggling back to Morgan's camp in that way; overweight, without any Union general to speak of. And not too anxious all of a sudden to hear what Captain Morgan might have to say about our little *sejour* in and around Nashville, Tennessee.

Chapter Nineteen

Shall await,
Like a love-lighted watch-fire,
All night at the gate;
A steed comes at morning; no rider is there;
But its bridle is red with the sign of despair.

Author unknown

There were no blue tea cups decorated with images from a fox-hunt waiting for us when we got back to camp...no, nothing of the kind. Instead, we found Captain Morgan at the head of a column of riders. I remember them as being four across, eerie and ghostlike in the bright moonlight bathing the Tennessee countryside. The last crisp notes of the bugler ordering everyone "To Horse" had just faded away. We rode up and saluted as best we could, conscious of the fact that even if everything went smoothly, we were still liable for a military chiding from the man who rode towards us now, menacingly, with a black plume flying from his hat.

"The least you could have done was to bring prisoners back on captured horses—assuming you couldn't find a general?" This Captain Morgan issued tauntingly.

He continued in his mocking tone, "Well, what do you have for the quartermaster? At the very least, you could have justified your absence—your *unauthorized* absence may I remind you, with a wagon-load of Colt revolvers, champagne and wine like Captain Gano and his Texans did when they showed up late. With which we could all celebrate your return in style. So then, what do you have in your haversacks that we can welcome you back with?"

"Devil" took the bait and like a scatter-brained idiot he offered Morgan some canned fruit and sardines we'd stolen from somewhere. Morgan knocked them from "Devil's" hand in such a violent way that even the horses started whinnying and stamping their hooves.

I felt it was time to speak up. I looked upon the man whose goatee had lengthened. Yet, besides his thinning hair and the freshly placed worry lines that had taken over his truculent forehead and fanned out from his eyes; yes, those same eyes which seemed as intimidating and demanding as when I had first met the man. "Captain Morgan, it was my fault, Sir. We came upon a farmhouse that we felt may have been the headquarters of a general and upon investigation as per your instructions, I encountered a woman that you may recall, you met once before back in Lexington. Also, you may recall Sir, she is an acquaintance of mine from my childhood back in Ireland." I also offered weakly by way of contrition, "She's married to a captain in the Yankee Army."

I did my best to explain our meeting at the farmhouse, and was as honest as I could be. Still in all, something was nagging at Captain Morgan to the extent he wouldn't let me finish.

Before I could continue Captain Morgan held up his hand for silence.

Then he pressed me on it in a very negative manner, "This "woman"?"

The way he pronounced "woman" made it seem like; *why would anyone bother with something so trifling as a woman with a war going on. Unless her name was Eve and she maintained a monopoly on all the apples in this part of the country?* Morgan continued, "This "woman"—doesn't she realize we are in a fight to the death or is she so resplendent that she still owns all of her own teeth?"

There were guffaws from the surrounding cavalrymen.

Then he caught himself, "This wouldn't be the same one that you've been whining about since the very first day I met you? Not the woman who's got you biting your own tail in the process. Well is it, 'Shakes'? You know the one I'm talking about; the one who'd make you a first-class pantywaist and have your full permission to do it too! "

Besides causing me instant embarrassment his question provoked laughter to emulate from the men waiting there on their horses. One of them even howled dramatically while making a sound like a captured wolf, his paw held rigid in a steel trap. I was caught alright and out in the open, in front of everyone whom I respected. In this case, *everyone* being the cavalry to my utmost dismay. Lest I need to remind the reader, the cavalry has never been known to be the forgiving kind where *pantywaists* are concerned. Nor do they ultimately enjoy a stalwart reputation for their limitless empathy to a troubled comrade-in-arms, especially when it concerns female companionship.

"As far as the "whining" goes, I'm not sure that is exactly—"

"Quiet!" He roared for the first time since we had arrived, showing his impatience.

"I don't give a damn if this woman is the Empress of China or makes lentil bean soup for Abe Lincoln! You've betrayed the trust I placed in you, 'Shakes', and now it's out of my hands."

"Well Sir, it's true we had no permission to be out as long as we were, still, I can explain—."

"What about spying *against* us? Were you out without permission so you could rendezvous with your Northern masters?"

Without waiting for a response, he pointed a gloved finger at Longfellow and "Devil", challenging the three of us, "It has come to my attention these men are active members of the Federal Northern Army along with your brother, 'Shakes'. They are on special assignment to spy on "Morgan's Raiders" and report back any such information that maybe helpful in the capture of one Captain John Morgan, Southern Confederate Army. Now do either of you deny that you have ever been in the Union Army?" Turning to me he added, "Is your brother as well, a member of the Union Army?"

Noticing our stone-cold expressions he added, "Don't just sit there like a bunch of damned pantywaists, answer me—damn it! Have either one of you ever been in the Federal Army?"

Longfellow apparently wanted to say something. Instead, he thought better of it, and ended up by spitting on the ground. Something he shouldn't have done for it further infuriated our captain.

"That's your answer—you, spitting at me?" Morgan cried out in disbelief. "And to your commanding officer as well? Why if I wasn't due to leave this very instant, I'd get down off my horse and take you apart with my bare hands—starting with those tomahawk moustaches you're wearing. For we don't tolerate that kind of disrespect down here, and I in particular, wouldn't mind showing you what a Southern gentleman's made of. You got that, Boy?"

I don't know why he said it for Longfellow was Irish like me. In any case, "Devil", true to himself, calculating there was going to be an eventual donnybrook of some sort made a balled fist while scrunching up his face like a round-cheeked rabbit.

Then fidgeting in his saddle he bellowed out, "This man's a Scotsman, a Scotsman I say! Death to the traitorous Scots!"

No sooner did he say this before half a dozen revolvers were drawn. And in a way that seemed to me, which did not reflect at all upon a Southern gentleman's code of conduct, upbringing, or any other way which could be construed as an estimable Southern attribute...for they were all pointed directly at us.

Captain Morgan spoke out, "Ellsworth and Gano, take these men and lock them up. They are hereby charged with treason, disobedience and misconduct before the enemy. And if we can't hang them for that then we'll just have to add spying as well. When I get back there'll be a general court martial and they'll be cashiered from the service first. That way their necks will feel a lot lighter when they're swinging."

I couldn't believe it so I stammered out our innocence. "Captain, we've only been living off the farms around Nashville. We've never come into contact with the enemy to pass along any information concerning your whereabouts, please Sir, you must believe me!"

Morgan wheeled his horse "Bess" around, for he had been heading back towards the front of the column, "'Shakes', I'd like to believe you. But you yourself, offered your own condemnation when you told me that your Irish girlfriend is now the wife of a Union captain."

I didn't respond I guess because I knew he'd have a better answer than anything I could come up with. It was like playing chess against a wizard.

So he answered my silence with this stinging rebuke, "If you couldn't capture a general you certainly could have brought back as a prisoner your rival so to speak, this Irishwoman's captain. If indeed, he is your rival, and not a fellow comrade-in-arms?"

"But Sir, he wasn't on the farm when we were there."

Now it was Morgan's turn to spit on the ground, "Wasn't 'on the farm' you say? And after what you just told me about her being dressed up, all formal-like, as if there wouldn't be a tomorrow? Otherwise, all dolled up for his return—what do you take me for 'Shakes', an idiot? Or is it too much to ask between combatants to lay a little trap and kidnap this Yankee captain, who it seems to me was due back at his farmhouse, at any moment, according to your story. For the life of me what do you think "Morgan's Raiders" is all about, or have you been blind these last couple of months to what we do? On the other hand, could it simply be that you are in cohorts with the Yankee Army? Thus, your Irishwoman's unreturned love is just a pathetic front for a convenient meeting place between you and your pack of Northern sympathizers, including your brother. Come on, 'Shakes', out with it now, *or* better yet you can wait until I get back. That'll give you some time to figure out an even better, whoppin'-good tale for your court martial!"

We were led away by Gano and Ellingsworth with Captain Morgan mentioning something about, "I can't wait 'till we get to Kentucky and away from these lying, poker-faced pantywaists."

This Morgan said as he started out the column at a brisk canter. As usual, for such a cloudless night and the beginning of a new raid, the sky started to rain. Although the sparse clouds up above couldn't match the dark ones in my heart. I should have been happy for at least I was inside and dry, but I wasn't. Instead, wishing with all my heart to be out on the trail and splashing through frost-lined mud, with a wet horse underneath me and a clear conscience within.

There were six grey-white tents placed in the middle of a clearing. These we were led to. Trees had been cleared away, and the tents placed on an elevated area where just about anyone in camp could see the goings-on. This was our prison, like fish kept in glass cases. Thus, we could walk around a short quarter-mile or so, but that was it. The three of us were fenced in, boxed in, facing who knows what when Morgan returned, in a word...trapped. And without anyone saying a word we all knew that it was my fault. On top of which, I had to live with the fact, Katherine had reputed my misconstrued accusations with her innocent-enough looking sorcery....It might seem strange to some people, nevertheless, I took considerable consolation in the fact that regardless of what might happen, including a possible public hanging, at least her hair was still in place.

Soldiers were brought over the next day by some sour-faced sergeant and I was told to work on their teeth.

"With what tools may I ask?" I inquired of the sergeant. For I hadn't brought any of my dental tools with me when I first joined up with Captain Morgan back in Lexington.

"Why don't you write your pals in the Union Army to send you some?" He sneered in a deep and menacing voice.

I didn't bother to answer him back for it would only have added *wood to the fire* so to speak. Eventually, the sergeant brought me some unsterilized tools that looked more pertinent for turning over a turnip patch than for working on a person's living mouth.

One of my first patients was a young lad of seventeen. He told me his name was Jeremiah Preston, he was from Virginia, and that he'd just about had enough of soldiering. That soldiering wasn't all that it was cracked up to be. This Jeremiah Preston was poorly dressed, with small rope cords tightened above each ankle, holding thin pant legs as closely as possible against his ankles to keep the cold out. His shoes flapped about like thrashing fish, as they both possessed a gaping hole in the front of each shoe, I suppose, so his toes could breathe. Still in all, he'd killed several men at the battle for Fort Donelson. Therefore, he figured, he'd see things through to the end, if for no other reason than his father had told him not to come home until the South had won. Then he showed me his mouth. It was as simple as an impacted wisdom tooth and would have to be extracted. We did the best we could with my two *nurses* "Devil" and Longfellow holding him firmly down on the cot. Still, he took to hollering like a cornered wildcat, and would have torn our tent to pieces if "Devil" hadn't leaned on the young man's windpipe with more pressure than was necessary, causing this Jeremiah Preston to pass out and lie still so I could extract the tooth. Afterwards, I had to remind "Devil" to ease up, that the operation was over. As a matter of course, we would all like to see young Mr. Preston alive and breathing once again. When he finally came to his senses this Jeremiah Preston claimed that my operation wasn't any more painful than a Yankee bayonet "across one's gizzards", I believe was the way he put it. In any case, he left our tent holding the back of his mouth with one hand and muttering something about how he could never seem to get enough air to breathe back in our tent. At that moment, he put the question to no one in particular, wondering aloud if by chance his lungs and back teeth weren't at the same time and in some strange way interconnected.

This went on all day long, with enlisted men and officers taking turns calling me a traitor. Yet, could I spare a moment to see why they couldn't chew properly, or to investigate an infernal abscess which wouldn't allow the pain-ridden individual, as well as everyone else in his tent, to sleep at night. I did the best I could, and was able to alleviate some of the suffering due to poor dental hygiene. Although, I had a hard time convincing a romanticized artillery man that spitting tobacco juice from a blackened gap in his front teeth would not help his teeth in the long run nor endear him forever to his beloved. He claimed that I was wrong; that I didn't know his fiancée the way he did. As a matter of fact, he told me, she chewed tobacco as well and what's more could spit farther than he could. I admitted that in fact he was right and I stood corrected; indeed, I had never met the down-to-earth, fortunate woman. Nevertheless, I was rather put about and thrust into a most delicate position when questioned sincerely by the same artillery man, if a young couple such as themselves, soon to be joined in the sacred rites of holy matrimony, shouldn't receive some sort of private instruction by a knowledgeable medical man such as myself. All this pertaining to the safe and regulatory practice of correct dental flossing, as a means of controlling the number of children they wished to bring into this world (a subject I don't recall touching on in school).

Towards mid-afternoon I drew the line on just whom or what I would treat, claiming I could do absolutely nothing for the mule that was thrust my way, other than shooting the poor creature. For the mule had sliced open his mouth something awful trying to chew a hole through a tin of bully-beef.

With this type of uninterrupted schedule I had no time to feel sorry for myself and our predicament. Although from time to time, I had to put up with the wishful thinking of my jailbird roommates who spent most of their days slowly putting together a plan to steal away to Mexico. "To Mexico we'll go"; Longfellow and "Devil" boasted while drawing together on a torn and stained bed sheet a map (showing Mexico to be but a day's leisurely paced ride from eastern Tennessee—heading due west I might add) where they insisted there was an abundance of tortillas and slew-eyed senoritas who had nothing better to do than to spend their lives waiting for this inglorious pair to show up. I told them regardless of what they could prattle about I wouldn't go—that we had done nothing wrong. Moreover, I intended to stay and see our honor and reputation restored. I don't remember which of the two said it. Nevertheless, one of them challenged me, telling me there was a Mexican soothsayer he knew of, living in some border town on the Rio Grande River that could restore my honor and my reputation, as well as anything else I felt I needed restored, for just a few paltry pesos in return. I responded in kind like any honorable dentist would have by telling the man (now that I think about it, it must have been McGoran who said it) that I would suture his mouth shut for free.

The next day I untied the flap of the tent's opening, not very enthusiastically, to see who my first patient was at that early hour. To my surprise I greeted the French Jesuit priest Father Alcime Stanislaus. He was in his clerical garments except for riding boots and a small, reddish-brown, leather hat, with an undulating, circular brim that looked to me like a Mexican cowboy's hat which had seen too much bad weather, and had rather shrunk to its current three-quarters size.

When he saw the priest and from the back of the tent, "Devil" whispered to Longfellow loud enough for me to hear, "It's a man of the cloth, now we're done for! He's come to give us the last rites of the church—and we ain't ever had a court-martial or nothin' like Morgan told us they'd do. Sure 'nough, they'll be hangin' us 'fore noontime! Let's take our map and try to escape—pronto!"

I hushed him up, telling him there would be no hanging at least until Morgan got back. Then I greeted the priest and beckoned him into the tent. Instead, Father Stanislaus asked me to join him outside. It seemed to me in a private sort of way, and therefore, not within earshot of my two apprehensive tent mates.

When he saw we were both heading outside to be alone, "Devil" took to arguing with us, claiming in a husky, bellowing voice, "I may have fallen away at times, still, I'm as good a Catholic as a confused Scotsman can be—and that's half our problem as Scotsmen; who is the patron saint of confusion anyway? Why if Saint Andrew was here right now, he'd have the lot of you skinned, drawn and excommunicated just for—"

I closed the tent on "Devil" McGoran and his belligerent musings over Catholic Canon law. Then, while walking slowly, carefully examined the grassless ground and waited for the Catholic priest to state his business.

"You're not here for anything you've done, but rather to make an example of you," the priest stated in a matter of fact tone.

I told the clergyman I didn't understand what he meant. Yet, for the first time in two days, I felt a small trickle of relief welling up inside of me while at the same time curious as to how a Jesuit priest could possibly know such matters.

By way of an explanation he informed me, "The word has come down from Richmond that Morgan and his men are completely out of control and are more interested in larceny and booty than in the war efforts. He has been sanctioned, called in effect a guerrilla, and threatened with disbandment and integration into the regular army. Morgan needed to shift the blame elsewhere while claiming his innocence, and you and the other two were the most convenient, coming back to camp as you did fresh off a non-authorized raid, as well as your conspicuous leave of absence. It was a perfect excuse for Morgan to lower the boom on you and your friends. As we say in French; *C'est le comble!*"

"Still, that doesn't excuse the captain from threatening us with a court-martial amongst other things?" Even then I was hoping we could come away with a clean slate.

"*Ah non, mon ami*, that is still something you are going to have to deal with. There most certainly will be a court martial, if only to help Captain Morgan distract Richmond long enough to win a few battles, thereby, creating a ground swell of support from loyal, die-hard Southerners."

Pausing for a second he asked me, "Can this be true what we have heard—you have fought for both sides in this war? This is something I do not understand."

He looked at me with those eyes which were at the same time calm yet quizzical, as if he had heard it all before thus nothing fazed the man anymore ...including treason.

"No Father, we never fought for the Northern Army. However, it is true that my two friends back there in our tent were at one time members of the Federal Army, although it only lasted for a few days sometime ago in New York City. They only did it for the enlistment bonus. Afterwards, they took off and ended up here, not so much out of conviction for the Southern cause or for spying purposes, but rather they have always lived this way—never staying too long in one place. Especially when the chow is lousy and they have to march a lot." I chuckled to myself at the thought of my two friends and their carousing ways.

He offered me some tobacco. We sat on two recently cut tree stumps that still smelled of fresh pungent sap and took our time rolling the weedy tobacco into cigarettes.

Father Stanislaus then said something that surprised me, "Back on the trail, our first raid together if I remember correctly—you seemed to want to?—How do you say it in English without directly insulting someone— *m'ignorez*—made a point of avoiding me—. Why was that if I may ask? Are you and your family of a Protestant belief?"

I told the man in all honesty that I didn't believe much in his religion. That it was impossible and somehow too far-fetched for someone like me to understand. This I told him with Katherine's stinging rebuke about my religious hypocrisy hanging about my ears. I tell you right now, the cock could have crowed a lot more than three times, right then and there, at me accusingly, and still had some left over—in fact a lot left over, just for good measure.

"Still, you have had some religious education?" The priest wanted to know.

"Well, I don't really know about all that. Some I guess. Our ma did what she could. Why?—Which Jesus are you for—? I mean which one do you pray to; the Catholic one or the Orange one? It must be the Catholic one—am I right, Father?"

The man laughed easily enough. Then when he saw I didn't appreciate being scorned by him, tossed me his pouch of tobacco and asked to be forgiven.

"But it's not like that at all." He told me.

"The hell it isn't." I answered back roughly. "You don't know the English perhaps like I do, but with their Orange Jesus a lot stronger than our Catholic one they made life hell for the Irish. And our Jesus was too weak and couldn't fight back, something about always "turning the other cheek", like we were all a bunch of—a bunch of "pantywaists" as Captain Morgan would say. What our Jesus doesn't understand is when "you turn the other cheek" on an Englishman, at the end there'll be bloody hell to pay which is one of the reasons I'm here right now."

I could tell the priest wanted to hear more. He seemed such a calm dichotomy from what I'd been living lately.

The man to my surprise was easy enough to talk to and so I did. I broke down and told him about my life. I don't know why but a lot of years seemed to pour forth from my memory that placid morning.

There were two things that seemed to hold his interest above all the other ones which I told him. The first was my unshakeable belief there were two Christs; that they were brothers and couldn't stop fighting one another, especially over Ireland. And the other thing which intrigued the French priest was the Irish concept of *Ne Temere,* which of course was initiated by his church, and therefore I was surprised he didn't know more about it.

"You mean there can be no marriages between young couples of mixed faiths in Ireland?" He asked, wanting to be sure he understood what I had told him.

"Sure enough there can be, well good and all—if you're willing to be damned for all of eternity, Father."

"Ah, c'est dommage—how we meddle so ungraciously in other people's lives." The priest sadly replied.

Talk about meddling....I thought of one Union captain...one Robert Singletary who had meddled so ungraciously in my own life that he had married Katherine. Then I hotly reminded myself how I would like to do some of my own meddling back with this captain...on a battlefield somewhere...with a meddling bayonet or two.

"Nevertheless," the priest mused aloud, "What if the *Ne Temere* law was put into place by the Catholic Church to actually protect the Irish people, instead of oppressing them?"

Optimistically I answered back, "That's why Katherine's not really married. How can she be for she's a Catholic masquerading as a Methodist? It seems to me she needs to be protected as well?"

"I'm sorry, Edward, but you've gone too far there."

"I'm simply stating the law—your Catholic law, Father."

"No, you're not, Edward. You're twisting the law to make it fit your desires. It's like when you told me earlier about your father leaving home, his wife and children, so he could enter the world of politics. You mentioned that he justified his absence by stating he was after a higher calling. Indeed, through his sacrifice Ireland would become independent from England, and therefore a better place to live for all of the Irish."

The priest paused for a moment, perhaps uncertain as to how to continue our conversation, "Please 'Shakes', forgive what I am about to say for it is not my intent to hurt you, still the truth must be told. Nonetheless, your father was wrong, just like you are wrong now, for if the man had truly wanted to better his country he would have started with the basic, perhaps unheralded, yet certainly the fundamental and unselfish task of taking care of his own family first, enabling man's basic desire for truth and charity to firmly take root in his own home. Once his responsibility to you was ended, when you and your siblings had become adults, then he would have been free to pursue his political ambition with a clear conscience but certainly not before. Then and only then can Ireland—indeed any country become a better place to live."

I didn't understand and told the priest as much, "When we have politicians that are capable of governing once their children are grown up?"

He smiled kindly at me. "No, not at all. You are missing my point. It has very little to do with politicians and their children becoming adults, but more so with people realizing their basic responsibilities and living them out with a deep caring unselfishness in spite of their self-absorbed natures."

I was amazed in that I had never heard anyone speak to me like this before.

At length, the priest became quite animated, as if to help drive home his point. A point that I had never heard broached before, "A father must take care of his own family which is really his first and only duty. However few there are that want to do such a thing. For there are no political hoorays, no speeches thanking you, no public acclaim for your glorious accomplishments; just the unrecognized, humble notion that you did what was right—what you were supposed to do—in quiet obedience to God."

He then added as an afterthought, "What a bunch of selfish and ignorant people we are. How can we possibly trust someone to govern us correctly if he lacks the basic moral insight to take care of his own family first and foremost?"

Rather defensively I asked him, "I don't understand what my father's betrayal has to do with Katherine not being married; remember it was your church that came up with the law—*Ne Temere?*"

"In the first place Edward, regardless of their respective religions, this couple in question—your Katherine if you will, although I don't like the sound of that at all, agreed to marry this man in her heart and without conditions. In other words, no one forced her into her marriage. God knows this, therefore, her promise and intent transcends anything man can and will do to dissolve their union. Including I might add, the Catholic Church's idea of *Ne Temere* as you have explained it to me. Which is why, just like your father tried to do, you cannot justify what you yourself want by citing some church law that may or may not be relative to your cause. As well, what if by some chance the law is wrong. It has happened before you realize, laws have been misconstrued from their original purpose. It is the intent of the people that sanctions their actions and not the other way around."

"What is in our hearts, then?" I repeated, underlining a certain amount of latent self-pity.

To this he agreed solemnly, "This is what I believe God sees while man cannot."

I was hurt and it showed.

309

The priest left his tree stump and motioned for me to walk beside him that we had talked enough for one day.

Maybe he had but I was too excited now, so I asked him what he knew of the Free-Masons.

Again he laughed, shook his head, and asked me what could possibly interest an Irish-rebel-dentist about the Free-Masons?

I didn't specifically mention Captain Morgan by name. But I was intrigued by the fact the subject was so hush-hush, and that every time I mentioned the name no one wanted to talk about it other than to tell me to leave it alone.

The priest gave me a short history lesson about the Templar Knights, the crusades and that after their disbandment, how the Free-Masons and their *Craft* grew out of the void left by the Templar Knights.

He couldn't see how it had anything to do with what we were living right then and there in our newly adopted country.

That is when I was able to tell him I had recently read an article in "The Summary" in which Jefferson Davis refuted his being a Free-Mason (although he freely admitted his father had been one).

Therefore I questioned the priest, "If as you say there is no relevance or significance to this secret society, why did Mr. Davis, with all he has to do to govern our country and keep it fighting, take the time to answer scurrilous remarks that have to do with whether or not the man is a Free-Mason—that it didn't make any sense. *If* as you say there is no connection between the Northern war of aggression and *Masonry*. Why would the man waste his valuable time—unless?"

Then I postulated what someone had told me recently about the rather singular interests of that secret society, "Unless of course, President Davis has a hidden agenda like the English."

Father Alcime Stanislaus looked around the clearing, peering up at the cloudless sky before answering. "Are all Irish paranoiacs like you, Edward?" He wanted to know, his blemished white face now reddened a light scarlet from the late morning, wintry, Southern air.

I answered back, "Only when it comes to the English and fighting for a just cause; to get those London-born leeches off of our backs—that would be defending our homeland at the same time, Father. I guess the Irish are finally tired of being manipulated by tyrants, that's all, in any shape or form!"

His cheeks puffed out like two water-filled bladders while the rest of his face lit up in amusement, "You know the French are not above a little manipulating now and then. Some might even suggest we are the royalist founders of just such a mischievous idea. *Ah, c'est trop beau!*" He chuckled to himself at the thought.

At which point, he lapsed into a satirical treatise on the destiny of France which appeared to me to be more about indigenous papal bamboozling, marital infidelities amongst European royalty who refused to bathe themselves, all to be washed down by cases of a marvelous Château Haut-Brion, as well as treating the resulting aristocratic gout amongst other important affairs of state.

Thus I was surprised when he told me, "Your Jefferson Davis in a very real sense of the word is a martyr. He gave up his honor and career as a United States senator in the middle of his life, when he certainly could have enjoyed the fruits of his labor. This he did, to take on the almost unbelievable task of forging a new nation out of the Confederacy with the Northern Federalists constantly breathing down his neck. Why if France had this man and his single-minded sense of purpose, as well as his Christian principles there would be no nation in Europe that could or would dare to stand against us."

"Let's start first with the Yankees!" I added solemnly.

We were twenty yards or so from our tent when we stopped to say goodbye. There was a slight breeze blowing in from the east, otherwise the plateau that we were living on was deathly quiet. It was even absent of the chronic sound of the horses stamping about, whinnying out their discomfort at the brisk cold and their lack of exercise. Thus I was able to listen and hear what the French priest had to say, clearly and precisely, almost as if I could never use the excuse I didn't hear anything because of our bucolic surroundings.

Father Stanislaus had his reasons for saying the following (which I certainly did not understand at that moment), "The only true way to the peace you are looking for is through virtuous living. It is not in Free-Masonry, triangular visions or society of itself, but rather in quiet contemplation of what is virtuous."

I suppose, in what could only be called the joyful anticipation of my lack of understanding at what he had just said that the priest concluded rather sardonically, "This means in cavalry terms—see God in everything—*mais la ferme—tu comprends?* But keep as much as possible *your big mouth shut!*"

He seemed to grow quite cheerful the more I looked dismayed.

Reaching for me, he took from his pocket a Catholic rosary chain of beads. Almost mystically, he pushed it into my hands telling me, "You'll be needing this—for from what I've heard from you today—you've vacillated long enough in what you believe."

At last, he walked away muttering to himself in French, "*Le Christ "Orange" et le Christ Catholique et en plus, ils sont frères? Mais c'est pas possible! Qu'est-ce-que c'est que ce monde où nous vivons!*"

To be honest and straightforward about things, I've spent the rest of my life contemplating what Father Stanislaus told me that day. As for the chain of rosary beads; I put them in my uniform's breast pocket and promptly forgot about it.

Oh, one other important matter before I forget—the day he gave me the rosary beads was six weeks before the great battle at Shiloh church. And yes, just in case you're wondering, this Irish rebel fought there.

Chapter Twenty

If you pause at the City of Trouble,
Or wait in the valley of tears,
Be patient, the train will move onward
And rush down the track of the years,
Whatever the place is you seek for,
Whatever your aim or your quest,
You shall come at the last with rejoicing
To the beautiful City of Rest.
                                        Author unknown

War has a way of deranging men. It starts in an obtuse enough manner with a lot of virtuous chest-thumping and lofty remarks aimed at pandering to those who would willing give up their freedom and lives because they still believe. They believe, unlike the hard-hearted politicians making the remarks, who can never understand what the simple folk want and need. Because they themselves have never been simple in their needs or called upon to believe, truly and sincerely believe like you and I. Instead, they take their pound of flesh today, ever eager to severe the Baptist's head for the sensual dance of the stepdaughter; wanting little more than to satisfy their lusty, as well as lowly desires, with no more thought for the little man than they did for the Baptist's head.

Therefore, the little man continues to fight their wars for them because the little man believes. And with this belief, therein, lies both his justification as well as his condemnation; that one cared enough to foresee a brighter tomorrow for his loved ones. That hope in a fruitful tomorrow for one's family demands any effort necessary to bring it about, as well as the callous understanding from the politician that because of this hope which he smirks at, the politician can count on the little man to make sacrifices until death.

These same sacrifices the politician wouldn't dream of making himself. Unless of course, it was to stare transfixed at the navel of the dancing stepdaughter while making asinine offerings, as if he were a god, not realizing in effect he is nothing but deranged. Not in some stupid philosophical ambivalence, but rather from the concrete idea that they should all be kings. And therefore, be able to do what they want, whenever and however they want without repercussions, never realizing for a moment that we are all held accountable when we take our pound of flesh.

Still in all, it is the deranging that scares me. I believe you would agree had you seen the chaotic battlefield at Shiloh, where there were so many dead and wounded, the Union General Ulysses S. Grant stated years afterwards, "I saw an open field, in our possession the second day, over which the Confederates had made repeated charges the day before, so covered with dead that it would have been possible to walk across the clearing, in any direction, stepping on dead bodies, without a foot touching the ground."

Simply put, it doesn't get more deranged than that.

It was the beginning of April and the recently promoted to Colonel, John Hunt Morgan had left our camp on a discreet furlough to Richmond, leaving his brother-in-law Basil Duke in charge. It had been more than five weeks which had passed since our confinement. There had been no court-martial, no proceedings against us, only a tempestuous silence. From our prison tent we could see and hear the slow and tedious preparations for breaking camp and on a large scale as well. This was not to be an ordinary raid, as if I could attribute the adjective *ordinary* to just such a thing as a raid when it involved wreaking havoc across the enemy's countryside. Nevertheless, we could see from the artillery being hustled into place, and the number of cavalry and foot soldiers scurrying about soliciting supplies from ordnance that something serious was about to occur, something we surely didn't want to miss.

I asked for and was granted permission to speak with Lieutenant Duke, with whom, I had no doubt I would be heard, if for no other reason than I had split a brace of ducks with him once. Then having pity on such a hungry man as Duke who couldn't cook to save himself, I smoked the birds slowly in an iron cylinder until their skins turned a glazed caramel. Yet when you bit into the meat, the juice escaped from all around the carcass until you could barely keep it in your mouth. And that's what had fascinated Basil Duke—the meat had been smoked, deep and to the bone, still it wasn't dry. By all rights he should remember me, or at least his stomach would, especially after eating camp food these many weeks.

When I walked into his tent the man was in a thoughtless rage over some

Enfield muskets that had been lost or stolen...Lieutenant Duke wasn't sure which. He had served too close to his brother-in-law, John Hunt Morgan for Morgan's traits not to have rubbed off on him, at least a little. To me, Basil Duke looked half-Chinese. Aye, from the Asiatic slits that formed his eyelids to the way he wore his beard in a long and wispy coolie style, only to be flaunted in thick brush strokes where his beard came to rest upon the first button of his tunic. He appeared angry and befuddled in a disheartening way. His hand continually rose to brush back some imaginary lock of black hair that had fallen over his brow. While at the same time, he was trying to read as fast as he could, as if he intended to find hidden in the letters on his camp desk the key to where the proverbial rifles were. I half-expected to be treated to tea and some dormant, oriental proverb such as; *if one wanted to know the whereabouts of the Enfield musket—well then, one must become an Enfield musket to know where such an entity would hide.*

Instead, upon seeing my person, Duke sighed strangely aloud, seemingly, as if to confirm that upon everything else going on around him he had to deal with the likes of me. I didn't care though for I had pulled enough teeth, stopped more than a half-dozen soldiers from haemorrhaging themselves to death, not to mention trying to keep my two fellow prisoners, McGoran and Mortlock from deserting to Mexico. Apparently they had finalized a plan, in which they intended upon arrival to write a letter to President Davis requesting pay status equivalent to Confederate State Governors. As they intended to annex Mexico and its inhabitants creating a ground swell, they claimed, that would make what had happened at the Alamo child's play...with or without Jim Bowie.

"Unless you can tell me where I can lay my hands on these rifles we're missing, or direct me to someone who can, you have no business being here!" Duke thundered out almost as if he had studied Morgan and could imitate the man and his gargantuan manners to a fault.

"No Sir, I can't." I echoed back apologetically.

Wiping his brow with one sleeve, Duke looked at me and asked me exasperatingly, "Well damn it all, what is it, what does a prisoner like you want?"

Then I brightened up, "I believe I may know where your rifles are, Sir. However, myself and the two other prisoners I'm with must no longer be required to be confined to our tents. If you can see your way through to granting us our temporary freedom then I trust we can come up with your rifles."

Basil Duke looked at me like a wild rabbit does, wondering if that dash into the cultivated hedge-row wouldn't be his last, but he jumps over the fence anyway trying to contain his doubts.

"You know where the rifles are?" He blasted his flattened hand across his thigh claiming, "Well, this beats all. Right now I can tell you that, 'Shakes'—if this don't beat all!"

"If you'll just cancel the "Confined to Quarters" edict that Captain—er, Colonel Morgan issued, we'll be right after your rifles. You can count on me, Sir."

Everyone knew there was no place for us to go, and even if we had wanted to, without horses we wouldn't make it very far. Thus I was granted permission to bring back the rifles. Although at the same time, Duke remained sceptical enough, and being an officer made a clumsy enough effort not to show it.

"Why can't you just tell me where the rifles are instead of making such a mystery about it—just who are you trying to protect anyway?" This he vented while running a hand through his silky beard, finally, stopping to tap the bottom of it just above his foremost uniform button.

"No one, Sir, I'm just playing a hunch for the moment."

One of the other officers in Duke's quarters, Captain Gano, muttered something about, "We've gone too long as it is on hunches alone. That's the only thing anyone knows in this blasted, dried-out, corn-eatin' army. We've got more hunches around here than battle victories."

Until Duke shot the man a glance, telling him to stow away his attitude.

At last, Basil Duke saluted me giving me permission to leave.

Longfellow accepted our freedom with uninspired joy, ""Just a hunch"— huh? What got into you? Now where are we going to find those rifles, unless we point out the ones they'll be using against us from the firing squad?"

Not to be outdone, "Devil" rose from his cot, and with outstretched, grimy hands downturned unflinchingly, to suggest cold and steely nerves were required at such a moment as this, confided to the two of us, "I'd better get to whittlin' pretty quick now."

Then he took a minute to think about it before asking, "Now just how many rifles did you say were missing, and were they the ones with flintlocks?"

"Put your carving knife away," I told him, fully realizing that with "Devil" whittling rifles out of wood, they were more than likely to resemble half-naked Shoshoni squaws doing their laundry down by the river, rather than anything the Confederate Government had ever issued.

I didn't sleep that night. Although, I guess my anxiety as to our almost-found freedom didn't keep "Devil" or Longfellow awake. Indeed, they had decided, it seemed to me by their ungrateful snoring, I could do enough worrying for the three of us without them sacrificing their nocturnal rest as well.

The next morning the flap of the tent was opened and a sentry beckoned curtly from the outside, "Lieutenant Duke wants to see you Edward Ruth, right away."

He marched briskly back and forth, just outside our sleeping quarters, waiting for me to get my rag-tag uniform on and to fall in behind. Quickly enough, in anticipation of what the lieutenant might want I worked my way into my boots and followed him.

When I reached his tent and was ushered inside, I found the lieutenant brisk and businesslike, certain I suppose that the rifles had been found.

"Well, where in the almighty-hell are they?" His eyes fixed on mine, as if he had finally decided to hang the three of us and be done with Irish riff-raff once and for all.

"We're still working on it, Sir."

I cringed a little when I thought of my two roommates sleeping, or as they called it; "sawing wood", seemingly, in such an inordinate amount, as if there would never be a tomorrow to wake up to.

Basil Duke appeared to be munching on imaginary food when he spoke next. His jaws continued to thump up and down yet there was no plate of food on his desk that I could see, "We are breaking camp to be in south-western Tennessee at a place called?" He inevitably hesitated while he consulted his overlaid desk map finally confirming his doubts, "A place called "Pittsburgh Landing". We cannot wait any longer for the rifles, but must move out at once. General Johnston has ordered it. Our departure is to be immediate."

"What about us, Sir?" I prompted Duke, sick and tired of imprisoned camp life. And even more exasperated from listening to my two compatriots tell stories about life, amidst the cactus and peyote-infused cantinas, down in Mexico.

"Do you know where the rifles are?" He demanded again.

I echoed back as honestly as I could, "Not yet, Lieutenant," half-wondering if maybe we couldn't ask "Devil" to whittle up at least a half-dozen rifles, just to be on the safe side, and keep the man happy while we continued our search.

"In that case I have no choice; you'll have to move out with the rest of us. We've no prison barracks to send you to at this point—at least no barracks with prison guards, they're all on the battle fields."

I told Duke, "That's fine with us, Sir—it's what we've always wanted—to fight for the Southern cause—to square ourselves up. Besides we never did the treacherous things that we've been accused of."

Duke answered in kind, "Don't forget, you're still a prisoner as far as

Morgan's concerned. As such, don't expect any special treatment from me. Just do as you're told and that'll go a great deal towards explaining your actions when he returns."

He ended up by instructing me in an almost kindly manner that we were to move against Generals Grant and Buell, in what could be a defining action of the war. In addition to which, he emphasized, the South could not afford to lose this battle.

At that point, I didn't care if we had to move out against the entire Northern Army or every Choctaw, Chickasaw, Cherokee, Creek, Seminole or any other Indian tribe that existed. We were free to move around at last and to do what we had volunteered to do.

I told him he could count on us; that when muster was called, we would be ready and in the forefront to do our duty.

"Very well, 'Shakes'. In the meantime, keep your eyes and wits about you, you never can tell what could be overhead," he warned me confidentially.

I answered back hopefully, "In the backwoods I don't think the Yankees can claim to be our equal, but I'll keep my eye out just the same."

Duke tried once again to make me understand, "Keep your eyes open towards the sky 'Shakes', for you can never tell what might be flying by."

"Sir?" I finally acknowledged that I had no idea what the man was trying to get at.

Consequently, Duke's face took on the countenance of an exploding Oriental balloon, bubbling and deflating all at once, "I'm not talking about the Yankees," he quibbled at me, "The ducks—the ducks—the smoked ducks—'Shakes', they're all heading north this time of year!"

To show what he meant he rubbed his flat belly while spasmodically winking at me.

On that recommendation I was excused and told to make ready to break camp with the others.

"Devil", Longfellow and I were assigned to Company F, the Second Regiment, Kentucky Cavalry, Captain Gano commanding.

We broke camp and headed west with Duke and Captain Gano leading us. Gano's Texans stayed in front, keeping up a cynical barrage of how one Texan equalled six to nine Union soldiers. The difference depended upon whether the Union soldiers in question had ever been weaned from their mothers' breasts or not.

It was early April. The rivers were running high from the volatile spring thaws which had just begun. There was broken timber lying across the trail, with cracked, dead and crooked branches, jutting up across the ground from the past winter storms that had to be cut up and moved out of the way. The underbrush was thick and continually scraped at our horses' bellies. The winds migrated through the valleys as if through a funnel, blasting us with such a force that it set us all to chattering, a haunting reminder the winter's chill, even then, wasn't quite over. Nevertheless, we moved on with a different set to our jaw. Indeed, this was no longer a devilish, hell-bent for leather raid with Morgan, but a formal battle in which we would all be tested. A battle in which, surprise would no longer be a factor; where the forthcoming events stood a damned good chance of being equal. Consequently, the best man would win and the other, the dead one, would go to a place called *W.L.P.P.* by the Irish—*Where the Little People Play.*

We carried two flags with us. One was tri-color; blue, red and white with circular stars enveloping a lone white star in the middle. While the other flag sported stars in the shape of a cross. The Texans blustered the cross on the flag would be the last thing a Yankee soldier would see. And hopefully, would inspire him to make a good confession in front of the Almighty, for his faults in this life. Above all, knowing he didn't have the advantage of being from Texas, which apparently (according to the Texans) included direct access to Heaven's door.

Upon hearing this, "Devil" decided that a Texan must be a direct descendant from the Scots. And wouldn't it be a *terrible* thing if the earth just opened up and swallowed the lot of them—Texans and Scots both at the same time, saving the world a lot of inopportune grief.

Longfellow noted to his friend, "Damn it all, McGoran—I don't understand it for one minute—you're a Scotsman and still you're talking like this, criticizing your own people—don't deny it now!"

To which "Devil" replied, a look of emphatic relief about him, "No, Longfellow, my good man, I'm no Scotsman—I'm from the highlands!"

We moved out this way. Sometimes making good time if the roads had proper drainage while other times we had to work like hell to get the horses and artillery pieces through the knee-deep muck that became worse the more we sloshed through it. We met scouts coming and going who told us Grant had assembled more than forty thousand troops and that Buell was on his way with more. It seemed as if every time we had fresh news the pace of the army quickened, as if we couldn't wait to get there and determine our fate. Longfellow mentioned to me that he had never felt so alive. I agreed with him. The early, spring-time, surrounding countryside seemed more beautiful, the smell of the back-country air more invigorating, the river's roar more uplifting, the beaver's harsh slap more definitive, the look on the men's faces more intense, more courageous than I'd ever seen them before.

In the late afternoon on the second day of our ride, the call came down through the line for silence. We obeyed and waited. We could see and hear a line of blue-clad soldiers not far away, gesturing toward the north and speaking in what appeared to be something other than English. We dressed our sabres and waited for the call which never came. It turned out to be the 18th Louisiana Infantry under Colonel Mouton, and one of ours that had come to join us for the upcoming battle. At the very least, Father Stanislaus was happy. For he took to jabbering away in French with the men from Louisiana while the rest of us looked on and wondered what they could possibly say in such a strange and lop-sided tongue.

That afternoon we pitched camp in Corinth, Mississippi. I was chosen to ride on ahead with "Devil", Longfellow and one other man who I didn't know. At length, he informed us he was one of Gano's Texans. We were to ride on ahead as scouts and find out what we could. Particularly, if we were able to surmise the North's ability to unload men, and what it would require to stop the ferrying of these same replacements, as they arrived by steamship, at a place called "Pittsburg Landing".

We rode out and rode hard, pushing our mounts to their lathering limits while covering a lot of ground. Otherwise, once or twice I believe, I heard Longfellow put forth the propitious suggestion that turning south would give us the unheralded advantage of watching the upcoming proceedings from somewhere south of the border, perhaps with a cold beer or two to slag our thirsts. I didn't pay any attention to his repeated; "Confederate Life from a Hacienda", as I had come to call his echoed Mexican overtures. Instead we rode on, only stopping when we came upon several burning brush fires with smoke rising rapidly from an engaging plateau. On the plateau, trees had been recently felled to clear away the rise, giving a perfect view to whomever was watching from that elevated spot. There was a hastily strung, slatted, wooden fence just below the rise. Two hundred yards in front of the fence we heard hidden voices, and these voices called out to us to identify ourselves. We looked at one another questioningly, trying to decide what to do.

Longfellow eased back from his forehead his policeman's helmet while he whispered to me, "They must be on our side, 'cause they didn't shoot first like the Yanks are akin to do."

"Devil" ushered us to quickly make up our minds about answering or not. For it was high time for chow, and he declared his stomach didn't know any Mason-Dixon Line when it came the moment to eat.

The caller who had asked us who we were, cried out again. Only this time, we heard the familiar sound of guns slipping off shoulders and firing mechanisms locking into place.

"Hold on, hold on," I shouted back emphatically, "We're with Duke and Captain Gano."

There was silence before the caller repeated, "Duke and Gano?"

Indeed, there was stern whispering from the other side, the side hidden from our view.

Eventually, someone shouted out, "We don't know any Duke or Gano—who *are* you?"

Not being able to contain himself any longer, "Devil" announced, "Well it ain't your Aunt Betty—you bunch of knuckleheads."

As a result, we distinctly heard one of them ask of the others, "Did he just say "Aunt Betty"? I wonder if she sent any of her plum-pudding?"

Eventually, three men emerged from the surrounding, milky-aired dusk. They were armed alright, but their rifles were now carelessly aimed, as if these men were also uncertain of just what to do. One was young. You could tell from the brown fuzz that surrounded his impish face it would still be a while before his beard formally declared itself. The second one smoked a pipe which protruded from his mouth like a burnished tuba. He kept looking around for somewhere to sit, as if his elongated legs that made him look to be on a pair of stilts could no longer bear his over-extended weight. The third one was darkly bearded, older than the other two, and owned the look of a somewhat amused professor taking in the proceedings while making sure his students did what they had been taught. The three of them were wearing soft blue *Union* Army uniforms belted at the waist, with short hats and brims, as well as carrying haversacks and belted bayonets. In contrast to us, their uniforms and shoes fit well, were not worn out, above all and in comparison to how we felt, the three Yanks appeared rather well fed and content about it as well.

"Hey, they're not Federal," the fuzzy-faced kid stated to each of his companions. At the end, glancing respectfully at the bearded leader, in case he had made a mistake.

As if to respond, the bearded Union picket took his hands out of his pockets and looked at all of us lumped together, as if he couldn't believe his eyes. Turning around himself, he let his eyes rest on the very tall man, who by now was stretched out against one of the hundreds of tree stumps that made up the field where we had met, smoking his pipe. The man leaning against the tree stump looked back at the bearded soldier, as if to say he wasn't going to move for anything in the world. That he was unbelievably comfortable, and that it was going to stay that way at least for the time being.

Given very little choice and speaking with that northerly, screechy voice which is so particular to the Yankees, the bearded picket asked us, "Anyone for coffee?"

"Devil" spoke out, "Your Aunt Betty taught you right Soldier, always be polite to strangers—." Then "Devil" brightened up before asking, "Say, do you have any *applejack* to go with the coffee?"

Upon hearing his Scottish accent, the Union picket, the one who was only wearing brown peach fuzz on his face, demanded of his fellow soldiers, "Them Southerners gotta whale of an accent now, don't you fellows think so? Say Soldier—," he asked, turning back to look at "Devil", "What part of the woods you from—Georgia maybe?"

I guess my friend decided to have a little fun with the Yankee picket for he answered back distractedly, "Only if Georgia is somewhere near Washington."

"Washington?" The picket repeated, with a certain amount of querulous disgust, "What is the likes of you doing in Washington?" He wanted to know.

"How's about advising President Abraham Lincoln." "Devil" added, looking like my dog "Blister" does, when he's found a milk bone with meat gristle still clinging to it.

The unevenly-tall, lanky, pipe-smoking picket, carefully rearranged his gangly legs.

Then with one locked arm posed on his knee for maximum comfort, his legs skewed out at almost forty-five degree angles from the tree stump, eyed "Devil" carefully before inquiring, "And on what subject did you carefully advise President Lincoln, before hightailing it down here with the rest of the Southern Army?"

Without any hesitation whatsoever, "Devil" answered the man, "I told the President, in order to win the war we gotta fester out the *ninnies* in the Northern Army. That there were too many of them and it was ruining the morale of his entire corps. Therefore I told the President; 'let me head down south, join the Confederacy, and when we come across Union lines instead of hollerin' out, 'Who goes there?', I'll ask around instead calling out 'If anyone has an Aunt Betty?'. That way we'll know who the real *ninnies* are with their Aunt Betties and homesick ideas of plum-pudding and what not. In that way, we can fester them out all at once without wasting too much time about it neither! That's the only way you'll have a more efficient army.' And what's more President Lincoln agreed with me—which is why I'm here."

The fuzzy-faced kid looked at the other two Union pickets before warning them dejectedly, "*We* mentioned something about "Aunt Betty". You figure he'll head back and tell President Lincoln about us—that we're *ninnies?*"

At length, the bearded leader took stock of the situation, and pulling his hands from his pockets, knelt down on the ground and started to spread a woollen blanket across the dirt, "Ah, they's only havin' fun with you, Kid. So Boys what'll you trade for?"

However, just then, the younger Union picket said something that quite startled me, as well as setting me to unspeakable fear, "You know his accent reminds me a lot of the 69th out of New York."

The pipe-smoking picket took from his mouth his smoking tuba, and answered him while pointing at me, blowing grey smoke at the same time, "Yes, that one's accent is exactly like theirs—give or take a shot of whisky!"

I knew my brother Paul Francis Daniel was with the 69th, so I asked with a certain reticence, my heart pounding in the act, "Is the All-Irish 69th Brigade from New York down here as well?"

I received my answer alright when he pontificated, "From what I hear they wouldn't miss it for the world. You know the *micks*[25]—always spoiling for a fight."

From that moment on and in contrast to what I had been thinking up until then; when I learned that I might be shooting to kill my brother on the morrow—the war took on a different—certainly a more deranged-like meaning.

We spent an hour or more swapping stories, as well as tobacco, coffee and a week old newspaper (depicting the inevitable Southern victory) that Longfellow had brought along. In exchange, we found out that the Union pickets were just like us. They were determined to fight. Although, they mentioned in an offhand sort of manner they wouldn't shoot our way if one of them identified any one of us. They seemed like a rather good pack of fellows. Still in all, I knew it was time for us to leave when "Devil" asked the pipe-smoking one if he wouldn't be interested in getting an extended leave of absence from the Union Army and coming with us to Mexico to pick out a site for the forthcoming, United States embassy. As the future governor, "Devil" attested to the fact he'd give him first choice on where to build the embassy, as long as he kept the Texans and Scots away as neighbors.

As we were leaving that stubbly and pockmarked field, the Texan who had accompanied us, took to making menacing overtures about how "Devil" had mistreated the Texans as a whole in front of the Union Army pickets. And he personally took it as an insult, and therefore wasn't going to stand for it any longer. He also wanted to know what "Devil" was going to do about it—the Texan's challenge that is. His dangerous eyes became puffy with anger until "Devil" calmed him down, claiming it was all just a planned-ruse. That he, "Devil", as well as everyone else around, knew if it hadn't been for the Texans and a handful of wily Portuguese sailors, why there wouldn't be any swampland, whatsoever, for anyone to fight over. "Devil" went on to comfort the man, explaining in so many words; that is why the mosquitoes flew around biting everyone—to show their appreciation for what the Texans had done.

---

25 A provincial term for the Irish male

This explanation seemed to satisfy the man, for he rode the rest of the way in grumpy silence.

We met back with the rest of the squadron coming up from Corinth sometime around midnight. We briefed a sleepy-eyed Basil Duke as best we could that from what we had learned; Buell and his army would indeed be ferried down the Tennessee River. That being the case, it was imperative to control Pittsburg Landing, and not allow them to land, thereby adding additional reinforcements to Grant's already swollen army.

Longfellow later mentioned to me, as well as some of the others that he had seen Colonel Morgan briefly at camp. He had seen Morgan rushing around like a whirlwind, with an army jacket pulled high up on his neck and over the lower part of his face, as if he didn't wish to be recognized. It was hard to believe to those of us to whom Longfellow had revealed Morgan's presence. We all wanted to know on the eve of such a great battle, why didn't Colonel Morgan take over once again as commander? What was the point of being there incognito? What could it possibly accomplish, except confusion perhaps? We had no doubt Basil Duke was competent enough. Still in all, he wasn't Morgan and couldn't see us through the morrow like Morgan could.

As for me, I became violently ill. I kept wondering about my brother and what would happen if we lined up opposite one another on the battlefield, the very next day.

We all went to sleep that way—wondering.

The next day, April 6th, a Sunday, we were up early. After eating a hurried breakfast of some sort of warmed-up army gruel, which had lumps in it that looked like cat's eyes staring back at you, we were told to take a reserve position with General Breckinridge's division. In a reserve position, we would then wait for our orders depending on further developments. Meaning of course— where we would be most needed to fill in the dismembered gaps. With Duke in command we waited on the right, holding our horses and listening to the frantic sounds of battle from the left and center coming from the whereabouts of Shiloh church. We were hearing for the first time what appeared to me to be sheer madness. I could only picture in my mind what was happening when the broken, intermittent crackling of fierce skirmishing took on the sustained volleying from the lines. As I mentioned earlier I couldn't see it, but there must have been hell to pay for both sides. The firing was continual. Smoke carried over the canopy of trees lying there like heavy cloud cover waiting to explode from the rain it carried. Except in this case they weren't clouds. But rather, an undigested force of man resulting from thousands trying to kill and maim one another. And yet, considering themselves one of the luckier ones if they were only wounded. I didn't see it myself, but heard later that many men on both sides took to crawling down to a place called "Bloody Pond".

Indeed, Northerners and Southerners on their knees and bellies, side by side, if they were still physically able to quench their thirst, staining the waters red while trying to stay alive.

At last, by noon, we were ordered into action. Duke bade us take up our positions and push if at all possible through to the right, where our boys were stalled. Knowing that we were finally moving seemed to help ease the tension, and we took to singing "Cheer Boys, Cheer", as we headed out amidst the thickening of gunfire. At length, we halted in front and just a few hundred yards away from a salty-looking ravine. A ravine that one of our corps commanders, I believe it was General Hardee had ordered Duke to assault the artillery position and wipe it out. Not only was the artillery well-positioned, but it was partially hidden from view by thick and tall, leafy, acacia brush.

I was privy to the conversation which went on between Duke (Duke, being a behind-the-lines-raider and thus having no experience in this type of warfare) and one of the men from another company.

Upon watching the blue-clad soldiers turn the guns from one degree to another with admirable precision before blasting away, Duke asked the man, displaying a certain lack of confidence in the matter before him, "Uh—tell me, Son, what's the best way to charge a battery?"

The soldier looked Duke plainly in the eye before responding, "Lieutenant, to tell you the God's truth, thar' ain't no good way to charge a battery."

Fortunately for us, General Hardee never issued the final order to attack that Yankee stronghold. Instead, we were called to press forward to the left of General Breckinridge's advancing infantry and attack the first enemy we came into contact with. It was at that point then, for me, that the sky and the ground collided together, and all hell finally broke loose. From then on everything became bellicose jabs or lightning-like flashes in my memory...a carousel of panic-induced movements. Luckily for all of us, at that moment, Colonel Morgan rode into our midst bellowing orders and waving his sabre, as if he hadn't been gone from us for more than ten minutes. His entry into the fighting buoyed me up as he always did, invigorated and fearless, an inducement to fight long and hard for the Confederacy.

I could see the Union boys directly in front of us. Some of them had taken their blue uniforms off and were only wearing stained, red undershirts while remaining hatless. It was a little afterwards, we found out red became a great target in smoke. They were slowly coming out of their wooded thicket while we on the other side were doing the same. Between the firing, men charging, stepping carelessly over the dead and wounded, horses falling down askew, and the incredible amount of noise, I saw something which profoundly shocked me. I watched as a Union captain turned from firing at us, to coldly point his revolver at one of his own men and ruthlessly shoot him down.

Someone, who had decided he'd had enough of the battle, and was running in the opposite direction from the fighting.

I thought of Katherine and what might have been if she hadn't married her stuffy, medal-weighted–down, wife-beating captain, and took a long time to aim and squeeze off a shot. I saw the Union captain go down.

Just then Morgan rode by.

He reined in "Black Bess" crisply, before looking at me strangely enough. He then fervently admonished me, "Give the English bloody hell!", before riding off.

Until this day, I cannot believe unless I had seen it myself, the level of continual firing which went on throughout that ungracious day. That's all I heard. We'd advance a little prior to backing off, essentially to ascertain our dead and wounded. Thereby, as a matter of course, determining we had won maybe four hundred or five hundred yards during all of the above mentioned madness. Still the battle raged on, the carnage was incredible. The men were lying about, some still energetic enough to call out for medical aid, the helplessness showing in their eyes when they realized none would be forthcoming. The luckier ones would suddenly shudder violently and stop their repugnant crying, to die alone. The poor bastards, I remarked to no one but myself—to die in such a way.

We somehow managed to fight our way through—through to what? I have no idea; nothing seemed to make sense except that a sense of fatigue had started to set in. I was having an arduous time firing my weapon, for the sweat was trickling into my swollen and tired eyes making it difficult to see. We came to a wide field where some of the Kentuckians were exchanging fire with Federal troops. Morgan gave the bugler the order to sound the charge.

Then he specifically called out to us, as if it were an immediate and unqualified order to be obeyed straightaway, "I want their flag."

At length, Morgan pointed with a gloved hand to something barely visible. Whatever it was, was hovering just out of sight, fluttering vaguely above the distant blue Union lines.

We followed the foot soldiers, coaxing our mounts to full gallop with sabres drawn and pointed menacingly. I for one, wondered what possible need could Morgan have for a flag at that moment in time, with the battle for Shiloh church still very much in doubt.

When I saw up close the flag that Morgan wanted so desperately, I almost fell from my horse. It was a rough reproduction of the Irish flag, the Leinster flag with the golden harp against a green background, and I knew damned well what that meant. That somewhere, opposite me, in this deranged mess was my brother, Paul Francis Daniel. I begged my God that He keep my brother well away from me, and if it were at all possible, to spare the two of us as well. Except first, I had to dodge a hatless, blonde man, who was coming at me with a drawn sabre. There were a dozen or more Yankees being led by this blonde, rustic-looking soldier. He was squatty-looking, undaunted even, with thick, bushy, yellowish locks, and slashing at everything in his way. In one hand, his sabre was cracking down on my rifle which I had shifted sideways to protect myself from his sabre. While at the same time and in his other hand, the intimidating Yankee was holding a pistol that as yet, wasn't aimed at me. Still in all, it was only a matter of time before his pistol was brought to bear on this tiring Irishman. His eyes never blinked, like an insomniac he was, but that he didn't keep thrusting and slashing at me. Aye, attacking all the time like a well-greased bevel gear, which wouldn't or couldn't stop meshing. I kept on protecting myself with my rifle...that's all I could do. The group of men he was leading caught up to the two of us, and I became separated from his maddening strokes. I don't remember losing my horse. But once again, they came at us like infuriated hordes—thus you didn't think, but only reacted to the next sabre thrust. As I rolled away from the blonde Yankee, there was my horse floundering in front of me; kicking at nothing, to finally laying quiet, dead. Yet, still more solders came running around and over me. Someone off to my right was clutching at his face and screaming. It was sickening. God heard my call that day and I'm not ashamed to admit it. The more the bodies caved in and fell, the more they protected me where I had slid from my horse, forming a barricade maybe eight or ten feet high. In the back of the barricade, deposited like a snug newborn I watched as the wave of spitting, bayoneting soldiers passed over. Their curried beckoning reached my ears, as the inimical horror went somewhere else. Then I was alone and at a loss as to what to do. For sure, thankfulness washed over me. Yet it wasn't over, it couldn't be over. Something that awful and evil, once unleashed, doesn't leave quietly, nor go back to where it came from without emptying itself completely.

I needn't have kidded myself. Within an hour they were back, stabbing and screaming just like before—like no one's business or the final apocalyptic dance...kicked up one notch. I waited until I saw more grey than blue passing by before standing up. There weren't as many men as the very first advance. Someone shoved me from behind. I looked over and Longfellow was right beside me proudly waving the Irish flag. So we'd done it! We'd done it alright, we'd taken the flag. I wondered where Colonel Morgan was and if he had seen the Irish flag—. Then perhaps, he would understand how the *children of the Gael* felt...now and forever.

Longfellow pointed to a slowly advancing blue line somewhere in front of us.

"They'se comin' back," he declared while waving the captured flag emphatically from side to side, as if to rub salt into the wounds of the oncoming Union Army.

What a deranged mess I thought to myself.

There was a rumbling like a steam engine train makes climbing up some desperately inclined mountain pass. Except in this case, the rumbling wasn't from a train, but rather, from directly in front of us by the oncoming, still-holding-strong Union Army. Besides the incoherent rumbling, there was enough dust being kicked up to resemble a Missouri-born and bred tornado.

It was afternoon now, probably late afternoon. Looking around me, I noticed the leaves on all the trees were dead. *Just-like-that-dead,* as if nature itself had given up all hope that this battle would end. There were piles of small boulders forming low walls for defensive measures which hadn't been there before. Or at least I hadn't noticed them before. The smoke lay lower and thicker than it had in the morning. The one thing that hadn't changed was the incessant caterwauling of the two armies. I wished I was drunk; good and busted drunk, it was the only sane way to handle all of this. Especially, what I saw next. In the one hundred yards or so that separated the two armies, I saw a patch of carrot-colored red hair on the head of a hatless Union soldier. My stomach turned inside and out, like I had the gastric-burning *runs* from eating left-out-in-the-sun Chinese food. I needed to sit down in the worst way. Yes, it had to be my brother, the one who was so crazy about fighting. Why this must be like heaven to Paul Francis Daniel, the legalized maiming of this entire conflict.

Like an uninvited guest, my thoughts raced back to our shed in Castlewarren and to our little game, my brother and I played, of *half-stump flurry.* The one I'm sure, the rats loved to play so dearly. Except now, it was one of the two of us, and not a rat, who had to make it past the half-circle. Then it was that I saw "Devil" carefully lay his rifle to his shoulder and take aim at my brother. He must not have recognized the Yankee he was aiming at to kill, was my brother. I wouldn't permit it. It would have been utterly unimaginable. So I threw my weight against the man while at the same time, I felt something biting and hot enter my breast. I went down first. "Devil" stumbled and pitched back after me into the same hole. Thus, he fell on top of me and perceptibly at just about the same moment as well, causing me to lose my breath. Yet, for all my screaming and kicking the man wouldn't move to get up off of me.

All I can say after everything went down, on that strange Sunday at Shiloh church is: it's too bad we weren't both busted-drunk, "Devil" and I... it's the only sane way to handle such confuted derangement.

Chapter Twenty-One

With luxury and pride surrounded,
The vile insatiate despots dare.
Their thirst of gold and power unbounded,
To mete and vend the light and air!
Like beasts of burden would they load us,
Like Gods, would bid their slaves adore;
But man is man and who is more?
Then shall they longer lash and goad us?
To arms, to arms ,ye brave!
Th'avenging sword unsheathe!
March on! March on!
All hearts resolved on Victory or Death!

Author unknown

The reason I could no longer find my feet as quickly as I would have liked to, was because "Devil" McGoran had been called home to *where the little people play,* and that was all there was to it at Shiloh. He was lying dead and on top of me. We were both caught, one on top of the other, in a shallow grave of dirt. I could hear men moving about, attending to the wounded who seemed to be crying out for heaven's own mercy and water. Always the incessant call came for lots and lots of water, as if the wounded soldiers hadn't had a drink in weeks. For some reason, I didn't want to move him for fear something would be disturbed. So I slid out as carefully as I could from underneath McGoran, with my shoulder and chest giving me undue fits of pain with every debilitating movement.

   Underneath his wire-thick, bristle-like, bushy, red beard crusted with dirt and clotted blood there was an ironic half-smirk still on McGoran's face. A last chuckle if you will, as if he'd convinced *the little people* or his guardian angel to stop for a small sojourn in Mexico, on his way home to the celestial

329

highlands....I don't know why...maybe just to see where he might have placed his governor's residency.

I was hauled up to a standing position by two strange Union soldiers. One of them took to covering my legs and thighs with lashes to get me to stand up, using the leather belt he had taken from around his waist. I couldn't walk. It must have been obvious to them. But they shoved me, whipped me and pushed me anyway until I could go no more. One last kick and I was gone, the fighting was over, the Irish rebel ceased to exist...enough was enough.

In my semi-consciousness, I remember them dragging me to a hospital wagon, pulled by continually bawling mules. Still in all, before throwing me face down inside, one of the soldiers shot and killed a threatening snake from underneath the wagon.

While thrusting the dead, still writhing, brown and yellow, diamond-backed serpent in my face, the soldier kept repeating, "You're going to get the same today or tomorrow, it'll be your turn, you'll see 'Reb'—you'll see—snaky bunch of bastards."

I overheard his companion tell the one who had shot the snake, "Leave 'em alone, Sergeant, he ain't going to make it anyway. Just look at that chest wound—will you? He's lost too much blood as it is. The man's a goner, let the poor rebel die in peace."

In the medical wagon, besides myself and what I can remember—there were four other wounded prisoners. It stays in my mind like a cliché from a photo camera; their moaning, the smell of burnt gunpowder encrusted within festering wounds, and the incessant horse flies buzzing about chewing into your solid flesh when they had a hankering for it, which seemed often enough. All of this taking place during the non-stop, vagrant sliding around inside the wagon, as the mules struggled through the churned up mud Shiloh and its surroundings had become. One of the wounded was sobbing bitterly (he really wasn't much older than I had been when I left Ireland) that he wanted his mother and pa right then and there, and he didn't give a particular damn about whether anyone knew how he felt about it either.

After a slippery, sickening ride of maybe three quarters of an hour we arrived at a field hospital set in amidst a half-dollar's worth of dry, scrub-filled, blue-tinted mountains where thin, rib-cleaving animals were grazing. Down below were a hodgepodge of dry canals and bleached army tents strung out for as far as the eye cou see amidst a scattering of sycamore, overland ash and birch wood trees. In other words, everything else, including the field hospital was out in the open with a wide, eight foot trench dug around the perimeter, within which were *chevaux-de-frise* (wooden stakes sharpened and set in a criss-cross fashion) to repel invaders.

We were all unceremoniously unloaded from the wagon and taken inside the field hospital. My shoulder and upper chest had stiffened and throbbed now with swollen and infected pain. I'd never felt anything like this before. Like a kind of searing, white, undulating heat had taken over my body, and everything before my eyes that I could visualize appeared filmy, kaleidoscope-like and granulated, as if I was half in my body and half out of it. When inadvertently my mind came to, lucidly, with something I could recognize as a simple idea. My single, unadulterated thought was for my brother Paul Francis Daniel and the confused hope he hadn't been shot. I instinctively knew I didn't wish to be in this world without him, he was my older brother and all that I had left.

One of the field surgeons, who, because of his stockiness, rotund caricature and sideways rolling-gait when he walked, reminded me of a white-smocked catapult, roughly cut my shirt away with a pair of scissors. In doing so, the doctor whistled in abrupt surprise, almost in shock, as if he'd been bitten, when he saw the wound or so I thought. He called out to another doctor to come for an overview. Or perhaps, more to the point, have some additional callous fun with another beaten and whipped Confederate soldier.

The other doctor was tall, with sharp features, olive-skinned like an Italian might be, with one curious brown eye sitting higher on his face than the other.

After sauntering over, initially annoyed from having to stop what he was doing, asked the one rather belligerently who had called him to assist, "What is it this time—do you want me to fix the leather strap in his mouth while you cut or what?"

The shorter, older surgeon grappled with his words, "That—that—won't be necessary—come have a look—in all my years of medical practice I've never seen anything like this before. I don't know what to make of it!"

Hesitatingly, with exaggerated gentleness, he pulled a third of a chain of Catholic rosary beads from the hole in my breast, just above my heart, the very same rosary beads which Father Stanislaus had given me. And there, tightly entwined several times around, within the miniature, silver-colored chain links was a Union-issued Federal Army bullet, like a fish caught in a silver net.

The field surgeon held the bullet, encrusted in the rosary, up to the overhead light and showed me what had saved my life.

"You must have one hell of a prayer-life, Rebel." The older doctor commented.

In my fatigued grogginess I could only half-imagine what he meant or what had happened.

Looking down at me curiously he asked, "Can I keep this to show the other doctors?"

I shook my head slowly back and forth, not knowing exactly why when I told him weakly, "No, Father Stanislaus may want it back."

Even though he probably wouldn't remember ever having given it to me in the first place. I caught myself thinking.

With an unqualified amount of vigorous restraint, the *catapult* doctor tried to wrest the bullet free from the chain (probably claiming his rights to a Union Army bullet I suppose). But despite his best efforts, it wouldn't come loose from the rosary. He tried more forcefully and renewed his efforts without success. The doctor must have wanted the bullet very badly. Giving up, he threw the whole, clinging, coagulated blood and steel mess in my direction while muttering under his breath, something about, how could the North win if the heavens were willing to help out the rebels with such pretentious miracles as this.

At length, the taller doctor inquired, "What should we do about his blood-letting and the fever?"

The *catapult* doctor responded, "I'm down to nothing on all medicines after what they hauled in last night. Suture him up, and let the doctors at Fredericksburg take care of the rest of him."

The taller doctor kept insisting, "That may be. Still, won't you look at the way his eyes are milky and half-shut? Then feel his pulse, he might not make it all the way to Fredericksburg."

The older one was already washing his hands and searching for a cot to lie down on when he countered, "Hell, if the man didn't die because a rosary saved his rebel ass, then I say let the Virgin take care of the rest of him a little while longer—at least until he sees someone at Fredericksburg."

Having said this, he walked over to a field cot and collapsed onto it. Within minutes he was asleep.

I don't know what happened after that—truly I don't remember. All I know is that my head was all astir, like it was full of bees with their collective, undulant droning. And from being destined for the United States Army hospital up in Fredericksburg, Virginia, someone decided, and so it was that we took the Mobile and Ohio Railroad to the great Mississippi River. There we boarded sternwheel steamers for the Rock Island prison barracks out on Rock Island, Illinois, of all places, a military prison. Upon arriving, we were given next to nothing to eat, no medicine, as well as nothing to warm ourselves from our various fevers. And all the time, we were told this was the Yankee way of saying thank-you for the Confederate treatment of Yankee prisoners down Andersonville-way in Georgia. A place of which I had never heard about, until much later, after the war had been unfortunately concluded.

I was certainly not myself then. The fever had completely taken over my body. And I'm not ashamed to admit to having asked the Virgin Mary; why had she stopped the bullet, only to bring a poor Irishman to this?

Word of my miracle got around the prison.

Some of the other prisoners bothered me to death with their incessant touching of any part of my body, as if I was a talisman and could work wonders. Instead of whom I really was; a miserably lonely *spalpeen* that wished with all his heart he had left everything back in Shiloh, including his cursed existence. One or two made the caustic remark he had never heard a miracle worker use such vulgar language or curse with such detailed profanity, as much as I did back then.

Now I'm not, or at least up until then, thought that I was much of a praying man. Still in all, I told Christ's mother more than once that it was a helluva thing to do, to bring a helpless Irish rebel to such a desperate state as this.

Sure, I was more than half-sick. But probably more to the point, crazy with fever and of being alone, like you realize you are going to die, you just don't know when it's going to happen. I knew "Devil" McGoran was dead and gone, but what had happened to Longfellow...was he still alive? Would he come for me? Afterwards, your undernourished, feeble mind takes over, playing all kinds of tricks on you, paving the way for despair to set in, like; *why would Longfellow bother to come—who was I to him? He probably didn't even remember me anymore.* Once you realize your thinking is lop-sided, it just becomes a question of; *let's get it over with, let me die in peace—enough with this crazy suffering.*

The prison smelled and felt exactly like the workhouses the Irish were stuffed into during the famine. For it was lined with cold and fetid brickwork. As if the ones responsible couldn't scrub out the smell of filth and sickness. Even if they had half a mind to do so, which of course they didn't. It appeared to this Irishman, as if the Northerners had learned their lesson from the English and committed it to memory so they wouldn't forget—. Aye, just like back during *the troubles*; one had the impression if we were left there long enough, with a minimum amount to eat, nothing to do, locked up in solitary confinement for twelve hours every day with no one to visit, then we'd slip away into death. Thus, we could be forgotten by our overseers, as quickly as they could find someone else to take our ignominious place.

There were several stories of cells used to house us, each lined with a grated catwalk. Since prison cells have never been used in the same sentence with *comforting* or *homespun*, then I won't say anymore about it. For me, I'd just as soon avoid any confusion of that place with the normal outside world we all avoided trying to remember, for it pained us so. On the other hand, the one thing we couldn't avoid was the penetrating, unrelenting wind which whipped-up off the Mississippi. For it blew through the place like an angry sea-witch, scattering everything that wasn't nailed down, and sending a man to bed with the shivers for days on end. Even to this day I can take the extreme heat or cold, but the wind is damned near unpredictable in what it does. They talk about a *Sirocco* in Northern Africa. Well as far as I can tell, they haven't come up with a name yet for a wind that whips around an ice floe out in the middle of the Mississippi River during winter. Then that same unforgiveable wind permeates your cell, leaving clinging, shivering ice slivers in its wake. In summertime it's just the opposite. Someone can be slathering a side of ribs; saucing those ribs down real well on the Iowa side of the river, and sure enough if it don't bring that smell right over to your cell, to just about drive you out of your mind from longing for pork-backed ribs.

I heard tell of one prisoner, who broke through the prison grounds and was so frightful and crazy in his unpredictable movements, the guards let him run right out the main gate and into the river to swim it off or drown. All because, he swore up and down he could smell gardenias from somewhere downriver. And damned if it wasn't what his wife used to stable next to their bed on her nightstand, before retiring at night—fresh gardenias—and the smell was driving this poor fellow to the point of no return. We did what we could. However, the freshly cut alfalfa-shoots we sprinkled liberally with lilac salve, didn't seem to help our homesick prisoner forget his sweet-scented domestic past.

Since it was a military prison and we were technically prisoners of war, we were given a certain freedom to move about during the day. Thus, we would get together as a group and be encouraged to play marbles, cards, checkers or chess.

One of the men, a gung-ho corporal from Virginia named Halyard, took it upon himself to try and reinstall basic, training-like, military discipline.

He seemed always on-guard, sententiously exhorting us amongst other army clichés, "We must never let the Yanks think they've broken us!"

Corporal Halyard initiated "group morale training" with the other prisoners, complete with mock short order drill and other presumptuous exercises. This he claimed, would help keep up our correct mental attitude until we were exchanged for Union prisoners or the war came to an end. One of my fellow prisoners soon discovered, and told the rest of us that Corporal Halyard was second generation West-Point. Only he had flunked out of that hard-line military school much to the dismay of his father, Colonel Halyard, for the beastly, undergraduate crime of *over-exuberance* in the line of duty. This Halyard fellow would try and muster the likes of us outside if the weather was decent. Once outside, Halyard would hand out a dozen or more wooden handles from discarded mops which he'd found, to see if he could get us to march in formation. It was either that, or some other insane and equally ridiculous idea like building a big enough forge to melt down our eating utensils and belt buckles to manufacture one gigantic cannon-ball. Upon which, we could conceivably threaten our guards with it—once we built an over-sized cannon, enabling us to fire the bloody thing.

If the weather was bad he would coerce us into listening to various military lectures he had dreamed up. Corporal Halyard would make up these innocuous handbills which he'd written out and finger-painted, before distributing them at meal times proudly, inviting us to such idiotic presentations as:

- *"How cleaning your musket—without first checking to see if it is primed and loaded, can bring you and your musket together, once more, for all eternity."*

- *"Why a sick horse should always be stabled downwind."*

- *"Ten ways to convince your commanding officer you're not as yet, fully prepared, for that frontal suicide assault."*

- *"If you're caught and interrogated in un-starched, soiled, button-less, long-winter underwear, never mind how your wife might feel—what would General Lee say?"*

There were other lectures as well. But by then, no one wanted to listen to Halyard anymore, except for a certain private named Samuel Abel. This private Abel was quite caught up with Corporal Halyard, and his current idea of disguising themselves as blossoming Wisconsin dairy maids, enabling the two of them to flirt with the guards until their wedding day, at which time they planned to escape.

Over time he was badgered so badly by a group of prisoners, insofar, as that every time one of them saw this Corporal Halyard, they would scream meaningless orders at him. Until finally, he ended up a recluse in his own cell, acting out *Hamlet* by himself while denying to anyone who happened to come by, he had ever been in the army. And thus, couldn't understand now, why he was in this insane Rock Island prison.

Once or twice I saw a doctor. I believe his name was Simeon, a Doctor Grant H. Simeon from someplace in *I don't give a damnsville.* He was a tall, meaty-faced, and somewhat stooped-over fellow, who wore bifocals and liked to cough in your face.

He would listen to your heart, take your body temperature, then satisfied that everything was as it should be stand up and proclaim, "I hereby, pronounce you fit for the service—. Oh that's right, you're a prisoner of war and not fit for much of anything!" Prior to staggering away, laughing over his little joke.

On the other hand, he was straight and to the point with all of us as to why we were imprisoned on Rock island, "Until the Southern Army considers Negro soldiers as legitimate prisoners for exchange, and not just to murder them or return them to slavery once they've been exchanged, then you will not be exchanged either. In which case, you'll be staying here with us on this "island paradise" until the war is over. So you'd better get used to the idea of seeing me around for quite some time yet."

Once to my unannounced pleasure, I received a letter from Colonel Morgan, who by then had made Brigadier General, the son-of-a-gun!
He wrote to me;

July 20, 1862

My Dear Edward 'Shakes' Ruth,
 We have received a list of our men captured at Shiloh, taken to Rock Island Barracks for medical reasons, and I saw that your name figured on this list. I know for a fact you fought bravely at Shiloh and were a distinct and honorable credit to the "Raiders", as well as to me your commanding officer.
 I beseech you, personally, to continue to hold your head up high. In that regard you will become an example to your fellow prisoners, as well as keeping yourself busy and free of the "doldrums" where many a prisoner has languished, due to a lack of activity or a victim of self-complacency. I would heartily recommend morning, afternoon and evening calisthenics (limit yourself to a brisk ten or fifteen minutes at each session due to a limited amount of caloric intake during your confinement), coupled with a stringent reading schedule if books are available. May I suggest, perhaps even forming discussion groups detailing the common books you are reading, if your fellow prisoners are like-minded. This you shall do until such a time as the Southern armies can break through and free not just you, but all her sons who are in prison and have sacrificed so much for the Confederacy.
 I have sent a separate note to the administrative staff at Rock Island Barracks, requesting they afford you every courtesy due to a citizen of a foreign power, which in your case is England (I am deeply apologetic in that I cannot write 'Ireland' at the present time). I have not received an answer back from the Rock Island prison administration. However, I can assure you, I will do whatever is in my power, including

writing letter after letter, until I am assured that you are being well taken care of.

I cannot write to you in more detail because this letter will have to be censored for obvious reasons. Still, I am duty-bound to inform you that we will not give up the fight, nor should you, until all Southern brothers-in-arms are together once more on the field of battle—this time victorious.

You will be interested to note that I am engaged to be married to one Martha Ready of Murfreesboro, Tennessee.

Your humble servant,
John. H. Morgan
Brigadier General, C. S. Army

So I've been forgiven everything at last while still in this Rock Island hellhole of mine.

'Aye, he is a kind and *dacent* man' (as my mother would have said) that Morgan he is. And as I mentioned earlier, and as you can see for yourself from his own letter, a blasted General to boot. Well, I don't believe me eyes now, I swear I don't—a general—well now, if that isn't something!

It wasn't long after receiving his letter, and beyond my comprehension that for some unknown reason my fever left me. For awhile anyway; only coming back on occasion when the wind brought before it the rather harsh and volatile Illinois winter. I became myself once again and we started to plan our escape. At first, we used our gaming sessions to get together and throw around ideas as to what was the best way to break out from such a sturdy prison. Indeed, we were planning to break out through mortar and brick walls which were several feet thick and constantly guarded. In any case, not all our *hashing a-rounds* were productive. For example, once when another fellow prisoner, upon finding out that I was country-Irish, suggested we all dress up as banshees (I have no idea how a banshee dresses). I would then teach everyone to scream frightfully like a banshee does while floating several feet above the ground in the open air (as if this could be done). While in effect, the guards, presumably being scared to death would *obviously* open the gates of the prison and let us walk out scot-free. In addition, according to this same inmate, if we kept our banshee screaming up an octave higher, complete with free train tickets as well. Needless to say, our banshee plan never came to fruition. As a matter of fact, I was severely criticized for the failure of this plan because I wouldn't come to share my knowledge of self-levitation (as if I could) with the other prisoners.

We were entertained more or less on a daily basis by a sergeant from Louisiana, with massive, humped shoulders and long, flung-out, gray locks like Moses. His nose was ghastly out of proportion and tweaked, making his face rather fierce looking, along with hollow cheeks creating a dispassionate, sallow bent about the man. He had big rolling eyes that would stare around the room every time he would make his move in chess, as if it was to be the death knell for his opponent, and he wanted everyone in the room to know. In addition to this, he claimed he was a descendant from the last of the Templar Knights' Grand Masters; that being Jacques de Molay. Indeed, he himself was a de Molay with his first name being Hattin. This unusual name he wore, as he explained, was a village in Palestine which the Templar Knights had fought for in the twelfth century. Aye, Hattin de Molay was a walking (or in this case a sitting) history book, if perchance, the only subject that interested oneself was the "Knights-Templar". Regardless of whom he played in chess, he would make his appropriate move or counter-move while at the same time offer some appurtenant threat, such as; Jerusalem was no longer safe from de Molay and the Templars. Seemingly, as if the chess board had suddenly become the Holy City, along with its *alentours*. Hattin de Molay was a good chess player based on the local, in-house, prison competition. Nevertheless, once in a while he lost and when he did—he swore before us all that Saladin's head would be his and his alone, as if what he threatened made any sense to the rest of us. In any case, it was fascinating theater to watch, and much better than staring at the ceiling of one's cell all day long while wondering about nothing.

Sometimes, he would be goaded by one of us standing around the table, "Who is it today, Hattin? Will the Egyptians fall? Why can't you and your knights keep the roads to the Holy City open? Who will face your wrath next—the City of Tyre? We can't imagine losing Tyre—that paragon of civilisation. Then how will we procure our dates and pomegranates?"

More often than not, Hattin de Molay wouldn't respond verbally, but with a bulging thumb keep hitting the chess board. In this way, motioning for the offending body to take the place opposite Hattin, to defend himself in chess, if he was as smart as his boasting mouth proclaimed him to be.

Hattin de Molay was the one who gave us the idea for a legitimate escape from Rock Island. And I'm not talking about a screaming banshee or a pregnant, over-sized cannon ball either. It must have been early September. As usual, we were sitting around with one newcomer, a man by the name of Whittle, Henry Whittle from Alabama, who had just arrived. This Whittle fellow while filling us in on news of the war (according to Whittle, things were not going well for the Confederacy) was having a game of chess with Hattin de Molay. Now surprisingly enough, de Molay was losing, and as was often the case to distract his opponent, he would start in on some subject which de Molay knew would interest the lot of us. In this way, de Molay bought precious time to figure his way out of his chess predicament. Which is why, in this instance, his subject was how to escape from Rock Island barracks, our current prison.

He leaned back in his chair and let his shoulder-length, grey hair fall grudgingly into place like he was a French musketeer. While at the same time, he tapped the top of his head and looked meditatively around the room, trying I suppose, to cull into play our feelings.

He suggested to the group surrounding him, "If it was me, not waiting or wanting to be exchanged—hmmm, let's think about it for a moment. Well then, I can see my way through to latching onto one of the grain ships that makes its way up here towards the latter part of September to collect the harvest from around these parts."

Henry Whittle challenged him immediately, "Listen de Molay, you can't just sneak up onto a bushel of wheat and go moseying on down the river like it was your everyday business."

"No," Hattin de Molay answered thoughtfully, "You're right, not only wouldn't the prison guards be a hankerin' to let you do it but it wouldn't be morally right, neither. You see, the Almighty has a way of punishing those who go about "moseying" this way and that way through life like it was their "everyday business"—. Why you have to plan and practice it 'till you gots yourself a certain aptitude for escapin'! Only then will you get heaven's blessing on your painstakingly, well-thought-out venture. Instead of this accursed "moseying" about—which is immoral and irresponsible to begin with!"

Taking into account our disbelieving attitude, he continued petulantly at first until we saw what he was driving at. At last, we too became excited until we found ourselves holding our collective breath, in eager anticipation of what de Molay might say next.

"Depending upon who had control of the city—one of the easiest ways for the Muslims or Christians to leave and enter Jerusalem, was to hide in a wagonload of whatever foodstuffs were being brought in for market on that particular day. All guards, even today, are always more lax when it comes to their stomachs, the Templars knew this and used it to their advantage. They also helped to consolidate the matter with a little financial donation to the guards as well. Thus, the messenger would conceal himself in a cart full of fruit or vegetables and *voila!* Enter and exit Jerusalem as he pleased."

He rubbed his two mutton-chop fists together as he spoke, "Now what say you-all to more of the same? Somehow, we have to find a way to get outside the prison by hiding ourselves in one of the wagons that come in here to collect the local produce. Assuming we could do this, all we would have to do then is collateral that with the time the ships in the river take on the harvests from around here, and there you have it—checkmate!"

With one swoop of his hand, he knocked over the chessboard scattering the two armies onto the prison floor. His opponent, Henry Whittle started to protest that his imminent victory had been but a move away. But alas, it was too late for Whittle, and besides, all of a sudden, Jerusalem...the Holy City... Rock Island Barracks was ours for the taking, or so we thought.

Then de Molay scared the lot of us. His daring, rolling eyes that looked like they came from a haunted monastery, or some such place, stared at those of us standing there.

At the same time, he insinuated our ineptness when he asked, crashing his fist down on the table to emphasize his displeasure, "Will no one go on this crusade with me—no one?—Damn your eyes!"

The room became eerily quiet as we tried to comprehend de Molay's mercurial question.

At last, someone next to me cried out in frustration, "What crusade? All I want to do is get home to my gal in Knoxville!"

After that, it became a homogonous sequence of events. First of all, we smuggled in a newspaper which gave the dates and times of the harvest pick-up and by which steamers. Accordingly, we planned our escape for a Friday afternoon. What with the kitchen deliveries and consequent filling up of the now empty wagon with local produce almost always happening on a Friday afternoon, just before the quieter weekend. We could hopefully, distract the deliverymen (perhaps even paying them off), hide several of the prisoners, and they could then make their way onto the main wharf. Upon reaching the wharf while waiting for nightfall, they should be able to stow themselves into a wagon, loaded to its sidings with a crop headed for one of the ships anchored just opposite the prison, out in the river. Perfect it seemed to all of us, until someone asked who was to go, since there could only be two or three prisoners at the most able to fit into one of the wagons.

We couldn't come up with any fair plan for deciding who should go, so we let things be and undecided—for the moment.

During all of this furious planning, one day, de Molay called me to his cell where he asked me pointedly, "Are you the defender of the land—the one the Virgin healed miraculously?"

I answered back that the only land I had ever defended, was the one with all the rocks in it. The plot of land which no one else would cultivate back in Ireland, so my pappy sent me to plant potatoes in the unforgiving soil. There was really nothing to defend I told him. However, I was happy to report I had oftentimes stood my ground against the hapless earth worms that came to burrow into our potatoes.

He paid little attention to my unintended sarcasm, "Listen to me, listen carefully 'Shakes', not everyone has been given the heavenly grace that you've been given. Do something with it or it'll be taken away."

I thought the man was crazy and said as much.

However, de Molay wouldn't relent. Instead, he recounted how men had gone to the fiery stake because of what they believed in. This they did, he insisted, regardless of what the hierarchy, including the pope, tried to coerce them into confessing.

I asked de Molay what did all this have to do with me, for there were no fiery stakes around that I knew of.

He remarked that I was pretty flippant in my attitude, but one day I would have to choose to believe, that I couldn't go on hiding behind my irreverent observations for ever.

I still thought the man was crazy. Nevertheless, this time I kept my peace, not wishing to offend someone who believed that he and Richard the Lionheart had a mutual voyage in view. Once my friend, de Molay, could extricate himself from our Rock Island prison. In the meantime, in order to placate the man, I assured de Molay should I find a follower of Mohammed trying to escape downstream in a bushel full of radishes; I would denounce him at once and promptly give his place to a Christian. He didn't see the humor in my quips, and made a vaunted point of trouncing me severely in chess that day.

The following morning, it was decided by our group that only two prisoners would go. There wasn't enough room in the wagon for more. De Molay told those of us prisoners gathered to listen that morning, at the same time insisting rather formally, the Irish rebel should go with whomever else the group decided upon.

I asked de Molay out of respect to come with me but he turned me down.

"Rheumatism has settled in all my joints; the voyage down-river wouldn't be good for it—the dampness and all. Besides, can you see me trying to nestle down inside of a load of barley or corn or wheat for that matter? T'wouldn't be long before I started growing a pair of ears like a rabbit while barking like a coyote—. No, I'm waiting on being exchanged like everyone else. Being exchanged is the only safe way of getting out of this place. 'Sides it gets you free grub all the way back to Louisiana."

I mentioned my surprise at his refusal, "But Hattin, just think? You could set into motion your idea of a last crusade. You remember—freeing the Holy Land like your ancestors did, once and for all?"

His grapefruit eyes seemed to light up with excitement then just as quickly die out once again, as if there was something infinitely wrong with what I had suggested.

Hattin de Molay countered me by growling back, "I'd like to chase the Muslims out of the Holy Land. Indeed, that would be fine, square, and my most sacred duty. But first I've got to do a little crusading back home in Shreveport. And that means chasing one Alicia Brownsfield—my mother-in-law—off the parlor sofa and out of my own house. Where she's been nesting since the day her daughter and I were first married, damn it all!"

Since de Molay wouldn't go, it was finally decided that Whittle should make the trip with me. At last, as if it was the next best thing to starlight after dusk, we were to leave in two days time, the upcoming Friday.

Chapter Twenty-Two

The fortunes of war often change, boys,
And trifles do oft turn the scale,
Tho' heavy the blow that we strike, boys,
We find that the truest may fail.

Author unknown

Looking back now, it was both fortunate and a godsend that I didn't go with Henry Whittle. Although, at the time, I was severely crushed. You see, my high fever caught up with me once again (probably from all the excitement of leaving) while at the same time, my shoulder and upper chest turned purple and throbbed most forcefully. In the meantime, Whittle got caught attempting to escape by the guards while scratching his way through a wagon load of turnips trying to breathe. Inevitably, he was returned to his cell where Corporal Halyard begged him to play the lead part of "Othello" to help him forget any further plans of escape.

Aye, it was a sad and loathsome bit of dirty business for us all back then.

I was shivering in my cell not three days after Henry Whittle had come back to join us, and before being sent to spend ten days in the *cachot* for his punishment. The fever was bad this time, real bad, causing my eyesight to fail, and something was happening to my skin, making it turn blistery blue and peel off in powdery, flour-like patches. I was in no condition to see anyone unless it was a doctor, which fortunately for me, one happened to call, and a godsend it was too. We were unlocked from our cells that Tuesday, and told to fall into line. It was announced that an inspection committee from the

United States Medical Corps had come to visit the prison, and make specific improvements. I couldn't move from my bed, the fever was that bad. When I didn't show up for the inspection muster, Hattin de Molay came with a guard to fetch me. I sat up alright, but as soon as I did a most horrific coughing attack settled in. Thus, I coughed and retched until I reached near-exhaustion from the effort. I became, as well, furious with myself that someone had , actually seen me like this, in such a state.... Boy, talk about raw, stubborn, Irish pride. Because I couldn't make it otherwise, de Molay picked me up in his bear-like arms to carry me to the inspection. He told anyone who would listen that I was going to see a doctor then and there. Furthermore, if the Yankees wanted proof that they were the worst bunch of uncivilized rapscallions who had ever existed, besides the Muslims in the year 1095, than he had the proof right there in his arms with me. Through sheer force of will I managed to stand up. Still in all, I clung to de Molay and wouldn't let go, for fear my legs would give out from underneath me.

As I understood it; no one from the prison, sick or otherwise, wanted to see the gloating Yankees.

A man standing next to us with a set of the most horrific bicuspids one could imagine, promised us all right there on the spot, he would sink his decaying teeth into the first Yankee doctor that tried to touch him.

Corporal Halyard threatened all of us with group ostracism if we so much as told the hated Yankees our name, or where we were from. In fact, he devised a hastily, thrown-together-at-the-last-minute plan, wherein, we would all make up fictitious names for ourselves such as *Morningside* or *Lancaster*. We would then lay claim while protesting as loudly as possible, we had all been falsely impressed from the British Navy.

I had no choice, and not a clue as to what to do when I was called to the front of the line, as soon as we entered with the others. The room we were ushered into was part of the main administrative building (which I had never been in before). As such, it was not damp, but dry, well-lit, and even had a painted surgical milk-green color on the walls. This fascinated me, as I had become convinced after more than eight months at Rock Island Barracks that anything other than mortar-grey was unbecoming to any surroundings whatsoever. There were people sitting at several desks waiting for us, with stacks of what looked to be medical folders in front of them. I could make out several doctors and a woman whom I took to be a nurse, for she wore the uniform of one, as well as the appropriately starched hat piece, usually associated with those of that caring profession. As a result, no doubt, of Whittles' daring break-out attempt, in each corner of the room a prison guard was posted, his hand resting lightly on his government-issued revolver.

The nurse spoke up first. She called out my name from her roster, as clinically and as sterile as one would before a marshal or a magistrate for that matter, where one's guilt had long been established.

Thus, it became of no further consequence, or of the least bit of interest to anyone when the nurse persisted, "Edward Ruth, if you are present in this room then make yourself known—front and center at once."

I found myself immediately afraid at the sound of her voice. I stepped back intuitively from both the nurse and her commanding tone. At the same time, I turned to look, alternatively, towards my right and left sides like I was mute or stupid. This I did, I suppose, to defray her attention from me, and what latest blow the Yankee government might have in mind to deal me.

The blurry-looking nurse examined once again her medical files for confirmation.

At length, with a sideways glance at one of the doctors, she repeated her initial order, this time explaining why, "If you are to be considered for exchange, according to the Articles of Warfare; the United States government insists on a full medical examination confirming that the above prisoner was in no way illegally treated or inhumanly abused during his incarceration."

This prompted someone to call out (I believe it was corporal Halyard), "A stage where every man must play his part—and his, alas—a sad one."

This of course inaugurated a baker's dozen worth of catcalls and hapless jeering from around the room.

Another inmate poked his entire hand through his holed and tattered shirt before professing, "It warn't no Yankee cannon that did this Ma'am. But I thank ye kindly just the same, for yer obliged thoughtfulness—. Mebbe I can wesh it now, 'fore I gets home."

Having uttered this last remark, the inmate took turns poking his hand through his shirt and cavorting around the room yelping like a...like a...well, like a banshee, until the guards came to control the poor bloke.

The nurse put her hands on her hips and glared at us all defiantly. As if she was a country-school teacher, and not above giving us all the deserved whipping she believed we truly needed.

Not knowing what else to do, I faintly raised my arm and put a hesitant foot in front of the other one. The nurse signalled immediately for two of the guards to come over to where I was standing or slumping...take your pick. Just like the instantaneous jolting of the fine meshing gears of an exact time piece, I was hustled from my place in line to an adjoining examining room. There I was unceremoniously dumped onto a cloth-covered table and told to strip down so I could be examined. Then the guards left, slapping their holsters in confirmation as they closed the door.

It must be noted that as I was leaving the main room where the doctors and other prisoners were still gathered, further names continued to be called.

Therefore, the shuffling of feet and men leaving the room was a background of noise to the poignant rallying cry of (now I am convinced beyond all doubt it had to have been Corporal Halyard); "But I do love thee and when I love thee not—chaos is come again!"

I was fiddling with my shirt buttons and coughing at the same time when the door clacked open and the nurse entered. I was anxious and afraid. Thus, I quickly resurrected my slackening posture while trying to make myself look like a soldier.

She came over to the table and to my surprise (for she wasn't accompanied by a doctor which was highly unusual back then) told me, "Here now, let me help you with those buttons."

That's all the nurse said to me....I swear to it.

Something jabbed inside of me as I tried to rub the milky film from my eyes.

"Katherine?" I asked weakly, suddenly embarrassed should I be wrong, and in my feverish state hallucinating like no man had ever done before or since, I'm thinking to myself.

"Yes, Edward, it's me."

Taking her time, she ran a hand over my face delicately, hesitantly circling my forehead while stopping at my eye socket afraid she might hurt me. She tentatively pulled her hand away from my eye, the one that Bailey Burke had fractured the corner of back in Ireland. She, then, let her hand fall to lay softly against my cheek as if the lady was feeling for my temperature. It felt so marvellous we could have stayed this way forever and I wouldn't have cared.

Like the ignorant fool I am, I asked once again.

This time in our own Gaelic tongue to be sure, *"Tà tũ Katherine?"*[26]

She replied in a soft and mothering tone which I had never heard her use before, *"Tà athas orm thũ a fheiceàil."*[27]

Afterwards, she laughed modestly, as if she understood my confusion. Reaching for a side pocket of her uniform, she took from it a letter and handed it to me to read.

She petted me on my arm and told me soothingly, "I'll be back in a minute or so with some ointment for that fever."

At first, I protested to no one (for she had left the room) that I couldn't see well enough to read. However, by rubbing my eyes and moving the letter back and forth, I finally made out after a fashion.

I opened the heavily creased letter and immediately looked to see who had sent such a note to Katherine, and why it should interest me. To my surprise, (although now that I think about it, I shouldn't have been) the letter was

---

26   Is it you, Katherine?

27   I'm glad to see you.

signed by none other than John H. Morgan himself. Only after staring at his incredulous signature for a minute or so, wondering to myself; *what in the heck do we have here?* Only then did I start to read it;

July 12, 1862

> *My Dear Mrs. Singletary,*
>
> *I am most distraught to have learned of the passing away of your husband Captain Robert Singletary at the battle for Fort Donelson. I became personally acquainted with your husband prior to my departure from Kentucky, and can confirm to you he was a brave and gallant warrior in battle. His passing must not go unnoticed by those of us who recognize in all soldiers the highest ideals of honor and valor, regardless of which side they fight for.*
>
> *Even though you and I do not share the same convictions during this unfortunate conflict, my personal condolences for your tragic loss transcend our differences during this particularly difficult time for you and your family. Please be assured of my sincerest sympathies, as well as my immediate assistance should it be required by you and your family. Insofar as this may be appropriate, I have written to my mother, Henrietta Hunt Morgan, that should you decide to return to Kentucky, her home in Nicholasville should be made available to you. Until, upon such time that you are fitting, and able to find suitable lodgings once again in our native Kentucky.*
>
> *I must now turn to a most difficult imposition, including a solemn request to be put forth, requiring your implicit sense of Christian charity and devotion to a woman's most worthwhile moral duty. It seems that one of my men and your fellow countryman, Mr. Edward Ruth, was injured and captured by the Northern Armies during what has since been come to be called "The Battle for Shiloh Church" in western Tennessee. I have confirmation that he is being held prisoner in Rock Island Barracks on Rock Island in the Northern State of Illinois. There can be no exchanging of prisoners at this point in time or in the foreseeable future, due to the breaking off in negotiations between our two governments for various, as well as confounding issues, for which we shall*

make no judgement thereupon. Therefore, at my own personal soliciting, I take it upon myself to beseech you to visit Mr. Ruth, and perhaps, endeavour to lend some comfort to a mutual friend who must certainly be in need of our assistance, be it corporal or otherwise. I have written the Rock Island administration for news of Mr. Ruth, however, without success.

Should you find it in your heart to do that which I have humbly requested, please remind "Shakes" (this is Edward's nickname) that he is never far from my thoughts and prayers. Indeed, he will understand should you accept to visit him in prison and show him this letter that once a part of "Morgan's Raiders"—one will always be a part of "Morgan's Raiders". As such, therefore, we endeavour to take care of our own.

In addition to the above, I would be forever in your debt that upon visiting Edward you would write to me, and inform me as to his well being. I am the one responsible for bringing young Edward into this war, and therefore, am most anxious for news of our fallen comrade.

Your humble servant,
John H. Morgan
Brigadier General, C. S. Army

I kept staring at Morgan's signature until the door opened, and I was no longer alone with my confused and depleting thoughts. Katherine came back into the room. This time followed by a grumpy, middle-aged doctor who proceeded with a lot of; "This shouldn't be this way", "I won't allow it" and "Entirely against military procedure". The doctor owned a furtive shock of thin white hair that stood up off his head like a wispy Indian Mohawk haircut. His wispy hair took to vaguely waving around with every step the man took, and seemingly, made as if to detach itself from the man's head, and fly-off of its own accord. He approached me hesitantly at first, trying to decide where to begin. At length, having made his preliminary diagnosis as to where to start his examination, the doctor aggressively plunged right in. He took to peering, pressing, and thumping my chest and backside until I found myself getting irritable with the man.

He eventually stood up from all of his chiropractic shenanigans and told Katherine perhaps sympathetically (I'm not sure), as if I wasn't there, "It's deep down in his chest—far too deep for me to be able to save the man."

Katherine must have shown some surprise (I couldn't see her face from the bed) for he quickly explained, "The pneumonia that is. And I for one can't understand how he could have stayed alive for as long as he has. Even without his lungs filling up, for his bullet wound still hasn't healed."

Apparently, Katherine displayed her displeasure, or whispered something which must have been construed as some sort of rebuke because the Doctor reiterated, "Well, just look at him won't you?"

He made a move as if to take my skeletal arm, but I moved it away from him.

Something clicked inside of me and I made up my mind. I announced to anyone who cared to listen to me that I wished to be taken back to my cell and left alone. I had finally figured out it was *the little people,* and they were most certainly up to their old tricks once again. Why of course, what else, or who else could it be? Katherine, as if it were possible, had come back cooing softly like a song-bird. Yet at the same time, I was supposedly sick and condemned to die? Aye, if it wasn't just like *the little people* to do such a thing...to play with a poor man's feelings in such a manner. I wasn't daft, it was them alright...up to their old tricks. Indeed, and as far as this Irishman's concerned, I for one, wasn't going to be duped, and I went ahead and said as much.

"Take me back to my cell, and enough of this nonsense," I croaked.

"You'll do no such thing. You're staying right here." The woman, who reminded me a lot of Katherine, kept saying.

Then she left the room.

When she came back, she had another doctor in tow. He was more of the conflicting idea that something could be done about my illness which appeared to please the nurse, who may or may not have been Katherine. I wasn't sure about anything any more. They made me swallow a most vile and disinfecting subterfuge; putting it forcefully down my throat while dissuading any rebellious commentary on my part. This of course, led me to attribute the medicine and their volatile manner of administrating it, as being part and parcel of the bedeviled witchcraft of *the little people* once more.

Eventually, I fell asleep.

He was killed, but not at Shiloh...her captain...what was his name again? I kept thinking or dreaming to myself, trying to remember if Katherine had been heartbroken, or even worse about his death. *I couldn't remember if she had been crying, or even, what she had worn to the military funeral...while the caisson trundled its way past the onlookers. The American flag on top completely covered with medals, more medals than I'd ever seen before...anywhere...except, perhaps, on a sultry afternoon, ages ago, somewhere else in a parlor room that I remembered being in once, in another lifetime.*

A parlor room, in which I was both happy and frightened to be in at the same moment in time.

How could that be?

Because Katherine was there, yet, so was his uncompromising shadow...the medals. The room was full of medals, and a solitary rocking chair stationed by an empty fireplace....What a curious legacy for a soldier....

Morgan had written Katherine's husband was killed but not at Shiloh. Then it wasn't... couldn't...have been my fault or "Devil's" or even Longfellow's—was it? Just one—for the love-of-mike—minute.... How could it be "Devil's" or Longfellow's doing? They were both down in Mexico, weren't they?—having a good look around in their new country. Aren't they both self-proclaimed governors or some such thing? On the other hand, hold on for a moment, just a minute here? "Devil" couldn't be there in Mexico if he was dead and lying on top of me here in Shiloh. Nevertheless, both "Devil" and I were calling out for Longfellow to come and lend us a hand, to help "Devil" become what?...un-dead? Is that how they said it..."un-dead"? But if "Devil" was helping to call for Longfellow that meant he wasn't dead by any means. Which seems to say that Katherine's husband, the good and saintly Captain Holmesby or Bicksby or Blowhard, something like that, wasn't dead at Shiloh either. Then if he wasn't dead, this meant that Katherine wasn't dead either or widowed or...or...ayeee! It was "the little people" again.... What did I do to deserve their meddling in my life?

How strange, how very strange indeed, all of this seems to be....

"Edward, Edward, wake up. It's me, Katherine—*cad é mar atà tù?*"[28] This she asked in our native tongue, as well as with more than a little trepidation.

"How the hell do you expect me to be, with Katherine *and the little people* all having a bloody good time of things, taking their respective turns, messing with my sanity?" I growled back, not understanding a single thing as to where I was, or for that matter, with whom I was speaking.

"To be sure, Edward Ruth, I'm never so surprised as to when I am with you. And to think of the shock I must go through every time I have to listen to the un-cordial words that come out of that *skibereen* mouth of yours. You should be ashamed of yourself!"

I answered back, finally, full of confidence in my situation, ""Ashamed of myself?" And to whom do I owe this great honor? For the last time I checked your *Highness*, I was in prison on some fog-engulfed island, crowded in with moping Templar Knights and crazy Shakespearean actors and—and—?"

28 How are you?

She wouldn't let me finish, for she cut me off once again.

She turned to some elderly-looking, practically-embalmed, medical man, "You see it now, Doctor, don't you? The fever must have done some permanent cerebral damage. For it has obviously left him as he is now, cool to the touch—touch him and see for yourself. In any case, he continues to drivel and babble on so, without making any sense a t'all. Please, come and feel his hand and forehead—see how they are both cool to the touch? Yet he goes on so, and babbles continually like he's dreaming, or worse—a confirmed idiot."

"Now, wait just a minute. I'll not be driven off like some market-day, fancy-showroom, meat-on-the-hoof heifer," I interjected, my self-dignity completely shattered.

"Oh Edward, do be quiet," Katherine told me resignedly.

For the love of mike, what in heaven's name is happening here? "The little people"—Katherine's voice—it does sound like her you know....Still in all, I'm not so sure anymore...?

"Katherine, is that really you?" I asked desperately, needing confirmation of something including the fact that I still owned most of my mental faculties.

Well, good enough then...I kid you not, it was indeed Katherine Louisa Maddox in the flesh.

For she took my hand almost forcefully so, and intoned a bit mockingly, "And to whom did you think you were speaking with just now—*the little people* I suppose, Edward?"

At length, she laughed I thought, much too smugly at the ridiculousness of her own suggestion, before bending down close enough to where I could smell all the fresh country-Irish which she possessed. Aye, that woman could play tricks on you alright, and then come off claiming it was all the fault of *the little people*....Well, I'll be daft and then some!

To my surprise, she ordered me to lie still, as I had been quite ill (isn't that just like Katherine to tell you something you already knew). It seems I had been feverish and semi-conscious for almost a week now. Otherwise, she would read to me if only I would lie still for a change, and stop them all from worrying so much about me.

This in truth was what that blessed woman did just then, and just about every afternoon afterwards as well. She came to visit and read poetry to me. To be perfectly honest about it, I can't remember a thing about her Gaelic poetry, except her poems seemed to employ the use of the words "lark" and "swoon" in every other line. I only remember that Katherine read them to me every afternoon, which I passionately waited for upon waking in the morning. It went on like that for quite some time as I recall. Indeed, it seemed such a blissful way to renew our friendship, with gentle poetry from the land of Erin. I got to be feeling better as well...a heckuva lot better.

Once or twice, she explained to me that after she had learned of the death of her husband, she went back to school and finished her nursing studies. Upon her graduation, she volunteered to visit and help where she could the prisoners of war held by the North. Those were the only times she ever referred to her married past. Other than that, we let our time together take whichever course it decided on. Aye, we had finally captured a precious moment, between the two of us, and were holding it carefully, joyfully, if even for a short while. Neither of us dared to force its hand. I was in prison and she had organized her life to where she could be close by as well. And it appeared as if she cared about me...what more could I ask for, or in effect, wait upon?

This was the strangest thing of all when I tend to reflect back...which I seem to do quite frequently. We'd gone around and around, like two punch-drunk fighters since the very first day we had met. Katherine, it seems, looking for something which was beyond my comprehension, with me, bumbling my way about, just trying to hold on and make some sense of my life. I suppose, quite honestly in retrospect, it was only because of the different paths which we had chosen that we were finally able to realize our mutual support and affection for each other. Indeed, that by highlighting our differences, and being damned stubborn about it in the process, we realized in the end, we both needed our Irish sameness...with or without the oatmeal biscuits.

Thus it was, that from the very first time we saw one another, once more in prison, we both decided to love one another, for the rest of our lives. It was that simple and that forceful. As well, without, either one of us having to say so... this would come later with time. She was blissfully sweet when she reminded me to speak in my Irish tongue...for I was losing my accent, something which before was abominably shameful for her to listen to.

Once, after having read my medical report, she asked me to show her the chain of Catholic rosary beads. The one Father Stanislaus had given to me; the one that had miraculously stopped the bullet at Shiloh. She didn't comment on it other than to hold it in her hands, before saying how glad she was. On more than one occasion, when asked about it by someone who'd heard about my past, I heard Katherine recount that the "rosary-stopping bullet" was "not the real miracle". Yet, she wouldn't explain then what the real miracle was, leaving it to the visitor and myself as well, to wonder what she meant. That's the kind of woman she had become...mysterious and fascinating.

I often took her vision in carefully when she wasn't looking. She may have been reading or fixing my medicine, thus, I could take my time looking at such a delightful woman. Her face was a bit fuller than before, yet the apparent fullness still couldn't hide the high-rounded cheek bones which made her laugh such an explosive and ebullient greeting. Her natural beauty, for she no longer wore any feminine war-paint that I could decipher was more distinguished, with a faint hint of hardship making her that much more endearing to me. As if she now knew what life was all about. Her red hair had turned a more gentle auburn color, with slight traces of gold hidden within the querulous thickness of it all. She was often given to sudden and uncontrolled mirth with me, as if she too had been liberated from some petulant prison. I think one of the things I appreciated the most; was the absence of her utterly senseless feminine flirting, which I had always found so distasteful in her. She appeared to me now, to be more kind and honest.

With her careful doting and my Irish stubbornness, my health seemed to improve.

Neither one of us spoke about it. However, it became quite clear to the two of us that we had both elected to join our lives together at some point in time. It was so obvious to Katherine and me, therein, we had no need to discuss the matter. Rather, we chose to invest heavily in the moment, letting things be, conscious I suppose that one day we would both take responsibility for how we felt just then.

One day, several of the men including de Molay, Whittle and Corporal Halyard came to visit. They were all wearing new britches. What a surprise! Katherine left us alone, for she had quickly surmised the quiet, nervous and anguished air in my room could only be attributed to her presence. They waited for her to leave before pestering me with all sorts of questions, including the most important one to a prisoner of war; "What did the nurse have to say about the conflict—which way is it going?"

"It doesn't look good fellows," I explained. "From what Katherine tells me, Grant has split the South in two, making it a war of attrition if nothing else."

"How can that be?" Corporal Halyard asked, looking dumbfounded.

De Molay pushed back his fountain of greying, matted hair before stating, more as a matter of fact than anything else, "Why it makes perfect sense to me. It's always the same; we go around making one helluva big stink about blowing the crap out of everyone and everything to defend our rights. But when it comes right down to it, we just can't keep up the supply lines, leaving our boys too far out in front without anything to fall back on. No one thinks these things through before it gets too late. For Grant it plays right into his hands, and must be like picking soft-bellied geese one at a time, right off the fence during mating season."

Henry Whittle told everyone in the room that if the war ended right then and there, then by rights, we wouldn't recognize the new world that the South would have to become, to please our new Northern masters.

"I won't stand for it!" Corporal Halyard rebuked.

"It's too late for that, me thinks," answered back de Molay.

At length, as if to justify the mournful turn of events, Halyard launched into some fuzzy-thinking scheme about taking the *Merrimac* right up the Potomac and kidnapping Lincoln.

"I don't know which is worse," de Molay imbibed, "Your sense of theatrics or your lack thereof?"

Corporal Halyard became in effect, ruffled, when he heard what Hattin de Molay had to say because he still wasn't quite sure as to how to take the man. Therefore, he countered cautiously, "I am happy to inform you that back at *The Point*, we covered just such a maritime contingency—"

But he was cut off by Whittle, who confounded us all when he asked, "And what contingency are you referring to my friend; 'to *Merrimac* or not to *Merrimac*'—that is the question?"

"In any case, it's not the *Merrimac* anymore but the *Virginia!*" Retorted de Molay, satisfied that even if we were losing the war we should at least get the names of our vessels right, probably before they all sunk.

Eventually, they asked me about Katherine. However, I didn't know what to tell them, half-afraid I suppose that anything I said on the matter would be like tracking mud across fresh snow. I told myself instead of the others; *it's best for it to lie there undisturbed, at least for the time being, perhaps when it is all said and done...the mud would come later.*

We had been in Rock Island Barracks all told, for a little longer than two years when the announcement finally came.

Katherine Louisa Maddox brought the news herself that we the prisoners were to be released and *not* exchanged, on the sole condition that we all swore sovereignty to the United States of America. And therefore, would no longer take up arms against her. On that condition and only on that condition would we be released and free to go.

I signed out on October 26, 1864.

I asked them to write on the release paper saying I was from Castlewarren, County Kilkenney, Ireland, but the officer in charge told me, "If you fought in the United States then you gotta be from the United States. Otherwise, the rest of the world would think we were runnin' nothing but mercenary camps like that frog Napoleon did."

So I read the following and signed it, deeply regretting that an Irish rebel hailed from Covington, Kentucky. On the other hand, I took solace in the fact that someone once wrote that nothing good had ever come out of Nazareth either, or so I'm told.

The document read; *"I, Edward Ruth of Covington, state of Kentucky do solemnly swear, in the presence of Almighty God, that I will henceforth faithfully support, protect, and defend the Constitution of the United States, and the Union of the States thereunder; and that I will, in like manner abide by and faithfully support all acts of Congress passed during the existing rebellion with reference to slaves, so long and so far as not repealed, modified, or held void by Congress, or by decision of the Supreme Court; and that I will, in like manner, abide by and faithfully support all proclamations of the President made during the existing rebellion having reference to slaves, so long and so far as not modified or declared void by decision of the Supreme Court: So help me God."*

I was let go from prison on that blessed day, and Katherine Louisa Maddox was there to take me away.

We drank tea and ate buttered scones until late in the afternoon on such a heart-warming day. With the faltering light she read to me. It was so cozy and warm, I started to fall asleep. Katherine woke me in her gentle way. Before the candle finally gave out, it was time to listen to another poem about a bird swooning or some such silly thing. I rather believe, it was about a lark this time as well.

The End

Epilogue

I was brought home from Harcourt's Paddock in the afternoon. Straight away I was put to bed, with a knot on my forehead the size of an egg, and more beguiling memories than I knew what to do with. They all seemed to come tumbling out of me, afterwards, whether I wanted them to or not. I don't know if the rock which hit me on my head, in a sense, broke the dam, or if it was the woman, who reminded me so much of my Katherine. Perhaps it was Fightin' Jim Sweeney, crooning out an Irish lullaby prior to the boxing match that did it. I don't rightly know. However, I do know it sure stirred up something frightful, maybe even tempestuous inside of me.

I eventually put my story down on paper without realizing that this story, like me was incomplete. Incomplete, in the sense, there was so much more. But then again, how do you define, or put down man's indefatigable spirit to surmount the challenges of life in writing, as if you could? Whether you can or you don't, doesn't change the fact that it does indeed exist; this omnipresent drive to acquit ourselves correctly, and if at all possible, honorably in this life.

Katherine Louisa Maddox and I married on a frosty day in January. When, as her father put it, "Let's all go back in the barn for rum-punch and sugar-cakes where it's warm. And you, Edward Ruth, can look at one of the plow-horses who doesn't appear to be chewing properly."

She and I produced eleven children. Two who died at childbirth, and the last one, appropriately named John Hunt Morgan Ruth, who doesn't live that far from me here in Lanesboro, Minnesota.

I guess what beguiles me the most when all is said and done, is that the human condition appears to be one of contradiction, at best. For example: let's say you're immigrant Irish, but to make headway in your new country you'd best forget about where you came from "Mick", or someone will slam the door on you with a note saying; "No popery allowed", and you'll starve for it. Otherwise, if your adopted homeland needs someone to dig a canal, police its unsavory neighborhoods or do stevedore work, it calls out for the Irish to do these tasks. Realizing, as a matter of course that an Irishman won't shrink from the job, or perhaps, is lacking in whatever it is which would cause someone else to think about it first, before saying they'll go ahead and do it. Another example if you will: you're Irish, so you fete the death of someone because you truly believe with all your heart they've gone ahead to a better place...heaven if you will. Yet, when all is said and done you sit home, alone at night with your thumb in your ear, weeping and wishing she was back. This is what I mean by being in a continual state of contradiction.

And how does one ever find peace in just such a state? I mean true peace? Does the body slow down its metabolism, and eventually leaves you gasping for something besides air...something that you've lived to regret? Or, maybe you don't because you know that you may have made mistakes and all.... Yet, you know a kind of peace because deep down you tried as hard as you could have, wanted to? Or, is there rather, just a series of intriguing innuendos which allow us a momentary respite from our seemingly unending state of contradictions? I don't know exactly (so I can't tell you). On the other hand, I have come to realize for myself anyway, it is not through satisfying our appetites that we come to a truce within ourselves. Yet, even that is of itself a contradiction. For if we cannot appreciate a spring day after six months of a drawn-out winter, or a beautiful being without having to lust after her, then we still have not succeeded. Long ago, someone mentioned something about balance in our lives and his words stuck with me; "Yes, everything but in carefully measured out doses." Or, rather not carefully measured out doses, which spells out contradiction once again, but rather a sagacious sense of when one has had enough. That for now enough is enough; even if what you're up to is basically a find and honorable thing to do like fishing or ball-playing, I must make time for other things. Fine then, how do we know when enough is enough? Is there a list somewhere like reading the Bible on a daily basis that will teach us? Indicate when enough is enough? How will we ever know?

I get up to rearrange the fire, for Minnesota unlike Kentucky, produces a cold that leaves you in a continual state of bone-marrow frigidness. A coldness, I've found out, which even slows down your thinking process. I believe it's due to the blood in your body becoming thick, like molasses because of the cold, and thus, can't circulate as quickly. This, to my way of thinking, makes you less alert than you would have been during spring or summer. You react and endure, waiting for what...spring? Better times ahead? Then you'd best learn if nothing else to *be resilient* while you're waiting.

If Captain John Hunt Morgan taught me one thing, it was to be resilient. For example, if the full moon tonight wouldn't let you attack your enemy because your line of approach would be lit up like noon-time daylight—not a problem. He'd tell us, "Boys, we'll wait until the moon and things above, change in our favor." Finally, when things came around to Morgan's liking, we'd attack alright, blasting everything in our path until we'd reached our objective. You can say what you will about John Hunt Morgan. No matter that; just don't forget to mention the man was resilient, resilient as hell... almost to a fault. When I heard what happened later, just after he was put under General Lee's jurisdiction, I cringed. A jurisdiction that Morgan argued would profoundly reduce his ability to decide things on the run. A spur of the moment decision-making process, if you please, in order to rapidly penetrate the enemies' defenses. Which is why I cringed, wondering if Morgan hadn't pushed his resiliency too far, provoking the end of his life's poem in Greeneville, Tennessee. By then, I learned Morgan was burnt out, a shadow of his former self, for he was starting to make costly mistakes like armed robbery which eventually ended in a court of inquiry. Too much reckless insubordination and not enough of this so-called "balance in life", I suppose.

I believe we moved to Lanesboro, Minnesota, in 1880. There I continued to practice dentistry after having decided to leave my practice in Maysville, Kentucky, and move west to "grow up with the country". Our son John, had moved there several years prior to our departure, so we evidently had a foothold out west.

Upon Katherine's bidding I became an American citizen on May 26th, 1880, which just goes to show you how quickly I adhere to what other people around me encourage me to do, including my wife. The clerk at the Mason County Courthouse solemnly declared that I had conducted myself, *"As a man of good moral character and therefore if I would renounce and abjure all allegiances and fidelity to every foreign prince potentate, State or sovereignty whatever and particularly to Victoria Queen of Great Britain and Ireland and Empress of India that I was hereby admitted and declared to be a citizen of the United States of America."*

What Katherine didn't know because I forgot to mention it to her was that I had actually taken out citizenship papers back in 1859. However, the war soon broke out, and my papers were lost in a fire along with some other personal effects.

It didn't take as long for Katherine to come back to her Irish roots and the Roman Catholic Church that we had both been baptized into. I believe women, somehow, know better about these things than men do. Aye, that once they've seen the error of their ways, they come back to the truth stoically, like a homeward-bound ship to port. Which in my case was a real blessing, as she never went about making me an object of her religious persecution with a holier-than-thou attitude. Instead, taking her own time, and through her own gentle holiness, patience and quiet simplicity made me realize that her path was mine as well. This she did, without hitting me over the head with it every time I went to say the "Our Father".

She later mentioned to me her prayers never went unanswered. This only convinced me that much more how profound a woman's strength and deep perception truly is. We, men-folk, by and large, want to be out in front, pushing and shoving one another to be the first in line, clamoring like all gang-busters about leading the parade.... On the other hand, a woman's redoubtable and quiet presence is a marvellous thing to witness. I would even go so far as to say a real blessing as well. The only thing my dear Katherine asked me to do was to join the *Father Matthew's Total Abstinence Society* which she said would help me to quit my affinity for the "pernicious bottle", as she liked to remonstrate. I did as she requested and became a better man for it. So I guess in a way she became a Catholic once again, and in return, my guardian angel and I gave up our distilled affection for "applejack", with its less than endearing consequences.

In Lanesboro, Minnesota, mostly at my dental practice, when people find out that I participated in the war of Northern aggression, I get asked about General Lee and President Davis all the time. However, there are only a few real history buffs who ask me about "Morgan's Raiders", or make the connection between the Northern Free-Masons and their Southern brotherhood.

Now, I know for a fact that Morgan was in spite of what he told me, a Free-Mason. Yet for all my research, I truly believed our President Jefferson

Davis when he said he was not a Mason and strictly abhorred any ties with that motley group (President Davis stated on more than one occasion he didn't have anything against the Masons personally as his father was one. I call them *motley* and take full responsibility for such a statement). Yet in regards to the rest, the President of the Confederacy was continually under attack as a traitor, in spite of his sincere and loyal beliefs. I have here on my desk a newspaper article that vilifies our President Davis by the defense and counter-arguments of General Lane, in which he must defend himself and President Davis from the most slanderous attacks one could envision.

The General stated; *"Then Sir, to whom do you allude to...Davis? Sir, I saw him on the battlefield. I was looking right in his face when he was wounded. I saw a shudder pass over him as the bullet struck him, precisely at the side end of his spur, and passed through the center of his heel. There was a perceptible simple shudder but not a murmur; just a shudder for the instant when struck by the bullet; but never, for a moment, did he lose sight of the enemy or the flag but struggled on through the battle to the end following the glorious stars and stripes, that emblem of the Union, that emblem of the Constitution, that emblem of protection to every State of the Confederacy under the Constitution as gallantly as ever did mortal man; and yet upon this floor there are some base enough to allude to him as a traitor. I have not words to express my contempt for any man that can apply such a term to such a man as Jefferson Davis. Jefferson Davis a traitor? Treason applied to him? He, the purest and bravest of patriots! He fought for his flag and country when the cowards and poltroons that now dare vilify him were supine at home. He will live gloriously in history when they are earth and forgotten."*

Jefferson Davis himself, further added; *"That as a citizen of the sovereign state of Mississippi, I obeyed her commands, and, as a sovereign cannot "rebel", neither lead nor followed a rebellion, great or small. As I had no Masonic standing, the assertion that it was not tainted by the imputed act of mine rest, not upon a fact, but upon a misrepresentation. Finally, Masonry could not have had much to do with securing my pardon, as I have never been pardoned or applied for a pardon, or appealed to Masonry to secure to me the benefit of the writ of habeas corpus that I might have the constitutional right of every American citizen to be confronted with my accusers."*

I get up to sift the now waning coals in the fire. Something in the fire or this day perhaps, has really gotten to me, bothered me in a way that hadn't disturbed me very much before. These memories continue to haunt me for they are bittersweet, and yet, at the same time, they weren't bittersweet when they happened to me. My brother, Paul Francis Daniel on many an occasion called life a curse, but no, I don't think so. Even my brother ended up changing his mind. After the war, he became a special agent with the Travelers Insurance Company of Hartford, Connecticut. There he met and married a fine colleen from the old country, who, from what he has written to me makes him, "Toe the line and chew with his mouth closed."

Aye, life is a blessing to be cherished and respected, requiring a sort of anchor that we can rely on when things become difficult. I stand next to our mantle, and besides reminding myself that I need to dust, and before I start to curse out loud because of such an unreasonable thought, I reach for a polished and painted jewellery box with raised emblems and an ivory insignia that I cannot recall the meaning of in which Katherine had placed the *miraculous* set of rosary beads. I take out the rosary which saved my life and immediately I am transported back to Shiloh. I have no questions about the battle which might need answering, nor do I have such a volatile memory that I cannot sleep at night because of the incredulous slaughter. If anything, I am in awe, and remember Shiloh and Ireland together like two pages from the same book...my Ireland, and our deep inculcated respect for all things sacred. It is a blind respect and trust, for we have been taught as *wee bairns* that we cannot understand nor even try to understand things which are far beyond our comprehension as simple folk.

An easy enough excuse to explain away a poor Irishman's faith?—No, I don't believe so. I finger the rosary and instinctively my hand goes to my breast and I wonder as I always do; why did she, the Virgin Mother do it? There were others more deserving certainly. I was not a great believer before the accident, and afterwards, I did not become a missionary preaching the Gospel all over the earth. I wasn't even like our very own sainted-Patrick, for Katherine, many a time, told me to drive the cockroaches from our kitchen as Patrick had the snakes from Ireland. Yet all I could manage, in the meantime, was to start sneezing violently from getting too close to where I had laid the powdery poison down.... A bullet stopped by a rosary.... They called it a miracle back then and I suppose it was. At the same time, I wonder if there wasn't a deeper miracle hidden back there in Castlewarren, Shiloh, Maysville, even Liverpool, that somehow I missed?

A log on the fire explodes in a crackle, the hiss of wet log sap like the steam from a locomotive escapes into the parlor reminding me I should think about bedtime. As a matter of fact, I still work as a dentist and have a few appointments on the morrow. This includes a pitiable Mr. Kudor, who remains convinced despite a thorough examination confirming the contrary that there lies permanently stuck between his second and third molar, the remnants of his Aunt Harriet's pigeon pie. Furthermore, this Mr. Kudor believes the bone won't come out until he apologizes to her, for calling her a "windless tribute to modern gossiping who has no peer in that regard!"

I go ahead and say the rosary by myself, something I try to do every night in thanksgiving...thanksgiving for having known my wife, as well as a multitude of other blessings including stopping the bullet. During my prayer I am reminded of something Katherine told me, once, way back when I was still in prison during the war, and she had come to pay me a most welcome visit. She mentioned that for her she didn't begin to experience life until she started to toy with the idea of becoming unselfish, "the lessening of one's self" as she put it. I corrected her by telling Katherine that she had already initiated her undiscovered role in life when she gave an oatmeal cookie to an urchin, who in fact was me back in our village of Castlewarren. She laughed a very long time when I reminded her of such an event. The thought or idea which she expressed was revolutionary to me back then, as it stood against everything I had seen since my days as a young *gossoon* back in Ireland. So there you have it. I guess I believe because I've seen with my own eyes the difference one can make when one sheds his own ego in the sacrifice of others. Isn't that something? Is this why there is so much suffering in our lives? If I see Bailey Burke again one day I'll have to ask him the same question.

Now, finally, for it is late and I still haven't ironed my pants and shirt for tomorrow, I must close with a letter from Jefferson Davis in which he recalls the Irish element in the Confederacy.

It reads as follows;

> "They were of two classes—those who were residing in the
> South before the war and those who, despite the difficulties
> of getting transportation came to us to fight for home rule,
> came at their own expense, joined the army without bounty,
> and, notwithstanding our poverty and destitution in all
> the material of war, served with patriotic fidelity and
> Irish gallantry wherever they were tried. At page 226 and
> following of Vol.2 of "The Rise and Fall of the Confederate
> Government", you will find a report of the battle of Sabine
> Pass, Texas, where forty-four men, commanded by Lieutenant
> Dowling, all of them Irishmen, achieved the most wonderful
> victory that I believe is to be found in the annals of military
> history.
> Respectfully and truly yours, Jefferson Davis."

At last, I snuffed out the remains of the fire before walking groggily down the hall to my bed. Wondering indeed, how I could convince Mr. Kudor there wasn't a pigeon pie bone in his mouth...at least as far as this Irish rebel could tell.

Bibliography

Akenson Don. *An Irish History of Civilisation.*

Allen Oliver E. *The Tiger.*

Black J. Anderson. *Your Irish Ancestors.*

Brooksher William R., Snider David K.. *Glory at a Gallop.*

Cap. Villiers Alan. *Men Ships and the Sea.*

Ealy Christine Kin. *This Great Calamity.*

Foster R.F.. *Modern Ireland.*

Gallagher Thomas. *Paddy's Lament.* Ireland, 1846-1847.

Ginna Robert Emmett. *The Irish Way.*

Hagger Nicolas. *The Secret Founding of America.*

Howarth Stephen. *The Knights Templar.*

Ireland of one Hundred Years Ago. (Author unknown).

Irish Dictionary & Phrasebook, Hippocrene Books, New York.

J. B. Lippincott Company Philadelphia, New York. *American Issues.*

Jordan Robert Paul. *The Civil War.*

Keneally Thomas. *The Great Shame.*

McPherson James M.. *Battle Cry of Freedom.*

Ramage James A. *Rebel Raider.*

Robinson John J.. *Dungeon, Fire, & Sword.*

Uris Jill and Leon. *Ireland A Terrible Beauty.*

Wagne Kerry Miller and Paul r. *Out of Ireland.*

Whyte Robert. *The Journey of an Irish Coffin Ship.*